**Coming Soon!!!**

# Coming Soon!!!

## A NARRATIVE

## John Barth

HOUGHTON MIFFLIN COMPANY
Boston · New York
2001

Its copyright info, ISBN, whatever:

For information about permission to reproduce selections from
this book, write to Permissions, Houghton Mifflin Company,
215 Park Avenue South, New York, New York 10003.

Visit our Web site: www.houghtonmifflinbooks.com.

*Library of Congress Cataloging-in-Publication Data*
Barth, John.
    Coming soon!!! : a narrative / John Barth.
        p.   cm.
    ISBN 0-618-13165-5
    I. Title.

    PS3552.A75 C6  2001
    813'.54—dc21     2001024988

Printed in the United States of America
QUM 10 9 8 7 6 5 4 3 2 1

Book design by Melissa Lotfy

The author is grateful for permission to quote from "The Life with a Hole
in It," from *Collected Poems* by Philip Larkin (Farrar, Straus and Giroux).

The chapter "Read me" first appeared in *TriQuarterly* 110/111.

## Its dedication:

*for Shelly*

Its disclaimers and acknowledgments:

The Chesapeake showboat called *The Original Floating Opera II* and all hands associated with it are purely imaginary, as is the author's association themwith: a hypothesis, a scenario—a fiction. However, for historical details of The James Adams Floating Theatre and Ms. Edna Ferber's connection thereto, the author gratefully acknowledges his debt to *The James Adams Floating Theatre* by C. Richard Gillespie (Centreville, MD: Tidewater Publishers, 1991).

# Menu

Its opening mini-icon:

# ▣ READ ME

Call me ditsy, call me whatchadurn please; just an old-fart Chesapeake *progger*'s what I am, with more orneriness than good sense—
else I wouldn't be sitting here a-hunting and a-pecking on "Big
Bitsy's" ergonomic keyboard whilst the black wind roars and the
black water rises and the power flickers and the cabin shakes. I'd've
hauled my bony butt across Backwater Strait to high ground over in
Crassfield whilst the hauling was still doable, before the storm-surge
from Zulu Two (stay tuned) puts Hick Fen Island* eight fingerfork-
ing feet under Backwater Sound.

"Whoa ho there, Dits," my mind's ear hears the gentle reader
gently interpose: "Where's Hick Fen I.? Where're Backwater Sound
and ditto Strait and mainland Crassfield? Who's Zulu Two, and
whaddafug's a *progger*, and who's thissere *EARL* character, that you
haven't even mentioned yet?"

All in good time, mon semblable et cet, which Yrs Truly don't
happen to have a whole skiffload of just now. Anyhow, old Ditsy-
Belle's a gal that likes her stories straight up, if you read me: Get
things going, says I, then cut to the chase, or old Dits'll chase to the
cut. *Once upon a time*'s about as far as we'll go in the way of wind-
up for your pitch. You say *It was a dark and stormy night*? We copy,
mate: now on with the story, ess vee pee.

Ditsy-Belle, Ditsy-Boy: I've done time in my time as mainly
male and ditto feem; have attained the age where what's between
my legs matters less to either of us than what's between my ears or

---

* Avg year-round human pop exactly 1 these days and holding. Median elevation
0 ft at mean high water, as we're ½ tidemarsh. *Max* elevation, just under Big Bitsy's ergonomic chair, an acrophobogenic 6 ft and sinking. Predicted storm-surge?
12 to 14 . . .

just twixt you and me. Which is to say, a certain high-density disk-in-the-hand that I progged from the bush this morning after Zulu One (a dark and stormy night forsooth) in the westmost marshes of B.E.W.A.R.(E.), the Backwater Estuarine Wetlands Area Reserve (East): a double-sided disk triple-zipped in a Ziploc™ baggie inside another inside another and hence bone-dry enough, as bones go hereabouts, that I could read its blot-free label through all three bags in the mucky marshgut whither it'd wended from wherethefuckever. To wit:

*COMING SOON!!!*

Not quite your classic message-in-a-bottle—of which, by the way, I have found none in seven decades of dedicated progging—but piquant, piquant, no? After Tropical Storm Zulu, however (now redubbed Zulu I), the marsh-pickings were uncommonly plump, and tempus was a-fugiting—the Weather Service warning all hands that Tee Ess Zee had made an unheard-of U-turn off the Jersey shore, regrouped and refueled, and was chugging more or less back our way as full-blown *Hurricane* Zulu; first time they ever reached the end of the alphabet, and with autumn prime-time yet to go! Anyhow, a chap can't just kick back in the cordgrass and thumb through a computer disk with his/her bareassed eye, capisce? So I tossed *CS!!!* in the crab-basket with my other objets trouvés and carried on with my progging, I did, figuring I'd cull and triage and boot up and peruse at my fatherfreaking leisure.

But stay: ¿Qué quiere decir, Q'est-ce que ça veux dire, Was bedeutet ein *progger*, prithee?

*A:* One (of any gender, both/all/none, in good old low-inflected English) who progs. And that's a long Oh, mind, as in *programmer*, not a shorty as in, well, *long.*

*Q:* And to prog? Or, as some may spell it, progue?

Let us begin with the Chesapeake Estuarine System, kiddies, and cut thence to the chase. Formed in its current configuration 10K years back, it was, at and by the end of the latest glaciation, with a probable prompt 35,000,000 years earlier from a mile-wide meteorite-strike 140 miles SE of Our Nation's Capital. The drownèd mouth of your Susquehanna River, is your C-peake Bay, and your largest mothering estuarine system in your USMFA, maybe your ditto world. At 300-plus kilometers north/south but only an average dozen-plus east/west and a mere measly average *three Ditsy-depths* top/bottom, she's as tall and slim and shallow as the female lead in a dumb-blonde joke, is Ms. CB. And she *is* a she, make no mistake as you could with me: Your Old Man River might just keep rolling with his one-track male no-mind, but our vagrant Chess not only ebbs and flows like the moonstruck mother she is — any old off-the-shelf ocean does *that* — but mixes salt and fresh till her average salinity just about matches that of the sack we all first swam in, or for that matter human tears. Add to which, her western shore's mainly high ground, her Eastern mainly low, and her *lower* Eastern mainly tide-marsh; add to *that* that her prevailing storm-winds are northwesterly, and in your southeast quadrant you've a proper progging ground: e.g., B.E.W.A.R.(E.).

Strike that, mate: A proper soggy prog-*bog* is what you've got. This brackish isle, this crab- and skeeter-rich wetland labyrinth: this . . . Hick Fen.

To prog, or progue ("origin and sense-history unknown," says my just-now-downloaded dictionary — but prog on, pal, and see below) = in general, to pick and poke about, to scavenge and to scrounge. More particularly, hereabouts, to beachcomb where no beach is, only the odd sandspit or low-tide mudflat 'mongst the marsh; to putt or pole or paddle one's shoal-draft johnboat, skiff, or own canoe* along the inches-deep but megamiles-long margins of the Bay's lee shore in leisurely but sharp-eyed search of . . .

Whatever. "Seek," saith Scripture, "and ye shall find," whereto your proper progger doth append "Amen — long's ye seek nothing in particular." Go ye forth a-progging for a certain length of half-inch braided nylon dockline or a spare red plastic fuel funnel, and you'll turn up a brace of used condoms like tired sea-nettles (but

---

* Hence Ditsy's non-Definitive Derivation: fr Fr *pirogue*, a dugout canoe, fr Sp *piragua,* ditto, corrupted fr Carib by Conquistadores and fr Fr by Br as once ruled the waves.

Day-Glo green, with ticklers), a snarl of fishermen's monofilament, a former spaniel, and the usual Big Mac boxes and Coors beer cans. Prog ye on the other hand for Whatever's Out There, and in addition to the routine assortment of usable lumber, salvageable gill-net, cork floats and other piscivorian accessories, doubler-crabs a-mating in the eel-grass, and yachtsfolk's hats sunspecs boathooks and personal flotation devices, you may turn up (to cite a few choice items from my own life-list) an entire summer tuxedo fetchingly entwined with a strapless ball gown, a former CIA clandestine-services officer with forty pounds of scuba weights 'round his waist and a 9 mm bullet hole abaft his left ear, a ship in a bottle (the latter uncorked and stranded one-quarter full of mucky Backwater; the former, a miniature square-rigger, storm-battered but still bravely afloat inside), a bottle in a ship (grounded and abandoned thirty-five-foot cruising sloop, both sails set, lunch half eaten on the dinette table, course plotted on the nav-station chart, and an unpopped liter of Dom Perignon in the wine-locker along with sundry inferior vintages, all which I liberated, finders keepers), and—different decade, different marsh, same old progger—a Ziploc™'d computer disk entitled

### COMING SOON!!!

Yeah right yes well: not as soon as Zulu II, was Ditso's guess, so I progged on for a spell, netted me a clutch of peeler-crabs, an orange rubber oysterman's glove (left hand, just right for right-hand shucking, and afloat fingers-up like a drowned waterman's last bye-bye), also the aforementioned brace of french-ticklered french letters (good as new once inside-outed, rinsed in Backwater Creek, air-dried, and recocked for firing; you never know who might turn up, and a girl can't be too careful these days with all them Ess Tee Dees floating 'round, d'accord?), and a pink glass fishnet-float, size of a canteloupe with net still rinding it, that must've blown either transatlantic from Portugal or transchesapeake from some gussied-up crabhouse across the way, as no waterperson hereabouts ever used such kitsch except for the odd decorative accent. Then I hustled home as the wind rerose and the sky redarkened over

4

B.E.W.A.R.(E.); hauled my progging-skiff (*Nameless*, I call her) 'bout as high as high goes on H.F.I., which is atop of my dock-deck and slip-knotted to my porchposts, ready to be jumped aboard of with my Getthehelloutahere bag atop Big Bitsy's workstation when cometh push to shove. Tidy anal-retentive that I am, I next stashed my take here and there as appropriate, and only *then* hauled my arse and the Ziploc™s three to my cobbled-up workstation and peeled off those serial containers the way Sir Summertux and Lady Strapless must've peeled off theirs, to have at the Thing Contained: the pearl within the oyster within the shell within the shucker's bushel,

*COMING SOON!!!*

Which doth remind me, that trebled exclamation, of lusty EARL&me a-hollering the like as we went to it once upon a time in yonder saltmarsh ("Your skiff or mine, hon?") or up on my dock-deck or over to her/his lab, wherever the rut smote either of us and whoever was that day's humper & who humpee. Sometimes a question, sometimes a warning to them as'd rather spit than swallow, most often a hopeful ejaculation, pardon my English, as me&him both were of an age more prone to ooze like the marsh we mucked in than to hey-diddly-diddle cow the moon. EARL! EARL! EARL!: mainly male through our joint marsh-tenancy, he was, as I was chiefly fe-, although our having each burnt her/his candle at both ends helped bring us together, you might say. E.A.R.L. is what his billcap advertised: the Estuarine Aquacultural Research Laboratory over to B.E.W.A.R.(W.) till the Navy reclaimed Westmarsh Island for an aerial gunnery target during the Persian Gulf Set-To. And "EARL"'s all the handle on that chipper chap I ever had or wanted, just as he in turn made do with hailing me, as boatfolk will, by the name of my skiff—old *Nameless?*—leaving off its first syllable by way of *tutoyer* (Less is More) as we came to know each other better.

Which I trow in very sooth is *why* we came, dear EARL and I, each for and/or in/on the other, depending on who et cetera in our Hick Fen hump-du-soir: *to know each other better*, not via names and résumés but in the King-Jim-Hebrew sense, the all but wordfree knowing of skin and eye and nose and tongue, of show-and-don't-tell, of scratch-and-sniff and lay-low-and-behold, of stroke and poke and squeal and sigh, of lick and split—of, in short and at length, the intercourse of Intercourse,

*COMING SOON!!!*

Not. But come it did and came, not so long ago, till it went with the wind of our Pentagon's latest, and the E.A.R.L. facility went with it, and pissed-off EARL with phased-out E.A.R.L.—not before, however, one glorious fuckitall joint progging of his half-dismantled aquacultural establishment, wherefrom we liberated not only a banquetsworth of prime tilapia and home-grown *Ostreae virginicae* (two of his graduate students' dissertation-projects down our pipes, EARL grumbled, shaking a free fist at the F-16s violating our airspace from their base at Patuxent, 'cross the Bay) but a Zip drive here, a modem there, here a keyboard, there a 17" color monitor and a laser printer and a CD-ROM gizmo and a hutch-topped workstation—all destined for recycling and replacement anyhow, so swore he. Thus came it to pass that before she could say Shucks or Shiver me timbers, old Dits was multigigabyte *wired*, man, and Big Bitsy (as we dubbed our only joint creation) was *online*—via what net-server, don't ask. Showed me how to up-and-run the sucker, dear EARL did, as I'd showed him a thing or three about snagging the odd out-of-season goose and rockfish, never mind how. Set me up proper for a different kind of progging, did the pearl of E.A.R.L.—that salty dog of B.E.W.A.R.(E.), that tongue-in-cheek namer (my tongue his cheek, then skiptomelou and all hands change partners all partners hands) of Hick Fen Isle, pop ⅺ 1 and holding: I mean a-progging through the warpèd woofs of your World Wide Web, a high-tech dreck-catcher if ever there was and a not-bad second-best companion on a dark and stormy night when there's not squat to do on H.F.I. except pick one's nose and suck one's home brew and watch sitcom reruns till the power goes, sometimes all three at once. Nowanights that menu's larger by one mighty item, with its own menus of menus of WWW menus. . . .

And here (some pages past) is where I came in: booted up Big Bitsy, unzipzip zipped and slugged in its slot that proggèd program, then open-sesame'd with mouseclicks twain its triply exclamatoried icon. Found in the window thus 4squared upon my monitor one of those Start-Here mini-icons called READ ME; clicketyclick and what to my wandering eyes should appear but the text you've just read (if you've read it, my dear)—I mean READ ME, "Call me ditsy," et cet—followed by the option-buttons below, wherefrom-among (skipping most of the text, as I'd read it this far already) I no sooner clicked ⓞ (for *On with the story*) than Z Two struck as if Z-squared: power down, storm-surge up, cabin shaking, lights out for the territory—and that's all she wrote.

Or almost all. Zulu Two's a humdinger, all right, fit to fin this tempest-tossed siècle with: But there's those of us as've weathered the stormfraught alphabet before, and learned therefrom a few things the hard way, and survived thereby to tell the tale, so to click; anyhow to run enough versions thereof to catch its drift. Will therefore now rebag(bag[bag]) this disk, refloat it off on the surge To Whom It May Concern, catch me a few raftered z's till Z has zed, then set out a-progging mañana after washed-away *Nameless* in hopes of refinding her and the porch she's moored to and/or EARL or/and who knows, maybe my own ventriloquizing self. Let me however just leave you, TWIMC, with this wrap-up sentiment, and then the option-buttons are all yours: It is one thing for an A-10 attack bomber to disappear into Colorado's wild blue yonder, or a multigigaton bulk carrier to break up in the Roaring Forties with nary a trace; you may invoke your Yew Eff Ohs and your Bermuda Triangles to your nutcase heart's content. But man & boy et alii I've worked the Bay since Hector was a pup—a-oystering, a-crabbing, a-haulseining, a-rod&reeling, even a-bay-piloting and a-hydrographic-charting a once upon a time. I know this Chesapeake the way I once knew my EARL's sweet bod, is what I'm saying: every blessed freckle and lump and cranny-hair. Even know her bottom, durned if I don't, I mean my Chessie's, the way some seasoned Bay-sailors know her top. And you can't tell *me* that there is or lately was (as this here disk claims) a great mothering *showboat* stuck on a shoal with all hands somewhere out there, that nobody's yet caught sight and

fetched the TV newscopters athwart of: Nosirreebob! But if somehow there subjunctively *were*, after all, so improbable a beastie as
*The Original Floating Opera II* aground out yonder on "Ararat
Shoal" and floating SOSs off in Ziploc™s while *en attendant Zulu*,
you can bet your bottom shekel she's history now.

But don't take Ditsy's word on't, mate, for I'm a coin as 2-sided
as this disk: For more on *TOFO II*, click LESS (you get the idea)
or whateverthefug else you opt. Hop to't now 'n click *something*,
though, luv: Curtains-time's a-*COMING SOON!!!*

<u>Its qualified recommendation of the more or less qualified "Novelist Aspirant" by the presumably still qualified Ditto "Emeritus":</u>

January 4, 1995

FROM:  Office of the Novelist You-Should-Excuse-the-Expression Emeritus

TO:  Whom it may concern

RE:  CONFIDENTIAL RECOMMENDATION FOR J. H. JOHNSON

Dear former colleagues and fellow readers of what follows:

This is to recommend, warmly but warily, <u>Mr. J. Hopkins Johnson</u> for admission to "our" graduate program in novel-writing, now yours.

Certain of you may know this young man better than I do. His parents are professors of medicine at our institution and cordial but casual acquaintances of mine, whose son I've come to know slightly through this acquaintance. Whether because of or despite the circumstances of his name and background (see Applicant Author's Personal Statement, attached), "Hop" Johnson appears to have been, on balance, a creditable undergraduate at this university. Although his general academic record is as unimpressive as was mine at his age and stage, he has managed to become something of a star not only of our popular B.A. program in creative writing but of our more modest offerings in theater, film, and video production as well. On his own initiative, moreover (but with my encouragement), he established and directed a noncredit Intersession course in Electronic Fiction — our department's first and thus far only venture into the problematic medium of interactive computer-fiction: literary hypertext.

Inasmuch as his undergraduate career happens to have coincided with the first phase of my academic retirement, when I was coaching only our M.A. candidates, I never taught Mr. Johnson directly in that period of his literary apprenticeship. Inasmuch as his *graduate* career, if he has one, will follow my complete academic retirement in June, I won't be coaching his advanced apprenticeship, either. For reasons set forth in his Personal Statement, however, he made known to me some time ago his "postmodern" interest (the adjective is his, as are the quotation-marks around it) in the late-19th-/early-20th-century American *showboats*, of all odd dramatic vehicles, and in particular the old James Adams Floating Theater, which cruised the Chesapeake from 1914 to 1941 and inspired or at least abetted Edna Ferber's 1926 bestseller *Show Boat* and that novel's subsequent famous spinoffs on Broadway and in Hollywood. Also and therefore, he told me (and more or less by the way, I suspect), he had come to know my own maiden novel, likewise inspired by the old Adams Chesapeake showbarge and written forty years ago, when I was the present applicant's present age.

Over the course of his latter undergraduate years, Johnson and I had a number of informal office-and-hallway conferences, in the course of which he apprised me in some detail of his family situation (see Personal Statement) and his summer internships aboard a showboat allegedly named "The Original Floating Opera II," and he pressed me to review his unfinished "fictionalized" account of those adventures. Against my own ground rules (for I was awash in my "regular" students' manuscripts and my own), review it I did, by reason of our shared interest in that bit of Chesapeakery; by reason also of my curiosity about any factual counterpart of his "TOFO II"; by reason finally, I confess, of some avuncular interest in the young man himself, who in certain ways reminds me (though I never had his chutzpah) of Yours Truly at his age.

What I read, actually, were bits and pieces and ever-changing prospectuses of a draft of Mr. Johnson's shape-shifting "novel," earlier than the redone but still-uncompleted version that he'll presumably be submitting herewith as his Writing Sample. Although unmistakably the work of an able apprentice in need of further coaching, those prospectuses and excerpts (lost-and-found computer disks, jokey "tables of contents" and manic "casts of characters," "orientation sessions" and pseudo-prologues) I found rather audaciously imagined, architecturally and ontologically intriguing (you'll see what I mean), and, on the whole, entertainingly written.

By the venerable device of prefacing his narrative with faked "documentary" material, the author pretends that his fiction is a factual account. By the less-venerable device of dating the ostensibly autobiographical action a few years hence, at our century's virtual end, he then evidently does the reverse: pretends that what in truth may well be a more or less factual account is "actually" fiction. Whether the reader finds engaging or tiresome such smoke-and-mirror tricks, a staple of Postmodernism, will depend on that reader's taste and experience. This late in the literary day, I myself find them off-putting in principle but still engaging when they're artfully done and relevant to the story's point. Hop Johnson's deployment of them meets those critera, in my opinion — or anyhow did so, last time I looked. He reuses such overused devices precisely because they've been overused; a "CPRtist of the done-to-death," as he once characterized himself to me, he plays the author playing the role of Author to spin out a novel in the form of The Novel, perfectly aware that that's just about where some of us came in, and resolved to tell a good story anyhow: one that, as he piquantly puts it, "will flap its fucking crutches and *fly*, man!" *Mirabile dictu* (again, in my opinion, last time I looked), he brings it off — but that is of course for you to judge.

In sum, the applicant is a bright, ambitious, and not untalented young man who — after an erratic high-school career, an aimless post-high-school interval, and a stumbling undergraduate start — not only "found himself" but distinguished himself, at least within our department, and who shows some promise as a budding professional. If occasionally a bit of a wise-ass and mischief-maker, he is no more so than were certain of our past graduate-level apprentices of whom we are currently most proud. His undergraduate professors report that he takes and delivers criticism well (but see my own comment on that, below) and that he is generally responsible in the area of deadlines and revisions (indeed, he revises *too* readily and frequently, in my judgment, preferring like the God of Genesis to trash and rebegin his fictional worlds rather than amend them). Moreover, I for one have found him to be by and large a personable and knowledgeable fellow, quite serious but prevailingly good-humored. I shall even say that I would enjoy being his official coach and mentor—perhaps more than his parents have enjoyed being his parents—were I not retiring from coach- and mentorhood.

Whence then my wariness about recommending this applicant for admission to our Master of Arts program? My reservations are several:

- I disapprove on principle of admitting our own undergraduates into our graduate programs. Better for them and for us that after four years of our tutelage, especially in a small university like this one, they move on to new turf, new coaches, a different air than ours—perhaps that of the world at large. Given Hop Johnson's background, this principle applies with particular force; he needs a fresh latitude & longitude, literal and figurative. On the other hand, such principles are made to be risen above where exceptions are called for. Four and a half decades after the fact, I remain grateful that such an exception was made in my own case back at mid-century, when—as I struggled to pursue my new-found vocation and support a premature family with whatever pickup work I could scrounge—a shift of environments would have sorely handicapped my search for the elusive muse. Despite his bachelorhood and his apparently boundless self-confidence, something similar may apply to Hop Johnson. Moreover, having permitted himself an extended *Wanderjahr* between high school and college (see Personal Statement), he is understandably now inclined to go straight on with his formal literary apprenticeship.

- His aforenoted inclination to reimagine, reinvent, and rebegin rather than to consolidate, revise, and refine may belie that same self-confidence. A target busily on the move, Hop inclines to agree with almost whatever critical objections I offer his manuscript and then to declare that he has anticipated those objections and has dealt with the "problem" already by scrapping that particular passage, episode, or character—even that overall design for the project! —or, on the contrary, that he intends to address the problem not by amending the text but by incorporating into it my critical objections before "the reader" can raise them. "I'll just put that in the show" is his characteristic response to criticism. I once called him, in this moving-target aspect, the Phantom of his own Opera. Replied Hop, "Cool, man: I'll put that in the show."

- Finally (anyhow next), I have reason to question the depth and seriousness of the Applicant's commitment—not to his art, whatever that turns out to be, about which he's serious indeed, but to our particular program and, for that matter, to Storytelling As We Know It, even to what has by now become the tradition of the Postmodernist novel (I mean those smoke-and-mirror tricks aforecited, the risky yanking of rugs from under readerly feet— devices that can make one long for Jane Austen, Charles Dickens, even Trollope and Henry James, anyone who'll just tell us a good story without forever reminding us that *it's only words on paper*). Even those devices—which for Hop Johnson are ironic quotations less from such playful proto-Postmoderns as Laurence Sterne and Denis Diderot, Edgar Poe and Jan Potocki, than from contemporary Postmodernists who themselves are ironically reorchestrating those pioneers—the Applicant deploys with a kind of impatience, like a bored virtuoso illusionist warming up for the main event, the Real Action.

For J. Hopkins Johnson, by his own acknowledgment, that action is elsewhere than on the printed page. Provisionally, at least, it is in the do-it-yourself labyrinths of "e-fiction," where the traditional job-descriptions of "author" and "reader" (or, one might say, of Daedalus and Theseus) are up for grabs; where narrative order deliquesces into virtual anarchy; where Beginnings, Middles, and Endings lose their longstanding sense and sequence, and such old standbys as plot-foreshadowings and reprises, climax and cathartic resolution, give way to ad-libitum jiggery-pokery: to "freedom from the tyranny of the line"—which, to some of us, is tantamount to freeing Theseus from Ariadne's indispensable yarn.

If that cyberspatial siren, e-fiction, is his true muse, I have asked the Applicant, why waste his time and ours with us? Why not apply instead to America's first officially designated Professor of Electronic Fiction and his lively program in that medium up at Brown University, to whom and to which I would readily recommend him? Replied JHJ, "I'm *doing* that, man! Here's their rec form; thanks in advance!" That is, it turns out, his first choice; but shifting up to Providence would mean severing his connection with *The Original Floating Opera II* and its dramatis personae (there is some romantic involvement there, his "novel" suggests, in addition to his wages as the company's all-purpose writer/performer/high-techie and his interest in "Postmodernist showboatery"). Given his spotty undergraduate transcript, moreover, he is justifiably less than confident that Brown will accept him with full tuition-waiver and teaching-assistant stipend, and so he frankly wants us as his backup: "A *close* second, mind you," he declares, and assures me that we would be his absolutely first choice if he happened to be "into a flat-out *Novel*-novel, you know?" or if we had any sort of program at all in — "even one measly adjunct professor of" — e-fiction.

I had better add that in Applicant's opinion, electronic fiction itself is but the transitional medium between printed literature (also theater, cinema, television drama, perhaps lived life itself) and the New Jerusalem of Electronic Virtual Reality. Enough said?

Not quite:

- My bottom-line scruple concerning this applicant is that his freewheeling showboatery inclines to appropriate not only certain field-identification marks of Postmodernist taletelling but, on occasion, the tellers themselves; that he now and then brazenly crosses the line between ironic quotation or parody and at least virtual forgery. "At *most* virtual," I suppose he would reply if confronted with this charge, and his correction may be well taken: Virtuality is Hop Johnson's stock-in-trade. But there is something about his *modus operandi* that reminds me of a computer virus: Once innocently admitted into your program, it busily self-replicates, impinges upon, and ultimately "eats" your files, takes over your script, mimics and then replaces your voice with its own or another — whatever it is that such a Phantom of the Opus does. Forewarned is forearmed?

Friends, colleagues, and any other readers of these pages: There it is. You may be certain that I have laid into Applicant on these matters: I've let him know that we are not pleased to be anybody's second choice; that I am supporting his application to us only with the understanding that I'll make no secret of my several reservations abovegiven, and that should you see fit to admit him despite those reservations (and any others of your own), he had better apply himself heart and soul to us and to our grand old moribund medium— "p-fiction," Hop calls it—or expect no further encouragement from Yours Truly down the line. I happen to believe that he'll honor his "cross my fuckin' heart, man" pledge to me to do that; Hop's a good boy.

Scratch that: Mr. Johns Hopkins Johnson is a prevailingly though not absolutely responsible, prevailingly though not perfectly scrupulous twenty-four-year-old man.

Tough call, this one. I'm relieved that the calling of it is up to Whom This May Concern and not to

Yours truly,

# Personal Statement

4/1/95

O invisible reverend judges of my fate:

The writer of my main and maybe only letter of recommendation tells me that over his 911 years at this 119-year-old institution he has read 123,456 of these Personal Statements from wannabe grad-student apprentice Nobel Laureates in print-lit and has come to prefer the straight-out short ones that say in effect *Do us both a favor and let me in, okay? I'm pretty good already, but I could use more practice with high-quality feedback if I'm going to distinguish myself from my comparably talented and no less hungry peers, which I damned well intend to do, in a way that will one day redound to your credit. You guys have a reputation for providing such feedback. End of statement.* And he glazes over fastest at the ones that suck up to him and his celebrated colleagues or, worse, attempt a Witty Parody of their prose (his own intricated periods, e.g., with their abundant parentheses, Teutonic Uppercasements, and hyperhyphenated compounds; their semicoloned members, and the archaizing coinages themin; their et ceteras, etc.). In between, he declares, are the Ha-Ha-Ho-Hum Histories (*I've known I was a Writer since the day I first managed to scrawl my name in block capitals on the wall of the Kreative Korner Pre-School in Crayola Burnt Sienna. Where, you ask, is Crayola, Burnt Sienna? A long way from Mount Parnassus,* etc.), the Magniloquent Manifestos (*We must liberate Literature from the twin tyrannies of Line and Page, from its bondage to the Binding, even to the Book—indeed, from its venerable vassalage to the Word! We must snatch the complacent Reader from the seductive snares of Story and mercilessly gestalt her with the whips of nonlinear Reality*, etc.), and other such categories of preening tedium, more familiar to him than to me. "The idea," he has apprised me, "is simply to give us some idea of what you sound like when you're not Making It All Up. Just tell us where you're coming from," he has advised me, "and why you want to do your Next Thing here instead of elsewhere." Never mind that in a sense (as who knows better than he?) we're *never* not Making It All Up; that in its need to sort out the instreaming flood of sense-data, human consciousness has evolved into a nonstop Scenario Machine or Ficting Factory, all of us the ongoing authors of the Stories-in-Progress of Our Lives. We know what he means. And never mind too, I hope, that as a matter of first-choice fact this properly prestigious p-lit program is *not* my #1 Druther. No doubt Herr Doktor-Professor E. Meritus, my first-and-last-ditch sponsor, has blown the whistle on that datum in his rec-letter—the 654,321st (and last) of his academic career, he informs me, but the all-but-first of mine.

Anyhow, here goes: My fairly famous mom and dad—professors of endocrinology and cardiology, respectively, at a certain *very* famous crosstown medical institution—so loved their joint undergraduate and med-school alma mater (and subsequent employer) that they named their only-begotten son after this dear damned distinguished place: *Johns Hopkins Johnson*, believe it or not, right down to that terminal *s* on the moniker's front bumper, which no ordinary taxpayer ever remembers. (Who would name a kid *Johns*? Only Our Founder's parents and mine.) Indeed, for that reason and others I grew up feeling as much this university's offspring as my busy folks', with duly and similarly mixed emotions regarding both. So enamored of their profession are Doctors Mom & Dad that, not a bit surprisingly, their one ambition for their One & Only from Day One (if not long before) was the big EM DEE, preferably to be by him pursued on location here in MD at the big JHU and then at the ever-so-bigger JH Medical Institutions—the mighty dog whereof you guys are the notable tail. Cardiology, endocrinology, general practice, even: The choice was mine, from Abdominojugular Reflexology to Zollinger-Ellison Syndromology, as long as my profession was MEDICINE.*

Alas for them, of all professions on Planet Earth that is the one that, having had such a lifelong taste of it, I had the least taste for. My prep-school passions (Where else but at next-door Gilman School, named for the Hop's first prexy and cloned from its red-brick-Georgian Homewood campus?) were not, as they were meant to have been, science, math, and lacrosse, but theater, computer hacking, video production, and rock drumming—the first two quite curricular if not Quite Right, the others extracurricular and All Wrong. I made a mini-career of straining the parameters of the school's dress code and was often suspended or otherwise disciplined, never unjustly, for rule-infractions large and small. When the subject of College came up at home, as it had done several times a week since before my conception, I declared to my long-suffering parents my intention to major in Anything Except Pre-Med and its associated sciences, anywhere except They Knew Where. Disappointed but by that time unsurprised, and perennially optimistic (also, I should add, sempiternally forbearing, in part because eternally overworking and fatigued), the folks offered me a deal: I might (1) attend at their full expense any college in the land to which I could win admission, so long as I chose that college's pre-medical curriculum, and then "go on" to med school anywhere ditto, likewise at their full expense. Or I might (2) major at their full expense in anything I chose at Johnnyass Hopkins, their hope being that this place's pre-medical ambiance would bring me to my senses; if it failed to, I would have to manage grad school on my own. Or I might (3) major in the nonmedical frivolity of my choice

---

* "What's the Jewish word for God beginning with *A*?" my secular-Jewish mom once asked at dinner. "*Adonai*?" supposed my *goyishe* but savvy dad. "That's Hebrew, not Jewish," mildly corrected Ma; "and I'm asking Johnsie." But Johnsie hadn't a clue, this first time up, and so "*A doctor*," he was instructed—to which Dad added "Adonai's the *big* Gee Dash Dee, son. The likes of us are only [*forming the initials with his hands*] *M*inor *D*eities, okay?" Et cetera, bless their self-ironical, ever-patient and good-humored, but earnestly hopeful hearts.

18

wherever I damn pleased if I financed my own education—with interest-free student loans from them, to be deducted from my inheritance upon their demise, inasmuch as scholarship money would not likely be forthcoming for the child of two well-to-do physicians: a fractious fellow whose high-school record had been at best erratic and who hopped, shall we say, from one nonacademic enthusiasm to another.

Given these reasonable, yea generous, alternatives, I chose (4) None of the Above and hit the road, sort of, as drummer and technical director of In Your Face, a Proto-Postindustrial Grunge band of likemindedly disaffected children of privilege, whose high-expectational parents lost sleep wondering what they had done wrong. When IYF autodestructed while still in rehearsal at the lead guitarist's (parents') Sea Island beach house, I dispatched the good Doctors Johnson briefly to heaven by agreeing to give pre-med a try after all—at UCLA, where, when not on the beach at Malibu, I chilled out mainly with the film majors and, to put it mildly, did not distinguish myself in biology, chemistry, and mathematics. I did, however, survive a screenplay-writing course and by the way confirmed what my (excellent) English teachers back in Crayola, Burnt Siena, had more than once mentioned: that I seemed to have A Way With Words. (Little did those teachers of Excellent English suspect that I would grow up—or down—to cry "Away with words!")

The question (one of the questions, anyhow) was, Whose WWW did I have? In addition to my being not a scholar and not an athlete, I was not much of a reader, either, except extracurricularly. But one does not escape such splendid schools as had been mine without taking on some freight of uppercase Literature—which, truth to tell, spoke to me, and which I resisted only in its curricular aspect, as part of my general posture of resistance. Given my penchant for acting, however (including Acting Up and Acting Out), whatever I wrote slipped into the style of whatever I had most lately been wowed by reading, or of what I fancied to be the genre I was working. Thus my term papers were not really *term papers*, but more or less skillful imitations of Term Papers; my freshman screenplays were mimicries of Screenplays. Even my frequent letters home—to my pals, ex-girlfriends, fellow failed In-Your-Faceniks, even parents (and I ought to mention here that, unlike your generic American teenager, I never much cared for telephones and always enjoyed writing letters [especially e-mail: :-)])—were trompe-l'oeil Letters Home.

A certain longstanding casual-but-cordial acquaintance of my parents—himself a professor of Something Altogether Nonmedical at "our" Homewood campus, whom I came to regard as a sort of benign or at least nonjudgmental great-uncle, and with whom (if not *to* whom) I corresponded from time to time, don't ask me why—remarked to me, when I remarked to him this Imitation business in one of my faux-epistolary epistles, that perhaps the only notable achievement of my nineteen-year-long Story Thus Far—namely, my ad-libitum but programmatic Posture of Rebellion—was exactly that: a posture, one more imitation, a Pretty Good Act. He mildly wondered whether, "under all that makeup and costumery," the actor had any clear sense of himself. He mildly wondered why, if imitation was my passion or at least my penchant, I didn't go flat-out for it and declare a major in theater, or, if School was my bane (which he declined to believe), go for the real thing, Theater Itself, however one does that. Could it be, he mildly wondered, that my penchant for imitation was the mere imitation of a penchant? In any case, he mildly but correctly imagined that the price of my Posture of Rebellion had been a waste of first-rate educational opportunity; that I was approaching my majority a good deal more ignorant of the world, of myself, and of Accumulated Human Knowledge than would otherwise have been the case. This state of affairs he found at least mildly regrettable, he told me, less for the ways that it would surely "impact" my professional fulfillment than in itself—since LIFE, as the bumpersticker sagely remarks, IS NOT A DRESS REHEARSAL.

But all of this was, of course (he mildly acknowledged), my business, as it was after all my life.

With a Nonjudgmental Sort-of-Great-Uncle like that, one scarcely needs parents, yes? His assessment, while not really news, sufficiently impressed me that I did what any self-disrespecting undergraduate would do: I dropped out of the UC part of UCLA, farted around awhile longer in the LA part (busboying in Beverly Hills restaurants with the rest of the cast and honorably returning my parents' subsistence checks uncashed), hitchhiked for a year through Europe and North Africa with others of my aimless ilk, and anon—my teeth at least mildly clenched, but *faute de mieux*—matriculated in January 1992 as a double-legacy second-semester freshman here at Eponymous U, with a parental-eyeball-rolling declared major in . . .

Three years later, on the far side of those suspension points, here we are—too late for "hands-on" coaching by Great-Uncle M. Irritus (whose hands-off attitude has been, on the whole, more to my liking), but not too late for me to run a few things by him, and him by me, extracurricularly. Did I finally and belatedly get my shit together? Did I find my voice, as they say hereabouts, and if so, is it a voice worth listening to, or at least worth finer-tuning at the graduate level? ("The muses," quoth Gr-U, "know nothing of such distinctions as Graduate and Undergraduate. All that matters to the muses is talent, disciplined one way or another into mastery. But *we are not the muses*, lad.") Alternatively, did my maybe-imitation penchant for imitation lead me down the path of a certain Hollywood waitress-friend who assured me, one smoggy night on the beach at Malibu, that "in acting, the crucial thing is Sincerity. Once you've learned to fake *that*, you've got it made"? That is for you Reverend Invisible Judges to determine.


Two final matters, Revs:

1. *P-fiction*. I happen to believe, as you may have heard, that the 300-year Golden Age of Bourgeois Literacy, epitomized by the ascendancy of The Novel as a medium of entertainment and art, peaked somewhere in the neighborhood of 1895 and has been inexorably petering through the century since, its market-share of audience attention reduced first by the movies and broadcast radio, then by television and the VCR, more recently by interactive computer networking, and down the road by Electronic Virtual Reality. I hap-

pen to believe, not that The Novel is dead (an overstatement by self-titillating Modernists in this century's first half), but that it is destined to become, with the rest of p-lit, ever more a pleasure for special tastes, like poetry, archery, opera-going, equestrian dressage. This prospect I neither applaud nor deplore; I merely bear it in mind and keep my portfolio diversified. Which consideration brings us to

2. *Showboats!!!* How comes it, you may well ask, that a self-declared part-time evangel of e-fiction and EVR, who regards "straight" novel-writing as a quixotic though harmless exercise in nostalgia, has been for some years arse-deep in, of all regressive media, showboatery? Specifically, in the erratic but always more or less sinking fortunes of *The Original Floating Opera II*?

The Short Answer is that en route to my certification as a Bachelor of the Art of P-Fiction I needed a summer job, and that in Great-Uncular conversation about *his* old Original Floating Opera and its historical prototype, I learned of its latter-day post-type: what we're calling *TOFO II*. Applied for and by-golly got a summer internship thereaboard, I did, and another in summer subsequent; worked me way up, I did, from all-purpose techie/deckhand/pit-drummer/bit-player to all-purpose techie/deckhand/pit-drummer/bit-player/*script-doctor* (the only doctor your son will ever be, folks) and involved myself, to put it mildly, with the vessel's fortunes, including proposals to convert it — should Postmodern Nostalgia fail, as is more than likely — into either a floating casino or a floating EVR-kade (my idea) or both. See Novel (coming soon).

The Long Answer comprises that pretty-straight novel-in-the-works itself, appended hereto and -roundabout as Applicant's Writing Sample: no sample, really, but the Whole Effing Story Thus Far (i.e., as of 9/9/99, an olympiad-and-then-some from "now"), to which I respectfully refer Yr Rev Invis Et Cets. It is a novelization not only of my adventures aboard dear dying TOFO Two but likewise of the script of The New Show (*END TIME: COMING SOON!!!*) that a certain Ms. Sherry Singer and I, with others of the Arkade Theatre Company's Script Team, busted our butts to cobble up in time for *TOFO's* "Final Season," climaxing on 11/11/99 in Baltimore's Inner Harbor: a last-ditch effort to Save Our Ship.

We missed—or shall I say, shall miss?—that deadline. See Novel.

So! *Do us both a favor and let me in, okay? I'm pretty good already* [if he does say so himself], *but I could use more practice with high-quality feedback if I'm going to* [etc.], *which I damned well intend* [etc.]. *You guys have a rep for providing such feedback. End of statement.*

[End of statement]

—except for an italicized postscript, clunkily echoing Stephen Dedalus's famous invocation of his mythic namesake in the closing lines of James Joyce's p-lit *Portrait of the Artist as a Young Man*, written at the virtual dawn of this now-virtually-sunset century:

P.S.: *Old "Great-Uncle," old artificer* [who in fact don't know Yours Truly from Adam], *stand by me nonetheless as I forge in the smithy of my word-processor the foregoing Letter of Recommendation in your name.*

Toot toot! Showboat round the bend!! *COMING SOON!!!*

*(The Phantom ;-)*

GET to story

HELL with story

Whatever

Its Applicant Author's aforepromised Writing Sample, or, just
possibly, *It!:*

# Coming Soon!!!

## THE NOVEL?

# Is There a Gee Dash Dee?

TO:  Sherry Singer, Director, Arkade Theatre Company, New Ark
     Productions, etc. etc.
FROM:  Hop Johnson, Script Team, *The Original Floating Opera II*
RE:  Draft script of proposed Orientation Session for New Hands,
     per Yr bright suggestion (wch = my command)

[*Suggest Newbies be seated front row center, Yr Sexy Self stationed
before orchestra pit w chalkboard on stand & pointer in hand. Suggest attendance at these orientation sessions be given High Priority,
and as many players be corralled from each of the several "teams"
as can be rounded up (wish I'd had such a session when I first came
aboard). Suggest playing tape of peppy-frisky showboat music while
audience assembles—perhaps our own PIT BULLS' Dixieland rendition of "Sailing Down Chesapeake Bay," available on CD from the
Galley, Concession & Bar Team. Better yet if band does these gigs
live, to supply fills and accents to what follows. Suggest YOU cut a
bit of a jig Yr Sexy Self as music winds up, or down. Then:*]
     YOU: Good [morning/afternoon/evening], everybody! And to all
of you Newbies from all of us Old Hands, a hearty welcome aboard
the good ship *TOFO Two*! WELCOME TO THE TEAM!
     [*Reprise "Sailing Down" etc. OLD HANDS stand, applaud NEW
TEAMMATES, sit.*]
     YOU: Now, then: Before we tell you who *we* are, let's find out
who *you* are! One at a time, guys, please: Stand up and look us in

the eye, tell us what name you go by, where's your hailport, and which capital-T Team you'll be working with. Let's start with this [great lummox/wee slip of a thing/wino derelict/whatever] here.

[*Suggest motioning each* NEW HAND *in turn to rise (perhaps with fanfare), face house, say spiel, be applauded, sit. E.g.:*]

NEW HAND #1: Herman Hunk! Altoona, PA! Galley, Concession, and Bar Team!

[*Polite applause. HH blushes manfully, nods, sits.*]

N.H. #2: Polly Morphus? From Morphusboro, TN? And I'll be working with the Thee-ay-ter Team? [*Sigh. Wink.*] Whatever the part requires . . . ?

[*Cheers, whistles, percussion, acknowledged by Ms. PM with perky flounce and flashy Quick-Change, perhaps into . . .*]

N.H. #3 (*a lean and grizzled squinting entity of indeterminate age, gender, and provenance*): Call me Ditsy, call me whatchadurn please, long's you don't call me too late for dinner, you copy? [*Percussion.*] I'm from way down-county and right proud of it, 'n I'll be doin' my durnedest to keep this old sumbitch afloat. [*Sits, without waiting for . . .*]

YOU: Maintenance and Engineering Team!

[*Applause, calls of "Good luck!" etc. Thus through the Newbie-roster, with appropriate* PIT BULLS *accents. Then:*]

YOU: Again we say welcome aboard *The Original Floating Opera Two*! I see CAP'N ADAM LAKE back there checking his watch already, so let's get this orientation-show on the road! [*Seriously but still cheerily:*] In just a short while, mates, we'll be casting off and getting under way for our [summer/seventh/Final/whatever] season, and I can guarantee you'll be busy bees indeed from the first All Aboard till we ring down the curtain at season's end, for it's Rule Number One aboard *TOFO Two* that no matter which quote *team* you're officially assigned to, *everybody lends a hand wherever he/she is needed!* Do I hear "Aye aye"? [*"Aye aye, ma'am!," "Right on, Sher!," "What'd she say?," etc.*] One hand for ship and shipmates and one for yourself, 'cause we're all in the same boat et cetera blah blah—and since you're likely to lose track now and then of which end is up and who fits where, we're going to take just a few minutes here to give you a shot of your place in the Grand Scheme of Things! [*Fanfare as* YOU *mime unveiling of chalkboard:*] Gents and ladies: THE BIG PICTURE! [*Gesture toward board; notice it's blank; mug appropriately to disappointed percussion. Then:*] Okay, so the BP needs a bit of filling in! So let's start with you guys, right . . . about . . . here! [*At very bottom center of board, write* YOU GUYS.]

> VOICE FROM ORCHESTRA PIT OR REAR OF THEATER, DE-PENDING: Bottom of the food chain!

> [*Laugh-track chuckles, percussion.*]

> YOU: Shame on you, Hop Johnson! That's our own J. Hopkins Johnson from the Script Team, guys: our newly-designated Writer-in-Chief and alleged funnyman as well as not-bad drummer with our very own PIT BULLS, whom we'll come to when we come to him—*if* we come to him. [*Percussion.*] "Bottom of the food chain," did he say? Let's say Salt of the Earth instead—Salt of the Chesa-peake, whatever! [*Touch pointer to* YOU GUYS.] What's the Base of the Pyramid, I ask you, if not the Foundation of the Whole Freaking House, am I right? [*Affirmative noises from* WHOLE F'ING H.] With-out whose steadfast and tireless support there could be no . . . [*YOU mug wide-eyed hesitation, hand over mouth.*] C'mon, Sherry: Out on a limb! [*Mug determination; point again to bottom of board.*] Without YOU GUYS down here, plus a few of the rest of us here in the middle, there could be no [*Tap top of board*] . . . no GEE DASH DEE up here!

> [*At top center of board, to reverent fanfare and more-or-less-affirmative murmurs from* WHOLE F'ING H, *write* G-D.]

> YOU: The All-But-Unnameable, right? Who no doubt is with us here in spirit, but couldn't be spared from Her infinite responsibili-ties to attend this session in bodily form. [*Mug prayerful reverence. Organ chord from pit.*] "Praise GEE DASH DEE, from Whom all blessings flow!" [*Another chord.*] "Praise Her-Slash-Him, to Whom net profits go!" And to Whom the ARKANGELS, whereof more presently, reportedly report. [*Two spaces under* G-D, *write* ARKAN-GELS.] Now, then: You may hear certain skeptical shipmates ask, Does GEE DASH DEE really and truly exist? Mightn't He/She have

once existed but then up and jumped ship some seasons back? [*From assorted OLD HANDS, cries of "Yes!," "No!," "Who cares?," "Call him/her Ditsy!"*] Or maybe She/He still exists, but has no present function? Technologically unemployed? Corporately down-sized? [*Laugh-track chuckles.*] Or maybe She has a present function, all right—like being Top Banana in the corporate food chain, high guy on the organizational totem pole, peak of the pyramid whereof YOU GUYS [*Point*] are the sturdy base—like, maybe He-Slash-She has a whole showboatload of present functions, but nevertheless happens not to exist? [*"Right!," "Wrong!," "So?," "Ditsy shmitzy!," etc.*] Me, whenever I hear somebody launch into one of those old theological tunes, I come back with one of my own, to wit: [*Peppy two-bar keyboard intro. Then:*]

> *As far as I can see,*
> *There ain't no* GEE DASH DEE. . . .
> *But there* might *be. Don't ask me!*
> *I just direct the* ATC.

Which is to say, the ARKADE THEATRE COMPANY! [*Applause, modestly acknowledged with sweep of Your hand to include seated fellow members of the THEATRE TEAM.*] Which goes just about *here* on our map of the world. [*Halfway between* ARKANGELS *and* YOU GUYS, *write* ATC: Arkade Theatre Company.] Note the Brit-style -T-R-E, okay? [*Whole-body shrug.*] That's how the Boss wants it spelled, so don't ask me, I just work here. And who am I? [*Ardent cries of "Sherry Singer!," which* YOU *wave off.*] We'll get to that; for now, just call us the T-R-E THEATRE TEAM! [*Applause.*] Thank you—to which team we shall in due time return, you betcha. Meanwhile, let's start in the middle of this here Big Picture and work both ways. [*Back to chalkboard; point to* ATC.] The ATC—which stands for? [*Audience dutifully choruses correct-for-the-most-part reply.*] Right you are—and that's *Arkade* with a *k*, mind you, as in Noah's? [*Chuckles, live or canned.*] The Arkade Thea-T-R-E Company happens to be the production wing of a two-winged birdie called . . . [*Write on board, above and to left of* ATC] N-A-P: New Ark Productions, Inc.! Or, as we call 'em here on *TOFO Two*, our ANGEL TEAM!

*[Your chalkboard now looks approximately as follows, YOU having deftly appended a question-mark to G-D, rewritten* ARKANGELS *as* (Arkangel Team) *without yet explaining those parentheses, and outlined the several still-unnamed branches of the organizational chart:*

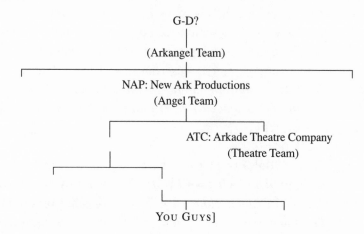

G-D?

|

(Arkangel Team)

NAP: New Ark Productions
(Angel Team)

ATC: Arkade Theatre Company
(Theatre Team)

YOU GUYS]

YOU: Nobody said Orientation was going to be easy! But *[Use pointer]* there's GEE DASH DEE up in Her/His heaven, maybe, and here's YOU GUYS front row center *[Applause]*, and here's *me*-guys of the ATC—

VOICE FROM DEPTHS OF PIT OR REAR OF THEATER, DEPENDING: Sherry M. Singer, Director and star! Let's hear it for Miz Sherry the Singer!

*[Fanfare & vigorous applause, natch, to which YOU mug Modest Acknowledgment.]*

YOU: Thank you, Hop Johnson, you smartass sweetie. Anyhow, up here is the ANGEL TEAM, New Ark Productions, whose Angel-in-Chief, I'm happy to say, is with us today *[If indeed she is, fanfare & introduce]*: Miz JUNE HARRISON, a.k.a. the distinguished *[former, and never* very *distinguished, but let that go]* actress quote BEA GOLDEN unquote! Stand up and take a bow, Ma!

*[If present & sober enough, YOUr alleged mother rises from her balcony seat, bows, & sits, preferably in that order. Indeed, if sufficiently unjuiced she might well attempt words of welcome to YOU GUYS, which it shall be the responsibility of her gorgeous & alco-*

31

*hol-abstinent daughter to contain within the time available, and good luck to You.*]

YOU (*wiping faux-tear from eye*): That's right, guys, we're a mom-and-daughter act. Long live nepotism, okay? [*Laugh-track chuckles.*] And that's before we even get to *Grandma* Harrison, way up on the Big Picture, as shall be seen. But as I was saying [*Back to chalkboard*]: New Ark Productions is a two-winged bird, of which we Theatre Teamies are one wing and the other is . . . anybody?

VOICES FROM HERE & THERE: Your father! The Dream Team! The Antichrist! [*Etc., until the aforehypothesized pert P. MORPHUS, shall we say, pertly raises her pert li' l hand and, pointered by Yr Sexy Self, ventures:*]

PM: FLOPCORP?

YOU: Brains too! FLOPCORP it is! [*Applause & salutatory music, fetchingly acknowledged by Ms. PM as You write FLOP-CORP opposite ATC and explain:*] The Floating Opera Corporation, or, as We Guys and You GUYS call it . . . [*Write in parentheses, after FLOPCORP:*] the SHOWBOAT TEAM, captained by who else if not our stalwart, our redoubtable CAPTAIN! ADAM! ANDREW! LAKE! From whom we'll now hear a word or three. Front and center, Cap'n Ad!

[*Applause & fanfare, naturally. Cometh forward. With deliberate step. From rear of hall. Our Stalwart Redoubtable. Winketh eye at Yr Sexy Self. Glanceth up & noddeth at Mme JH-a.k.a.- "BG." Checketh wristwatch, as is his tic. Then in captainly wise addresseth the assembled. More or less thus:*]

CAPT. AD.: I'll make this short. [*Rechecketh watch.*] Like Sherry said, your ATC is an arm of your New Ark Productions. Which is just one division of your Dorset Tradewinds Enterprises Incorporated. . . . [*Not having quite said that, above (Arkangel Team) You quickly chalk in the full corporate name preceded by the initials DTE. CAPT. AD. noddeth approval & proceedeth:*] Now, then. DTE's directive from your Tidewater Foundation . . .

[*Pauseth; frowneth at You, who mug an embarrassed Oops and —above DTE, under G-D?'s presumable backside—quickly enter Tidewater Foundation (G-D? Team), such that the BIG PICTURE now looks thus:*]

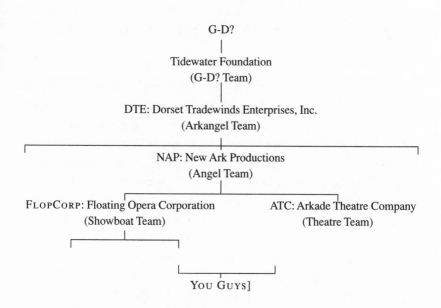

G-D?
|
Tidewater Foundation
(G-D? Team)
|
DTE: Dorset Tradewinds Enterprises, Inc.
(Arkangel Team)
|
NAP: New Ark Productions
(Angel Team)
|
FLOPCORP: Floating Opera Corporation          ATC: Arkade Theatre Company
(Showboat Team)                                         (Theatre Team)

YOU GUYS]

CAPT. AD.: As I was saying there: DTE's directive from your Tidewater Foundation is. And I quote [*Readeth from notes*]: "the economic and cultural enhancement. First, of the gated community of Dorsettown-on-Choptank, Maryland. And Second, of the Chesapeake tidewater region generally." Close quote. To this end, DTE saw fit 'bout a dozen years back. To establish a subdivision called New Ark Productions. [*YOU point, with pointer.*] And to charge it, Number One [*CAPT. AD. sticketh up left thumb*]. With publicizing the fair town of Dorsettown and DTE's various other enterprises. Such as your Tradewinds Park, your Snug Harbour Retirement operation, and your *TOFO Two*. Which we'll come to shortly. [*Beebusy, to the subdivisions of DTE YOU add* Tradewinds Park *on one side of* New Ark Productions *and* Snug Harbour, Inc. *on t' other.* TOFO II *finds its place farther down the Great Chain of Being, under* FLOPCORP'*s right hand or foot as viewed by YOU GUYS.*] And Number Two [*CAPT. AD. raiseth forefinger beside aforeraised thumb*] with making a profit for DTE, or at least not losing their corporate shirts. [*Laugh-track chuckles.*] I want you New Hands to remember that second charge of New Ark's. When you hear loose talk about converting this showboat into a floating casino or a video arcade or what have you . . .

FROM REAR OF HALL OR, POSSIBLY, DEPTHS OF PIT: Floating cathouse!

[*Percussion.*]

CAPT. AD. (*Scowleth sternly*): So: Dorset Tradewinds Enterprises' directives to New Ark Productions are One, *publicity.* And Two, *profit*—quote "or at least not loss" unquote. [*Glanceth at wristwatch.*] To carry out these directives, NAP formed two very different branches. Like Sherry here said. Each one with its own responsibilities. Your Arkade Theatre Company [*Putteth hand on sexy shoulder of You*] is a not-for-profit, tax-exempt concern. Eligible for subsidy from your Tidewater Foundation. It's even permitted to operate at a loss. Although you can bet that Miz Harrison up there at New Ark and *her* bosses at DTE would obviously rather see a break-even or better yet a small surplus at season's end. Now then. Your ATC [*Pointeth to board with aforespecified forefinger*] officially leases *TOFO Two* from your Floating Opera Corporation for its April-to-November season. But it also does fund-raisers and publicity events ashore in the off-season. Your FLOPCORP's responsibility, on the other hand. Is to maintain, manage, and operate both your *Original Floating Opera Two* [*Pointeth to abbreviated name on board*]. And her tugboats, *Raven* and *Dove.* [*To left of TOFO II, YOU duly enter* Raven & Dove (Propulsion Team). *Continueth CAPT. AD., after glance at watch:*] Some folks might think all FLOPCORP does is schedule this showboat from one town to the next. So Sherry and her team can strut their stuff. [*YOU strike an appropriately stuff-strutting pose, to ditto accompaniment.*] But besides leasing *TOFO Two* to the ATC and getting it where it's s'posed to be, both safely and on time [*Tappeth wristwatch*]. We're responsible for the food and beverage concessions. Including three square meals a day for the company and crew—

YOU (*presuming for first time to interrupt*): GALLEY, CONCESSION, AND BAR TEAM!

[*Applause. Any GC&B Teamers present briefly stand at Your prompting, not forgetting New Hand HERMAN HUNK aforehypothesized. Sit.*]

CAPT. AD.: And likewise for renting out this showboat off-season for other purposes. No wisecracks, please. To sum it all up, as director of your Showboat Team [*Pointeth to* FLOPCORP *on board*] it's my job to make a profit, or at least not lose money, for your NAP [*Pointeth*]. And as skipper of your *TOFO* Team [*Pointeth*], it's my job to get you where you're s'posed to be. Number One [*Thumb*], safely! And Number Two [*Forefinger*], on time! Needless to say [*Consulteth watch*], these two objectives sometimes pull in opposite directions. Ten minutes, Sher?

YOU (*saluting smartly*): Aye aye, sir! [*Applause for* CAPT. AD., *who curtly noddeth acknowledgment & leaveth theater, to relief of several.*] And speaking of pulling in different directions together, it's time you NEW HANDS said howdy to our PROPULSION TEAM! Will CAP'N HARRY KANE of the tugboat *Raven* please rise and be howdied!

[*That Stocky Swarthy Ruggedly Handsome Trim-Mustachioed Energetic & Resourceful but Impatient & Impulsive Fellow duly does (preferably from down in the pit with us BULLS) and moreover fetches forth in mid-howdy the trusty trumpet never far from his skipperly hand, blows a near-perfect, ear-piercing high C, nods shortly as if to say "Take that!," and follows in* CAPT. AD.'s *wake, presumably to man his Ravenly station, leaving us PIT BULLS for the nonce brassless.*]

YOU (*rubbing Yr perfectly perfect gold-ringed earlobe*): Hoo! After a piercer like that I can wear *two* pairs! That's HARRY JAMES KANE of the mighty *Raven*, guys, blowin' up a storm—as you'll be hearing him do now and then onstage and down here in the pit with our boat-rockin' PIT BULLS BAND, whose music you've been grooving on between my lines! [*Four-bar blast of* PIT BULLS, *taped or live, horned or polled. Then:*] But now I ask YOU GUYS: What's a raven without a dove, or a twin without his/her twin? Meet CAP'N ELVA KANE of the good tug *Dove!* Elva-babe?

[*That Rangy-Tough Yet Placid/Serene/Regressive/Meditative/ Gently-Aging New Ager—Wouldn't you say, Sher?—unhurriedly withdraws her concentration from what appears to be reverse macramé (like nighttime Penelope, she's unweaving stitch by stitch some item of head-shop stitchery), refocuses unhurriedly first upon*

the NEW HANDS *each in turn, as if truly sizing them up, and then,
beamingly, upon You, with a small nod of approval, assent, whatever. Applause.*]

YOU (*gesturing toward Tugboat ELVA*): Massage therapist,
herbal tea–meister, organic dietitian extraordinaire, supporting actress in the ATC, and absolute boss of the good ship *Dove*—that's
our New-Age Elva/Nova! And take it from Sherry the Singer, mates:
When it comes to tea and sympathy here on *TOFO Two*, with Nova
Kane you'll feel no pain! [*Laugh-track chuckles.*] But if you're ever
aboard the *Dove*, better mind your Pees and Cues, 'cause up there
in her pilothouse our Super Nova can be a Bossy Nova indeed!
[*L-T CHS, as You do a little dance-turn to two bars of bossa nova
rhythm.*] Just kidding, Cap'n Elva! ELVA KANE!

[*Applause. CAPT. ELVA unhurriedly stands, unhurriedly gathers
up her unwarps & antiwoofs, smiles a benediction upon the company, fetches forth one of her trademark perverbs—e.g., "It's always darkest before the storm" —and with a meaningful look at
You (the meaning whereof is none of this draft-scripter's business),
unhurriedly exits, presumably to her skipperly sanctum sanc-
torum.*]

YOU (*sighing after her*): "Able was I ere I saw Elva!" [*L-T CHS.*]
But time's a-flying, mates, and so as CAP'N HARRY KANE likes to
say, Let's chase to the cut! What's left to be filled in on our mighty
BIG PICTURE? [*To chalkboard, upper left:*] Here's our GEE DASH
Presumable DEE, right? Who presumably begat Grandma JANE
HARRISON's Tidewater Foundation [*Point*], bless her philanthropi-
cal heart! Which in turn begat Mister ANDREW S. TODD's Dorset
Tradewinds Enterprises! [*Point.*] Which, as CAP'N AD LAKE told
us awhile back, is a three-legged beast whereof Ma's New Ark Productions [*Point*] is the middle leg here, excuse my French, flanked
on one side by Dorsettown's busy *Tradewinds Park* [*Write it in, to
left of* NAP, *unless You did that already*], with its *motel* and *marina*
and *convention/exhibition center* [*Write in*]; and on the other [*to
right of* NAP] by *Snug Harbour, Inc.* (and that's Har-*B*-O-U-R,
mates, for the same scrutable reason that we're the Arkade Thee-A-
T-R-E Company). Which corporation in turn—Snug Harbour, Inc.

—comprises both the *Snug Harbour Retirement Community* [*Write SH Ret Comm*] and the *Snug Harbour Assisted Living Facility* [SH Asst Liv Fac], just across the creek from Tradewinds Park. And you'd better believe that these cash-cows are the legs we truly stand on, mates, pardon my metaphors—I mean us middle-leggers dangling down here from the Angel Team. And this is where YOU GUYS come in! [*Add the remaining sub-items as You call them off, working from the bottom up:*] As you've told us already, some of you'll be pitching in with *TOFO*'s GALLEY, CONCESSION, AND BAR TEAM, others with its MAINTENANCE AND ENGINEERING TEAM—which overlaps ATC's PRODUCTION TEAM, 'cause it handles *TOFO*'s sound and light systems. The Production Team—stand up, guys; let's see your smiling faces [*They do, if present—especially peppy MORT SPINDLER, whom we'll get to in chapters to come—and are applauded & percussed*]—also takes care of set design and construction, publicity and scheduling, and liaison with our ports of call, not to mention box-office ticket sales. Busy, huh, guys? And then there's our COSTUME AND MAKEUP TEAM [*Applause & percussion*], our knockout SCRIPT TEAM [*At least a dollop of appreciative A&P, okay?*], also our DIRECTING AND COACHING TEAM [*Make a mock-shy little curtsy, You Sexy Thing, to well-merited-indeed applause*], and—what the whole shebang finally comes down to as far as the audience is concerned—the PERFORMANCE TEAM! Musicians, actors, dancers, entertainers—here's what we're all about! A-one! A-two! . . .

[*From somewhere off—maybe* Raven'*s pilothouse—comes another high note from* HARRY KANE'*s trumpet, as if to set the pitch for the* PIT BULLS' *rendition of (Irving Berlin's) "There's No Business Like Show Business," to which rousingly amplified accompaniment* YOU *lead your Performance-Team accomplices—notably* JAY "OBIE" BROWN *and* HOLLY WEIL, *whom we seem to've neglected to introduce, and the aforeneglected, nothing-if-not-versatile "*DOCTOR SPIN*" Spindler, sorry there, guys—in song & dance before & around the now-completed* BIG PICTURE, *flourishing Your pointer smartly like Fred Astaire's walking-stick and slightly altering the original lyrics as appropriate, e.g.: "There's* NO *bizness like*

SHOW*(boat) bizness, / Like* NO*(boat) bizness we know," etc. Your*
*chalkboard now displays in all its taxonomic splendor the relation*
*of* G-D? *to* YOU GUYS, *viz.:*

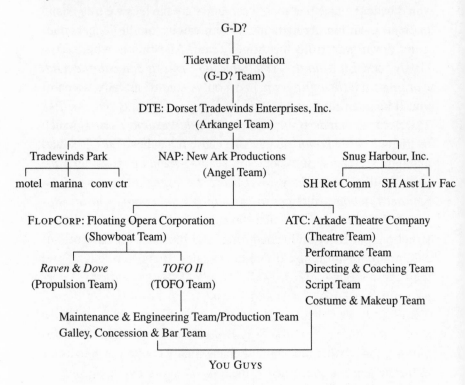

G-D?
|
Tidewater Foundation
(G-D? Team)
|
DTE: Dorset Tradewinds Enterprises, Inc.
(Arkangel Team)

Tradewinds Park     NAP: New Ark Productions     Snug Harbour, Inc.
(Angel Team)

motel   marina   conv ctr              SH Ret Comm   SH Asst Liv Fac

FLOPCORP: Floating Opera Corporation     ATC: Arkade Theatre Company
(Showboat Team)                          (Theatre Team)
                                            Performance Team

*Raven & Dove*     *TOFO II*               Directing & Coaching Team
(Propulsion Team)   (TOFO Team)               Script Team
                                            Costume & Makeup Team

Maintenance & Engineering Team/Production Team
Galley, Concession & Bar Team

YOU GUYS

*Your dance becomes a procession through the theater aisles, the*
*mimes a-miming, jugglers a-juggling, clowns a-clowning, singers*
*a-singing, quick-change artists a-changing quickly, etc., and all*
*hands a-joining the parade. Just as it makes its way up onstage, we*
*hear the twin whistles of* Raven & Dove, *joined by the (taped) faux–*
*steam calliope of* The Original Floating Opera II. *This last roars in*
*just as all hands chorus "Let's* GO / On-with-the (SHOW! BOAT!)
SHOW! / Let's go-o-o / On . . . with the show!" —*and overwhelms*
*all other sound with something of a blastingly oom-pah-pah charac-*
*ter, like maybe a faux-steam-calliopish "Over the Waves"?* CAPT.
AD.'*s swarthily loudspeakered voice orders "All hands make ready*
*to cast off!"* OLD HANDS *give* NEW *a final welcoming embrace/pat-*

on-tush/whatever, and the company disperseth to a grand crescendo of the (taped) calliope, YOU blowing kisses broadcast themward as they go, until the theater is empty except for gorgeous YOU, lingering reflectively before the BIG PICTURE, and perhaps YRS TRULY, lurking in the margins & 'tweenlines of this Draft Orientation Script. Music fadeth. Then, in the Cavernous Silence:]

YOU (as if to Yourself, contemplating the BP's top line while holding pointer behind Yr sexy back): But of course, there may not be a GEE DASH DEE. . . .

[Your eyes wander to the chalkboard's lower RH corner. Bending for a closer look (and thereby affording the house voyeurs a shot of the Toothsomest Tushie on the Ark), YOU gasp—theatrically, shall we say?—drop the pointer, and draw back in floating-operatic dismay at what some prankster hath there inscribed, to wit:]

—Copyright © Y2K-minus-1 by (THE PHANTOM ;-)

Dear Hop o' My Thumb, love o' my life, fly i' my ointment, pain i' my butt—

Get *real*, hon, wouldja already? Deep-six this supersophomoric dreck and just show the newbies around, s.v.p.—then get yrass cracking on The New Show, sweets, or we're up Merde Creek sans paddle for real.

Come to think on't, though, something along these lines might just possibly *work* in the show itself, no? An Orientation Scene, ostensibly for the New Teamies (acted by themselves) but actually for the Audience (ditto, assuming there *is* one), to get us a bunch of exposition done? And to introduce not only Capts. Ad & Harry & Elva, but Mort & Jay & Holly & the whole freaking Cast of Several?

She's serious! Think about it, cheri, yes? And get back pronto to yr

Sherry

P.S.: So okay, there may or mayn't be a "Gee Dash Dee," Hopperino mio—but *there ain't no Phantom aboard of thissere Opera!* Right? RIGHT???

**WHERETO HE IN TURN APPENDETH THESE
READERLY OPTIONS:**

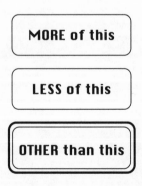

MORE of this

LESS of this

OTHER than this

# A Cast of Several

Dramatis Personae of *TOFO II*(*quod vide*)'s "The New Show" (q.v.), a.k.a. END TIME (q.v.), and thus ineluctably of the "novel" *COMING SOON!!!* (q.v.). Listed here in the order of their appearance in the alphabet, inasmuch as the order of their appearance in TNS/ET/*CS!!!* is as yet undetermined and in the nature of the case —the e-novel/script's "interactive" aspect, for example—may well prove indeterminate.

**Abel:** In the book of Genesis, second son of Adam (q.v.) and Eve (q.v.); slain by his elder brother Cain (q.v.). *(Played in TNS/ET/*CS!!! *by any expendable Extra [q.v.].)*

**Adam:** In Genesis, the first man. *(Played in TNS/ET/*CS!!! *by Capt. Adam. Lake. [q.v.] or equivalent.)*

**Adams, Capt. James:** First owner and first captain of the first Chesapeake Bay showboat, actually a showbarge originally named *Estelle*, later named *Playhouse*, then *Adams Floating Theatre*, then *James Adams' Floating Theatre*, then *James Adams' Show Boat*, then *The Original Show Boat*, and ultimately *The Original Floating Theater* (see also *Cotton Blossom*, *AOAUFO*, and *TOFO II*). Probable inspiration for Cap'n Andy Hawks (q.v.) in Edna Ferber(q.v.)'s 1926 bestselling novel *Show Boat*, with which freshwater skipper the brackish Capt. Adams is sometimes conflated. *(Both roles played, in both The Old Show [q.v.] and The New, by Capt. Adam. Lake. or [the virtual] An-*

drew S. *"Todd 'Cap' n Andy' Andrews" Todd [q.v.], depending.)*

**Andy, Cap'n:** Confusion-compounding nickname of Andrew S. "Todd Andrews" Todd as well as of Edna Ferber's Andy Hawks, skipper of her fictional *Cotton Blossom Floating Palace Theatre.*

**Angels** (a.k.a. "The Angel Team"): G-D?(q.v.)'s minions; also, the CEO and other officers of New Ark Productions, Inc. (NAP), a division of Dorset Tradewinds Enterprises, Inc. (DTE). *(In TNS/ET/CS!!!, played occasionally by larking New Arkers, more usually by Extras either feeling angelic or directed thus to appear.)*

**Antediluvians:** In general, those who lived before the Flood (q.v.). In particular, those doomed by G-D? to drown therein, having been denied passage on the Ark (q.v.). *(Played in TNS/ET/CS!!! by expendable or recyclable Extras.)*

**AOAUFO:** *Adam's Original and Unparalleled Floating Opera.* In the Novelist-now- "Emeritus"(q.v.)'s first novel, *The Floating Opera* (1956), a Chesapeake showbarge modeled after James Adams's Floating Theatre (see above), and in turn the putative model for *TOFO II* (see below). *("Played" in TNS/ET/CS!!! by* TOFO II.*)*

**Ark:** In Genesis, an unpowered vessel of 300 cubits length and un-specified displacement, designed to save a minuscule remnant of G-D?'s first draft of the human comedy, discarded by the Author, together with assorted other fauna two by two and so presumably sexual in nature. In history (and spelled with a terminal *e*), a sail-ing ship of "300. tunne & upward," the larger of two vessels car-rying Lord Baltimore(q.v.)'s first English colonists (q.v.) to the Province of Maryland. *("Played" in both aspects by* TOFO II.*)*

**Arkangels** (a.k.a. "The Arkangel Team"): Chairman and board-members of Dorset Tradewinds Enterprises. Also, to be sure, G-D?'s minions-in-chief. *(Played in TNS/ET/CS!!! by senior Extras.)*

**Armoire, The Chink in the:** One of "The Phantom"(q.v.)'s several quasi-racist aliases. See also Woodpile, The African-American in the. *(Player unknown, in the nature of the case.)*

**Ballet, Corpse de:** Self-deprecating self-designation of the versatile Morton Spindler (see Spin, Dr.) in his capacity as *TOFO II*'s dance coach and dancer-in-chief. By extension, the dancers *en bloc*.

**Baltimore, Lord:** By decree of His Majesty King Charles of England, Scotland, France, and Ireland, Lord Proprietary of the Province of Maryland. *(Played in TNS/ET/CS!!!, lord-proprietarily, by Capt. Adam. Lake.)*

**Cain:** Firstborn son of Adam and Eve; slayer of his brother Abel. *(Played in TNS/ET/CS!!!, with considerable reluctance, by Capt. Harry Kane.)*

**Caliban:** In Wm Shakespeare's play *The Tempest* (q.v.), a disagreeable entity. *(Played in TNS/ET/CS!!!, with relish, by once-and-future old-fart Chesapeake progger Mr./Ms. Ditsy, currently of T II's Maintenance & Engineering Team.)*

**Colonists:** Passengers on Lord Baltimore's vessels *Arke* and *Dove* (q.v.); first English settlers in Maryland except for sundry trespassing Virginians. *(Played by Extras.)*

**COMING SOON*!!!* A NARRATIVE** (also THE NOVEL?, the computer disk thus entitled, and perhaps eventually THE MUSICAL): An extended prose fiction-in-progress. *(Played in TNS/ET/CS!!! by itselves: the Container as the Thing Contained, or vice versa.)*

**Cotton Blossom:** The Mississippi showboat in Edna Ferber's novel *Show Boat*, subsequently (1927) morphed into a hit Broadway musical by Florenz Ziegfeld, Oscar Hammerstein II, and Jerome Kern (q.v. all; stage version successfully revived 1930 and 1995), thence into a series of successful Hollywood films (1929, 1936, 1951). In the novel, the original musical, and the first two film versions, the vessel is an unpowered, tug-tugged barge like the *James Adams Floating Theatre* (see Adams, Capt. James, above), although curiously outfitted with pilothouse and steering wheel in the 1929 film. In the 1951 film and the 1995 Broadway revival, *The Cotton Blossom Floating Palace Theatre* has blossomed into a mighty self-propelled, steam-powered, steamboat-gothic sternwheeler. *("Played" in both The Old Show and The New by the unpowered, no-wheeled showbarge TOFO II—much closer to the original James Adams' Floating Theatre on which*

*Ms. Ferber did her novelistic and perhaps romantic homework in 1924 and 1925.)*

**Dove:** The smaller of *TOFO II*'s two tugboats, the larger being *Raven* (q.v.); also, a pinnace "of about 50. tunne," the smaller of Lord Baltimore's first-expeditionary vessels to Maryland in 1634, the larger being the *Arke* (see *Ark*); also, in Genesis, the bird sent out by Noah (q.v.) from the Ark to check the height of the Flood. *(In TNS/ET/CS!!!, "played" in its second aspect, occasionally in its third as well, by its first.)*

**Dunyazade:** In *The 1001 Nights*, younger sister of Scheherazade (q.v.). *(In TNS/ET/CS!!!, played by the temperamental, not-untalented, disingenuous ingenue starlet of the ATC, Ms. Holly Weil—when Holly will.)*

**End Time:** In roman caps/lowercase, the Last Days before Apocalypse and the Second Coming, famously scripted by "John of Patmos" (q.v.) and anticipated by many toward the close of the first millennium of the Christian era or, that failing, the second. In small caps, working title of *TOFO II*'s make-or-break New Show. *(Played as needed in that same show by any sufficiently terminal-appearing hand.)*

**Eve:** In Genesis, the first woman. *(In TNS/ET/CS!!!, played variously by Sherry Singer and Capt. Elva Kane.)*

**Extras:** Extras. *(Played by Extras.)*

**Ferber, Edna:** Pulitzer-prizewinning American novelist, short-story writer, and playwright (1887–1968); author of the novel *Show Boat* (1926) and other bestsellers. By her own description, "a nice little Jewish girl from Chicago" in residence aboard the *James Adams Floating Theatre* during portions of its 1924 and 1925 seasons. *(Played variously in both The Old Show & The New by "Bea Golden" and Holly Weil—if Holly would.)*

**Finn, Huck L. Barry:** In The New Show's politically corrected echoes of Mark Twain, young white raftmate of "(Young) African-American James" (q.v.) on Old Man River. *(Played variously by Hop Johnson or Mort Spindler.)*

**Flood, The:** In Genesis, the Deluge; in *TNS/ET/CS!!!*, both the Deluge and the anticipated storm-surge from Hurricane Zulu (q.v.), as well as the disastrous but more gradual rise in sea levels consequent upon global warming. See also Storm, The. *(Played in TNS/ET/CS!!! by any sufficiently wet Extra.)*

**G-D?** (a.k.a. Gee Dash Dee?): In Genesis and other stories, including END TIME, the All-But-Unnameable CEO of the universe. Author and occasional destroyer of world. May or may not exist. *(Played if necessary in TNS/ET/CS!!! by the virtual Andrew S. [etc.] Todd or some other ontologically debatable alpha entity.)*

**Hammerstein, Oscar, II:** American lyricist and librettist (1895–1960); author of the "book" for the 1927 musical-comedy version of Edna Ferber's novel *Show Boat*. *(Played in both TOS & TNS, heavily, by Capt. Harry Kane.)*

**Hawks, Cap'n Andy:** In Edna Ferber's *Show Boat*, owner, skipper, and bandmaster of the showboat *Cotton Blossom*; father of Magnolia (q.v.). *(Played in both TOS & TNS by either Capt. Adam. Lake. or the projected presence of "Cap'n Andy" Todd, depending.)*

**Hunter, Charles M.** (1885–1951): In history, director, script doctor, and character actor on the *James Adams Floating Theatre*. In *COMING SOON!!!*, alleged author of *Show Barge* (q.v.: *TOFO II*'s Old Show), said to have been latterly renovated by the Novelist "Emeritus" and subsequently adapted and transformed (or pirated) into The New Show by Novelist Aspirant (q.v.) J. Hopkins Johnson. *(Role played in TOS, allegedly & anonymously, by the N.E. himself, who however maintains Plausible Denial.)*

**Hunter, Beulah Adams:** Wife of Charles Hunter, sister of Capt. James Adams, and (in her prime) female star of the *James Adams Floating Theatre*; billed as "The Mary Pickford of the Chesapeake." *(Played in both shows by Sherry Singer.)*

**Israelites, The:** In *TOFO II*'s New Show, not to mention the Bible, the children of Israel led by Moses out of Pharaoh's bondage. Also, in both Old & New shows, the characters Edna Ferber, Oscar Hammerstein II, Jerome Kern, and Florenz Ziegfeld (q.v. all). *(Played variously by Extras and by Hop Johnson, Mort Spindler, & Holly Weil—unless Holly won't.)*

**James, (Young) African-American:** The politically corrected nickname for Huck L. Barry Finn's not-all-that-young raftmate in The New Show. *(Played, spiritedly, by our versatile self-styled "blacktor" and dancer Jay "Obie" Brown.)*

**Joseph, Senior African-American Citizen "O. B.":** The politically corrected nickname for Jo, the not-all-that-senior African-American deckhand aboard Ferber's *Cotton Blossom.* Probably modeled on Joe Gunn, cook aboard James Adams's *Original Floating Theater*, and memorably baritoned in the musical versions of *Show Boat* by the likes of Paul Robeson and William Warfield. Also called "O. B. Joe." *(Played, without conviction, by Jay "Obie" Brown.)*

**Kern, Jerome:** American composer of musical comedies (1885–1945), including Oscar Hammerstein II's adaptation of Edna Ferber's novel *Show Boat. (Played in both TOS & TNS by J. Hop Johnson.)*

**Kit & Kaboodle:** American slang for "the whole works." Stage name for Sherry Singer and Hop Johnson in their "utility team" aspect and played by same, if called for, in *TNS.*

**Magnolia (Hawks Ravenal):** In *Show Boat*, daughter of Cap'n Andy & Parthy Hawks, later wife of Gaylord Ravenal (q.v.) and mother by him of Kim Ravenal (q.v.). *(Played in both TOS & TNS by Sherry Singer.)*

**Miranda:** Ingenue female lead in Wm Shakespeare's play *The Tempest. (Played in TNS/ET/CS!!!, disingenuously, by either Sherry Singer or Holly Weil—if etc.)*

**Noah:** In Genesis, builder and skipper of the Ark. *(Played in TNS/ET/CS!!! by either the televised projection of Andrew S. "Todd 'Cap'n Andy' Andrews" Todd or by Capt. Adam. Lake. in propria persona, depending.)*

**Novelist Aspirant:** J. Hopkins "Hop" Johnson, co-author with Sherry Singer and others of The New Show END TIME/*COMING SOON!!!*; author and promulgator of the e-fiction computer disk *COMING SOON!!!* THE NOVEL?; possible co-author (with Novelist "Emeritus") of *COMING SOON!!!* A NARRATIVE. *(Played by himself, playing himself.)*

**Novelist "Emeritus":** Author in years past of bonafide novels alleged to have inspired such "real-life characters" as Andrew S. "Todd 'Cap'n Andy' Andrews" Todd, Jane Harrison, "Bea Golden," and the showboat *TOFO II*—for all which he disclaims responsibility. Unofficial & perhaps unwitting sometime mentor and perhaps current rival of Novelist Aspirant Hop Johnson. Putative rewriter, in his partial retirement, of "Charlie Hunter's" recently discovered old playscript *Show Barge*. Self-declared author of COMING SOON*!!!* A NARRATIVE. *(Played in TNS/ET/CS!!!, if we can snag him, by his partially retiring self.)*

**Patmos, John of:** In Christian tradition, author of the Book of Revelation, a.k.a. Apocalypse—with whom, in TNS/ET/*CS!!!*, "Noah's daughter" pleads postdiluvianly to rewrite our story's ending. *(Played by old "N.E.," if etc.)*

**Phantom, The:** No opera complete without one: the Chink in the Armoire, the African-American in the Woodpile, the Spider in *TOFO II*'s Website, Virus in the Program, etc.; the residual and inevitable element of chaos, mystery, and mischief in even the best-regulated systems, not to mention in *TOFO II*. *(Role aspired to by Hop Johnson, but played by who knoweth whom? ;-)*

**Prospero:** Elderly wizard in Wm Shakespeare's play *The Tempest*; father of Miranda. *(Played in TNS/ET/CS!!! by Capt. Adam. Lake., unless the Novelist "Emeritus" can be persuaded. . . .)*

**Raven:** The larger of *TOFO II*'s "twin" tugboats, skippered by Capt. Harry Kane. Also, in Genesis, the bird first sent out by Noah to determine the height of the Flood. Also, in Edgar Poe's poem "The Raven," a one-liner blackbird. *("Played" in that 1st aspect by itself; in the 2nd & 3rd [if called for, in TNS/ET/CS!!!] by Jay "Obie" Brown, with sigh, shrug, and croak.)*

**Ravenal, Gaylord:** In *Show Boat*, dashing gambler lover & subsequent wastrel husband of Magnolia Hawks; father of Kim. In "Charles Hunter's" *Show Barge*, ditto—but of Jewish rather than *goyishe* ethnicity. *(Played in both TOS & TNS by Hop Johnson.)*

**Ravenal, Kim:** In *Show Boat*, daughter of Magnolia & Gaylord Ravenal; born aboard *Cotton Blossom* at the confluence of the Mississippi and Ohio Rivers—the juncture of the states of Kentucky, Illinois, and Missouri, whose initials form her name. In *Show Barge*, potential fruit of alleged Chesapeake romance between Hunter and Edna Ferber, the initials secretly standing for Koshered In Maryland. *(Played in both shows by Holly Weil, or by Sherry Singer if Holly etc.)*

**Sailor, Sindbad the:** In *The 1001 Nights*, an often tempest(q.v.)-tossed merchant mariner. *(Played in TNS/ET/CS!!! by Capt. Harry Kane.)*

**Scheherazade:** In *The 1001 Nights*, 1001st virgin bride of the Caliph Shahryar (q.v.). *(Played, sexily indeed, in TNS/ET/CS!!!, by Sherry Singer.)*

**Serpent, The:** In Genesis, reptilian tempter of Eve in the Garden. *(Played in TNS/ET/CS!!! by any suitably serpentine, temptive Extra—perhaps Holly W., if Holly w.)*

**Shahryar:** In *The 1001 Nights*, King of the Islands of India & China and husband/deflorator/murderer of 1000 young women, up to but not including (in that last capacity) Scheherazade. *(Played in TNS/ET/CS!!! by Capt. Harry Kane or Capt. Adam. Lake.)*

**Show, The New:** a.k.a. END TIME and, optimistically, COMING SOON!!!, or TNS for short: the ATC's last-ditch attempt to rescue *TOFO II* from bankruptcy. Co-authored by Hop Johnson & Sherry Singer, among other hands, TNS/ET/*CS!!!* incorporates elements of The Old Show with additional echoes of Genesis (the Garden, Cain & Abel, the Flood), *The 1001 Nights*, Shakespeare's *Tempest*, the historic arrival of Lord Baltimore's first colonists in Maryland, Mary Jane Holmes's *Tempest & Sunshine* (see "Sunshine" & "Tempest," below), Mark Twain's *Huckleberry Finn*, and the end of the world as prophesied in Revelation. *("TNS" played in TNS/ET/CS!!! by Sherry Singer.)*

**Show, The Old:** The ATC's less-than-successful next-to-last-ditch *chef d'oeuvre* for *TOFO II* in its latter seasons. Entitled *Show Barge* and allegedly authored by Charles Hunter of the old *James Adams Floating Theatre* (and latterly renovated by "The Novelist Emeritus Character"), TOS concerns Edna Ferber's brief residencies aboard the *Floating Theatre*, her possible affair with Mr. Hunter, and her inspiration therefrom for the novel

*Show Boat. ("TOS" played, in The New Show, by June Harrison/"Bea Golden.")*

**Smoke & Mirrors:** Colloquial term for deceptive "special effects"; also, in The New Show, a comedy/dance/illusionist act darkly parodic of *Tempest & Sunshine. (Played, Amos 'n' Andy style, by Jay "Obie" Brown and Ms.* **SPECIAL EFFECT!** *[q.v.])*

**SPECIAL EFFECT!:** A buxom female student-intern Techie (perhaps our Ms. "Polly Morphus"?) whose specialty is "special effects" and who aspires to become one herself. *(Played in TNS/ET/CS!!! by* **HERSELF!***)*

**Spin, Dr.:** Nick- and stage-name of Morton Spindler, publicist & PR man for Dorset Tradewinds Enterprises (DTE) generally, and in particular for *TOFO II* in its make-or-break "final season"; also dancer and dance coach in the ATC, and occasional actor as well. *("Played," with his characteristically undentable, indefatigable pep & optimism, by himself!)*

**Storm, The:** In TNS/ET/*CS!!!*, a tempestuous entity whose shifting aspects include the biblical Deluge, the tempest in Shakespeare's *Tempest*, the several sea-storms in Scheherazade's Sindbad stories, and Tropical Storm/Hurricane Zulu. *(Played by any sufficiently tempestuous Extra—perhaps the team of Holly Weil &* **SPECIAL EFFECT!***)*

**Sunshine:** In Mary Jane Holmes's bestselling 1854 American novel *Tempest & Sunshine, or, Life in Kentucky* and the popular showboat melodrama based thereupon, the perennially optimistic, good-natured sister of "Tempest" (q.v.). *(Played in TNS/ET/CS!!! by Sherry Singer or, on occasion, by Mort Spindler in drag.)*

**Tempest:** When preceded by the article "The," a play by Wm Shakespeare, elements of which have been absorbed into that hopeful last-chance mishmash The New Show, or, END TIME (*COMING SOON!!!*). Also (sans article), in the 19th-century novel-&-play *Tempest & Sunshine*, the terrible-tempered sister of sunny "Sunshine." *(Played in TNS/ET/CS!!! by Holly Will/ Would/Won't/Weil.)*

**Todd, Andrew S. "Todd 'Cap'n Andy' Andrews":** Director Emeritus of The Tidewater Foundation (TTF, the "G-D? Team"); Board Chairman Emeritus of Dorset Tradewinds Enterprises, Inc. (DTE, the "Arkangel Team"); President of the Owners Association of the Patmos Tower high-rise of DTE's Snug Harbour Assisted Living Facility in Dorsettown-on-Choptank, MD, USA. Sometimes mistaken for G-D?, despite his disclaimers that he is at most the Arkangel-in-Chief. Enjoys modeling himself upon, assuming the name of, and promoting confusion with the protagonist of "The N.E. Character's" old *Floating Opera.* *(Played, in life and in TNS/ET/CS!!!, by himself—or, rather, by the closed-circuit-televised image himof, as the chap disinclines to physically-present appearance.)*

**TOFO II:** The marginally persisting Chesapeake showbarge *The Original Floating Opera II*, a pet project of Dorset Tradewinds Enterprises and gently subsiding vehicle for the Arkade Theatre Company. *("Played," in TNS/ET/CS!!! and generally, by its marginally floating self: Container-as-Contents again, or v.v.)*

**Woodpile, The African-American in the:** Another of The Phantom's several quasi-racist aliases. Ignore it, Reader.

**You:** The Gentle Reader, spectator, clicker of the mouse, sinequanon, mon semblable etc. *(Played by Yourself, s.V.p.—if not in TNS/ET, then most indispensably in* CS!!! THE NOVEL?*)*

**Ziegfeld, Florenz:** American theatrical producer (1869–1932) of, among other successes, the 24-year annual *Ziegfeld Follies* and the 1927 musical *Show Boat. (Played in both TOS & TNS, at risk of stereotypecasting, by Morton Spindler.)*

**Zulu, Hurricane:** Tropical Storm #26 in the 1999 Atlantic hurricane season, 1st striking the U.S. mid-Atlantic as T. S. Zulu and then, after a rare turnaround off the New Jersey coast, threatening to return on 9/9/99 as full-fledged Hurricane Zulu *(a.k.a. Zulu II, "played" by itself, for keeps)* and destroy us all.

---

**ON with show!**

---

# *Part I?*

# 1.1 Commencement

Okay, patient Readers of J. H. Johnson's foregoing PERSONAL STATEMENT and associated crapola: I did all that, back there between 1/4 and 4/1/(19)95 — and it worked, sort of. True, the Reverend Invisibles up at John Carter Brown's university were not amused by my faked credentials, although no doubt they got the Postmodernistical point. They were, however, sufficiently taken with the interactive e-fiction version of this opus (disked themto along with the present more-or-less "straight" version, up to and including the "page" just before this one) to wait-list me for admission to the wired-up wing of their M.F.A. program — sans fellowship or tuition waiver. The Doctors Johnson, bless them, relented, as loving parents incline to do, and offered after all to underwrite my stay in Providence. But hey, they'd underwritten already enough stuff for, and written off enough guff from, their maverick heir, whose wayward youth had given them one Bad Heir Day after another. I would've turned down with heartfelt thanks this latest overgenerosity of theirs even if Backup U hadn't come through for me at the last minute: no teaching assistantship or stipend, but admission to its Fairly Famous Straight-Writing Seminary with a full tuition waiver and no threat of prosecution for forgery. It's a slot they keep in reserve, I was told, for special cases.

Story of my life, and fine with me: Although I've learned at last to respect real brainies and even real academics, with both whereof Eponymous U abounds, I am neither of those meself. Huck Finn among the high-tech humanists, that's Yrs Truly. Could no doubt have played the teacher, but I would've been Playing Teacher, and while I agree with Aristotle (here's our U rubbing off on me, or seeping through) that a person not naturally courageous, say, might acquire that moral virtue by practicing it, I had been too recently a practiced-upon undergraduate myself to relish learning my lines at freshman expense.

Inquired Doc Dad, when I ran this scruple by him, "How d'you think we learn heart surgery, 'Son?" Short for Johnson, actually; there's an unvoiced apostrophe before that *S* that only a 'son can hear. "We start with cadavers and go on from there."

Added Doc Mom, "The fact is, Johnsie," Yup, she calls me that, "a university's undergraduate college is like a teaching hospital, with freshmen as the patients and Teaching Assistants as the interns. In a good one, the master surgeons are always standing by, and the patient gets first-class attention."

True enough, I dare not doubt, and altogether necessary if we're to have a next generation of surgeons and of teachers. Aside from my principled reservations about TAships, however (not to mention the circumstance that I hadn't been offered one), the need to support myself gave me more excuse to maintain some postseason connection with *TOFO II* and its Cast of Several, in particular with one Ms. Sherry McAndrews Singer. So: Thanks again, folks, but no thanks. Come May, I commenced from Namesake U as a confirmed Bachelor of the Arts—with Departmental Honors, remarkably, despite my lackluster performance in other neighborhoods of academe. My patient progenitors applauded and, for all their presumable heart-pangs when the ranks of new M.D.s came forward to be consecrated, gave their blessing to my summer work-plans (same old story: *TOFO II* [!!!]) and to my return Home as a Graduate Writing Seminarian in the fall. I evacuated my rowhouse flat in the roach-rich student warren of Charles Village, just off-campus, and bade bye-bye to Sybil, my apartment-mate: a Practicing Lesbian doctoral candidate in Sapphic Lit who had done wonders for my lit'ry education* in return for my sharpening her savvy in the CD-ROM and database-sifting way. I stowed my stuff for the manyeth time at the Drs. J's more-than-ample manse in nearby manse-rich Guilford, where the bedroom of my misspent youth was still lovingly maintained for me despite my protestations of unnecessity (there were, they counterprotested, abundant other bedrooms for any other houseguests, whereof that workaholic couple were too busy to have more than rare, if you follow my parenthesis). I then restuffed my spanking-new cherry-red Jeep Cherokee with what I needed for the summer (graduation gift from Guess Whom, bless them, to replace its hard-used high-school-graduation predecessor, originally bronze but weathered by harsh climes and inconstant maintenance to a sort of burnt siena), flip-phoned Coach Singer of *TOFO II*'s Theatre Team to let her know that I was sprung from college and COMING SOON(*!!!*)—

"Not soon enough for me, Hopsy dear," Sher deep-throated in her testicle-twitching contralto. "We're in shit to the Plimsoll, per usual." Reference to Mr. Samuel Plimsoll's mark for the maximum safe loading of seagoing vessels; check out his website.

In my Mickey Rooney/Andy Hardy mode, with just a dollop of Florenz Ziegfeld, "So let's put on a show!" I exclaimed—or, rather, Exclaimed.

A loopy Zsa-Zsa Gabor now, "Ve're *doink* dot, dollink," Sher came back: "Dot's da trobble essactly."

"So here comes *Your Old Kit Bag*," I sang, "to *Pack Up Your Troubles In*"—the venerable Yank war song, I forget which war.

"*Come on, Lucifer, light my fag*," growls Sherry back, parodying two songs at once, from two very different eras, and then adds a third: "I'm smiling already, lad; *Smilin' Through. . . .*"

"*If folks only knew*," I et cetera'd. We kept that up for a while, as is our wont when in our "Kit & Kaboodle" mode (see CAST OF

---

* Particularly in the area of her dissertation topic: *Feminist Soma(tics): Objectifying/Commandifying the Body, or,* I'm Afraid of Virginia Woolf. But we went through Dante, Blake, and Proust together, too. Syb modestly classifies herself as a Practicing Lesbian because she's new to girl-on-girling, having Come Out only as a graduate student, and thus "needs practice."

SEVERAL); tossed the banter-ball back and forth in a bit of Free Improv on *TOFO*'s campy repertoire until the Mary Pickford of the Chesapeake — also its Ava Gardner and its Kathryn Grayson, not to mention its Whoever's Hot Just Now — got down to business: "Do me and New Ark Productions a little favor on your way down here, Hops, okay?" Reference to be explained anon (or click Ye back, wired Reader, to *Its draft orientation session:* IS THERE A GEE DASH DEE? etc.).

"Thy wish, et cet."

"The Angels," Ref To Be Xpl'd (or click Ye etc.), "want you to make a little detour to Solomons Island to check out the competition, okay?"

"What's to check? Last time I looked," which had been but a mere month earlier, "old Coming-Soon-Exclamation-Point [*RTBX'd*] was dead in the water."

Chirped Sher, "Don't feel so fit meself, mate, come to that," and off we went into a Kit-&-Kaboodle Down-Under cadenza until she said "Just take a peep anyhow, Hops, you dig? For FLOPCORP's sake [*RTBX'd*], for Christ's."

"For yours, luv. Done."

"*Mwah.*"

— kissed the dear indulgent Doctors *hasta la vista,* I did, and in less time than it takes to unpack the syntax of this sentence, with just one detour instead of its several I Cherrykeed me over and down to Dorsettown-on-Choptank, on Maryland's lower Eastern Shore, where trouble-rich T Two was in process of getting its act together for the season already under way.

*Click* **D** *for Detour,* **N** *for Next Instalment of this hopalong narrative,* **A** *for an Alternative (yea even Emerital!) view of the whole down-spiraling, double-helical show.*

| D |

| N |

| A |

# 1.2  Same Old Story

*In the beginning,*
the idea seemed good. Anyhow feasible. The "American century," for better or worse, was 95 percent expired; the current Gregorian millennium, 99.5 percent. I myself was getting no younger: Although just a bit more than half through the 120-year span allotted us mortals in Genesis 6:3 and reneged on ever since (but latterly confirmed by some gerontologists to be the inherent human design–life), as of my upcoming birthday I would be 93 percent through the "biblical" threescore-and-ten. In any case, approaching age sixty-five I was a freshly retired academic and still able senior-citizen novelist with a respectable output behind him and a not-unreasonable itch to add another, perhaps final item to that shelf before the curtain closed on this staggering century, to look no farther. My mean production-time for a book — I had perpetrated some dozen plus — was four years: one olympiad, an American presidential term, and the traditional interval between undergraduate matriculation and the baccalaureate. Allowing another half year to see the manuscript through the press, in 1995 I had just time enough to bring the thing off, His Latest Last, if the muse and I got cracking on it promptly.

All well and, as I've mentioned, good: a wrap-it-up novel, let's say, whatever "it" might turn out to mean, and then — whatever. For the how-manyeth time, I opened to a virgin page the venerable, battered, much-prized, anything-but-virginal looseleaf notebook in which I had first-drafted Everything Thus Far. I popped my customary earplugs in, uncapped and filled my never-failed-me-yet old fountain pen, and . . .

Well, now. From back at mid-century, in my earliest college-teaching days, I recollected a particularly tiresome category of freshman composition that we entry-level English Compers called the Nothing-on-My-Mind, What-Am-I-Going-to-Write-About, How-I-Came-to-Write-This-Paper paper: process as content; something wishfully out of nothing. "Writer's block" I find about as interesting as impotence, not to say constipation. The Void, at least in its aspect of blank paper, has never troubled me—See how I chatter on? Although from one quadrennial project to the next I've seldom foreseen what the next will be, forty-plus years of unbroken productivity are reassuring.

In this instance, moreover, it was not that there was in fact nothing on my mind; there was if anything too much. I have alluded already to those fin-de-siècle and millenarian currents, more or less apocalyptic, much astir by the mid-1990s in the media, the popular imagination, and my own: TERRIBLE EARTHQUAKE TO BREAK OCEANIC EARTH CRUST UNDER PACIFIC OCEAN BY A.D. 1996; 8 COMPELLING REASONS WHY CHRIST IS COMING

"VERY, VERY SOON"; et cetera. Onstreaming nature, I reminded myself, knows nothing of such human measures as olympiads, centuries, millennia: The seasons recycle, the tide ebbs and flows, Ol' Man River just keeps rolling along. My busy/idle fancy, however, inevitably conflated those wind-ups with a range of other declines and expirations—not least my own aging, Q.E.D., but including the arguable downslide of American society, civility, civic-spiritedness, "family values," and the rest; our deplorable ahistoricity; the usurpation of civilized attention from the realm of print, first by the movies, then by commercial television and the videocassette recorder, latterly by computer-interactive pastimes and pursuits. Were we not, moreover, warming Earth's atmosphere disastrously with our fossil-fuel combustion, destroying its protective ozone layer with our fluorocarbons, overrunning the planet with our own species at the expense of others, ravaging the rain forests, fouling the waters, and what have you, or what once had we? The sinking of the very ground beneath my feet did not escape my concerned attention: As I wrote these words, the mean water-level of Chesapeake Bay was rising at the rate of 3.4 millimeters annually, about double the global sea average, and the likeliest explanation appeared to be that our Delmarva Peninsula was subsiding by that differential as we simultaneously melted the polar icecaps with our car and chimney-flue exhausts and overpumped the underlying aquifer for our farms, residential developments, and businesses. The Bay's islands were vanishing before our eyes, or already had done: Cacaway and Clements and Cows, Poplar and Punch, Sharps and Swan, Tippety Wichety and Turtle Egg—old friends going, going, gone. Its once-vast and still ecologically indispensable wetlands were fast shrinking: The Blackwater National Wildlife Refuge, my virtual birth-marsh on Maryland's lower Eastern Shore, had in my thus-far lifetime lost more than a quarter of its crucial marsh-acreage. . . .

Et cetera, even before one got to politics, "ethnic cleansing," terror international and domestic, the black-marketing of weapons-grade plutonium (perhaps of nuclear weapons themselves) out of the former Soviet Union, the emergence of dreadful new diseases and the declining potency of our antibiotic defenses themagainst—

all more or less on *my* mind, if not quite on my muse's. I didn't attempt to deconflate these several conflations; to wonder how much of my concern for the environment's and the culture's attrition projected an oldster's concern for his own: Whether the sea rises or the land sinks is all one to us dwellers on the verge.

In such a pass, your millenarianists might cry "Repent!," your old Noahs turn amateur arkwright (and your young Mickey Rooneys/Andy Hardys exclaim "Let's put on a show!"). It is not, however, principally to warn, correct, lament, or save the world that I make up and set down stories, but rather to add to the human inventory of its artful artifacts; not to preach, teach, engage, escape, celebrate, or bear witness (although I may by the way do any and all), but chiefly to discover what my muse has up her sleeve, let's say, by way of encore. If (to change the metaphor) having delivered, she declares a postpartum respite before reimpregnation, I'm patient, as a rule. The well (to change the metaphor) refills. One is a writer; one takes up one's trusty pen, boots up one's trusty computer, whatever. One invokes one's ditto muse. One writes.

Doesn't one. . . .

*Meanwhile,*
in my house anyhow, that muse being once again a touch dilatory, the season opportune, the water rising and/or the land subsiding, one may simply say "Let's go sailing," as one has simply said in ear-

lier such passing impasses: A-sailing down the Chesapeake let's go, whither the wind listeth, but playing that wind to one's purpose as, with the wind's assistance, that purpose discovers itself. Just so, in Gemini-time '95, amid the circumstances here set forth and others not, my mate and I embarked, as is anyhow our pretty regular wont, on an open-ended, un-itineraried, bye-bye-springtime/hello-summer cruise aboard our aging but sturdy, well-maintained and eminently Bayworthy vessel, to see where we would go and to pleasure in the going there: process as content. Also, as with dim-because-distant stars, to turn my attention's eye from what it sought, in hopes of better seeing it.

Same old story.

To have no itinerary, mind, is not necessarily to have no direction. Inasmuch as we dwell in the great estuarine system's upper reaches, our general vector was, as usual, south; we would crisscross the Bay as conditions suggested from Eastern to western to Eastern Shore, river to familiar river, anchorage to new or old-favorite anchorage. We would linger here, poke about or put ashore there, romp right down when the wind said Romp and, when the wind said Lay-Day, lay over in some fine foul-weather cove with music and love, food and wine, books and notebooks. Southeast, southwest, southpureandsimple we would mosey, southstayput, southwhatever, but ever more or less south, out of Maryland's and into Virginia's waters, probably, until we reached either the Atlantic's threshold or waters too jellyfish-rich for swimming (depends on the winter-spring rainfall) or some psychological/calendrical turnaround-point (my mate could south right on to the Caribbean; alas for her, a fortnight of such a-musement tended to fill my bill, especially as we'd be another sennight sailing home).

'Tis a tale (thus far) the like of which I've told more than once upon a time before and shall not here retell: the musely recovery-time, the shrug-shouldered embarkation—a tad less insouciant this time, as Time was of the essence of this otherwise-undefined idea. Clock and calendar were running; those several endings aforenoted were coming soon, coming soon. No cause for any *reader*'s concern, but a genuine problem for the recidivist talester, and one that in the nature of this case could only grow more acute. Before anyone could ask me, I asked myself So what? If the product comes on-line a year or three late—in 2001, say, or -2 or -3—'twill be a touch anticlimactic and minus a few timely first-pub tie-ins, per-haps. A few years farther on, however, none of that will matter, any more than it matters now whether So-and-So's end-of-*nineteenth*-century novel appeared in 1899, 1907, or last semester. Is it any good? is what matters, or still good when its time is history? Mean-while the world's miseries ongo; its problems multiply and exacer-bate, and folks would rather watch television anyhow—so so what?

The so so what, I then replied to me, is that given *enough* years nothing will matter, and therefore the number does, for now. More-over, Earth's general human problems are only one six-billionth mine, whereas mine are mine entirely; *that*'s so what—and I'm not complaining, you understand, just reporting the news and getting on with the story. Same Old Story? Sure, maybe—but it's *this* S.O.S. this time, which goeth thus:

That off yet again sailed Miz and aging Mister So-and-So, feel-ing just so-so thereabout but gratified as always to be under way, fuel- and water-tanks topped off, food- and beverage-lockers stocked, all plain sail set on a nice close reach in a sunny late-spring sou'westerly—Hi ho hum!—bound finally who knew whither (all hands know where we're all bound, finally) but immediately down-creek, down-river, down-Bay, prevailingly south via whatever zig-zags and partial retracements, south and south and still farther south. That after a dramaturgical sufficiency of such southing, through weather clement and in-, winds fair and contrary, ditto tides, gear glitches and mishaps mainly minor, sweet swims and sweatsy slogs and languid Happy Hours—in a word, the usual—they fell afoul of (choose one from Column A)

A

*humongous storm*
*shoal-draft sea monster*
*stowaway secret sharer*
*disconcertingly familiar stranger*

which surprise encounter fetched them, one way or another, to
(choose one from Column B)

*B*

*uncharted isle of aspect fair*
*and beckoning-but-sinister*
*interior*
*ditto creeklet, through trackless*
*fenlands wending who knew*
*whither*
*unsuspected compartment in*
*their so-intimately-familiar*
*vessel, as in dreams one*
*discovers strange but oddly*
*déjà-vuish rooms in one's*
*own house*
*spacetime wormhole debouching*
*ultimately upon itself but*
*more immediately upon*

the same old story.

In fact, however, in *this* fiction it came to pass that, having me-
andered pleasurably and all but uneventfully as aforeforecast from
our Chester River starting-place on the Bay's

upper Eastern Shore
across to
the Magothy River on its western,
thence down to
the South River (likewise western),
thence across to
the lovely Wye and Miles
and in lazy stages down to
the Choptank
and
the Little Choptank
(there being no good western-shore anchorages in that stretch),
we made the long downward crossing to

63

the Patuxent, where, needing a pit-stop to replenish our consumables, we poked into marina-rich Solomons Island, an old favorite of ours and of most other Bay sailors. The afternoon being by then late and sultry, the usual Chesapeake summer-thunderstorm brooding off to northwestward like a season's preview, we decided to postpone our business till morning and make for a certain snug, attractive, fairly secluded nearby anchorage to refreshen ourselves with a swim after the long day's passage and with rum-and-tonics before dinner.

I pause to let the Bay-knowledgeable here scoff: A snug, attractive, fairly secluded, water-clean-enough-to-swim-in anchorage in yacht-infested, facility-jammed Solomons Harbor? As well look for a patch of old-growth forest in Manhattan! Yet nonetheless and cross my author-"emerital" heart: There is, of the former at least, at least one, or at least there was as of that late-spring mid-Nineties afternoon and this writing: one known, for all we knew, but to ourselves, as we had reanchored there on every revisit since first discovering it some years before and had yet to have to share it with a fellow "gunkholer," as we shallow-draft, let's-poke-in-a-little-farther types are called. Even in fiction I won't say where in fact it is, this improbable *Ankerplatz*; chances anyhow are that by the big Two Zero-Zero-Zero it will have been "developed" into history. Meanwhile, however—in the so-swiftly-diminishing interval until then —there remained this solitary, charming one-boat cove, really all but unspoiled, woods right around, couple of houses yes, but far enough off to be unobtrusive upon our view and we on theirs as we swam sans swimsuits in the believe-it-or-not quite-clean-enough-to-swim-in water: nettle- and turd-free, to the eye at least; of a crudless Chesapeake olive color and an agreeable temperature; nowhere much more than a fathom deep, but plenty wide enough to swing one's shoal-draft cutter on a sixty-foot anchor-scope if one planted one's hook carefully; waterfowl and small swimming turtles, even, to be observed occasionally as one lounged and nibbled and sipped, watched and read and listened in the still steamy, after-all-stormless P.M.—and farther than this, deponent saith not, lest he give the game away with overmuch specification.

Thither we headed, past wall-to-wall marinas, waterfront restaurants and condominiums, She at the helm and He making ready our ground tackle, through throngs of other cruising vessels inbound, outbound, merely roundaboutbound, or moored already in the crowded harbor; also tenders rigid or inflatable, azip twixt mother-ship and shore; also the handsome clippereplica *Pride of Baltimore II* (replica of a replica, actually, of a nineteenth-century Baltimore Clipper, its immediate predecessoreplica having predeceased it some years since in a vicious "white squall" off the Bahamas, to the eponymous city's sorrow and not-inconsiderable mortification)— the handsome vessel apause in its PR peregrinations, presumably, to grace some convention-in-progress at one of the harborfront hotels. Also, just across the busy Solomonian waters therefrom . . .

"I don't believe it," declared the helmsperson, who saw it first and pointed. Her friend the talester herward turned, aft from his foredeck anchor-prepping, then followed her point starboard-bow-ward, to where . . .

Carramba. Gott in Himmel. Sacré bleu and shiver me timbers.

"*I* don't believe it, too, either."

In or by a ruined former boatyard over there, not far from the half-submerged ribs and shivered timbers of some large wooden former vessel, upon a larger-yet former cargo barge evidently of some naval provenance (US NAVY YRB-7 in fading but conspicu-ous white block capitals on its square black bows), hulked a ruined two-story superstructure of some boxy former function (floating temporary office-space, it will turn out, in Philadelphia's now-for-mer Navy Yard), half its window-sashes gone, light blue corrugated-metal siding here peeled, there missing, walls and roof plentifully unsheathed to studs and rafters, the whole a spectacle of large-scale dilapidation like some former ark abandoned on some sea-level Ararat (as, after all, Noah's mount was when he went aground there and dismounted) but bebannered boldly across its second-story bow-end balcony:

## FLOATING THEATRE
### *COMING SOON!*

Well, now. Having gawked and grinned a bit and then grinned and gawked some more, I left off flaking down the rode (sounds like a dope-stoned ambulation, but it's nautispeak for arranging the anchor-line to run out smoothly) and stepped aft to fetch up the ship's camera; then decided Hell with that, we'll shoot the thing mañana en route to our pit-stop; for now let's simply gawk and grin. We did that; made a portwise circle, even, the better to g&g yet further before motoring on to our confidential cove to drop the hook and P.M. ourselves as aforespecified. Indeed, to that catalogue of anchored pleasures we added another: Once swum, showered, air-dried, dark-rum-punched and pâté-canapéd, we hitched to our little dinghy its little outboard motor and took a little outboard-dinghy ride down-harbor to reinspect that unexpected huge outlandishment and, in passing, to photograph it after all in the long last light:

## FLOATING THEATRE
### *COMING SOON!*

Well! Well! Well.

*Back presently aboard,*
to the customary ship's-log entry of our anchoring-time and -place I added a note on this improbable, portentous, but perhaps fortuitous coincidence,* together with a bare-bones description of that formidable, all but bare-boned ruin 'round the bend:

## FLOATING THEATRE
### *COMING SOON!*

We made a fine hot-weather cold dinner — chicken/rice salad, soy/sesame-sauced fresh asparagus, cherry tomatoes, calamata olive bread, jug chablis — and dined upon it belowdecks in our underpants (cabin a touch stuffy, but we had been on deck all day) to the tune of muted FM jazz. Postprandially, we returned upstairs to let our skin breathe the evening air and to watch another T-shower rumble usward from west-northwest. When this one, unlike its fore-

---

* A multiple coincidence, really: For where had one seen recently that same exclamation (trebled!!!)? And whence had its apprentice exclaimer (characteristically hyperbolical) filched the floating image thus appended?

rumbler, crashed onstage with its flashy sound-and-light show, we retreated below from the blitzing rain and ended our pleasant day snugged up with book (her) and notebook (him), in which latter — Beck's *Dunkelbier* in one hand, pen in the other — he mused furiously further, more or less as follows, upon that most unlikely

## FLOATING THEATRE
*Coming Soon!:*

# 2.1 Detour after all . . .

*Detour* now, is it, O Opter of the Options, Clicker of the Clicker, Mastress of the mighty Mouse? Detour it is, then, even as Mlle Sherry Singer directed back there in (my) Chap. 1, "Commencement"—where last we saw your Novelist Aspirant & apprentice narrator hip-hopping south and east and south again on wings of desire, also of show biz and of modestly gainful employ: from Johns Hopscotch U down to *TOFO II* in springtime '95 . . . with but one detour, to Check Out the Competition.

RsTBXd there were back then, as I recall: References To Be eXplained as we hopped along, the way we novelist-types used to do it in years of yore, before Hypertext happily hit the fan. "New Ark Productions," "Angels," "FLOPCORP," "old Coming-Soon-Exclamation-Point"—the whole Kit & Kaboodle of *T 2*'s Big Picture. . . . But hey, here we virtually are in '999, no?—the all-but-end-of-the-road for p-fictive one-thing-at-a-timery. So, Reader luv: Do all three of us a favor and scroll back as aforesuggested to Is THERE A GEE DASH DEE? (Yrs Truly's draft orientation script for Newbies), if You haven't already done; then it's on with our Detour, all references tidily explained.

But stay: What say? No Coming-Soon-Excetera to be found back there on Sher's chalkboarded Overview? One pat on head + cookie coming up Youfor, sharp-eyed Caller of the Shots! Takes three to tango, says JHJ: in the Old Days, Author/Text/Reader (p-fiction's genderfreed analogue to Father/Son/HolyGee); in the

Interactive Now, Programmaker/Program/Progger, shall we say? In any case and by any name, O Implicit Subject of the commands OPEN/ENTER/QUITcetera, Yrs Truly is truly gratified to gather You're still awake and tracking us in our cherry-red Cherokee, a-jeep down I-97 back in 5/95 from Baltimore toward Annapolis, the Bay Bridge, MD's subsiding Eastern Shore . . . and problem-fraught *TOFO II*, stalled in her hailport: what we're calling (that being its name) Dorsettown-on-Choptank.

With just one detour, to check out a certain Coming-Soon-Exclamation-Point.

A space/time detour, actually, beginning, as beginnings should, with Time. As if *The* [not-so-]*Original Floating Opera II* hadn't problems enough, from falling attendance-rates to failing bilge-pumps—because really, who needs a *showboat* in the Terabyte Twilight of the Terrible Twentieth?—rumor'd reached us some seasons past of (gulp) *competition*! Not just competition from alternative media, mind: The obvious question—how to float, in the Age of the Internet, an enterprise so retro on the face of it as an old-time showboat—had been Square One for what we're calling the Arkangel Team at least since 1990, when Dorset Tradewinds Enterprises (see Big Picture) established New Ark Productions (s.B.P., s.V.p.) to rebuild/renovate a certain earlier honorable failure called—and here we go—*The Original Floating* Theatre *II*, itself inspired by the aforecited fictional *Adam's Original & Unparalleled Floating Opera*, inspired in turn by James Adams's historically original *James Adams' Floating Theatre* (the apostrophe comes and goes with successive refurbishings after successive sinkings—always, interestingly, in November), which likewise inspired, as afore-established, Edna Ferber's *Show Boat*. When canny Captain Jim sold his rig in early '33 after eighteen on-the-whole-successful seasons, it was in part because he saw the handwriting on the wall—i.e., those moving (and now talking) images on the screen, which along with automobiles and network radio were making tidewater-folk too mobile and relatively sophisticated for *Tempest & Sunshine* and *Smilin' Through*, even in the depths of the Great Depression. The vessel's subsequent owners tinkered with name- and menu-changes and kept *The Original Show Boat/Original Floating Theater* in ever-declining business through another eight seasons and yet another sinking (1938, November). Their 1940 season they advertised as "final," whereafter *TOFT* was to be beached somewhere on West River, just below Annapolis, and converted into a moviehouse: If you can't lick 'em, join 'em. In the event, however, she was sold down the Bay, so to speak, to a Georgia contractor for conversion into a wartime cargo barge. Under tow theretoward in the Savannah River—in jinxed November, wouldn't you know, 1941, just three weeks before Pearl Harbor—she caught fire and burned, first to the waterline, then on down to her very keel-timbers when the ebb tide left her high and relatively dry.

And that was that.

Or 'twould've been, had not Fact and Fiction, fifteen years later, resumed their tangled tango that had commenced with Ferber's fictionalizing the *Adams Floating Theatre* into her *Cotton Blossom Floating Palace Theatre* and then later, in her 1937 autobiography, misremembering Cap'n Adams's showbarge as *The James Adams Floating Palace Theatre*—by which time the showboat (no longer Adams's) had been renamed *The Original Show Boat* to capitalize on Ferber's fame. Along now ('56) comes Great-Uncle Ennie, as I here dub my sometime mentor the Novelist (semi-retired and thus, let's say) Emeritus: In those days a mere Novelist Aspirant like mere Yrs Truly nowayears, he makes his professional debut as aforeremarked with a tale inspired by kidhood memories of the original *Original*. No pot of gold like Ferber's, his yarn nonetheless inspires or helps inspire the more-or-less-Real World to come up in the mid-1960s with *The Original Floating Theatre II*, and our factfictional tango resumes.* More particularly, so the story goes, a wealthy Eastern Shore couple whose fortune had been made first in the pickle trade (yup, You read that right) and then in the manufacture of Army C-rations during World War II had salted away their profits into the philanthropic Tidewater Foundation (see Big Picture), safely out of the Internal Revenue Service's reach. With an eye to bolstering the

---

* See (our chap's) Chap. 2.2, coming soon.

fortunes simultaneously of their failing local shipyard, in which they owned an interest, and of their stagestruck daughter June Harrison (a.k.a. "Bea Golden": See CAST etc.), they cause their foundation to seize for arrearages an old steel barge originally used for transporting petroleum products on the Bay but currently laid up at "their" shipyard, and they then commission that same yard to build expensively atop it a Picturesque replica/evocation/hybrid of the Adams/ Ferber/Unc-N.E. showbarges, trimmed in hippie Haight-Ashbury Victorian for a quaint modern touch. Their worthy project saved neither the shipyard nor June Harrison Mack Singer Bernstein Golden's theatrical career. It did, however, help nudge into being the much more successful Dorchester Tradewinds Enterprises, and upon that same DTE, or vice versa, sired our problem-laden *TOFO II*.

But we're getting ahead of our historical Detour! *The Original Floating Theatre II*, 'tis said, toured the Bay through several High-Sixties seasons with a mix of old flicks and live nostalgia-pieces (the inevitable *Tempest & Sunshine*, *Smilin' Through*, and *Six Nights in a Bar Room*, abbreviated from Ten to suit the audience's postmodern attention span), along with some defanged Sixties political satire, all featuring Ms. Golden. 'Twas last glimpsed in fiction bound from Solomons Island (which Yrs Truly was last glimpsed in fact detouring *toward*) across the Bay to Bloodsworth Island in 1969 with a film-company aboard, bent upon reenacting there the 1814 British attacks on Washington and Baltimore. It is heavily implied by the Novelist-then-not-yet-"Emeritus" that the showboat will be zapped in mid-reenactment by a stray air-to-ground missile from one of the warplanes at nearby Patuxent Naval Air Test Center, which uses Bloodsworth for a different sort of rehearsals — but never mind that.

Still with us?

In "fact," however, if one may so put it, *TOFT II* carried on fitfully for another four or five years thereafter, until the Arab oil embargo of the early 1970s inflated its operating costs unacceptably (your Novelist Aspirant sniffs an uncertain irony here, given the barge's petrochemical origins and the consequent circumstance that even nowadays, after a rough Bay-crossing, the house still sometimes faintly smells of oil; stay tuned). In 1975, the year Yours Truly himself was launched and commissioned on his erratic life-trajectory, The Tidewater Foundation *de*commissioned and sold at considerable loss—read Tax Write-Off, I suppose—its floating exercise in nostalgia, the posttype of Adams/Ferber/N.E. and prototype of *TOFO II*/N.A. . . .

*COMING SOON!*

*(!!),* if Yrs Truly ever gets that groundbreaking, ballbusting e/p-fiction past its sundry fartings around and on with Part I of a gen-You-wine Story.

And was *that*, then, that? No way, saith JHJ: The new owners—Baltimoreans a tad ahead of the times—de-Victorianized *TOFT II*'s trim and converted the theater-space into a floating indoor racquetball-court-cum-fitness-center, moored for a time in Baltimore's Inner Harbor with the hope of attracting downtown office workers to tune their abs and pecs during lunchbreak. Just about broke even, 'tis maintained, until the Rouse Corporation's Harborplace development so revitalized the area that rents and dockage fees ate the owners' lunch. So they towed the rig south to Alexandria, just across the Potomac from D.C., and later down to Norfolk/Portsmouth, on the Chesapeake's lower lip. But the Alexandrians and Norfolk/Portsmouthers, too, while not altogether uninterested in the odd waterfront racquetball set or pec-deck workout, were even more interested by 1980 in following Baltimore's example (and Boston's/New York's/Philadelphia's) of converting their once-working waterfront into urban amenities and tourist attractions, now that the steamboat age was history. Each time the Rouse Corporation or its likes worked their profitable wonders upon those venues, the Floating Fitness Center's overhead rose until its profits sank. The Me Decade found *Sea Gym* (its last-ditch dubbing) mothballed somewhere in the maze of Norfolk/Portsmouth/Newport News marine facilities, awaiting her next Prince Charming.

He arrived in the form of President Ronald Reagan, determined to arms-race the Soviet Union into bankruptcy by giving the Pentagon carte blanche. So freely flowed Defense Department dollars in all directions from D.C., and on such long elastic leashes were our manifold intelligence-gathering operations run, the dormant oil-barge/showboat/fitness center next awoke (unless it was a shadowy dream) to find itself converted into floating "office space" by "a Pentagon subcontractor" for "a government security agency." Perhaps for use as a port-to-portable safe house in and around that massively military neck of the tranquil Chesapeake? Deponent cannot say; only that to *TOFT II*'s sometime smell of oil was added, in these spend-'em-to-Hell years, a faint whiff of intrigue: *parfum de fantôme*, I've heard it called.

By me.

And who captained this seldom-seagoing safe house for this unspecified "government security agency" through this still-obscure interlude in its floating history? Why, who else but our doughty and deliberate Adam. Andrew. Lake. — the virtual Dash, as shall be shown, of Gee Dash Dee — who in his twenties had worked aboard *TOFT II* (where, one hears, he became June Harrison/"Bea Golden"'s paramour-in-chief), and in his early thirties had foreman'd in the Baltimore shipyard that converted her to her subsequent athletical employments — we mean the showbarge, not its fading star — and in his latter thirties had steered her (had anyhow floated herwith) into Spook Harbor, shall we say. When then the Evil Empire imploded and the Bush Administration set about modestly downsizing our gargantuan military establishment, the associated "peace dividend" threatened even to tweak a bit our pantagruelian intelligence community. Specifically, 'twas rumored at the turn of the Nineties that the *S.H. NoName*, let us call her (as she bore in that hush-hush period no visible identificatory tag whatever), was slated either for shedding her superstructure and returning to her original function of petrochemical transport or — *nota bene*, patient putter-up with this almost-finished historical detour — for sale to out-of-state gambling interests bent upon towing her to Biloxi/Gulfport for conversion into a floating casino: an idea whose resurrected spirit spooks us yet, and whose implementation may, alas, be COMING SOON!!!

Enter here, however, like an antique god on wires, the GD of Gee Dash Dee in the very senior personage of one Mr. Andrew S.

73

Todd, General Director (Emeritus) of both The Tidewater Foundation and its busy implementation-agency, Dorset Tradewinds Enterprises. A curious piece of work himself (who claims to've been so struck by his resemblance to the "Todd Andrews" character in *The Floating Opera* that he modeled his subsequent self thereupon: Life imitating Art, and sometimes outstripping same), AST and his DTE have caused into existence the Planned Community of Dorsettown-on-Choptank, with its Tradewinds Park hotel/marina/convention center and its Snug Harbour Retirement (sub)Community and Assisted Living Facility — including the high-rise Patmos Tower, in whose upper reaches dwelleth, if not finally the Big G, at least His/Her Arkangel-in-Chief aforespecified, and, in a penthouse suite himabove, his ancient co-Arkangel and erstwhile bedmate, Ms. Jane Harrison, mom of June and grandmom of (sweetnsexy) Sherry Singer. Our lay gospels differ on whether the Word came from AST/"TA" himself or was into his General-Director-Emerital ear murmured by Ms. June Harrison Slash Quote Bea Golden Unquote (by this time prodding her gifted daughter Sher's theatrical ambitions while not altogether relinquishing her own) or by Cap'n Dash Himself, our own Ad. A. Lake., who, if he wants his aging polymorphous vessel and his ditto polynomial lover within reasonable commuting range each of the other, has got to come up with Something New. In whichever case, the fortuitous or strategically arranged conjunction of Capt. Dash and Mr. GD (= G-D?, no?) catalyzed into existence New Ark Productions — Whereof we think You've heard? — and its corporate subcreatures FLOPCORP and Arkade Theatre Company, authorized by DTE to reconvert the "security agency's" Floating Black Hole into (*Ta-da!*) . . . *The Original Floating* Opera *II*, to distinguish it slightly from its less than distinguished predecessors.

End of time-detour, and here we are!

Or here we'd be, riding high and sitting pretty, the hottest ticket in tidewaterland with our touch-all-the-bases mix of post-postmodern high-tech low comedy, avant- and derrière-garde, *TimePast & Sunscreen*, *Tin Knights in a Ba-roooom!*, *Smilin' Through Cyberspace*, and the rest of our front-edge-retro rep (not a little of it cobbled up by Kit & Kaboodle)—here we'd be, mates, says I, were't not that (a) nothing we-all floated either quite flew or quite flopped. The Less-Than-Original Floundering Opera is what we came to call ourselves as we flubbered through Season One ('93) and flatfished through Season Two, and here we are (back in '95) up Dorsettown Creek sans paddlewheel, our third season semi-stalled before the summer solstice, even, and rumors reaching us already that Patmos Tower's powers-that-be are having Seriously to Consider re-reconverting us to floating casino or EVRkade if we can't, you know, get our act together?

Or here we'd be, but that (b) we're not there yet, forasmuch as just as Baltimore's successful Harborplace development spawned clones (though not direct competitors) up and down the seaboard, so our scarcely-successful-but-not-quite-sunk-yet Floating Floundery appeared now—i.e. then, in spring '95—to have engendered dot dot dot: *Competition!* To check out which, at request of Boss Singer, Yrs T finds himself, with Your mousely consent & cooperation, negotiating "now" the Space part of this spacetime detour: not straight east from Annapolis across the Bay Bridge and down to *TOFO II*, no, but on south along the Bay's high western shore to Patuxent River and Solomons Island (attainable by causeway at that river's mouth). Where what to his reconnoitering eyes should appear but

*COMING SOON!,*

exclaiming meward from clear across Solomons Harbor in two-foot-high italic majuscules as Line Two of a billboard-size white banner whose entire message read

**FLOATING THEATRE**
*COMING SOON!*

—said banner affixed at second-story-balcony level across the squared forward end of a hulking, bulking, barge-borne entity the size of a . . . well, of a floating we-know-what.

The potential Competition. More specifically (for I had, as You'll recall my mentioning in [my] Chap. 1, popped down from Baltimore but a month before on behalf of FLOPCORP to investigate reports of its materialization) The Chesapeake Bay Floating Theatre Inc.'s *James Adams II*. Condition unchanged, as far as I could see from across Back Creek, where I had parked at a strategically positioned harborside restaurant to recon and anon eat lunch: a dilapidated former floating two-story office building, by the look of it, not unlike how our *TOFO II* might have appeared between its safehouse phase and its shaky current resurrection. No sign of activity aboard or around it in the cross-creek marina on whose scrappy margin it was moored. With a Polaroid brought along for the purpose I snapped a few for FLOPCORP's perusal and then strolled some blocks upcreek to the Calvert Maritime Museum to stretch my legs, pee, and put a few confirmatory questions to the museum's infolady before lunch.

Being after all still in my narrative apprenticehood, I'm late remarking that this late-May day was in truth a lovely temperate-zone late-May day: mid-seventies at forenoon's end on Gabe Fahrenheit's quaint old scale, the air fresh and dry for these parts from an inland westerly that floated fair-weather cumuli over Solomons toward the Bay. Azaleas, rhododendrons, and maybe lilacs round about the funky clapboard cottages and sidewalkless smalltown streets . . .

Enough of that, not my line; take my word for't, s.V.p., that it's a salty, yachtsy, still unselfconsciously picturesque place, is the Isle of Solomon: no Nantucket or Martha's Vineyard, but a largely ungentrified marina-biz and working watermen's community wherein those oyster tongs, crab pots, and net-floats stashed beside yonder backyard shed are not decorative accents but implements awaiting their seasonal deployment, and here we are at the marine museum with its *de rigueur* screwpile lighthouse beside the main building, and its well-mounted displays of Chesapeakery past and present, and its obliging infolady (currently preempted by another visitor), and its public pissoirs, to the male whereof I repaired to make water before making inquiries re what was new, if anything, *James Adams II*–wise. As Robert Frost invites, You come, too, Comrade Reader— and never mind, here in Virtualville, if the door-sign doesn't apply.

The single urinal being bespoken, so to speak, by a lanky elder gent in cut-off jeans, shortsleeve sweatshirt, deck moccasins, and canvas sailing hat (we novelists note such details even when offline, or invent them to suit), I stepped into the toilet stall, where, after my customary brief uncertainty whether to raise the horseshoe-style seat or leave it down and aim more carefully — for in the former case, having handled the seat, oughtn't I really to go wash my hands before as well as after handling my equipment?, which I knew I wouldn't; and in the latter, oughtn't I to wipe my inevitable droplets off that seat for the next customer's sake?, which I knew I wouldn't either — I opted for the second as usual, fetched forth the male instrument of urinary relief and erotic gratification, and deployed it briskly to the frequenter of those, reminded as oft I am, a-pissing, of that steady stream one notes discharging from the sides of moored vessels, usually just above the waterline, e.g. *TOFO II* and her stout tugs *Dove* and *Raven*. Have several times thought to ask Captains Ad. or Elva or Harry what exactly it is, that liquid incessancy — bilge water (but then why unceasing, except in *T II*'s leaky case?), engine-cooling water (but then wherefor when the tugs' engines are shut down, and wherefore on the engineless showbarge?), or what? — but have yet to remember so to do in their august presences. Peed then, retucked and -zipped and, leaving seat-cleanup for him who next thereon must sit and ought routinely to wipe it anyhow, don't You agree?, I exited the stall and washed my hands posturinarily like the good doctors' son I am, noting side-of-my-eye that the old guy was still at it, and hey hold on now no not possible but bedamned if it wasn't —

"As your decades pass faster," GreatUnc Ennie observed from over there, "your water passes slower. Don't put this episode in your novel, Hop: too implausible a coincidence for fiction."

Well, I'd be hornswoggled, I responded in effect. As wouldn't You, dear invisible witness to this unlikelihood? Be, I mean, hornswoggled? I held out my still-wet-from-washing right hand to shake his; having shaken His, he tucked and zipped, raised a cautionary finger, and before shaking my hand washed both of his while I blow-dried mine. When then I made again to shake, he dangled his palms-down to indicate Wet and took my place at the hand-dryer as previously at the wash basin. *Hornswoggled*, he further observed . . . dryly, shall we say, as he dried and I stood by (thus as it were reasserting our mentor/mentee relation after my unintended display of superior urinary efficiency), is a curious early-nineteenth-century American slang term of unknown origin that he was pretty sure though not absolutely certain meant "hoaxed," "bamboozled" (an even earlier slang term, also of unknown origin), or "hoodwinked" (from an old term for "blindfolded," thus "deceived by false appearances") rather than, as in my usage, "flabbergasted" (eighteenth century, origin unknown) or "dumbfounded" (seventeenth century, sense obvious)—and what an odd, agreeable coincidence, our piss-pathcrossing!

He now pushed up on his nosebridge his plastic-rimmed eyeglasses, I on mine my wire-rims, and we shook hands. A coincidence, moreover, it developed as we chatted out of the Men's, of motive as well as of presence, for sometime coach and ditto coachee were both bent not only upon bladder-voiding but upon inquiry-making as well, at the infodesk whereto we now made our tandem hearty way; and our separate queries both had to do with the same certain

### FLOATING THEATRE
#### *COMING SOON!*

—which he, he now told me, had learned of the existence of ("*of* the existence *of*"? He guessed so) just yesterP.M., when he and Missus, off a-spring-cruising now that school was out, had sailed into Solomons for the night. Over and above his historically established connection with tidewater showboats, whereof he was aware I was aware, it was that banner's lower line that'd caught his eye, both because of the irony of ("*of* the irony *of*"? Guess so) its blazoning from so no-time-soon a wreck and because . . . well, for another reason as well, pardon the repetition, which—the second reason, not the repetition—would take some explaining. And me?

Yes, I acknowledged: I guess I take some explaining, too.

Not what he meant, as of course I knew. We were at the infodesk now, where, I having been-here-done-this just a month before and there being that other infoseeker ahead of us still engaged with Miz Hooper the Nice Infolady, I showed him, with respect to that afore-savored irony, a Solomons Island Welcome handout available from that same infodesk, wherein, on a schematic map of the island's fifty-nine several numbered attractions, Item 52 was *Chesapeake Bay Floating Theatre*, and in the categorized map-key overleaf, under ART GALLERY & CULTURAL ATTRACTIONS, along with *19. Calvert Marine Museum* itself (*Local maritime history fish and fossils. New river otter exhibit.*) and other listings was *52. Chesapeake Floating Theatre (James Adams II) Calvert Marina. Oct–March. ETA Spring 1995.*

I.e., right now (i.e., right then).

"Well I'll be hornswoggled," allowed GreatUnc, and again pushed his specs up, a thing he does from time to time whether or not they've slipped down.

"Me too," said the infoseeking woman who had been engaged with Miz Hooper but now turned smiling to greet her husband, as it turned out, and his not-really coachee, whom GreatUnc said she might recall his having mentioned last night: that e-fictive novel-in-the-works? et cet. We were introduced; shook hands. Nice lady about my mom's age, I'd bet, but livelier and younger-looking, who I was now informed had been checking out *JA II*'s advertised ETA while her semi-retired-novelist-quote-emeritus husband peed. "*She*'s hornswoggled, too," she declared, indicating Miz Hooper, who nodded cheerful agreement, waggled one handsworth of fingers at me in recognitory greeting, and pushed *her* (rimless, octa-gon-lensed) eyeglasses up. Contagious as a yawn, the gesture went 'round.

Then He: "D'*you* happen to know what's what, Hop?"

In general, I was tempted to tease, or floating-theatrewise? For we know he knows, does Unc N.E., of my eyebrow-raising curriculum vitae. But I simply said instead that I could indeed background him a bit, as they say, on the *JA II* as of April last, when it had looked to be no farther from its ETA than its current lightyears' distance. If, as I gathered, Miz Hooper had heard nothing since then —

"Not a blessed word," affirmed she.

Opined my erstwhile coach, "They seem a fair way from coming soon," indexfingering the brochure.

"I wouldn't hold my breath," Miz Hooper admitted.

— then I could pretty quickly update all hands, if they wanted updating, before I headed on Eastern Shoreward to my summer's adventure.

The at-least-for-the-present alpha male of us rubbed his beard; pushed up — anyhow at — his specs; checked watch and wife. "Tell you what, lad: We'll stand you lunch at the Drydock Restaurant, just down the road, and you fill us in on your James Adams Two over yonder."

*My JA II?* But I upped my wire-rims. "Sure." And I here pass the ball to You, luv, sans prompt:

> **Lunch à trois,**
> **him her me;**
> **they get the check.**

> **Lunch à deux,**
> **novelists only;**
> **she takes a walk,**
> **he gets the check.**

# 2.2 Coming Soon!?

*Yes, well: Don't hold your breath.*

Thus mused this anchored Elder Talester through the shipboard evening, night, and morning after reaching Solomons Harbor. Mused, I mean, upon that Portentous-Ironic Mid-Cruise Coincidence aforeremarked: portentous-ironic in yonder barge-banner's bottom line—*COMING SOON!*—given the tentativity of these busy musings and the condition of the vessel thus bannered; just plain coincidental, with maybe a dash of irony but no more than a smidgin of portentousness, in that banner's top line—FLOATING THEATRE—and in the phenomenon itself, hulking and peeling downharbor there in end-of-century fact as if conjured for my benefit hugely forth (with substantial loss in translation) from mid-century fiction.

From *my* mid-century fiction, to be precise, although subsequent investigation would reveal more direct other sources. Briefly: My first published novel happens to have been suggested by my chancing upon a photograph[*] of a certain tug-towed tidewater showbarge called, more or less, James Adams's *Original Floating Theater* (contemporary photographs and playbills give roughly equal time to the Brit-spelled *theatre* and the Yank *theater*). I recalled having seen the thing in my boyhood, tied up at Long Wharf in my hometown on

---

[*] By A. Aubrey Bodine, in his album *Chesapeake Bay and Tidewater* (Baltimore: Hastings House, 1954).

the Choptank; the showboat worked the Chesapeake and adjacent waters from 1914 to '41 and played Cambridge, Maryland, in 1930, '35, '37, '38, and '40, when I was, respectively, age zero, five, seven, etc. The Portentous-Ironic Coincidence of "Adams" and "Original" sufficed for my story's genesis; it concerned an affably nihilist fifty-four-year-old bachelor lawyer with heart-, prostate-, and other problems, who in 1954 (when I myself was a healthy young husband, father, freshman-composition teacher, and aspiring novelist, writing the story on summer vacation in modest rented lodgings within sight of Long Wharf) tells of a June day in 1937 when he attempted to take his own life and numerous others' by blowing up what I renamed *Adam's Original & Unparalleled Floating Opera*; of the entire unsuccess of that attempted suicide/mass murder; and of its would-be perpetrator's subsequent shrug-shouldered conclusion that, given his amateur-nihilist premises, there is finally no more "reason" for autodestruction than for continuance.

Got that? Anyhow, it seemed a good idea at the time, and five books later I saw fit to recycle the *Opera*'s undead narrator, one Mr. Todd Andrews, into an enormous, intricated fiction meant to be my U.S. Bicentennial novel, but so long in the muse's womb that it bade to become my personal semicentennial novel instead. A tale of recyclings, of second halves, -acts, and -revolutions, it was set at the volatile end of the American High Sixties. Among its incidental inventions was a replica of the James Adams Floating Theatre denominated, with Portentous Irony, *The Original Floating Theatre II*: thus our present bemusement, let's call it, at that great floating coincidence off yonder.

Not to mention . . .

My imaginary *TOFT II*, a parallel to *The Original & Unparalleled*, was kept just barely afloat by heavy subsidy from a local philanthropic foundation. Were I reimagining the thing today, I would ratchet up the Recycling theme by seeing to it that the old movies with which it padded out its recycled stage-melodramas were the several Hollywood versions of the 1927 Ziegfeld/Kern/Hammerstein *Show Boat*. Were I reimagining the thing today, I would tisk at the Vertiginous Coincidence that one of the most popular of those old showboat melodramas, *Smilin' Through* (1920, produced on Adams's *OFT* in '29, '34, and '38), echoes repeatedly, in advance, the title of my *second* novel, from 1958: "I'll be there waiting," goes its title song, "just at *the end of the road*"; and the play's wrap-up line (spoken by the dead lovers from beyond the grave, and not a dry eye in the house) declares that folks would "go smilin' through the years if they knew what they'd find at *the end of the road.*" Italics mine; tongue-tisk, too, at the yet further Vertiginous Coincidence that the male lead in another of those perennial melodramas, *Ten Nights in a Bar Room* (like *Smilin' Through*, a staple of the James Adams repertoire), is named Joe Morgan—as is a chief character in *The End of the Road*! If I were reimagining *TOFT II* now—

But I *am* reimagining it, no? Or, rather, was already busily so doing then, at anchor somewhere in Solomons Harbor in late spring '95, recycled Life having bidden thus ponderously to imitate recycled Art:

## FLOATING THEATRE
### *COMING SOON!*

*Later in this same chapter,*
motoring past the lifeless hulk next morning en route to our postponed pit-stop, "Don't hold your breath," my mate and I joked at its breathless banner. But my breath was mildly bated as—our vessel resupplied and our dockside queries unproductive of info—we strolled into salty Solomons to learn what we could learn.

*The coincidences*, I was still musing as we strolled:

- *Item*: Just the year previous, in 1994, I had published a novel/memoir entitled *Once Upon a Time* and subtitled *A Floating Opera*. A little life-tale written under the aspect of Vocation, it is, wherein the author-narrator loses track of his muse (such things happen). He finds himself obliged like the skipper of a grounded ship—or like lost Odysseus/Aeneas/Dante—to go forward by going back, the long way 'round (such things happen), and regains his missing Sinequanon by reinvocation of her maiden visitation himto: i.e., the original *Floating Opera*.

- *Item*: Three years before that, in 1991, when the aforecited *Once Upon* novel was just a-germinating, a theater-historian acquaintance of ours in Baltimore published a history of the old James Adams showboat,* which excellent opus no doubt reinforced the "Floating Opera" theme in my *Once Upon a Time*. Having delivered that novel/memoir (a problematical genre, inasmuch as one's interest in the two categories proceeds from antithetical presumptions: If you retail to me over lunch the "story" of your love affair in Lisbon, my interest in it presumes your account to be factual, even though in fact you may be exaggerating, omitting relevant details, even flat-out lying. If on the other hand you write a novel about its narrator's love affair in Lisbon, your story must interest me despite my presumption that it's a total fabrication—even though I may happen to know that in fact it's not. Et cetera? And *nota bene*), my muse amused herself postpartumly with a collection of nonfiction pieces and another of short stories, as if to reschool herself in the mattersome distinctions between fact and fiction, Life and Art. It was while this latter volume was "in press," as they say—that is, in this same spring season that sees us "now" strolling Solomons Island—that my wife and I retired from our decades-long teaching careers, and I scratched about per usual to see what Miz Muse might have in mind for her next encore, and drew the aforeillustrated blank, whereupon off we went a-sailing as is anyhow our late-spring wont, Same Old Story etc., and here we are: a-strolling up C Street from our pit-stop marina, meandering right on Calvert (pronounced *Call*vert), left on Langley, right on Main . . .

"You left out one Item," either Muse or Mrs. would surely have reminded me hereabouts (they are not the same female entity, al-

---

* Typical of the vessel's protean denomination, in the jacket photo (from 1937) of C. Richard Gillespie's *The James Adams Floating Theatre* it's called THE ORIGINAL FLOATING THEATER, as also in "my" Bodine photo. Capt. Adams had sold the showboat five years before, and its new owners had renamed it. It will turn out to have been Gillespie's history that, in another quarter of tidewaterland, inspired the Solomons Harbor showboat-project before us.

though their Venn Diagrams, so to speak, most certainly and fortuitously overlap), had our stroll not just then fetched us to the *Callvert* Maritime Museum, where we hoped to learn more about that largest of these several Items, just down Back Creek from our strolling-ground.

I know, I know, I would have replied to whichever, and might have further murmured,

- *COMING SOON!!!* For what else than that same jumped-up exclamation had entitled a certain shape-shifty, media-straddling "novel"-in-"progress" fragmentarily submitted earlier in the year as the Writing Sample of a certain applicant to the M.A. program of my university's Writing Seminars? Which fiction (so I presumed it, submitted as it was to our resident fictioneers rather than to our poets or our creative nonfictors) featured a faltering showbarge dubbed *The Original Floating Opera II* (*TOFO II*), to no small extent inspired — so both the aspirant author acknowledged to me and his opus to its Reader — by its aforementioned predecessors. This circumstance I had mentioned in passing, at the time, to both Muse and Mrs., and both — preoccupied otherwise, as was I — had in effect replied Mm.

As had I.

What I had *not* bothered then to mention, to my mate at least, and did not now (for we are entering the marine museum, with its *de rigueur* Chesapeake screwpile lighthouse — those distinctively hexagonal and homey nineteenth-century clapboard bungalows topped with fresnel-lensed beacons and mounted on auger-tipped steel beams drilled originally into the Bay-bottom shoals thus beaconed, more recently into the grounds of sundry bayside maritime museums as the Coast Guard replaces the old lighthouses with unmanned, automated navigational markers), was that that same brash and fragmentary, edge-of-the-envelope-pushing "novel" had presumed further to include —

But "Hi," my wife was saying now to the whitecurled bespectacled lady at the Information desk, and I put these itemized musings on Hold while we put our question herto. Our guess, the InfoMs replied in effect, was as good as hers: She understood that "the folks in charge" of that cross-creek project were campaigning to raise funds for it, but she "[hadn't] the faintest" whose project it was or what its current status might be. Maybe this leaflet will tell us-all something? From a pile atop her counter she handed each of us a CALVERT COUNTY MD/SOLOMONS ISLAND EST. 1867/WEL-COME leaflet and helpfully perused one herself — wherein, sure enough, listed under the subhead ART GALLERY & CULTURAL AT-TRACTIONS along with the marine museum itself, a nearby sculpture garden, and a commercial arts/crafts/framing establishment, we jointly found *Chesapeake Bay Floating Theatre: (James Adams II) Calvert Marina. Oct–March. ETA Spring 1995.*

"Spring Ninety-five?" the infolady wondered aloud. And adjusted her rimless eyeglasses. And consulted her wristwatch.

Recommended we: "Don't hold your breath."

*At this juncture,*
I suppose, if whom I'd come to think of as the Novelist Aspirant were "writing" this account as e-fiction instead of Yrs Truly as p-, you the "Reader" — Mouseclicker, Option-opter, whatever — would be offered a menu of alternatives:

HOLD

EXHALE

DETOUR

or some such. But until and unless you opt out altogether — always your privilege — the narrative hands you're in are mine: aged, yes; pen-calloused, even, and a tad conventional (welcome aboard, friend; make yourself comfy and go at your own pace, but leave navigation and steering to the skipper, s.v.p., and I'll return the favor when I'm *your* passenger), but at least professionally experienced. Respire therefore as it pleaseth you while your narrator takes you on a short detour, to relieve himself both physically and otherwise. The room's marked MEN, but come along regardless: Our medium here is language, the original virtual reality, which seeth not nor hears nor smells/tastes/feels, but only *names*, and nameth neither more nor less than what the situation calls for.

Namely, in our case, not the mechanics of narratorial urination, but Narrator's by-leaps-and-bounds-growing realization that here — I mean out there, on that weathered banner on that battered barge — was the circle-closing, de-siècle-finning, last-hurrah novel-notion I'd been looking for, and for which already my recharged muse was coming up with "secondary inspirations"—scenes, situations, incidental felicities, and "bits"—at a flow-rate exceeding . . . never mind what. In those relevant earlier *opera* of mine, e.g. (it now occurred to me), despite the echoes of Genesis in "Adam's" and "Original," I hadn't really exploited the showboat's now-to-me-obvious associations with Noah's Ark and the biblical Flood, so readily tie-innable with our planet's current sea-rise and the millenarian fascination with apocalypse. The cities of Newark in New Jersey and Delaware, I thereupon realized for the first time as I stood leisurely a-pee—the former pronounced almost monosyllabically *New*rk, but the latter a distinct "New Ark"—must both have been founded and named by settlers in a spirit the opposite of Louis XIV's: instead of "Après moi, le déluge," "Après le déluge, nous!" Imagine a showboat, I invited my muse or she me, a-pissing, that, unlike the unlikely hulk down yonder, is an already-established but ever more precarious and quietly desperate enterprise, along the lines of . . .

Voilà, of course, the rub: the inconvenient circumstance that along with what he's rather brazenly calling *The Original Floating Opera II* (that being, he has claimed, the vessel's name), it has to have been this same quixotically bannered FLOATING THE-ATRE, this would-be *James Adams II*, that inspired young J. "Hop" Johnson's half-hatched hybrid COMING SOON!!!, a work whose ontological status—fact or fiction?—now appeared as dubious as "his"

*TOFO II*'s. But fact or fiction and e- or p-, it had been his idea before mine, no?

Well, no, actually; anyhow not quite, by the young hopeful's own acknowledgment. Just as Ms. Edna Ferber and I, thirty years apart, had each borrowed our fictive showboats from James Adams's factual one, and I then twenty years later had "borrowed" mine for reorchestration as *The Original Floating Theater II*, so either Hop Johnson or his (alleged) summer employers had modeled their *TOFO II* on one or both of my inventions. With my permission, explicit or implied? To me (a-pissing) that perhaps debatable point seemed *beside* the point: Absent written contracts with clauses of exclusivity, any shrug-shouldered, half-tacit "permission" from me for another's borrowing — echoing, spin-offing, whatever — from copyrighted-by-me material most assuredly did not preclude my own recyclement thereof. Consider the title of Johnson's graduate-application effort, *COMING SOON!!!*: A venerable cliché of showbiz hype (framed on one wall of my house is a 1930s handbill from the old *Original Floating Theater* with that same breathless exclamation), its deployment by the hopeful promoters of the unlikely-appearing *James Adams II* in no way precluded Hop Johnson's hopefully borrowing it therefrom to entitle his equally unlikely "novel." Should I choose now to borrow back what had after all been from me borrowed — choose even to entitle my re-reorchestration thereof with "his" same title — who could cry plagiarism? Especially if my borrowing from his borrowing from myself reaches print before his. . . .

Urination, Reader, like sentence-writing, proceeds in (sometimes intermittent) streams, whereas thoughts are thought in (sometimes gestaltic) flashes. In less time than it takes to tell, much less to write the foregoing, I thought and considered not only all that but, further, that all of it elaborately evaded the real issue. To wit: In forty-plus years of teaching, writing, and teaching writing at assorted American universities, I had taught thousands of students and coached hundreds of apprentice fiction-writers, and in the inexorable course of things had seen all but a very few of them and their hope-fraught manuscripts pass into oblivion, as almost certainly Mr.

Johns Hopkins Johnson and his bright but erratic and fragmentary *COMING SOON!!!* would likewise pass. Among those thousands of quickly forgotten manuscript pages I had more than once espied an incidental image, observation, or plot-idea that, as a working writer, I admired to the point of envy: Wish *I*'d thought of that!, et cetera. But on a principle as absolute mewith as not exploiting sexually the teacher/student or coach/coachee connection, I had never once in all those decades sneaked so much as a simile from my students' work into my own. Was I then now — academically retired and leisurely a-pissing — to violate that virtually sacred principle and (the idea here flooded, shall we say, upon me) not only reappropriate Johnson's central image and appropriate his (appropriated) title, but even make a chief character of the chap himself? Brash and callow young Novelist Aspirant, say, attempting his First while canny old Novelist "Emeritus," say, attempts his Last, may the better (or faster-to-the-punchline) talester win, and Devil take the hindmore?

Unthinkable!, I thought, enthusiastically. Whereupon, as if conjured from this . . . stream of consciousness? . . . there emerged from the flushing toilet stall behind me its brief occupant, whom I'd heard enter the Men's and, *faute de mieux,* said stall some paragraphs past. Younger than Yours Truly and therefore quicker at our common business, the fellow set about now washing his hands at the basin beside me, and I recognized that I had, most implausibly, in speaking of the Devil . . .

*Aristotle on the subject of coincidence in fiction,*
I made note to myself as I tucked and zipped and presently shook hands with the Very Fellow I Had Been et cetera. Had he read the *Poetics*?, I asked him presently. Still your best how-to manual around for storymakers.

"What a coincidence." His rejoinder was, by the sound of it, exclamation-mark-free. He grinned and pushed up his wire-rimmed specs, a habit of his. "I just happened to be thinking in there," nodding toilet-stallward, "about Aristotle's take on the role of coincidence in a story's plot. So hi!"

Hi indeed.

Eyeglasses up. "What an et cetera!"

Indeed. If he's going to be a Character, I suppose I'd better describe him: A wiry, sharpfaced entity is J. Hop Johnson, shorter and edgier than me. Non-noteworthy thin brown short-cut hair under a black-white-and-orange Baltimore Orioles cap; dark eyes bird-quick behind those wire-rims and brighter with mischief than with any distinctive color. Jeans and T-shirt, the latter labeled PIT BULLS RULE!, a name I'd heard somewhere but couldn't place, and logo'd with the eponymous animal behind a set of drums, on the head of the bass whereof appeared said label. His generation's inevitable running shoes, clean, no socks. Left lobe gold-ringed. His manner a characteristically good-humored mix of impudence and well-brought-upness. Enough of that. He was here in Solomons, he informed me, *en detour* to my natal turf and his summer job, his present purpose to check out the progress, if any, of what my wife and I had fortuitously happened upon (so I now told him) just the evening before — and whence I now understood him to have borrowed the title of his proposed M.A.-thesis-novel.

"Unless those turkeys borrowed it from me," he countered, and reminded me — *pointedly*? I wondered — that he'd staked his title-claim the previous autumn, when he'd begun drafting his more-or-less-e-fictive Writing Sample for application to our graduate fiction-writing program, and others.

Mm-hm, said I to myself, and of him inquired — as we made our way out of the Men's and toward the museum's Information desk, where waited my wife — whether he knew anything more than did the woman there officially stationed (who knew no more than did the WELCOME brochure [which knew next to nothing, and some of that mistaken]) about that so-called *James Adams II*, in which, for obvious reasons, I had a certain interest.

"Sure. A little."

My wife: Hop Johnson, one of our Writing Seminarians. Hop Johnson: my wife.

"Hi." "Hi." "You're the electronic one?" "I guess."

Eyeglasses up; even the information-lady followed suit. Then earnestly advised Johns Hopkins Johnson "Forget about that Welcome brochure, guys. The showboat you *really* oughta check out is TOFO Two, not that old rat-bin over there."

"Tofo Two," my wife repeated.

One hand on my shoulder as if to give credit where due and the other raised as if on oath, "The Original FlOpera Squared," he to her vowed: "*Going Soon*, unless our luck changes."

She and I exchanged a considering look. Tell you what, I told the lad then: We're tied up at that marina/restaurant complex couple of blocks down the road from here, just across from old Coming Soon. . . .

"The Drydock?" Right. "That's where I'm parked! What would Aristotle say?"

So why not join us for lunch—

Our treat, my wife put in, still teacher to the bone and generously predisposed toward all species of the genus Student.

—and fill us in on these assorted showbarges of yours.

"Mine?" Eyeglasses up. For James Adams Redux, he declared, he took neither credit nor responsibility, it being The (potential) Competition. As for "his" dear *TOFO II*, wouldn't I acknowledge that its existence owed more to me than to him?

Its existence: That's what needs discussing, I suggested, before we get to paternity claims. Lunch?

"Look here," proposed my wife the teacher and facilitator extraordinaire: "The forecast's clear, and we're in no hurry to get under way. Why don't you writer-types have your lunch-talk while I grab a bite on board and do some laundry in the marina laundromat? Maybe I'll borrow one of their bikes and get some exercise." Sailboat-cruising, she explained to J. H. Johnson, was sporadically strenuous but by and large not physically exercising—as perhaps he knew?

"Nope."

I protested: Meals ashore, like meals aboard, are one of the sport's pleasures, and of the latter, thanks to her, we'd had a tasty series. . . .

"So I'll walk to the Drydock with you and pick up a sandwich to go."

"In *my* novel," Hop Johnson told her here, "you'd have mouse-click options at this point. Like *Lunch à trois* or *Lunch à deux, you and your husband, while the kid gets lost. . . .*" With a grin: "Or *Lunch him and me while* you *get lost,* excuse me—"

"What?" she came back, mock-offended: "no *Lunch à deux me and yeux while* he *gets lost?* But I here click *Lunch à deux novelists only.* Enjoy."

# 2.3 Ontological Lunchbreak: Novelists Only

*On the proper role of coincidence in fiction*
—more exactly in storymaking, for the subject of his *Poetics* is dramatic, not narrative, art—with characteristic reasonableness Aristotle declares in effect that since real life now and then includes unlikely coincidences both idle and consequential (Fancy meeting *you*, of all people! *Here*, of all places! *Now*, of all times! etc.), a storymaker may legitimately deploy such a possible-though-improbable happenstance to begin the tale or to give its plot-screws an early turn. Thereafter, however, the Plausible (even when strictly impossible) is ever to be preferred to the Possible-but-Unlikely; and in the *resolution* of a plot, most particularly, coincidence ought to be eschewed. Fate in fiction, decrees the great A, ought to flow from character and situation, not from chance; let no god on wires drop down at climax-time to rescue the storymaker from whatever dramaturgical corner his want of experience, talent, or judgment has painted him into.

Thus Aristotle; and "Sound advice," opined our Novelist "Emeritus" to our ditto Aspirant as the three of them—Mr. N.E. & Mrs. + young Bachelor of Arts N.A.—strolled back through May's-end tidewater sunshine from the Calvert Marine Museum toward Zahniser's Marina and Drydock Restaurant, the eldest of the trio reflecting, even as he opined, *Life is short and, for some of us, already three-quarters run. We strut and fret our hour upon the stage; why should anyone at the forty-five-minute mark spend even a single*

*second reviewing, with someone not after all his student, Aristotle's*
*position on the role of coincidence in fiction?* While the next-eldest,
or next-youngest, in effect reflected, *Good old Aristotle: Two thou-*
*sand three hundred years old, that little lesson is, and as sound as*
*the day his students first made note of it. What a goodsome business*
*altogether, teaching and learning! If a person had only one hour*
*from birth to death, she should spend her first thirty minutes learn-*
*ing as much as she can of what human experience has scraped to-*
*gether, and her second thirty teaching as much of the best of that as*
*she can to other people, kids especially. Plus I love my husband,*
with whom in her undergraduate years, decades past, she had first
read Aristotle's *Poetics* and *Nichomachean Ethics,* and who himself
—reflecting now on her characteristically unselfish response to Hop
Johnson's hypothetically preferred option buttons—appended to
his above-reflected reflections *Plus I love my wife.*

"Yup," agreed the youngest thosethreeof, adding however "But I
can think of half a dozen ways to turn that dictum on its head," and
to himself reflecting *Way cool, man! Here I am at age five-and-*
*twenty talking Aristotle with Old-Fart GreatUnc Ennie and his Re-*
*ally Nice Wife in Solomons Island Maryland at eleven forty-five of a*
*May's-end morn in Nineteen Hundred and Ninety-five, and okay,*
*I'm aware that when he was my age he was six years married al-*
*ready (not to this one) with three kids and a subsistence-level teach-*
*ing job and his first novel in second draft, while I'm just a late-*
*blooming young-fart prospective grad student with neither wife nor*
*kids nor steady girlfriend even and my parents still paying much of*
*my freight, but all the fucking same I bet I can write, if that's the right*
*word for it, a quote-unquote novel at least as good as and maybe*
*even more capital-I Important than any of his. Plus I'm hungry.*

Speaking of the Chesapeake Floating Theatre *James Adams II*
Coming Soon!, he sort of added, here's what he knew about it,
from a reporter for the Calvert County *Voice* whom he'd met while
doing research in a Fells Point grad-student bar just a few weeks
past: It seems a local theater-type who happened a couple years
back to be between projects, as they say, happened to read a just-
published history of the old James Adams Floating Theatre—

"We know the author!" the woman thosethreeof exclaimed. "What a coincidence!"

Yes, well.

"The title," her husband added, "if I've got it right, is *The James Adams Floating Theatre*. Something catchy like that."

"Yeah, well. So the guy—not the historian guy but the theater-type guy?—decides what we need around here's an old-time Chesapeake showboat, okay? As if we-all hadn't launched one just across the Bay that very same year?"

"Yes, well . . ."

"So he cobbles up a theater company, and he stages shows here and there onshore to promote the project and raise start-up money, and somebody donates him that old Navy-surplus office barge, and he wangles a feasibility-study grant from Maryland's Department of Feasibility or whatever and then a hundred-K challenge loan from the state legislature if he can shark up another hundred K to match it by fiscal Ninety-seven, and *that's all she wrote*, said my girl reporter —or anyhow *meant* to write now that she'd thought of it." He conned his walking-companions' expressions, found them neutrally attentive, pushed up on his slender nose-bridge his wire-rimmed specs. "We TOFO-Two types think he's dead in the water, natch; a nice enough guy, we bet, but get this: When his company did a quote-unquote *Evening with Rodgers and Hammerstein* to raise money for their J.A. Two, they actually did *Rodgers* and Hammerstein instead of Kern and Hammerstein! Like, *Oklahoma!* and *South Pacific* instead of *Show Boat*?"

"Mm-*hm*."

The young forthholder batted his forehead and turned up his palms. "I mean where's their fuckin' *brains*, excuse me? But then get *this*: Instead of parking our TOFO Two right across the harbor here and blowing the new guy out of the water, our airhead Planning and Strategy Team left Solomons Island *off* our itinerary last season, as if to give him a sporting chance! Go figure!"

Pointedly observed Mrs., "And yet you said they sent you down here to check out the competition. . . ."

"Right!" Hop Johnson skipped briefly backwards before her and twiddled his ringed left lobe, the better to expostulate: "That's 'cause Doctor Spin has got our shit together now, excuse me, competitionwise." By whom he meant, he said—back in place now and glancing appreciatively herward between side-of-the-eying his own maybe Competition, all as the trio doglegged Drydockward from the marine museum three abreast, the two males flanking the fe-— Mort Spindler, one smart cookie, Expediter- and Facilitator-in-Chief for Dorset Tradewinds Enterprises, who he Hop was much relieved to hear had been assigned virtually fulltime this season to the ailing T Two. As for *J.A.* Two: All signs indicated that that project was stalled, if by no means necessarily abandoned. It would pose "us" no threat *this* season, for sure, and with Mort Spindler and Holly Weil and a couple other way-cool newbies on board, the Arkade Theatre Company would have nobody but itself to blame if the Maryland legislature didn't decide that TOFO Two—which, mind, so far from *costing* the Free State's taxpayers, was raking in the state's 5-percent sales tax on every ticket sold—was showboat enough for Chesapeake country. "Plus," he pointed out as theythree cornered into Zahniser's Marina's parking lot, "*we* can play ports in Virginia or wherever the playing's good, the way Adams's Original used to do? But if that state-supported sucker ever leaves Maryland waters, Mort's got us a protest campaign all loaded and cocked. Which your J.A. Two won't ever, 'cause we're going to see to it she never leaves Back Creek."

"Mm-*hm*," hmmed the Novelist herein called Emeritus.

"Well, you're an impassioned casemaker, for sure," his wife granted the Novelist Aspirant, who appreciatively agreed while trying in vain to read his elder counterpart's mind. "But what *I*'d like to know," she went on (halting their forward progress here, as they had reached the inboard end of Zahniser's "A" dock, at the outboard end whereof their vessel was tied up), "is how my husband and I have managed to live for sixteen years just two rivers up from the Choptank, plus half-time in Baltimore too, and to read the city newspaper every day and the Kent County one every week, and never to've even *heard* of this TOFO Two of yours."

His question exactly, sort of, her husband affirmed, and to his wife added "Some of us suspect he's making it all up."

She: "Well, novelists do that." And to the N.A., "You *are* one, too, right?"

"Apprentice grade," the young man cheerily amended, raising his right forefinger and with his left pushing up weknowwhat. He took his ease against the nearest parked vehicle, a red Jeep Cherokee, and added "*Novice* grade, actually, so I prob'ly didn't make it *all* up." To the N.E., "Hardly any of it, actually: just that old-fart progger on Hick Fen Island who finds the computer disk, and even he's less fictitious than I wish."

"Computer disk," wife wondered. And "What's a *progger*?"

"Inside joke," said husband: "Novelists only. Sorry."

Not a problem, she assured them—and then in fairness reminded all hands that Mr. and Ms. Themselves hadn't managed to hear tell of the *James Adams II*, either, until they'd motored past it just yestereve.

"There you are!" exclaimed the Novelist Aspirant.

Not the same thing as an up-and-Floating Opera Two in their virtual backyard, the Mrs. went on, but still. "Anyhow, here *we* are, so bye."

"No sandwich to go?" her Mr. wondered, for she was turning dockward; and to his counterpart-aspirant, "We're tied up out there."

"Cool, man!" Craning at the double row of yacht-filled slips: "Which one's yours?"

"Come see," he found himself by Mrs. invited, but GreatUnc Hubby intervened: "You can see it from here; it's the one across the end of the pier there." Wife sees he's a touch discomfited, can't quite guess why ("Just don't want the kid in our *story* that much," he'll explain later, unable himself to say further just why), doesn't press her invitation. But Aspirant takes it upon himself to say "Just a quick look-see, okay? I don't know a yawl from a whatchacallit. Ketch?"

And so out to pier's end they stroll, Mr. N.E. trailing theytwo by reason both of dock-width and of mild reluctance while his mate, ever the teacher, explains that a yawl's mizzenmast is stepped aft of the helm, in the boat's very stern, while a ketch's is stepped just forward of the helm—except in center-cockpit vessels, come to think of it, whose mizzens may be aft of the helm but forward of the aft cabin.

"Mizzens," echoed the Novelist Aspirant.

"But ours is a cutter." She pointed. "One mast instead of two, stepped farther aft than on a sloop, but two headsails instead of one. There's more to it, but that'll do for Lesson One. Catboats and schooners come later."

"Much obliged." Grinning her to Him. "I wish I knew *everything!* Don't you?" Eyeglasses up; earring twiddled. "Shouldn't a novelist know everything? At least the *names* of everything."

She: "Sure."

Himself: "Yes, well . . ."

He Junior, twiddling lobe-ring: "Anyhow, way cool, guys! So: Postmodernism has been good to you, right?"

Uncomfortable with this turn of their talk as well as with J. Hopkins Johnson's characteristically half-mocking tone (and trying to remember whether the placement of male earrings was a sexual-orientation code), Coach Emeritus declared that what had been good to him and his were forty-plus fulltime hardworking years in the U.S. university system and two teaching salaries under the same roof; that given the facts of trade-fiction life in fin-de-siècle America, he counted himself blessed to be in print at all; and that he counseled his apprentice-novelist coachees, or used so to counsel them, to plan their economic lives the way poets must, not mistaking their vocation for a profession. Live on your salary, he used to advise them, he declared, wherever it comes from, and regard any book-royalties as manna from heaven, for paying off house-mortgages and kids' tuitions—

"Or buying a nice sailboat," the younger man teased, "once those other items have been manna'd off."

"But count on nothing, Hop. You can *hope* for a major score, as your poet-friends can't: Hope for a million-buck advance on royalties and the moon to boot—but *expect* zilch, and chances are you won't be far off."

Scribbling with his right forefinger onto his left palm, "Wait'll I write that down, Coach." But it was a poet our N.A. then quoted, the late and by-the-muse-much-lamented Philip Larkin: *"So the shit in the shuttered château / Who does his five hundred words . . ."*

*"Then parts out the rest of the day,"* the N.E.'s wife joyously picked up, and the pair together *"Between bathing and booze and birds . . . !"*

*". . . Is far off as ever,"* the senior themof then reminded the junior, who however gestured toward the couple's probably handsome old cruising cutter and said "Not so far off after all, looks like from here! But I guess even you must envy the ones who manage to combine literary quality with real popular and commercial success?" He named names.

"Are you needling us?" Wife wanted to know.

"Hey, no, really!" Eyeglasses up, twinkly-sharp eyes a-dart thembehind from her to Him. "But you wouldn't be *disappointed*, would you, if your next one hit the charts again? First time in thirty years?"

"You *are* needling!"

"He can't help himself," Husband informed her: "It's his nature."

"Sorrysorrysorry," apologized Needler, but couldn't help adding "What *is* your next, anyhow, or is that a trade secret? What's in the pipeline for us You-fans?"

She, though not really incordially, "Nunnayerbeeswax, buster"; and He: "No interviews, Hop, okay?"

Okay, okay, replied Novelist Aspirant, and apologized again— to Missus especially, whom he saw to be the thinner-skinned in these matters. He truly *was* a fan, he assured her; that's how he'd gotten involved with showboats in the first place. Plus he couldn't help thinking, like, *I showed you mine*, you know? *So now you show me yours.* But just kidding, of course (for he saw her face flash indignation): He didn't need reminding that he'd showed his because her husband was the doctor, so to speak, and himself the patient et cet, "And look here, guys, I've worn out my welcome, and anyhow that's all I know about old J.A. Two, so why'n't I hit the road now and let you do lunch *à deux* after all. Really cool-looking cutter there, man, ma'am."

Wife's look to Husband said *she* had no problem with that suggestion, but Hub declared No, he wanted that aforeproposed ontological lunch-conference still, whereto however she should by all means consider herself both invited and welcome. Lunch *à trois*.

"Thanks," she decided, "but I think it'd better be Novelists Only." Her tone was genuinely cordial now, the seasoned teacher excusing an unruly but promising student—whose hand she then shook, pleased to've met him, good luck with graduate school and first novel, have a good life et cetera.

"You sure?" Husband asked her. "Not even a take-out?"

She meant to take her ease on a cockpit cushion with grapefruit and good book, Wife replied; they two should go ontologe themselves till the cows came home. As long as *they* two got under way no later than three, three-thirty, say, there'd be time still to sail upriver to St. Leonard's Creek for the night. Enjoy.

*Ontological lunch menu:*

"Crabcake on crackers and iced tea with lemon, please."

"You, sir?"

"Same."

"Have wine if you want, Hop. When we're sailing, I never drink till the hook's down."

"Iced tea's fine." Eyeglasses up. "The hook's the anchor?"

"Knock it off now, okay? The faux-naiveté?"

"Sorry there." Earring. "But I *do* wish I knew the names of everything."

"Likewise. *All trades, their gear and tackle and trim . . .*"

"That's the *other* Hopkins, right? Compliments on your wife, by the way, as well as your sailboat. Your *cutter*. She's all right."

"Agreed."

EGs up. "Like, I liked the way she came back at me for 'needling,' and then put it right aside. And I meant what I said back there, man: You've been my mentor, like it or not, more than you're aware of. I wish you really *were* going to be the doctor for my COMING SOON!!! novel, though it's not really sick. Just growing pains—"

"*Genug*, Hop. We're here to do ontology: the ontological status of The Original Floating Opera Two."

"What's to say?" Elbow on table, cheek in hand, eyes bright, like a pensive Jiminy Cricket. "One of these days I'll learn to *invent*, like you—though even yours didn't come from nowhere, right? Meanwhile I just log it like it is, plus some fills and flourishes here and there."

"Um-hum."

"Um-humarooney, man! *TOFO*'s economic status might be uncertain. Her aesthetic status is, for sure; even her *hydrodynamic* status if we don't upgrade her fucking bilge pumps! But ontologically? There she blows, as real as Dorsettown-on-Choptank and Snug Har-B-O-U-R and Patmos Tower and old quote-unquote *Todd Andrews* and you'n me. Maybe more than me."

"Todd Andrews?"

"I know I know I know. That's why I put him in quotes: 'As real as quote-unquote *Todd Andrews*.' Now we understand each other, right? In *your* new novel they'll be figurative quotes; in mine they're not. Hey: great crabcakes."

"Quite okay crabcakes and not-bad fries. But that means your novel isn't one. To the extent that *they're* real, your novel isn't."

"Novel shmovel," declared J. Hop Johnson. "Fiction shmiction, as long as it floats. Let the librarians decide where to fucking file it."

"Or the libel-and-plagiarism courts. But that's a different lunch altogether. Some vinegar for these fries, please, miss? Thanks. So let's talk about this quote-unquote *novel* of yours, beyond the bits I've seen."

"Sure thing, Doc. Just let me unzip here. . . ."

Sip of iced tea. What he had in mind, in fact, declared the younger themof then—or should he say in quote-unquote *fact?*—was a First Novel that would also be the first of its kind, one foot plunked squarely in each of electronic- and print-fiction, one hand in each of capital-F Fact and Fiction, what did *he* care? It would quote-unquote *involve* a talented but scattered young aspiring novelist trying to quote-unquote *write* his first ditto-ditto *novel* in the age of the World Wide Web: a first novel itself involving an uncertainly functioning showboat named *TOFO II*, just like *TOFO II*. This N.A., let's call him (and he *is* a him, *faute de mieux*), has a promising central metaphor—the sinking showboat—and some bright, more-or-less-manic bits, such as he Hop had back at application-time. He even has a tentative wacko cast of characters—wait'll you meet 'em!—but no real capital-S Story. He therefore resolves—*this*'ll interest you, Doc—to appropriate and reorchestrate, or shall we say update and improve upon, his quote-unquote *mentor*'s first novel (published long before N.A. himself was born), at least *its* central metaphor, as well as its author himself, come to think of it: a foil-character whom let's call the The Novelist Emeritus. Okay, so it's a brazen and ungrateful invasion of privacy blah blah blah, but who gives a shit? Not the N.A. character, who'll deal with that question if and when his quote-unquote *novel* goes online and/or hits the stands, or his quote-unquote *mentor* sues. His program meanwhile —like his crabcake-eating, iced-tea-sipping author's—is to log his adventures aboard *TOFO II* and then, somewhere down the line, to recast them as capital-F Fucking Fiction. Okay?

"Somewhere down the line . . ."

"You got it. Now you show me yours."

"Nope. I'm the doctor, remember? More iced tea, please, miss? Thanks."

"I wish. But you're not, *tant pis*, remember?"

"Granted." Stir and sip. "Even so, I don't discuss work in progress, especially in the first trimester. Bad luck. Could we have our check, please, ma'am?"

Luck shmuck, boldly declared then Johns Hopkins Johnson. If *he* were writing his GreatUnc's Next, he might as well say, it'd be about that aforeimagined Novelist-Emeritus type, who wants to do a quote-unquote *Last Novel* to close the circle on his career. So he goes back to his personal Square One and latches onto this *J.A. II/ TOFO II* business? But the problem is, some smartass young applicant to his university's M.A. program has already staked out that turf (in fact, so to speak, it's the twerp's Writing Sample that gives the old fart his basic idea), and so he's conflicted, as we say nowadays: Chances are the kid's so-called novel will come to nothing, like most grad-student M.A.-thesis novels—like the old guy's own, come to think of it, which it embarrasses him even to *remember*, remember? And yet the little shit *did* get there first . . .

"Except he didn't," pointed out here Dr. E. Meritus, and fished forth his Visa card, "seeing as how he more or less lifted *his* central image from the N.E. guy's first novel. First *published* novel, not counting half-assed apprentice work."

All smiles. "*Now* you're talking, Dad! So in *my* version I'm just now deciding to borrow that N.E. character from *your* version— maybe just exactly the missing element I've been looking for! Novelist Aspirant versus Novelist Emeritus, First Novel versus Last, e-fiction versus p-, all played out aboard TOFO Two! *Coming Soon*, man!"

"Maybe call it *Ejaculating Prematurely*," advised the other, figuring 15 percent of $16.40-rounded-down-to-the-nearest-buck equals $2.40, rounded in turn to the nearest buck and added to the Visa total equals $18.40; "that's *my* novel you're outlining."

"Way cool, man!" In *his* version, it now occurred to its author (said author declared), The N.E. Character not only discovers that *T II* really exists—which he maybe knew all along but pretended not to or resisted acknowledging, for reasons yet to be worked out —but gets himself involved with the showboat in some important way, to try to unstick his stuck Last Novel. . . .

"Keep me out of your cottonpicking novel, lad, s.v.p.," here warned or advised The N.E. Character. "In fact, keep *yourself* out of it, is my advice. Even old Edna Ferber says somewhere that it's usually a mistake for the writer to put him/herself into the story."

"No shit!" All delight and earring-twiddle. "Ferber says that?"

"In her autobiography, I believe, which I read as homework once upon a time."

"Hot damn! We both know it's negotiable advice, but I like it that Ferb herself said it: the horse's mouth! I'll put that in the show —or did you already put it in yours?"

"Would it matter?"

All delight et cet. "Now you're talking, man! Up your old eyeglasses and go to it!"

The elder realized that he was in fact pushing up his specs not unlike the younger (such tics are contagious), to whom then he declared "No criticism necessarily intended, Hop, but you can be sure that any novel of mine on this subject of ours will be a very different piece of work from yours."

"Not a problem! So the two'll add up to one metanovel, like the e and p versions of mine." Or like, come to think of it, he then thought and added, *TOFO II*'s tandem tugs, mighty *Raven* and sturdy little *Dove*, which he hoped to remember to do a chapter on, or at least a cadenza, somewhere down the road: Being of different sizes and thrusts, they're obliged to tow T Two from somewhat different angles, to correct each other and average a straight course. "That's *my* metaphor, remember," he warned.

And not a bad one, the check-picker-upper granted, and added that his lunch-guest was welcome to it, inasmuch as he himself had no taste for collaboration. A friendly rivalry, if anything, was what *he* saw ahead: a cordial-but-serious contest, which may the abler penperson win, each taking every fair and no unfair advantage of the other. Agreed?

"You say," said bright-grinned J. H. Johnson. "*I* say all's fair in love, war, and art."

"Amen, then, lad." Retrieving credit card and hip-pocketing wallet: "As the bumpersticker says, OLD AGE AND CUNNING WILL DEFEAT YOUTH AND STRENGTH."

"Touché, man. But YOUTH AND STRENGTH AND CUNNING WILL DEFEAT OLD AGE AND CUNNING, and anyhow you're not *that* old."

"Nor you that young. But AGE, CUNNING, AND STRENGTH WILL DEFEAT YOUTH, WEAKNESS, AND INNOCENCE, we bet."

"Could be. But YOUTH, STRENGTH, AND CUNNING WILL DEFEAT AGE, FATIGUE, AND FATUITY, excuse me, and my bumpersticker can whip your bumpersticker's ass."

"Don't bet the farm on it, fella. Up your eyeglasses and on with the show?"

"Up yours and thanks for lunch, Doc. I mean it. Gotta run now."

Warmly then the pair shook right hands, adjusted each his own spectacles with left, and rose from table. Elder excused himself to visit the Men's before returning to wife, vessel, and annual-spring-cruise-in-progress; Younger decided he'd best do likewise before

Jeeping Eastern Shore– and summer-jobward; and so the pair found themselves once again parallelly peeing.

"It won't be the better *pen*person who wins, by the way," J. Hopkins Johnson informed the wall above his urinal. "I'm strictly a keyboard man."

"Too bad for you," in his cordial-rival neighbor's mid-piss opinion: "You've lost hold of a basic metaphor."

"A technologically outdated and politically incorrect one, no? Anyhow, take your sweet time there, Unc: That's what the old meta's for. Me, I'm off to TOFO Two." Wherewith he zipped and flushed and washed hands and was, leaving his slower-flowing senior to declare to *his* stall-wall his shaken but not yet abandoned conviction that whatever the status of Chesapeake Floating Theatre *James Adams II* COMING SOON!, and whoever the "author" of this now-concluding "scene," *The Original Floating Opera II* existed mainly, if not only, in their paired imaginations.

¿No?

No!

Either way, on to
PART II,
shall we?

Its second part!:

# *Part II*
## *1995–1999*

# 1995.1

*In the fullness of time,*
the chap who's being called "N.E.," "GreatUnc Ennie," and suchlike, but who if I were narrating this chapter in the first-person
singular would now be called simply "I," zipped and flushed,
washed one hand with the other and vice versa, dallied awhile
before a nautical chart of the Patuxent posted outside the restrooms,
then exited the second-story marina restaurant and made his way
down and out onto the transient-vessel pier to rejoin his patient partner and resume herwith their customary school's-out sailing cruise.
Her he found, per her aforedeclared intention, duly at ease on a
cockpit cushion, her back propped against the cabin bulkhead and
the bezeled faces of our vessel's flush-mounted depthsounder, ane-
mometer, and knotmeter. And reading, as it happened, not after all a
good book, but one of several piled-up back issues of *The New York
Review of Books.* For just as among the pleasures of sailing in general is the literalization of commonplace metaphors — getting to
know the ropes, making headway, giving oneself leeway, battening
the hatches, riding out the storm — so among the pleasures of extended sailboat-cruising is the opportunity to clear the decks, so to
speak, of accumulated reading matter.

"So how was your Ontological Lunch," she wanted to know,
"Novelists Only?"

I stepped aboard. Haven't quite digested it yet, I think. I'll give
you a report. Yours?

Nothing ontological about grapefruit and tortilla chips, she supposed. "Anyhow, your self-designated mentee seems to've gotten our moneysworth. He came out to say thanks and bon voyage, and we talked for a while."

He did? You did?

"A bit fresh, that one." Since she wears reading glasses only, it is your narrator's mate's pleasantly compensatory habit to shift them *down* on her nose when speaking, the better to focus her speakee. "Smart, though. And lively."

Better fresh than stale, her husband supposed.

"And anyhow a student, so a priori half excused. A fortiori? Ipso facto?"

Dealer's choice. What'd he say?

"Oh . . . how much he enjoyed *really talking* with you, et cet." As we spoke, we set about our routine preparations for undocking: exchanged reading- for sunglasses, secured loose gear above- and belowdecks. "Explained to me what a *progger* is."

Mm-hm.

"Pointed out his red Jeep Cherokee up in the parking lot, on the grounds that quote *we'd showed him ours, so et cetera* unquote. Explained to me who the Pit Bulls are when I asked him about his T-shirt. . . ."

He had time to say and do all that?

"He told me you were occupied in the Men's room."

Told *me* he had to hustle on over to that showboat of his.

"Which it turns out really *does* exist, apparently?"

Yes, well, maybe.

"Let's not forget to check the engine again before we cast off."

Roger that. For we had reached the point in our routine where, all gear secured, she fetches the engine ignition key from its keeping-place atop the companionway binocular box, slugs it into the switch, and takes up her position at the helm. He then for his part steps down the companionway ladder into the cabin proper and over to the navigation station, where, leaning across the chart table to the electrical-switch panel, he twists the big battery-selector switch to ALL. *Batteries okay*, he now reports upstairs, and his mate advances the throttle two-thirds, checks to make sure the gear-lever is in Neutral, switches the ignition On (whereat the low-oil-pressure alarm whistles its test signal, and various engine-panel warning lights routinely flash theirs to let us know they're functional), then presses and holds the Start button until the cranking auxiliary diesel engine catches and rumbles to life. Promptly throttling down to idle-speed, she peers over our transom to verify that the engine's cooling system is discharging raw seawater as well as diesel fumes out of our exhaust pipe and back where it came from instead of into our dinghy. Then—not routinely, but in this instance—we listened together for any trace of the irregular clanking that had troubled us the day before but went unreported, as did some other things, in Chapter 1.2 ("Same Old Story") above.

None. All the same, Narrator returned to cockpit, lifted the engine hatch cover, and visually doublechecked that their recently-installed new alternator's drive-belt guard—inadequately secured by the engine mechanic just prior to this cruise, with alarmingly loud consequences presently to be set forth—was now behaving itself.

*All set*, we agreed, and went on with the so-familiar but always quietly stirring procedures of Casting Off and Getting Under Way. Harbor chart, binoculars, and logbook ready-to-hand in the cockpit. Instruments switched on and reading properly. Dinghy drawn up short astern (but not under that exhaust-water discharge), clear of snagging on wharfpiles or boat-neighbors. Masthead vane consulted for wind direction, and docklines "singled up" accordingly. In this instance, a mild breeze on our nose and negligible tidal current promised simple extrication from between the vessels snugged fore and aft of us along the pier's cross-T: She at the helm, having verified that our rudder is centered fore and aft, releases the steering-wheel brake; he on the dock casts off first (in this instance) our stern- and then our bow line, permitting us to lie to a single breast line against our fenders and the padded piles. That final line too he then un-clove-hitches and tosses aboard, holding six tons of sailboat momentarily in position by the mast-shrouds as one might steady a (willing) horse by grasping its saddle. All set?

She glances again to make sure our way is clear of harbor traffic. "All set."

Off we go, then. He gives a small shove and pulls himself up from dock to gunwale as the light wind catches and swings our bow out; she at the same time shifts into Forward, then gooses the throttle and expertly turns the wheel just enough to clear the boat moored ahead of us without swinging our stern against the wharf or, as we slide past it, that neighboring vessel. Were we setting out from our home pier rather than from a mere marina pit-stop, we would at this point salute Poseidon with three blasts of the ship's conch shell — our Conch of Departure — and perhaps have the hornpipe from Handel's *Water Music* piping from the tape player. As is, a simple *"Hasta la vista*, Solomons Island" does the trick; once we're clear, our helmsperson ups the throttle to maybe 1800 rpm and turns her attention to maneuvering through harbor traffic and channel markers toward the Patuxent proper while her mate uncleats and coils and stows our docklines, retrieves and stows the inflated neoprene fenders, lets the dinghy out to trail us quietly at the full length of its painter, and sets about raising the mainsail for our run upriver. We are, once again and welcomely, under way.

Or were, rather, that end-of-May 1995 midafternoon. As he drafts this paragraph nearly three years later, on a rainybleakchill mid-March '98 morning in his creekside workroom — our boat still hibernating in a nearby boatyard, its spring commissioning not even begun, and that "cordial contest" between novelists "Emeritus" and "Aspirant" so momentously escalated since their Ontological Lunch — the innocent pleasures of sailboat-cruising seem to Narrator distant indeed, in both directions. But back then upstream we turned, once clear of Solomons Harbor, and he lowered our centerboard halfway and raised our forestaysail and cranked out our big genoa and trimmed all three "plain sails" to suit our heading, and she shut down the engine after first gunning it to blow out accumulated diesel soot, and he ducked below to switch the batteries to 1 and warned us *Drawing five feet* and switched the depthsounder alarm to eight feet to give us a bit of margin, and we settled down, more or less (since river-sailing, unlike open-water passage-making, requires continual course adjustments and sail trims), to enjoy a lazy close reach up under the highway bridge toward our night's anchorage in handsome St. Leonard's Creek, some miles upriver.

Bliss. Until "He also said," she said, resuming our dockside conversation, "that he really looked forward to collaborating with you on your new quote-unquote *showboat novel*, and that you'll soon be hearing from quote-unquote *Doctor Spin*, if not from quote-unquote *Todd Andrews* directly. What's *that* all about, or shouldn't I ask?"

Oy, forget it, her mate advised or hopefully requested: The guy likes to tease.

"He is a bit fresh." But, splendid woman, she didn't press her question. We went on with our reach upriver, our day, our spring cruise — a near-three-weeker, as it turned out, but south only as far as the Virginia shore of the Potomac, where (this season) the stinging sea nettles were already arriving to put an end to swimming and turn us unhurriedly back north. Routinely for the next several days, whenever we ran the engine — to enter or leave an anchorage or pit-stop, to make headway in calm air, or simply to recharge our batteries — we listened for Trouble and happily heard none. The season's first Atlantic hurricane, Allison, threatened from the Caribbean but fizzled out. We sailed and motored, read and swam, made meals and love, danced naked on our cabin-top in mid-Bay warm light rain to irresistible reggae, and made no further mention of (although the he of us may have made a few surreptitious notebook-notes upon) Ontological Lunches or ditto Engine Trouble. . . .

Until, as sometimes-corny Fate would have it, we reentered Solomons Harbor en route back up-Bay, a week and more since we'd left it, intending as before to overnight in our special spot, ride out what bade to be another thunderstormy evening, and reprovision next morning for some days ahead — and almost exactly as we motored into view of Chesapeake Floating Theatre *James Adams II* COMING SOON!, we heard again a certain tremendous clatter under our cockpit sole, as if the Yanmar diesel were autodestructing. The woman of us, at the helm as usual while her mate on the foredeck furled sails and made ready the anchor tackle, immediately throttled down and shifted into Neutral; the man of us hurried herward, damning some but not all marine diesel mechanics. When in short order it became clear that the clatter, though reduced, was nowise eliminated by these measures, we hurriedly decided to shut the engine down at once (without its usual clean-out revving, which we feared would do damage), coast on our remaining headway out of the main harbor-channel, and drop anchor any old where while we took the Next Step as we had been earlier instructed. A simple measure, actually, neither long nor in present circumstances difficult; we duly thanked Zeus and Poseidon that this Engine Trouble theme was being reprised in calm conditions and sheltered shallow water rather than Out There in a half-gale. Okay, so the sky's fuzzy off to northwest behind that looming hulk with its weathered exclamatory warning, and the forecast mentions a line of T-showers already in the D.C. area, headed our way. But this time, unlike last, it should take no more than an anecdotesworth of tinkering to get us back up and running and safely tucked into snug harbor.

*Click ye therefore back,*
so to speak, if you will, Comrade Page-Turner, to Chapter Whateveritsnumber, "Same Old Story," which with your indulgence Narrator will now, as the computer-graphics people say, Enhance. On the cusp of age sixty-five he was there then, you will recall, and his muse mute — for the nonce merely, all hands assumed, and so set forth as there set forth, a-sailing, till she refind her voice and ipso facto his. In itself no large concern, this postpartum pause, as it was both precedented and indeed postpartum, he having delivered to his publisher just the autumn past Book Two of a two-book contract. In short, an at least normally busy time, musewise, it had been — for that is what your professional-writer types do: conceive, imagine, invent, execute, revise, edit, and deliver, then copyedit and galleyproof while conceiving and executing the Next Thing and managing as best they can the business side of their vocation. While also, be it added — if one is one of those American-style writer/professors — teaching one's undergraduates, coaching one's graduate-student apprentices, keeping regular office-conference hours, and abetting the operation of one's department, even one's university, for that is what your writer/teacher types do. While also, to be sure, together with one's indispensable mate (a hardworking professional academic herself), maintaining house and grounds and vehicles and vessels and connections with family and friends, managing house-

hold finances, planning and enjoying meals and vacations, reading books and running errands and recreating, endeavoring to be if not a remarkably good citizen at least not a bad one, and dealing as best two can with life-problems of assorted kind and magnitude—for all that is what your modern-day married middle-class middle-aged types do.

Nothing novel or untoward in any of this.

So what was new? Well: As established in Chapter "S.O.S." and again above, our chap *was* turning sixty-five, a voltaged passage-marker like birthdays twenty-one, forty, and threescore-and-ten. Although we fortunate First Worlders are on average living longer and retiring older these days (as witness the university's shifting its "normal" retirement age from sixty-five to seventy, with ample provision for even later out-to-pasturing), he had been at it for forty-plus years, and so at age sixty had reduced his teaching load and scheduled spring '95 as his final academic semester. In order to liberate them both from the traditional academic calendar, by the rhythms whereof they had lived since kindergarten, his mate likewise retired, and over Spring Break they duly scouted Florida for winter quarters in the years ahead, that being what your North American pensioners do. That same spring—just at Passover season, as heavy-handed, Aristotle-be-damned Coincidence would have it—His annual medical checkup disclosed an alarmingly high Prostate-Specific Antigen count: a false alarm, as later tests would confirm, but unsettling enough for the month thembetween, and his first real brush with the Dark Angel's wingtip-feathers. Not long whereafter, He and She both critiqued their final student papers, met their last classes, packed up their campus offices, farewelled and were farewelled by their separate longtime valued colleagues, shut down a bit earlier in the season than usual their "teaching house" in the city and shifted to their weekend-and-summer retreat on Maryland's Eastern Shore. Except for the present instance's aspect of finality, this was their established spring routine; the real tug, they imagined, would come in September, when the rest of their world went back to school and they didn't, ever again. Meanwhile, they would settle into their customary, pleasant School's-Out routine: She managing their affairs, planning their travels, scheduling their visits and visitors, dealing with service people, doing the lioness's share of property maintenance and meal planning, and in the interstices catching up with her reading and other recreations; He doing his usual measure of the above (long- and well-married couples have these things calibrated equitably, generously, and flexibly) while conceiving and executing his Muse's Next Thing. . . .

And here they were: Gemini-time '95; rhododendrons, lilacs, and azaleas finished, roses full abloom, tidewater just warm enough now for swimming, boat belatedly in commission (needed a last-minute engine overhaul) and ready for the usual extended June cruise—even in late May this time, maybe, now that they're off the academic calendar; coffee mug and fountain pen filled, earplugs in, notebook and first-draft looseleaf binder open to virgin pages. . . .

Dum dee dum dum.

Been there, done that: have awaited more than once before Ms. Muse's pleasure, patient with her not-yet-pregnant pause. Nothing alarming nor yet even disconcerting, just the familiar once-every-four-years-or-so *kenosis*, an emptying out given extra resonance this time by those other life-changes, but not to worry, dum dee dum dum, he'll just review this earlier-stalled project here, shelved some years back in favor of those others now completed and delivered. Still nothing doing there? Not to worry. Back on the shelf with it while he composes miscellaneous thises and thats for ditto periodicals and makes his last overnight lecture-trip of the academic year, for he has nowise retired from those occasional junkets to other campuses—an agreeable and profitable scenery-change which his wife is now free to enjoy with him if she so inclines—any more than he has retired from noveling. What the question bade to become was, Had noveling retired from him? For it were folly to fancy, were it not (he fancied), that a writer who does not die prematurely, but goes on breathing air and filling pen through his sixties and seventies and who knows maybe eighties and nineties, will ipso facto enjoy continued serial inspiration. Who's to know, except after the fact, which routine musely pause will turn out to be her menopause?

So hell with this, let's go sailing, and off we went, per "S.O.S." except for a detail there withheld and now to be supplied: that in addition to our routine preps for an extended cruise, we had arranged for the purchase from and installation by our local marine diesel mechanic of a heavier-duty alternator for the vessel's newly overhauled engine, to the end of topping off its twin deep-cycle battery banks more efficiently each time we switch to ALL and fire up the powerplant. And that the busy fellow had promised but failed to deliver same, pleading peak-season overload, until we nudged and nagged and finally deadlined him—this weekend or forget it—whereupon, on the virtual eve of our casting off, he got himself out to our pier, made the installation by twilight and flashlight, gave it a quick test run, and pronounced it shipshape.

*Then* off we headed, hi ho hum, south and south et cet, He with one skipperly eye on the ship's ammeter (way up on green when we're under power, as it should be) and t'other on the Muse's (nothing doing, just that abstract inclination, aforeremarked, toward a wrap-up-the-century-and-millennium-at-least yarn), while at the same time resolving to turn his attention *away* from all that wrap-it-up pack-it-in business, really rather morbid, no? *Carpe diem!* Give Muse a breather! Relax and enjoy!

We have mentioned, I believe, Aristotle on the subject of Coincidence in plot construction? Real life, however, is a shameless other matter. Bad enough that back at April launch-time, in midst of that Passover prostate scare, the boatyard crew had been unable to give our always previously reliable diesel its routine start-up: "Sucker cranks," they reported, "but won't catch," and recommended a costly, time-consumptive complete removal, overhaul, rebuilding, and reinstallation of the dozen-year-old engine—whereto we consented, He rolling his eyes not so much at the expense and delay as at the hamhanded symbolism. *The spring sailing season from Hell*, our ship's log calls the ensuing serial delays and screw-ups, too tedious to itemize—and then adds, appreciatively, *but better than having cancer*. Likewise with the Muse's engine trouble, which anyhow would surely mend itself in time as ever thitherto; keep on cranking that sucker and anon she'll catch, yes? So off we cast—earlier than usual for the Big Spring Cruise, we being no longer calendar-bound, but with only one prior shakedown sail on account of those delays; new batteries, newly renovated powerplant, and, finally, that hotdog big new alternator in place, and for pity's sake let's hear no more of Engine Trouble either lit or fig, okay?—and en route down-Bay from our first night's anchorage, when after a morning's light windward sailing the breeze drops at lunchtime off Sharp's Island Light and we decide to motor on down at least to the Patuxent, maybe even as far as the Potomac, south and south and still farther south—there comes suddenly from the engine compartment a most fearful machinegunlike clatter. Alarmed, we shift to Neutral (and back to past tenses) and shut down fast. Becalmed and adrift then in mid-Chesapeake, we managed to determine by visual inspection that a certain bolt, meant to secure the drive-belt-guard on that new alternator, had backed off enough from normal engine vibration to permit the metal guard (intended, we supposed, to keep exploratory fingers attached to examinative hands) to wobble down against the teeth of the gizmo's cooling fan. Why no lockwasher to secure it? Negligent mechanic, we supposed. Why for that matter but a single attaching-bolt instead of two at least? Skimpy design, we supposed. No proper-size lockwasher in our fairly ample spare parts kit, but at least it was no great chore in those calm conditions to reposition that guard and retighten its bolt. Seeing no sign of damage beyond a few nicks on guard and fan-teeth, we then cautiously restarted and resumed our southing—toward Solomons Harbor on the Patuxent, rich in marinas and *a fortiori* in diesel mechanics. He radioed ahead to one such, described our problem, arranged to have it looked at and tended to first thing next morning, inasmuch as our ETA was past quitting time for the marine-mechanical fraternity—and *then* at afternoon's end we putputted as aforementioned: past Cove and Drum Points and the ongoing military roar of Patuxent Naval Air Test Center, into the wide-mouthed river, into the yacht-and-workboat harbor and Back Creek, past the marina (now closed for service work, as predicted) and Drydock Restaurant a-port and that improbable COMING SOON! thingamajig a-starboard, on up to our confidential cove. Where we anchored. Swam. Rechecked that mothering bolt. Fetched wine and hors d'oeuvres wherewith to thank Poseidon for not doing us worse. Relaxed, sort of. Updated the log on Episode Latest of Spring Sailing

Season from Hell while reminding ourselves how truly luxurious were such problems as these. Dinnered. Enjoyed T-shower. Made in a different notebook first furtive, tentative notes on yonder *Coming Soon!*

And next morning made that pit-stop aforenarrated, whereto now needs appending only that the clearly more knowledgeable marine diesel mechanic whom we there consulted approved our emergency measures, added a lockwasher to the vagrant bolt, partially exonerated his up-Bay colleague by shifting blame to the engine-manufacturer ("Happens all the time. Damn furriners"), wondered only half rhetorically how useful such a belt-guard was anyhow on an engine in a closed compartment, as who but a damn fool would poke his damn fingers into that neighborhood while the damn engine was running? And advised us that should that sucker back off again, we could just as well take bolt and guard off altogether and pitch 'em into the damn Bay, for all the good that sucker does.

And so we now did, anchored temporarily just off the square bows of *Coming Soon!*: removed bolt, lockwasher, and maybe-unnecessarily-protective-but-anyhow-malfunctioning guard and tossed 'em — not overside, to be sure, but into that earlier-noticed spare parts box, just in case. And thus ended our Engine Trouble, not only for the rest of that cruise and our 1995 sailing season, but to date: i.e., as of the drafting of the wind-up of this extended anecdote in now-late March '98, our three-years-older vessel and its ditto scribbling co-skipper not yet recommissioned for their upcoming Next Season, nor *TOFO II* for its.

We'll see.


*Point of anecdote, s.v.p.?*

Yes, well: in the first place, obviously, to supply the literal sense of those portentous Engine Trouble rumblings earlier in this chapter. And in the second place . . . well, if Narrator were Aesop and the above a fable, its approximate moral would be

> *Things meant to protect may merely impede,*
> *And must sometimes be ditched if the tale's to proceed.*

Something like that? As he was to be reminded less than a fortnight after our return from that extended cruise — on balance another good one, declares the ship's log, despite those engine troubles, some adverse weather, and inadequate breezes toward the end,
so that we motored (untroubledly) through its whole last day, from
lovely Luce Creek on the Severn, down past the Naval Academy and
through the throng of becalmed day sailors off Annapolis, up under
the dual spans of the mighty Bay Bridge, around Love Point and
into the tranquil Chester, our home river; thence up our wide and
handsome tidal creek to home, high-volume Handel thrilling from
the tape player. There over the next hours and days we unloaded and
unpacked, reopened house and grounds, resumed mail and newspaper delivery, apprised family and friends and agent and editor of our
return, caught up on suspended business, and settled into our summer routine.

Dum dee dum dum.

Until — sorry there, Aristotle — at the turn of June/July it came
to pass that in swift succession he received (1) his final salary check
from the university, which was to be in all likelihood his ultimate
such from anywhere ever; (2) the first batch of his assorted pension
and annuity checks, paid from funds in which he and his serial
employers had invested through the nearly five-decade span of his
salaried life; and (3) — even as with the expectable mix of feelings
he registered (1) and (2) — a late-morning telephone call of muse-
stirring consequence.

Muffling her cordless phone against her chest, "Morton Spindler?" his wife asked him doubtfully. Our workday practice is for
her, whose metabolism and morning business are by and large less
damageable than his by interruption, to take our forenoon
phonecalls while he's At It and to request callers-for-him to leave a
message or call back later unless their business is urgent. "He says
he knows you quote *very well indeed . . .* ?"

He frowned, too — more puzzled and skeptical than bothered.
The name sounded only faintly familiar, but it was almost morning's
end, and Miz Muse still tiresomely recalcitrant, so what the hey.

Hello?

120

"Mister B?!" More exclamation than question in the caller's tone. "Am I talking to the author?"

You said we know each other?

"Heck no, sir! You don't know *me* from Adam, but I've been reading *you* since college, man! The whole shmeer! And now we're talking one on one! Mort Spindler here!"

What can I do for you, Mister Spindler.

"S.O.S.!" Enthusiastic laugh—"Save Our Ship!"—then down-to-business serious: "Actually, Mister B, I'm calling from Patmos Tower, down in Dorsettown? On behalf of a gentleman that you *have* known since Page One: Mister quote-unquote *Todd Andrews*, of Dorset Tradewinds Enterprises?"

Now the caller's name came back. No games, please, Mister Spindler—

"Call me Mort! Anyhow, we know who we mean, right? Or is it *whom*? You're the professor!"

Mister Spindler.

"Sorrysorrysorry! *Any resemblance to actual persons living or dead* . . . ! Not to worry, sir!"

Could we maybe get to why you're calling, Mister Spindler.

"*Mort*, man, please! As in *mortmain*, whatever mortmain is? *Morte d'auteur*? Just kidding, sir! But hey: Our mutual pal Hop Johnson tells me you're between projects just now, as we say in show biz, and maybe considering a sequel to your *Floating Opera*? Maybe even in collaboration with him? Which sounds to me like a winner of an idea if there ever was one—but hey, I've got a better one yet!"

He certainly hoped so, Narrator here declared, inasmuch as *that* one struck him as about as cockamamie as they come. The very word *collaboration* rang of treason in Narrator's ears: infidelity to the muse. Moreover, if circumstances such as he could in fact no-wise imagine should ever lead him to extend his collaboration beyond the longstanding and ongoing one with Her, that extension would never till Hell freezes over be to a green and erratic talent like Johns Hopkins Johnson—no insult to that young man intended.

"Gotcha, sir! Absotively posilutely! But what if, instead of Hop

Johnson, your co-authors were none other than Edna Ferber herself and old Charlie Hunter, of James Adams's original *Original* ?"

Narrator begs Caller's pardon?

"Five minutes!" Morton Spindler entreated: "Give me five minutes, and I'll tell you a story that's a Book-of-the-Monther in itself!"

Narrator doesn't *write* Book-of-the-Monthers.

"Rightrightright you are! For better or worse, eh? Richer or poorer? Just teasing, sir! But perfectly seriously now, Mister B: Listen up to me for just five freaking minutes, and I swear you won't regret it!"

Sigh. Your clock is running, Mort my man. And in fact Narrator here cradled phone between jaw and shoulder (a thing he's not adroit at) in order to set the rotating bezel of his watch, a habit picked up from outdoor barbecuing and sailboat navigation. Shoot.

*"Bang bang!*

"Just kidding, sir." And the publicity director of Dorset Tradewinds Enterprises and, *a fortiori*, of *The Original Floating Opera II* then delivered himself at length, though with professional efficiency, of a story-cum-pitch in fact not uninteresting, as follows:

Was Narrator aware that the Ferber/Kern/Hammerstein/Ziegfeld *Show Boat* musical was enjoying a smash-hit new Broadway revival this year? Narrator was. And that back in the summers of 1924 and '25, Ms. Ferber had come down from NYC to homework her *Show Boat* novel aboard the *James Adams Floating Theatre*? Narrator was. And that the showboat guy that she'd been closest to during those visits, and that had given her the most material for her novel, and that she'd corresponded with now and then for years after *Show Boat*'s success in various media, was Jim Adams's brother-in-law Charles Hunter, the *Floating Theatre*'s artistic director and husband of the quote *Mary Pickford of the Chesapeake*? Yeah, well: Narrator guessed he vaguely remembered some of that. So go on.

First, some history! This Charlie Hunter was an all-'round smalltime showbiz type from West Virginia — musician, actor, whatever-the-part-requires kind of guy, you know? Self-educated, maybe a bit heavy on the cigarettes and booze? Back before World War One he worked the Ohio Valley showboats and vaudeville tent shows and even circuses, including one of Jim Adams's, where he met and married Jim's sister Beulah in 1911. By his own claim, it was Charlie who persuaded Jim to try his luck showboating in tidewater country, where he'd have no competition, and then advised him on the design and construction of the *Floating Theatre.* But be that as it may ('cause our man Charlie was a bit of a story-improver, you follow me? Like you, sir! Only different?), he and his bride were on the showboat team from at least its second season, 1915, and Charlie took charge as Jim's artistic director from the 1920 season till he and Beulah jumped ship in '36. By that time the boom was over, right? Both for showboat biz and for the country at large! Automobiles were making folks more portable, and movies and radio were making them less innocent. Vaudeville acts and blackface minstrels and old-time mellerdrammers couldn't hardly cut the mustard like they used to, and on top of that the moviehouse owners in every little tidewater town were leaning on their local officials to jack up the dockage fees for showboats and the license fees for traveling tent shows, to cut down the competition—plus they cranked up their local parsons to preach against the wicked influence of carnival and showboat types, not to mention the money that they quote *took away from the town* unquote! For a while, back in the late Twenties and early Thirties, the popularity of Ferber's novel and then the musical and then the first movie version were good for Adams's business; in 1932, when Ziegfeld revived the musical on Broadway, with Paul Robeson singing "Ol' Man River," Jim even changed the boat's name from the *Adams Floating Theatre* to the *Adams Show Boat,* to capitalize on the connection. But that same year he evidently saw which way the wind was blowing, shrewd cookie that he was, and after FDR's inauguration in the spring of '33, he unloaded the showboat on a rich widow-lady from St. Michaels who was smitten by the novel and the musical and was looking to buy a fun business for her grown-up foster son. So she renames the thing *The Original Show Boat* and gives it to the guy to be captain and manager of!

Narrator knows most of this: Nina Howard and Milford Whatsisname . . . Seymoure, was it?

"Seymoure it was! Whose benevolent foster-mom was sort of a

precursor to our Mister Andrew S. quote-unquote *Todd Andrews* Todd—but that's another story! So Jim's out of the picture now, right?, managing his real-estate interests up in Philadelphia. But Charlie and Beulah Hunter and most of the rest of the troupe stay on, and it's business as usual in tidewaterland—except that things get tougher every year on account of the fees and taxes and disappearing audiences and now the Depression. So what does our Charlie do, sir? He goes Postmodern!"

Beg pardon?

"I figured *that* would prick up your ears!" In very truth, Mort Spindler explained, he believed that Charlie Hunter's playscript-treatment *Show Barge*—which we would get to presently, not to worry!—could fairly be called Postmodernist, anyhow proto-Postmodernist? As he was confident Mister B would agree. But what he meant just now was that more and more, from the turn of the decade until the end of the 1936 season, the *Original*'s stock-in-trade became *nostalgia*, for showboats in general (and the quote *innocent American past* that they evidently represented) and for Ferber's and Ziegfeld's *Show Boat*s in particular. How much of Charlie's *Show Barge* script is factual we can't say for sure—Milford Seymoure carrying on like Cap'n Andy Hawks of the *Cotton Blossom*; Beulah Hunter, plump and forty-plus, trying to bring off Irene Dunne's film rendition of the ingenue Magnolia Hawks—but it's a matter of record that the showboat's orchestra did tie-in broadcasts for local radio stations, playing tunes from the Kern/Hammerstein musical, and that Charlie himself gave publicity talks both aboard and ashore about "Edna's" residences on the *Adams Floating Theatre* and his own helping out with the first Hollywood version of the musical. When the second film version appeared in '36, he even tried to coordinate showings of the movie in local theaters with the showboat's scheduled itinerary, pitching to the moviehouse operators that cooperation would benefit both parties more than competition. "How does that grab you, Mister B?"

It grabs me as mildly interesting and probably doomed to fail. Does that make it Postmodern?

"Zingo! Can I quote you on that, sir?" But the quote *proto-Post-*

*modernist* part, Morton Spindler quickly explained, comes now, with Charlie Hunter's playscript-scenario. What happened, he reminded Narrator, was that when the Hunters jumped ship in '36 (most likely on account of differences with the showboat's new musical director, who liked slightly quote *racier*, more *up-to-date* material than *Tempest and Sunshine* and the rest), they set up a traveling tent show called The Original Show Boat Players and competed directly with the Howard/Seymoure *Original Floating Theater*, as it was now renamed, by playing the tidewater towns before the showboat got there. They enjoyed a couple of moderately successful seasons, but in the not-so-long run both enterprises suffered, inasmuch as both were being swallowed by their real competitor, the movies. By the late 1930s, scarcely enough audience remained to support one "show boat" company, whether afloat or ashore, much less two. So what does our Charlie do?

Our Charlie?

"He *is* one of us, Mister B, as you'll soon see!"

One of *us*?

"But first, more history!" It was his personal guess, Mort Spindler declared, that after twenty-one consecutive seasons aboard the floating theater, the Hunters much missed their aquatic-thespian life, and that despite his differences with the showboat's new management, Charlie felt strongly that they must join forces against the common enemy, or both would go under. What we have, Narrator's caller was now ready to confide, is an unfinished playscript-scenario entitled *Show Barge*, discovered among the late Charles Hunter's effects, which playscript—by a route that not even its canny current possessor could reconstruct with any certainty—had found its way from Saginaw, Michigan (where Charles Hunter ended his days as pianist and bartender at James Adams's brother's establishment, the Show Boat Inn), to Dorsettown-on-Choptank, Maryland, and the Patmos Tower archives of Dorset Tradewinds Enterprises, Inc. Although the possibility could not be ruled out that Charlie intended the thing for his own short-lived Original Show Boat Players, it was Caller's personal conviction that the script was meant to be a gesture of rapprochement to Milford Seymoure and a last-ditch stratagem to save the faltering *Original Floating Theater*, as well as to get himself and Beulah back aboard in the roles of—Here we go, Mister B! —in the roles of Charlie and Beulah Hunter!

Are we there yet?

"Fun-ny! Mister Todd warned me you're a joker!" But Narrator would admit, would he not, that in the age of André Gide's *Counterfeiters* and Luigi Pirandello's *Six Characters in Search of an Author*, it was surprisingly uptown for Charlie Hunter to do a script in which he plays the role of the smalltime showboat actor Charlie Hunter? And should Narrator object that his doing so brings us up only to 1920s Modernism, what about the fact that by Act Three of *Show Barge* Charlie and Beulah are actually *playing themselves playing the roles of Charlie and Beulah*?! And that the audience gets to decide how the play will end?! Are we there *yet*, Mister B?

We could be getting warm, Narrator acknowledged. Might one ask why you're calling, Mister Spindler?

"Ask you may, sir, and answer I will! And the quickest way for me to do that is to summarize Charlie Hunter's own synopsis of his lost-and-found *Show Barge* story. You with me?"

Provisionally.

"Here we go, then! Act One: The Good Old Days! (These section-titles are Charlie's, by the way: Act One, *The Good Old Days*; Act Two, *Smilin' Through, or, Tempest and Sunshine*; Act Three, *Show Barge*, like the play itself! How he meant to do the titles in the production proper is one of the things left unsettled—put 'em in the program, maybe? Anyhow . . .) By the quote *good old days* he means the high-rolling Twenties, between the disaster of World War One and the Crash of Twenty-nine: automobiles ever more popular, but railroads and steamboats still thriving too. Movies still a novelty —and still silent until Jolson's *Jazz Singer* in Twenty-seven. Vaudeville and tent shows and showboats still riding high, including Jim Adams's *Floating Theatre*, where Charlie and Beulah are knocking 'em dead with *The Balloon Girl* and *East Lynne*. Enter Miz Edna Ferber from NYC in the autumn of Twenty-four: ex-journalist, successful playwright, popular fiction-writer and conscientious backgrounder for her novels, willing to do quote *whatever it takes* to get the story and get it right! She's a single woman, late-thirtyish like Charlie (Beulah's a few years younger), strong-minded liberal, independent, adventuresome, and down-to-earth; she got the idea for a Mississippi showboat novel from one of her New York showbiz friends, and it appeals to her 'cause she's a midwesterner herself— a quote *nice little Jewish girl from Chicago*, by her own description. But the Big Muddy's a long haul from the Big Apple, and so here she is in tidewaterland: too late in the season for an extended visit, but although Beulah Hunter doesn't much take to the new arrival, Edna and Charlie hit it off just fine from Day One. Bear in mind that except for the occasional smalltown haberdasher or moviehouse owner, Ferber's probably the first Jew the guy's ever known up close and personal (this theme gets important as the play goes on). He and Beulah've been happily married for a dozen years, but Charlie finds himself fascinated, charmed, *attracted*! As is Ferber, although she's also drawing him out as a potential character and a goldmine of showboat lore. The pair have long conversations, not only about showboats but about her New York theater experience and about their quote *cultural differences*—apropos of which, Charlie tells her the story of a couple he'd heard about on a Mississippi showboat —white fellow married to a mulatto gal?—that when they were charged with miscegenation by a redneck sheriff, the guy pricked his wife's finger and sucked a drop of her blood and claimed that now *he* was a Negro too, which in fact he was under Mississippi's quote *one drop* law. . . ."

That's the Julie/Steve subplot in *Show Boat*, right? Ava Gardner as Julie LaVerne in the 1951 movie version (Julie *Dozier* in Ferber's novel).

"Bingo, sir! Did you know by the way that Lena Horne was dying for that part, which everybody at MGM agreed she was perfect for, but in Fifty-one Hollywood still didn't dare show a real black or mulatto woman married to a white guy, so they settled for half-Jewish Ava Gardner instead? Which has its own kind of accidental fitness, as you'll soon see. But on with the story! Back goes Edna to NYC, and back go Beulah and Charlie to being the Mary Pickford of the Chesapeake and her supporting-actor husband. The following spring, to Miz Pickford's discomfort, Miz Big Apple comes back aboard the *Floating Theatre* for a two-week stay — selling tickets in the box office, helping out any way she can, even playing walk-ons now and then to soak up as much atmosphere as possible — and she and Charlie are tighter than ever. She's got big ideas indeed for her new novel, she tells him, thanks mainly to her conversations with him: It's going to be not just about Mississippi showboats but about what nowadays we'd call *interethnicity*! The white/mulatto Steve/Julie couple with their showstopping drop-of-blood business will serve as a bridge between the New England WASP couple Captain Andy Hawks and his priggish wife Parthenia on the one hand and the quote *earthy* black couple Jo and Queenie on the other! (Did you know, by the way, Mister B, that in Ferber's novel Cap'n Andy himself has a drop of Portuguese Basque blood in him, which is s'posed to account for his gamy high-spiritedness? And that *Parthenia* is Greek for virgin? But of course you did!) What's more, get this: Ferber intends Gaylord Ravenal to be the Jewish lover and husband of *shiksa* Magnolia Hawks, so that their daughter Kim (who in the novel grows up to be a Broadway star) will be an interethnic analogue, you should excuse the expression, to the mulatto Julie, who's been Magnolia's best friend and drama coach till she and Steve have to jump ship! How's *that* for a story?"

Ava Gardner, Narrator happened to know, was the daughter of Scotch-Irish-Baptist North Carolina sharecroppers: Not a Jewish gene in her, *tant pis*.

"Interesting! But listen to *this*: In Charlie's *Show Barge* play — which we're still in Act One of? — Ferber decides that if she's going to get it right about Gaylord and Magnolia she's got to go to bed with Charlie, even though the gender-eths are reversed! What the hey, she's a novelist, right? She can leave *something* to her imagination! The quote *mingling of their essences* she sees as symbolic of Steve and Julie's drop of blood. Well! Beulah Hunter senses that something's in the air; she's suspicious and inclined to draw the wagons in a circle! Edna tries without much luck to get on the woman's good side, 'cause she respects and half envies their successful marriage. We don't know much at all about Ferber's actual sex life, by the way: She was a fairly homely, stocky woman, never married, lots of friends of both sexes, but no real mention in her autobiography of either male or female lovers. Could be she was nonsexual? In the play, of course, she's a goodhearted but iron-willed *femme fatale*, and damn the torpedoes, *pour l' art* she'll do whatever the part requires! Charlie's attracted, but he's also shy as well as honorable, plus loyal to his wife and maybe a bit prudish to boot— we remember that he and Beulah left the showboat when Milford Seymoure's new music director wanted to do more short-skirt, high-kick routines. Anyhow, he and Edna talk all around the subject, and at one point, noting that neither of them has kids, Edna tells him that quote *her novels are her children.* 'By whom?' Charlie asks her (good dialogue-bit here), and Ferber tells him that if she ever delivers one about showboats, it'll for sure be by him! At that point they kiss, and in my humble opinion Charlie the playwright misses a trick here by not reprising that One Drop theme, but what do I know? Edna then tells him that she now has just about all she needs to conceive their showboat-novel child except for one thing—*one drop*, you might say? And she proposes a midnight tryst that night in her cabin—which in historical fact happened to be Charlie and Beulah's cabin, loaned out to their famous visitor during her stay! So if Charlie the character takes her up on her proposition, he'll be humping Edna in his marriage bed—but Charlie the playwright misses *that* trick, too.

"So Act One closes with a split-scene set: Edna's in her cabin Stage Left scribbling notebook notes and waiting to do quote *whatever it takes*—which I see as a leitmotif for her character, you know? Reprised now in a tender key on account of she's not just your hardboiled get-the-story type anymore, but half in love with her dear rube Charlie, okay? While equally fascinated and maybe half creeped out at the exotic prospect of sex with the uncircumcised, excuse me! At the same time, we see Beulah Hunter Stage Right in *her* cabin sleeping the sleep of the innocent, or more likely pretending to, 'cause she's not blind to what's afoot footsiewise, and she knows that her husband has gone out on deck to quote *get himself a drop to drink.* The fact is, she's pretty sure she's pregnant at last with their first child, but she hasn't told Charlie yet 'cause she's made up her mind that if he and that Broadway flapper do what it looks to her like they're about to, she'll abort the pregnancy! This would have to be some sort of extended soliloquy, I guess?

"Anyhow! Up on the *Adams Floating Theatre*'s deck we see Charlie pacing between the two cutaway cabins in what the script calls *tortured indecision* near the famous water barrel that will figure as a trysting-place for Gaylord and Magnolia in Ferber's novel, and that Charlie had told Edna about from his own courtship of Beulah Adams years ago! Somehow we learn that he's just made guilty-conscience love to his wife, prob'ly thinking of hot-stuff One-Drop Edna the whole time, so maybe his tortured indecision includes a drop of performance anxiety, too! If this was an actual floating-opera *opera*—as maybe it ought to be?—we'd have Edna singing her *Whatever It Takes* theme Stage Left and Beulah her *Just One Drop* theme Stage Right, while Charlie paces between them singing some Tortured Indecision riff. Then as the curtain closes on this trio he plunges his dipper deep into the water barrel, let's say, and swallows hard! You with me, Mister B?"

*More or less,*
Narrator replied, and checked his watch.

"And Less is More, right?" came back the indefatigably ebullient Morton Spindler. "That's why I'm synopsizing Charlie Hunter's synopsis, which we really *really* need your help on, Mister B!"

Yes, well: He had helped already, Narrator pointed out, by correcting Caller's mistaken impression that the late actress Ava Gardner was part-Jewish. . . .

"Right you are, sir, and thanks a bindle! It was the name *Ava* that threw me off, plus my wanting her to be One Drop Jewish to fit the cross-culture theme in Charlie's *Show Barge* play—of which comes now Act Two: *Smilin' Through!*"

Mister Spindler, Narrator here put in: If I rescue Ava Gardner for the Jews, will you skip the rest of Charles Hunter's playscript and tell me exactly and briefly what this phonecall is for?

"Rescue Ava Gardner?"

In connection with some recent showboat homework of his own, Narrator then confessed or declared, he had glanced through the autobiographies both of Edna Ferber and of Ava Gardner (quite similarly-rhythmed names, he now remarked, having spoken them aloud in such proximity for the first time), and it presently occurred to him that inasmuch as Ms. Gardner's second husband, after the Irish-American actor Mickey Rooney, had been the indisputably Jewish-American bandleader Artie Shaw (who used to call her, fondly, "Avaleh"), then by the Ferber/Hunter One-Drop Principle she shared her husband's ethnicity—and he hers.

"*Zingo!*" Morton Spindler enthused. "We've *gotta* have you on board, Mister B! And you've gottagotta*gotta* hear me out, because TOFO Two—*our* TOFO Two; *your* TOFO Two—is in just about the exact same deep shit that Milford Seymoure's *Original Floating Theater* was in by Nineteen Thirty-five and Act Three of Charlie's *Show Barge*. How 'bout if I summarize my summary of Charlie's summary of Act Two, and then we'll get to Postmodernism and where you come in?"

Oy gevalt.

"Did I hear you say *oy gevalt*, sir?"

So let's hear Act Two, please: *Shlepping Through*?

"Fun-*ny!* You're our *man*, man!" The second act of Charles Hunter's unfinished and never-produced *Show Barge,* Caller quickly went on, was in fact no more than a scenario entitled "Smilin' Through, or, Tempest and Sunshine" and spanning the years 1927–36; the playwright had evidently not decided which episodes were to be dramatized. What actually happened on that curtain-closing night in 1925 is left unstated, but we observe that two years later, when Ferber's much-acclaimed novel has been made into Florenz Ziegfeld's even more acclaimed musical, Charles and Beulah Hunter are still (and will remain) childless. As for Edna's "child" by Charlie, its putative sire notes upon reading it that the "Jewish" theme is absent from *Show Boat* entirely: Gaylord Ravenal is as *goyishe* as Magnolia Hawks; the only traces of the "interethnicity" that Ferber had solicited his assistance with are the Steve/Julie One-Drop subplot that he'd supplied her and a somewhat patronizing sympathy for the black characters Jo and Queenie. All the same, Charlie's privately pleased to regard the book as his and Edna's collaboration; he so treasures the hundred-dollar thank-you check sent him by Ferber upon her return to New York that over Beulah's protests he pastes it into his autographed copy of the novel and vows never to cash it. As for Beulah: Relieved as she is to be rid of her rival, she clearly still smarts at her husband's infidelity, literal or figurative—all the more when she hears him speak of the novel's missing interethnic theme. Having associated Jewish Edna Ferber with the Big City, she now comes to equate the Big City—especially Broadway and, presently, Hollywood—with Jews. "The Israelites," she comes to call Ferber/Ziegfeld/Hammerstein/Kern and company, particularly after the latter two, planning their musical, pay an evening's visit to the *Floating Theatre* in Crumpton, Maryland, in the fall of 1926. Unwittingly thereby she leads her husband to regard Ziegfeld's *Show Boat* as the half-Jewish offspring of his and Edna's half-Gentile novel-child—analogous to what the Broadway star Kim Ravenal would have been if Ferber had held to her original idea of a Jewish Gaylord! Indeed, when baby Kim, in Ferber's novel, is named for the confluence of rivers, or "mingling of essences," at Kentucky, Illinois, and Missouri where Magnolia gives birth to her aboard the *Cotton Blossom Floating Palace Theatre*, it pleases Charlie to read the acronym as Koshered In Maryland—for so he feels himself stirringly to have been.

"Comes now a plot-thicknink!" Morton Spindler here exclaimed in mock-Yiddish accent. None too soon, in Narrator's opinion. History tells us, Caller declared, that the Hunters spent January 1927 in Hollywood, where Charlie worked in some uncertain capacity with the scriptwriters of Carl Laemmle's unsuccessful first film version of *Show Boat* (it had the bad luck to be filmed as a silent by Laemmle's Universal Studios just as Warner Brothers was revolutionizing the medium with Jolson's *Jazz Singer*). Beulah hated the place, no doubt in part for its associations with Ferber and "the Israelites," and the couple soon returned east to the *Adams Floating Theatre*. But Charlie made no secret of his hope to attend—perhaps even in Edna's company!—the much-anticipated Broadway premiere of

Ziegfeld's musical, scheduled for autumn of that same year but delayed until late December. Again in historical fact, that hope was thwarted by the circumstance that on Thanksgiving Day '27 the *Floating Theatre* sank in sixteen feet of Chesapeake tidewater off the entrance to Norfolk Harbor—the first of her four November disasters—and all hands were too busy salvaging the vessel and replacing their ruined possessions to go traipsing off to the Great White Way. The misfortune was reported in Ziegfeld's opening-night programs and misattributed to fire; in fact, while under commercial tow to its winter quarters the barge struck an unidentified submerged object that stove a large hole in her bottom. In Act Two of Charlie's *Show Barge*, however, there is a strong suggestion that Beulah Hunter, jealous of her husband's continuing interest in *Show Boat* and its author, somehow engineered the sinking itself in order to prevent his attending that Broadway premiere (but how, Mister B? The season was over, and the Hunters weren't even on board at the time!), or at least that she was inspired by the accident to arrange the subsequent Black Novembers—in '29, '38, and '41.

Whatever the facts of this first sinking, we know that it cost the Hunters their "trunk"—the itinerant actor's indispensable wardrobe of costumes for sundry character-roles—and that in order to replace it our Charlie felt obliged to write to "his" Edna for permission to cash that hundred-dollar check, which he'd vowed to keep forever in token of their connection. In the play, he cashes it only at Beulah's insistence; she resents his even writing for permission instead of just liquidating the hated souvenir! No reason, by the way, to think of Beulah as an anti-Semite in the usual sense, Morton Spindler believed: She simply feared and resented anything associatable with what she saw as an ongoing threat to her marriage, and while she goes "smilin' through" this second act of *Show Barge*, it's painfully clear to her that having cashed her rival's check, Charlie goes right on cashing in on his past connection with the author, both to keep the Adams showboat afloat and to keep that connection alive. He writes letters to Edna; Beulah intercepts her replies. He proposes changing the *Floating Theatre*'s name to *The Adams Show Boat*, and maybe even mixing some short flicks with the stage routines, despite Beulah's opposition to that tainted medium. In October '29 the stock market crashes, and one month later the floating theater sinks again, this time in the Dismal Swamp Canal.

Is Beulah cutting off her nose to spite her face? Each of these setbacks threatens to put Brother Jim out of business—but they also demand Charlie's full attention to salvage the operation and keep it going. In the fall of 1930, in hopes of beating their quote *November jinx*, the troupe decides to spend the winter playing city audiences in Washington instead of hauling south as usual for lay-up till spring. This is Charlie's brainchild: He'd planned to close the season as usual in mid-November down here in Cambridge—where you'd just been born, Mister B, right?—but suddenly he's telling the local papers that they'll cross the Bay to the Potomac and Our Nation's Capital instead, and that Miss Ferber herself is expected to attend their D.C. opening!

But it doesn't happen, and here the Movies-as-Villain theme comes back, Stage Center. In fact, the D.C. fire marshal and harbor police denied Adams a license, on the grounds that the showboat's exits weren't in compliance with the District's fire code; in the play, this becomes another and more sinister instance of the film lobby— the quote *Israelites*, Beulah would say—manipulating local officials to cut down the competition. So Charlie moves across the river to Alexandria and provides free bus service from D.C. to the *Floating Theatre*; but Edna doesn't show for the opening, and instead of playing the big city all winter, they shut down by Christmastime and never return to the upper Potomac again. Next season Charlie stages an anti-film propaganda play called *Tildy Ann*, having to do with the movie-biz conspiracy to tax traveling rep companies out of business; the thing's a bigger hit with Beulah, who plays the Cinderella-type orphan Tildy Ann, than it is with the audiences, who'd rather go see a movie. And Charlie himself, of course—even Charlie-the-character—remains half in love with the quote *Jewish medium* that's killing him. By '32 he's wondering again whether they can't somehow combine the two; that same year Ziegfeld revives his *Show Boat* musical on Broadway, an even bigger hit than before, and Charlie finally persuades Jim to change the *Floating Theatre*'s name to the *James Adams Show Boat*—but having done so (over Beulah's protests), Jim decides it's time to cut his losses and sells out to Nina Howard and Milford Seymoure. The boat gets renamed *The Original Show Boat*, to Beulah's chagrin; the new owners press Charlie to chuck *Tildy Ann* and *Smilin' Through* and do more quote *Ziegfeld stuff*, which half appeals to our Chas except that he's got Beulah the aging ingenue threatening hellfire and damnation if he doesn't stick with *Tempest and Sunshine* and Company. Come 1936, MGM releases the second film version of *Show Boat*—the one starring Irene Dunne and Helen Morgan, with Paul Robeson as Jo. Charlie's last-ditch proposal (in the play, anyhow) is to echo the movie-musical as far as possible onstage without actually infringing copyright, and to coordinate the showboat's itinerary with local showings of the film, just as he tried to do in fact. Milford Seymoure nixes that as too legally risky, and ups and hires himself a new music director, while also insisting that his wife Rachel take over Beulah's role as the Mary Pickford of the Chesapeake! That night, on the same split set as at the end of Act One, beside the famous water barrel, Beulah supposes to Charlie that they'll have to quote *just swallow hard* and go smilin' through life's tempests as well as its sunshine. But Charlie's not buying it: Can't he maybe cash some final check with Miz Edna, he wonders aloud, by persuading her to persuade Ziegfeld to let him stage actual scenes from *Show Boat* on *The Original Show Boat* without paying royalties? In his opinion, he declares, it's either that or quote *jump ship*—and with that, Beulah runs to the rail and literally jumps over the side into Ol' Man Choptank, or Ol' Man Chester, whatever! Curtain closes on Act Two with Charlie hollering first to the audience *Help!*, then to the empty Stage-Left cabin *Edna, help!*, then to the heavens *Omigod, help!* as we hear Beulah's Voice Off calling *Help! Help!*—and then Charlie hollers *Beulah! Beulah darling!* and springs over the railing after her!

"Splash! End of Act Two!

"Still with me, sir?

"Mister B?"

\* \* \*

*Yes, yes,*

Narrator presently admitted: He was still listening, Lord knows why, to what has to be the longest phonecall of his life. As theater, the two acts of *Show Barge* thus far synopsized struck him as more pathetic than dramatic, a mishmash of historical-biographical detail. To him personally, that detail was not without interest; but unless this alleged playscript had a lot more zing to it than its circumstantial summary suggested, it did not speak well for the late Charles Hunter's prowess in the medium.

"Right as rain, sir! Which is exactly where *you* come in!"

Narrator thought not. For one thing, he had a novel to get written before the century's rapidly approaching end. For another, writing plays was as alien to his muse as writing verse: He was, *tout court* and for better or worse, neither a dramatist nor a lyricist, but a Narrator. Even to a nontheater type like himself, however, it was clear that Hunter's *Show Barge* was, among its other failings, architecturally humdrum. Why didn't its action begin in the middle of things, for example, as Horace wisely recommends? Why not open Act One sometime in the mid-1930s, say, with Captain Milford Seymoure calling all hands onstage for an emergency meeting and announcing that *The Original Floating Theater* is in deep shit: movie operators conspiring to jack up license and dockage fees, audiences bored with *Ten Nights in a Bar Room* and corny band concerts and vaudeville acts when they've got Jean Harlowe and Clark Gable and the Three Stooges onscreen, and now the *Show Boat* flick itself. *We're going under, guys*, Cap'n Milford says in effect: *Twice already this barge has sunk and been refloated, but what's taking us down for keeps is those damned quote* mechanical entertainments, *as Cap'n Jim Adams used to call 'em*—which he did, by the way, Mort, in the broadsides he printed up against the movie operators who claimed he was taking the townsfolk's money out of town. "Flesh and blood actors and musicians," Adams said, are "of more benefit to your community than five thousand feet of celluloid and a phonograph," et cet. *To think*, Cap'n Milford goes on, *that it was right here on this very showboat that Miz Edna Ferber started it all, and now her damn movie's sinking us!* So that gets the Charlie Hunter character to reminiscing out loud about those two happy summers when Ferber did time aboard the *OFT*, and how he supplied her with all those pure-gold anecdotes and characters for her quote *kid-in-the-making*—or, as dear Edna liked to put it, their very own K.I.M. . . . Split-set flashbacks here, maybe, to establish the One Drop theme and their romantic involvement, which Charlie swears they put behind them for the sake of his marriage and on account of their quote *cultural differences*. I hear a few bars of Kern/Hammerstein's "Make Believe" during Charlie's flashback-soliloquy, segueing into Beulah's "Smilin' Through." Then the Charlie character proposes to the Cap'n Milford character that the best way to stay in business is to stage a mini-version of *Show Boat* itself as their main feature, with himself as Cap'n Andy Hawks, Beulah as his wife Parthy, and Milford and Rachel Seymoure as the lovers Gaylord and Magnolia, plus the *OFT* itself as Ferber's *Cotton Blossom*. A sure-fire hit! Problem is, Charlie knows very well that they can't possibly afford such a high-royalty item as Ziegfeld's *Show Boat*, unless—aha!—unless he prevails upon Ms. Ferber, on the strength of their old quote *connection*, to prevail upon Flo Ziegfeld to make a special exception in their case and grant them permission to do the show *gratis* forever, no royalty at all! He'll write her a letter, he announces, and bets they can start rehearsals at lay-up time —in November, dot dot dot.

So everybody's gung-ho about Charlie's idea—except Beulah Hunter, who's pretty sure that things got serious indeed back there in '24 and '25 and wants no more connection between her husband and Miz Broadway (little reprise here of Kern's "Life Upon the Wicked Stage"?). But for the good of the order she reluctantly agrees to let Charlie write his letter, which of course he narrates aloud as he composes it, about time rolling on like Ol' Man River and carrying all hands with it, et cet. He reminds his dear Edna and the audience of that uncashed-hundred-dollar-check business and how he'd cashed it with her blessing after Black November Number Two. Now they have a different kind of November on their hands, he tells her, one even more serious, and he's obliged to ask for her permission and help in cashing quote *another kind of check* unquote. . . .

\* \* \*

*"Dynamite!"*

Morton Spindler here cheered. "Out goes Charlie Hunter's Act One right now, along with Hop Johnson's half-assed revision of it, and in goes yours—assuming your permission, sir! And the really amazing thing is, the scenario you've just ad-libbed happens to be a perfect set-up for Charlie's Act Three, where Nineteen-Thirties Postmodernism hits the fan! Or should we say *hits your fans*? Just joking, sir!"

*Entendu.* And having wasted much of a morning's writing-time already, Narrator supposed he'd hear the wretched thing out, with one stipulation: that Mort Spindler then make it clear what any of this had to do with anything beyond moderately interesting historical trivia about a fifty-year-old bestselling novel of small literary merit, its perennially popular musical adaptation, and the passing of showboats: a minor episode in the history of American entertainment.

"So you say!" cried Morton Spindler, but vowed to fulfill that stipulation in spades, as it was of course the whole reason for his calling on behalf of Mr. quote *Todd Andrews*, Dorset Tradewinds Enterprises, the Arkade Theatre Company, and *TOFO II*. Fasten your seatbelts, guys, and hold on for Act Three of *Show Barge*, entitled . . . "Show Barge"!

Oy. On with it.

1937! Show trials in Moscow, riots in Sudetenland! Dos Passos's *U.S.A.*, Hemingway's *To Have and Have Not*, Steinbeck's *Of Mice and Men*, Picasso's *Guernica*, Disney's *Snow White and the Seven Dwarfs*! Charlie and Beulah change into dry clothes and put together their traveling tent show called "The Show Boat Players," with the idea of hitting Milford Seymoure's ports of call just before the showboat gets there and stealing what's left of his audiences. For one season they get away with it, still doing their standard old-time rep stuff, but by '38 Milford's on to their trick and does some schedule-switching of his own to beat the Hunters at their own game. Come November of that year Beulah must've worked her famous curse again, 'cause on the sixth of that month the *Original Floating Theater*, as it's been renamed, hits a snag while under tow in Roanoke River, NC, and goes down for the third time! Remarkably enough, Milford's able to salvage and refurbish the thing despite its not being insured—the wealthy stepmom in St. Michaels, maybe?—and they announce they'll be back on the Chesapeake in '39. In fact, the hex seems to rebound on the hexers, 'cause their tent show loses money that year, and Beulah, in her middle forties now, decides her Mary Pickford days are over. Charlie-the-actor has always played what were called *characters*, which his aging doesn't much affect, but Beulah either can't or won't play anything but ingenues, less and less believable as time goes by and the pounds pile up. That same year Ferber publishes her memoir, *A Peculiar Treasure*, where if you've read it you know she gets a bunch of stuff wrong about the *Adams Floating Theatre*, including even its name. To Charlie's great relief, however—in the play, this is—she doesn't Tell All about her and him and their *mingling of essences*, or anything else about her love-life if any. All the same, reading her book is like hearing her voice again up on deck beside the water barrel; he feels the old flame stirring, and even wonders whether there's a real-life Kim somewhere—maybe in some New-York-Jewish equivalent of the Chicago convent school that Gaylord and Magnolia's Kim was raised in?—a Kim with a famous mother and an anonymous father! Fact is, the Jewish aspect of Ferber's memoir much moves our West-Virginia-*goyishe* Charlie; it opens his eyes to the war in Europe, which he'd scarcely been paying attention to, and to Hitler's round-up of the Jews, which he'd known nothing about. He admires Edna's outspoken pride in being both American and Jewish, and her clearsightedness not only about the Nazis but about the Soviet Union as well, at a time when most liberals were still defending Stalin. The book persuades Charlie that some sort of apocalypse is *coming soon*, excuse the expression! Now he associates the decline of the old traveling rep companies in general and showboats in particular with the quote *end of everything*—while at the same time remaining half in love with the quote *Jewish medium* that's driving them out of business. In the spring of 1940, with Beulah out to pasture, he tries working both sides of the street with what he calls the Charles Hunter Vaudefilm Show, a mix of vaudeville acts and short flicks. It doesn't fly. That same spring he gets word that the Seymoures have given up their city-smart stuff and've gone back to the old melodramas, camping 'em up in ports like Baltimore and Annapolis and playing 'em straight at the smalltown landings. Which we forgot to mention, by the way, was another bummer for the showboat biz: that as cars and trucks and buses put the Chesapeake steamboat companies out of action, the old piers and landings that every river-town used to depend on were let go to ruin. Add to this that after FDR declared a national emergency in '39 and began shipping war materiel to Britain, German U-boats began to be spotted now and then even off the mouth of the Bay! Anyhow, word reaches Charlie that the Seymoures are half considering 1940 as the showboat's make-or-break season; that if they don't at least meet expenses they'll beach the thing somewhere and convert it into guess what: a movie theater!

But all this is just more of your historical-biographical yadayada, right? Until Charlie sees his opportunity and wangles himself a quote *emergency meeting* with the Seymoures aboard *The Original Floating Theater*—a perfect reprise of that meeting in your revised Act One! He admits to all hands that his Vaudefilm Show is doing no better than the Seymoures' rep shows, but that he has a plan that could save the showboat yet! Cap'n Milford's skeptical, but says Let's hear it. So Charlie announces that after reading Miz Ferber's *Peculiar Treasure*, he's written a quote *peculiar kind of play* called *Show Barge*, having to do with Edna's two visits to the Adams *Floating Theatre*, her involvement with him, and the genesis of her *Show Boat* novel. This play deals boldly with issues of racial and ethnic prejudice, he declares—bound to make a great stir in tidewaterland and bring the folks flocking to see—as well as with the theater-versus-film rivalry, the socioeconomic and technological changes of the 1920s and '30s, and the approaching worldwide cataclysm. What's more, it does all this with a flashy mix of live drama and projected film-clips: the best of both worlds! *Show Barge*'s first two acts are finished, he says (which is doubly true, since he's saying this in Act Three): Act One dramatizes his and Edna's collaboration and quote *romance*, along with their nobly resisting adulterous temptation. Act Two dramatizes the success of *Show Boat* as novel, play, and movie, in contrast to the *Floating Theater*'s November Curse and failing fortunes, the Uncashed Check bit, and his and Edna's split-set correspondence, so to speak; it affirms their shared conviction that *cross-fertilization of the media,* or shall we say *mingling of essences,* is the last best hope for showboats and rep shows, not to mention blacks and whites and Jews and Gentiles. As for Act Three (which we're actually in the midst of, remember; now is that Postmodern, or what?), it's finished but not ended, Charlie says, as he'll presently demonstrate. Meanwhile, he offers the play free of charge to *The Original Floating Theater* for what he suggests ought to be billed as its quote *possibly final season!,* with himself in the role of Charlie Hunter, Beulah as Beulah, Cap'n Milford Seymoure as Cap'n James Adams, and maybe Rachel Seymoure as young Edna Ferber? Unless (as he hints might be just possible) he can call in his final IOU and persuade Miz Edna to come play herself! Wouldn't *that* put the *OFT* on the map!

Well, Milford pricks up his ears, all right, and so does Darrel Hulit, his new music director and leading man — who already has his eye on the Charlie Hunter part, playing opposite some sexy Edna Ferber! But what they all want to know is, How does Act Three end?

*That's for the audience to decide,* Charlie tells them — at the same time telling the audience too — just as it's up to the audience to decide whether the *OFT* goes rolling along for another showboat season or hits the beach as just one more movie theater. He has three different endings waiting in the wings, so to speak, he says, and the audience can vote right now which one they'd like to see. What's more (he adds with a chuckle), if they're disappointed with their choice they can round up their friends and come vote for a different ending tomorrow night, and a different one yet on the night after that!

Ending Number One, he then explains (speaking equally to the audience in the theater and to his audience onstage), is straight-up live theater: Edna Ferber (played by whomever) puts quote *New York and all that* behind her and returns to the *OFT* and the quote *man she's loved since the day she first met him, and to whom she owes so much*! They confess their old affair to Beulah, who in sorrow and anger tries to sink the showboat yet again, but relents in the nick of time! Edna blesses the couple and leaves them together, and the *OFT* goes smilin' through the seasons with Miz Ferber's gorgeous daughter Kim in the starring role of the Magnolia Hawks of the Chesapeake! Her aging godparents, Charlie and Beulah, wind up their careers in the character roles of quote *Old Cap'n Adam and his First Mate Eve*, with some devilish moviehouse owner as the Serpent in the Garden who tries to scuttle the showboat every November in order to lure Kim to Hollywood and sink his competition; but with the help of her godparents, her famous mom, and her unknown dad (whom Kim thinks of as the Phantom of the Opera), she sends the villain packing, and the showboat jest keeps rollin', it keeps on rollin' along!

Ending Number Two, on the contrary, is a straight-up movie, in which we see Ms. Ferber in New York summon Charlie to join her in Hollywood to make the movie *Show Boat II*. For the sake of his marriage and the *OFT*, Charlie loyally declines, but the very next November the showboat is torpedoed by a German U-boat off Cape Charles — Charlie/Charles, right? — and has to be beached there before it sinks. Beulah, alas, is among the victims of this sneak attack, which bids to plunge the USA into World War II; Charlie luckily survives and teams up with Edna to do that *Show Boat* remake in quote *his late wife's honor*, starring Kim Ferber-Hunter in the dual role of Magnolia Hawks and Kim Ravenal. The stranded *OFT* is converted into a movie theater and chosen to premiere the film, which goes on to become a great success despite the misfortune of the showboat's burning to the waterline from a quote *mysterious fire in the projection room* on opening night, in November, dot dot dot!

As for Ending Number Three, it's what Charlie describes as quote *cinestage*, a mingling of the essences of live theater and film. It begins onstage like Ending One, with the difference that when the lovers remorsefully confess their long-ago affair, Beulah Hunter generously forgives and blesses both her prevailingly loyal husband and his one-time, one-drop lover. Charlie spends his winters thereafter with Edna in Manhattan and Hollywood, making such top-drawer films as *Show Boat II* (starring Kim as quote *Kim*), and the rest of the year with Beulah aboard the *OFT* in their smash-hit production of *Show Barge*, a cinestageplay combining the best of both cinema and live theater!

"'So which'll it be?' Charlie asks the audience at this point," Morton Spindler reported to phone-weary Narrator at this point: "'How many for Ending Number One? Number Two? Number Three? Okay, we hear you! The people have spoken, Cap'n Milford: *On with the show!*'

"So whatcha think, Mister B? Whatcha say?

"Mister B?"

*Number Two,*
Narrator presently responded.

"Beg pardon, sir? You mean the second ending sounds best to you?"

Afraid not, Mister Spindler. What Narrator thought (Narrator felt regretfully obliged to say) was that whether this *Show Barge* play, as exhaustively "summarized," was in truth a last-ditch literary relic of the late Charles Hunter or some screwball improvisation of J. Hop Johnson — the opera-phantom of the phantom *Floating Opera II* — it was in Narrator's not-inexperienced judgment a three-act crock of Number Two, excuse him.

His enthusiasm clearly if but briefly dampened, "No apologies necessary!" Morton Spindler insisted: "We could camp it up, the way the Seymoures did *Tempest and Sunshine*! Or you could redo the script for us as straight comedy — the Edna and Charlie show! — and still make their point about cross-fertilization of cultures and media, or genes and genres. Hey, I like that: *Of Genes and Genres!*"

Yes, well. But what was this quote *you could redo the script for us* malarkey? Narrator had his hands full as it was, planning his end-of-millennium novel as it were, from which he'd been distracted for so long already by this interminable phonecall that he was half surprised the world hadn't packed it in already.

"*Coming soon!*" Mort Spindler intoned. "Not too soon for you to repent, though, sir! I mean *relent*, of course! Here's the bottom line, Mister B — if I may?"

Perhaps, Narrator suggested, his caller could condense that bottom line into a one-liner? After which they both could get on with their usual—and separate—businesses?

"Zingo! Let's see now: How's this? Our mutual acquaintance JHJ was telling me about his conversation with you on Solomons Island recently—*On* Solomons Island? *In* Solomons Island? *At* Solomons Island?"

Whatever, Mister Spindler. And?

"*And* when he got to describing the differences between his COMING SOON!!! novel and yours, as he saw them—actually, the differences between him and you as writers, I suppose?—Hop said (just joking now, sir, as I'm sure you'll understand!)—Hop said, quote, *My problem is that I think the world is my oyster, whereas his problem* (that's yours, sir) *is that he thinks the oyster is his world*! How's *that* for a bottom-line one-liner?"

Narrator promised to take it, whatever it might mean, under advisement. All done now, then, yes? Or was it All done *then now*, yes?

"*You're the one*, Mister B! Whether or not you need us, we sure as shootin' need you!" Whatever one took Hop Johnson's tease to mean—and it *was* a tease, Caller reassured Narrator, though of course not *merely* a tease (he himself, he declared, took it to be a friendly jibe both at the younger writer's self-confident ambition, or ambitious self-confidence, and at the older writer's inclination toward tidewater settings for his fiction)—in any case, as he was saying, such serial, portentous coincidences as the prospective *James Adams II* versus the established-but-troubled *Original Floating Opera II*, and then the rival-twin novel projects of whom Johnson jokingly called the quote *Novelist Aspirant* and the quote *Novelist Emeritus*, right down to their coincidental path-crossing in/on/at Solomons Island, backdropped by that COMING SOON! banner— and then the crowning, coincidence-topping coincidence of Mister Andrew quote *Todd Andrews* Todd's happening to turn up Charlie Hunter's forgotten old playscript in the Dorset Tradewinds archives (which the quote *N.A.* was conscientiously now homeworking, by the way, for his novel-in-progress), just when he, Mort Spindler, was scratching his head for a gimmick—no, scratch that: an *inspi-*

*ration!*—to turn the tide, so to speak, of the ebbing fortunes of
*TOFO II* . . . !

Too true to be good, not to mention syntactical, Narrator ventured (reminding himself to ask who on earth this "Andrew Todd
Andrews Todd" person might be, whom he believed Hop Johnson
too had mentioned during their Solomons Island Ontological
Lunchbreak)—and was immediately, enthusiastically agreed with.
"Stranger than fiction, right, sir? *Anyhow* . . ." What he and Mr. Todd
and Sherry Singer and the whole Arkade Theatre Company hoped,
Mort Spindler said, was that given this ultimate coincidence—the
spooky parallels between the *OFT*'s situation in the 1930s and
*TOFO II*'s in the 1990s; between Edna Ferber's association with the
*OFT* and Narrator's with both the *OFT* and *TOFO II*; even between
the movies-as-enemy back then and TV/VCRs/web-surfing and
such nowadays—given all these, it had occurred to the present
caller that quite a few birds might be nailed with one stone, excuse
his mixed metaphor, if the Novelist Emeritus, excuse the expression, saw fit not only to quote *homework* his own COMING SOON!!!
novel with a Ferber-like residency aboard *TOFO II*—which, after
all, owed its existence in large measure to him and Ferber—but also
(here it comes, sir!) to finish and polish Charlie Hunter's proto-Postmodern *Show Barge* play as *TOFO II*'s make-or-break Feature Production for next season, thereby (a) helping to rescue a struggling
but truly worthy enterprise, while (b) leaving its would-be competition scuttled in the starting gate, excuse the mixed metaphor; also
(c) reacquainting himself with his native neck-of-the-woods, which
Caller gathered (from Hop Johnson) that Narrator was considerably
out of touch with (if he didn't even know who quote *Todd Andrews/*
Andrew S. Todd was!); and at the same time (d) maybe getting the
jump on Johnson's COMING SOON!!! novel by making use of the Fer-
ber/Hunter story in Narrator's own version! Leave the Novelist Aspirant—indisputably talented, but maybe a touch too big for his
britches?—scuttled in the starting gate, so to speak! Or at very least
(e) keep an eye on the (wink wink!!) competition!

"Whatcha think, sir? Shall I zip you the script?"

Not necessary, Mister Spindler.

"Right on, sir! You'd rather take my summary as a Henry-James-ian *donnée*, would you, and start from scratch?"

Would rather scratch this whole conversation, Mister Spindler. No offense intended.

"Nor none taken! Disappointed, of course, 'cause I know Hop won't do half the job for us on his own that you and he could do *mano a mano*, each sparking the other. . . ."

Perish the thought.

"*Bang bang, Thought, you're dead!* Just joking, sir! Fact is, I might as well say it, it occurred to us that a project like this might be good for *you* as well as for us. In trouble or not, *TOFO Two*'s a lively operation, as I can testify — quite a change of pace from my PR work with DTE or your graduate-student seminars! C'mon'n *let your guard down*, man; maybe stir up the Muse's juices, you know? Get the old oyster out of his shell for a bit!"

Shuck off, Spindler.

"Zingo! But you haven't hung up on me, Mister B; I appreciate that. So here's my proposition: C'mon down to Dorsettown-on-Choptank — *D-o-C*, we call it, as in *What's up?* Or as in what TOFO Two's tied up at? Come look us over; say hello to Mister Todd, who's made a career out of your Todd Andrews character, and to Sherry Singer and Cap'n Ad Lake and the Kane twins and Yours Truly Doctor Spin, and let me show you that Charlie Hunter's playscript isn't something Hop Johnson and I cooked up. Give us half an afternoon, okay? *Half an hour*, even! We may not convince you that we're really worth your time and attention, but at least we'll convince you we're real!"

Mister Spindler, Narrator declared: I'm your quote *Novelist Emeritus*, remember? The Reader and I are less interested in whether you're real than in whether you're worth our time and attention. No zingos, please.

"Bullseye! Tomorrow lunchtime?"

No lunches.

"Not even a freebie? *After* lunch, then: Over the bridge to Cambridge — hey, there's a redundancy for you: *bridge to Cambridge!* — then follow the signs to D-o-C, as in *Doc Spin*! Big mother showboat at our Tradewinds Marina, raring to go, all flags a-flying, steam calliope a-steaming; couldn't miss her if you tried!"

He would in very truth, Narrator earnestly promised Caller, earnestly try.

"Tease tease tease! But all teasing aside, Mister B: Mister Andrew S. quote *Cap'n Andy* quote Todd Andrews Todd and I would purely love to have you aboard. I can understand how important it is for somebody quote *in your position* to keep his guard up with callers like me and propositions like this. But I truly believe that for both our sakes it might be better this once to *let your guard down*! Maybe just toss that sumbitch guard overside and full speed ahead! You follow me?"

*Yes, well:*

Advice perpended, Mister Spindler. Cheerio now.

# 1995.2

So hi ho again, Readerino mio! And hey: Thanks a bunch for booting Yrs Truly up instead of out; for clicking himon, repaging him — whatever 'twas Y'all must've just now up & done, or we wouldn't be left-to-righting here again together, would we now? Just You'n Yr Young-Fart Alternative Narrator Johns(let's hear that *s*!) Hopkins Johnson, Bachelor of Arts and Novelist Aspirant. See Hop run!

On and on. His ontological free lunch and Solomonian detour done, his Competition duly checked out (we mean *TOFO II*'s would-be rival checked out and off, while Your Novelist Aspirant's ditto checked in — and picked up the check), he Jeeps Youwith up past Annapolis and over the Chesapeake Bay Bridge, bound for what we're calling (that being its name) Dorsettown-on-Choptank, *T II*'s home port on the *mar* of Delmarva Peninsula: Maryland's (ta-da!) Eastern Shore.

Two years earlier or six ago (summer '93), when in this present buggy's predecessor he'd Jeeped down from Baltimore toward his maiden internship aboard that newly commissioned and already problem-fraught vessel, he had zipped through the intervening geography with history-blind undergraduate eyes. While to my mentor-in-spite-of-himself, e.g., and perhaps even to others as well, this river-reticulated peninsula is attention-worthy in its own right, to urban sophomores like the then JHJ it was a featureless flat stretch of four-lane highway to be traversed on cruise control at illegal speeds through feed-corn and soybean fields, past charmless towns of peeling clapboard and downscale strip development, to reach the Atlantic party-beaches on its farther side. *This* time, however (summer '95), having done his alma-materish homework for that cyber-novel-project allegedly in progress, as he crossed the CBB's four-mile eastbound span he was able to review the so-familiar estuary and the Del*[aware]*mar*[yland]*v*[irgini]*a P'nin beyond it through less sophomoric eyes: how in the Bay's prepontine days, when ferries laboriously shuttled a few dozen cars per trip twixt Sandy Point on its western shore and Matapeake on its Eastern—not to mention the time before horseless carriages—it had effectively made two cultures of its two shores, the more isolated Eastern tilting Britward in our Revolutionary War and Dixieward in our Civil. When Ms. E. Ferber choo-choo'd down from Manhattan in the Twenties to homework *her* then novel-in-mind aboard James Adams's showbarge, and Kern and Hammerstein made their follow-up visit to musick the thing for Flo Ziegfeld, the steamboat landings to which spur railroads fetched those fancy folk were peninsulated indeed: a world away from Baltimore and Washington, another universe from NYC. Narrator's freshly-juiced historical consciousness now savored the musical Algonquin names—Chesapeake, Matapeake, Choptank, Nanticoke—by him taken hitherto for granted, that are that lost people's sole memorial; likewise the English names—Kent, Talbot, Dorchester, Worcester—that supplanted them. That curious preposition on the official welcome sign at the Bay Bridge's eastern end —Kent Island: First English Settlement Within Maryland—he could now appreciate as shorthand for a mid-seventeenth-century set-to: William Claiborne's interloping Virginians had run a profitable Indian trading post there until Lord Baltimore's newly-arrived Marylanders cannoned them out of it at the aptly named Bloody Point, and so "the first English settlement within Maryland" had not been a settlement of Marylanders.

Ah, history—in the undergraduate study of which, our lad had managed only a gentleman's C. After his *de rigueur* dropout tour of Mother Europe some years since, where the seventeenth century is fairly recent news, everything in the US of A had struck him as cobbled up the day before yesterday. Now, however, he felt alive to the decades-thin layers of our phyllo-crust American past: the refugee Catholic first colonists of Mary's-Land and their Protestant successors, who moved the capital from St. Mary's City to Anne-apolis; souvenirs of the Revolution here, of the 1812 War there, of the bloody Civil and already far-off First and Second World dittos, reverberating through place-names (Caulk's Field, where our guys nailed Lord Byron's cousin in an 1815 skirmish; Union Folly Road, self-explanatory), from smalltown monuments that he'd never really registered before, and from the state historical society's markers, which he now further educated himself by actually *pausing to read.*

History, history, dum dee dum dum. In the seven minutes of his Bay Bridge transit (the ferry crossing here used to take forty-five, plus waiting in line, loading, and unloading) Yr N.A. reflected serially, one minute per reflection, upon the countless English, Irish, and continental European immigrants, his own forebears themamong, swarming hungrily up-Bay to Baltimore from Bremerhaven, Southampton, Cork, and sundry Mediterranean ports of exit in the decades before WW I; upon such luxury liners as the *City of Baltimore*, which till WW II had shuttled between that city and Le Havre (eighteen days, round trip $180); upon the Merchants & Mariners coastwise cruise ships that until 1950 had sailed from Baltimore up to Boston and down to Havana, with intermediate stops; upon the sudden death of the Bay-ferry lines in '52, when the first span of the bridge from which he now reflected these reflections opened to traffic; upon the more protracted demise of the passenger steamers that had once worked every bend and landing of the Chesapeake's forty-plus rivers, but that by '62 ran only, and for the last time, between Baltimore and Norfolk; likewise upon the festive beach-excursion steamers — *Annapolis, Bay Belle, Emma Giles, Tolchester* — that shortly followed them into History's scrapbook. Having used up six already of his seven reflective minutes, he does not even here mention the handsome flying boats — Glenn L. Martin's Clippers, built locally and named after their square-rigged Baltimore forerunners — that briefly but seriously looked to be the next major advance in air travel, until the advent of jetliners in the 1960s blew them into obsolescence even more abruptly than the railroads had blown the nation's barge-canal system a short century before. No time to reflect themupon, as Narrator had saved (and now spent) his final Baycrossing minute envisioning "Captain" Adams's great boxy Eastern-Shore-gothic *Floating Theatre* nudged by its twin tugboats to those same failing steamboat landings, from Chesapeake City at the Bay's tippy-top down to Norfolk/Portsmouth at its bottom and well beyond, through Albemarle and Pamlico Sounds to the Carolinas and even Florida, fraught with melodrama, farce, and vaudeville in the dicey decades (day before yesterday) when the movies were doing to those homely entertainments what television and VCRs later did to the movies, more or less; what now web-surfing and Internetting are doing to TV, and what EVR will eventually etc. So goeth (teched-up, tockless) Time.

What next? Maybe we'll all rediscover *reading*? Don't hold Your breath, dear disappearing Reader—but do, pretty please, read on:

How, his historical reflecting done, as he zipped south on U.S. 50 and across the merely two-mile-long Choptank River Bridge to the towns of Cambridge and Dorsettown ("bridge to Cambridge"? "town of Dorsettown"? Apprentice license), he dwelt for two final minutes, one per bridge-mile at a mile a minute, upon the Wisdom of Solomons: that Novelist Emeritus chap's considered reply to the Novelist Aspirant's challenge, toward the close of their ontological Drydock lunchbreak, that at year's end they combine their separate versions-thus-far of the Ur-novel *COMING SOON!!!*, divide the interleaved manuscript randomly between the pair of them, and "grow" each half into a separate whole, like bisected flatworms.

"No."

Ah, the succinct gray wisdom of (maybe-timidified?) experience! Whereagainst—just You watch, hon—he would pit the unconstrained green wisdom of callow chutzpah and leave the old fart farting in the starting gate, You betcha.

"It's been done already," had declared Great-Uncle Ennie over crabcake and iced tea: "All that reader-be-damned crapola has been done, and good riddance to it. *You're coming late to a party that's been swinging for two-thousand-plus years already*, Hop: That's your Square One."

So we recycle! had retorted present company: Recombine! Make it new!

Quoth GreatUnc, "Ezra Pound was saying that sixty years ago. *Make It New* is old hat, lad."

So we make it new! said lad said back: New hats from old!

Bite of crabcake. Sip of tea. "Sows' ears from silk purses, more like. But on with your story, and I'll on with mine, and never the twain shall merge."

You're *in* mine, Novelist Aspirant had then declared straight out. As am I. And you're welcome to put me in yours.

Shake of head. "I think not, thanks. Mine's *fiction*."

Fiction shmiction, boss. (Winding up for pitch, or punch.) In my upcoming chapter, you get the wake-up call from Patmos Tower: our PR man Mort Spindler, calling on behalf of quote *Todd Andrews.* . . ."

"Spare me. Could we have our check, please, miss? Thanks."

Suspend your disbelief, man!

"Not willingly."

Save Our Ship!

"*Sauve qui peut.* 'Scuse me now? Got to pee."

Sigh. Thanks for lunch then, Dad—and listen up for that call, okay?

*No,* had replied the Novelist Emeritus—signing the check, retrieving his credit card, and rising to another sort of summons: He had long since gotten the only call that mattered, he declared, back when he was present company's present age, and in response thereto had conceived and delivered Adam's Original and Unparalleled *Floating Opera* together with its purely fictitious protagonist, Todd Andrews. Should he now choose to embark upon some late-career reprise themof, he needed no wake-up call from any save that first and ever-since-faithful caller, his muse. "Bye, now."

*Coming soon!* our Irrepressible Apprentice had called after him.

"You say," had replied his withdrawing host.

And *He's ready,* now opined Hop Johnson to that aforespecified Mort Spindler—for here we are in Dorsettown-on-Choptank, Maryland; in the Snug Harbour office suites of Dorset Tradewinds

Enterprises; in Doctor Spin's newly-set-up base of operations in the FLOPCORP division of the Arkade Theatre Company branch of same—docked immediately outside whereof, in all-but-imminent Casting Off mode at Snug Harbour's Tradewinds Marina, awaiting only the three of them (for there is a third besides Hop and Mort, standing by for proper introduction Youto), flags a-flying, faux–steam calliope a-faux-steaming . . . *The Original Floating Opera II*!

Casting off: aye, Mate. Supercool as our B.A. Narrator aspireth to be, and jaded as he may look forward to becoming, in his seasons aboard *TOFO II* he has never tired of watching—sometimes from ashore, sometimes from aboard, sometimes alone, sometimes with Sherry Singer (Ah, there you are, lass; stand by for introduction after this Casting-Off cadenza, s.v.p.?)—the showboat dock and undock from its landings up and down the Bay. Each has its peculiar routines and intricacies, known best if not only by our Captain. Adam. Lake. and sub-Captains Harry and Elva Kane; never mind those refinements just now. And as we are after all a *show*boat, some of the usual associations of these procedures are reversed: When, e.g., we cast off to resume our tour, it means that the show is over, not beginning; and when we break or end our voyage by docking, the show begins! In this, though, come to think of it, we are not unlike Mediterranean or Caribbean cruise ships with their serial ports of call, or such archetypical voyagers as Odysseus, Sindbad, and Huck Finn, their actual sea-passages usually mere intervals between their more significant adventures ashore. All the same, whether we're casting off as now from Dorsettown-on-Choptank in late spring to begin our Main Season or from any of the river towns and cities along our summer circuit, and whether we're tied up all winter or merely overnight, and whether Narrator is helping with the dock-lines or merely standing by aboard barge or tugboat, he never fails to feel a ritual twinge of excitement, a twinge of ritual excitement, whichever, as our shoreside electrical and water umbilici are disconnected and stowed, and one by one our hefty hawsers—bow and stern lines, spring lines, breast lines—are slacked off from their on-deck cleats, unhitched from their wharfside piles or bollards, and hauled aboard for "flaking down." One crewmember ashore, under normal conditions, lets go the lines in whichever sequence Cap'n. Ad. on the barge's bridge in his step-by-step wisdom seeth fit — a matter less of wind direction, as might be the case with smaller vessels, than of our situation at the wharf-du-jour: whether we are clear ahead or astern or perhaps bracketed fore and aft by other moored vessels and require sidewise undocking before getting under way. On *TOFO* herself, normally, one hand forward and another aft on the landward side fetch in the lines as each is cast off. Tighter or trickier circumstances might require several hands ashore and one at each hawsepipe aboard, so that all tethers can be untethered simultaneously and simultaneously retrieved. As a rule, however, with *Raven* and *Dove* positioned outboard to hold *TOFO* steady, a single dockside hand (not infrequently, these seasoned days, Your Narrator) lets go each line in its appointed sequence as bullhorned himto by Captain. Ad., moves then unhurriedly to the next and next, and, when the last is loosed — unless the caster-offer be a shoreside stevedore, as might be required by union rules in city ports, or some member of the Theatre or Management Team who'll be preceding us by car to our next port of call or who for some other unimpugnable cause is not coming aboard — steps or leaps across the slowly widening space from which the gangway has already been removed.

But wait! Where are the circling, keening ospreys, the ubiquitous kvetching gulls, the squawking mallards and gawking bystanders, the bobbing cormorants and harbor trash, the impassive great blue herons surveying all? There, there, there they all are, and our Dress-Ship flags a-flutter and loudspeakered calliope a-blare, as Cap'n. Ad. signaleth by bullhorn or handheld VHF radio his captainly imperatives to the Propulsion Team. Who-all — after sounding the appropriate whistle-signals as required by law even when not by circumstance to let the world know that we're casting off, backing down, making way — by their combined and meticulously coordinated backing, filling, nudging, tugging, extricate us from our berth into relatively open water.

A real rush, Mate, all this, and more to come, for now the Undocking Team gives way to or becomes the Getting Under Way

Team, inasmuch as—unlike your freighters and your cruise ships, which need tugboats merely to undock them before proceeding under their own power—*TOFO II*, as you may've heard, is engine-free. Her undocking-tugs shift position now to become her propulsion proper, a transition that calls for further adroit-indeed maneuvering. Each bridles a mighty towline to one square corner of the barge's bow, the Kane twins conferring with Cap'n. Ad. by bridge-to-bridge radio but signaling each other as needed with their private whistle-code. Cap'n Harry hitches his larger and more powerful *Raven* to *TOFO*'s leeward bow, if any wind blows, and pulls straight ahead, thus causing the barge to "correct" somewhat to windward and offset its leeway. Cap'n Elva's smaller *Dove* tows from a shorter line on our windward bow and steers slightly off in that direction as well—just enough so that their combined pulls and vectors tow us straight ahead. In different wind and sea conditions and on different headings they position and angle and throttle their tugboats differently, but seldom if ever are their courses exactly parallel or their towlines equally long; and although *Dove* will typically be steering on more or less of a tangent to our course, the net pull is dependably straight toward our next waypoint: "Like," in Elva's own words, *"ever straight forward though never straightforward."*

Come landing-time, the sequence is reversed: Towlines are shortened as we leave the Bay and enter one of its abundant rivers; to negotiate narrow channels, the tugs will even lash right alongside, *Raven* always pulling from either our port or starboard bow, *Dove* either pulling from the other or pushing from the appropriate stern quarter (Cap'n Harry won't, under any circumstances, push; "Never again," he is said to say; "don't ask.")—and then, by dint of masterly nudging from *Dove* and ditto backing and filling from *Raven*, *TOFO II* is teased up to and into her new berth. Even the whistle-code may be dispensed with: The twins appear each to know precisely what to do when, in synchrony with the other. At such times, 'tis said (by Sherry S., still narratively standing by for introduction; and we must take her word for this infobit, inasmuch as Cap'n Elva permits none of the male persuasion into her pilothouse while casting off or docking, welcome as we may be otherwise), *Dove*'s skipper talks more to the showbarge than to Cap'n Harry, addressing it by the name of their evidently stillborn or misdelivered brother. For we have established, have we not, that the dizygotic Kane twins were originally either trizygotic triplets or monozygotic male twins plus dizygotic sis? Forgot to tell You that? Sorry there. "Come on, now, Abie-babe; *there* you go, bro," et cet. Together then they hold the mighty barge delicately in place while *TOFO*'s Docking Team hurl monkey's-fisted light lines ashore to crewmates, dockside stevedores, or, in the smaller towns, eager boys and tomboys hopeful of free tickets—though liability risks in litigious America have all but ruled out that happy volunteer labor, an asset in times past to traveling carnivals and chautauquas as well as showboats. These light lines haul the heavy eyespliced hawsers through their hawsepipes to be dropped over piles and bollards, their slack then taken up with the aid of some final fine-tuned tugwork and their inboard ends made fast and coiled. Comes then *TOFO*'s faux-steam-whistled *All secure!*, which prolonged faux-jubilant blast signals too our faux–steam calliope to burst into amplified musical faux-huzzahs. Gangways are run out from ship to shore; depending on wharf space, dockage fees, and Cap'n.-Ad.-alone-knows what other considerations, *Raven* and *Dove* either snug themselves along our outboard side (*Raven* always forward) or berth themselves separately nearby—*et voilà*: Showboat no longer COMING SOON!!!, but here.

Berthing has, forsooth, its savors: the sometimes intricate maneuvers themselves; the gratifying release of that All Secure signal; the anticipation of stepping ashore if it's that sort of place, of welcoming day-visitors aboard, and of the evening's show. As one approaches Old Fartity, perhaps the end even of a good voyage is as welcome as its commencement, whether despite or because of its analogy to the end of life's larger odyssey. But for those of us not yet, shall we say, *emeritus*—and, one suspects, for some who are—it is Casting Off that most stirs the spirit: the checklist routines, engine start-ups, whistle dialogue, and assumption of positions; the aforenoted shift from Shore to Internal power and water (if it's that sort of place; if not, we make our own) and subsequent disconnection of white water-hoses and yellow power-cables; and then, and then—our Sherry in her unfailing Offwego excitement hugging

Your Narrator, whose own excitement is thereby unfailingly complexified — that serial letting go and hauling in of docklines until inch by inch the crevasse begins to widen between pierside and slabsided *TOFO II*, and the shoreside linesperson, most likely Yr Narrator, makes the long-looking and perhaps daring (if he's been delayed a few seconds or is testing his nerve or just showing off) leap across that gap from wharf to gunwale and into the hands if not quite the arms of his arkmates; and Cap'n. Ad. soundeth his compressed-air steamwhistle, and *The Original Floating Opera II* is cast off and ready to make way.

On with the season! On with the voyage! On with the show!

On with the story: *Let's put it in the show*, Narrator proposed to Ms. Sherry Singer's starboard breast that night in her against-ship's-rules-candlelit cabin, his spunksoggy safesexsheathed stopcock withdrawn at length, so to speak, from her scrumptious, for-the-nonce-slaked snatch, but his sweatwet phiz still shmooshed into her sweatsweet shirtless shirtful.

"Put what?" Her estrogenic voice rich in his hair.

This Casting Off bit. The way I see it, see, we Theatre Teamies are ourselves a cast of more or less cast-off castaways, yes? So we open The New Show with a whizbang Casting Off scene.

"Ah." Then: "Nah."

C'mon, it's a winner, mnyum mnyum mnyum. We can touch all the bases in one swell foop.

"You've *touched* all the bases, Hopsie, and swell it was. What bases? Ouch."

Sorry there. The Noah's Ark base, for one, he explained, unmouthing her right-hand nip, so to speak, to speak. When Unc Ennie's *Show Barge* fiasco flops and we take over with Kit & Kaboodle's New Show, we stage *TOFO II*'s casting off for its advertised Final Season — spring 1999, say? — and we conflate *that* with *TOFO I*'s ditto back in '41, which turned out to *be* its final season. Then we conflate those with the Ark's lift-off in Genesis as the floodwaters rise to drown Gee Dash Dee's first draft of the human comedy. . . .

"I don't think so. Mm, that's a good lad. Now the left one."

Left one, right. So as the world goes under and the left-behind-ones scramble to get aboard like Vietnamese losers from our embassy rooftop in Saigon Seventy-five, we see Cap'n Noah bull-horning his crew to cut their lines and run, like Aeneas deserting Dido. . . .

"There was no wharf in Genesis, Hops. A launch-pad, maybe?"

Right you are. So the Ark's onboard Lift-Off Team patrols the gunwales with fire axes, chopping fingers off Passenger Aspirants while the faux–steam calliope does "Over the Waves." Granted, there's no Propulsion Team in Yahweh's version, just the ravens and doves themselves, two by two; but that ties the Ark in with Great-Unc Ennie's *Floating Opera* as envisioned by his Hundred-Percent-Fictional Todd Andrews character: an ongoing show drifting in and out on the tide, so the spectators onshore catch snatches here and there, excuse the expression, and have to fill in the gaps for themselves. Plus get this: Noah's lift-off can segue to Lord Baltimore's *Arke* and *Dove* casting off from Britville in 1632, which we'll exploit with special performances on Saint Clements Island on Maryland Day!

"Maybe."

What's this Maybe? And we haven't even gotten to the Ferber/Ziegfeld tie-in yet! Instead of Kern/Hammerstein's opening with the showboat's *arrival*, we start with its *departure*, Gaylord Ravenstein already aboard and hot to trot with *shiksa* Magnolia! I see Mort's Corpse de Ballet rigged out as a line of Showboaters along the ship's rail and another line of cheering Spectators ashore, including Just Plain Bill and Poor Shmuck Steve and One-Drop Julie. To simulate Casting Off, the Showboat line dances slowly backward from the Spectator line as the Pit Bulls play "Sailing Down Chesapeake Bay," and we've touched every relevant base right from Square One!

"What I think," declared the talented, resourceful, and spectacularly naked director of the Arkade Theatre Company, co-conceiver of The New Show *End Time*, and frisky Kit of the versatile stage duo K&K, "based on what I've been hearing mainly from you? Is that the base you're really touching here is the renegade apprentice and Novelist Aspirant's declaration of independence: his casting off of parental and mentorial authority and of capital-T Tradition; the changing of the guard, the passing of the torch, and like that? And/ or, contrariwise, the casting *out* of fledglings from the nest, even the floating off of baby Moses in his basket and baby Perseus in his seachest, e.g. In the case of you versus your quondam coach and current rival, just who cast off whom seems a toss-up to your present fuckee. In either case, however, what I think is maybe okay we *will* put a Casting Off sequence in The New Show—but not as an opener: Maybe close Act One with it and then reprise it in the finale? But TNS should definitely definitely open with an Arrival scene to echo the *Show Boat* movies, despite any contradictions like hooking up umbilicuses at the voyage's end. We start our show with the showboat's arriving to start *its* show and the new millennium gearing up for curtain time, and we cast off singing bon voyage to the audience as the curtain closes on the Terrible Twentieth. Okay?"

Okay.

"Okay. So now you've fucked me and I've fucked you and we're both going to fuck the capital-C Competition. How about that introduction you promised?"

Okay: Reader, meet Sherry McAndrews Singer, whose kit drives the whole kaboodle. Ms. Singer, the Gentle Reader.

"*Enchantée*. We've met before, I believe. . . ."

You have, unless Dear Gentle is starting this novel *in medias res*. You did a star turn way back in *Its Draft Orientation Session* and made a follow-up cameo appearance in *Its Prospective Players*, plus a voice-off phone bit in *Its Fresh False Start*—but with your clothes on in at least the first two of those three encounters. On the phone, who can tell?

"*I* can tell," said Sherry McA. Singer, agilely making a bidet of her in-room washbasin before slipping her entirely noteworthy physical self back into clothes. "But I won't. If you and Dear Gentle can't tell by listening whether or not the girl you're chatting with is bareassed, *tant pis* for you. Now, then"—T-shirting her splendid bubbies, patting her short-cut amber-waves-of-grain hair just so— "efficient little welcome-backer that I am of selected teammates, I seem to recall that before you launched into this Casting Off and

Humping the Director sequence, we were sitting in Morty's FLOP-CORP office discussing when and how to bait our hook for the Novelist Emeritus. Maybe scroll back?"

Roger that, sweetnspiciest of mates, and right readily wilco. Indeed, your still-afterglowing Kaboodle will not only scroll but *dolly* back, for a longer shot of what led up to what was afoot back there at Casting Off time, and of where in tidewaterland we-all are now. In years of yore, although its itinerary varied from season to season, Cap'n Jim's *Original Floating Theatre* used typically to go into rehearsals in March at its winter base down in Carolina waters and then in April begin playing its leisurely way north, stopping five or so days per port to run through a repertory calibrated by Charlie Hunter from long traveling-show experience: perhaps a "heart interest" play on Night One, with sufficient "afterdraft" to hook the townsfolk without giving them their fill; next night a "family comedy" pitched especially at the ladies, it being thought to be they who would bring their menfolk back for more; on Night Three a mystery, maybe, or a western, to change the pace: something entertaining but of not more than middle weight; then on Night Four, the "feature night" (typically a Friday), an all-stops-out melodrama with the most elaborate sets and costumes in the repertory; and on closing night a flat-out farce, to leave 'em laughing. Not until August or September would the showboat reach Maryland waters and work river by river up to its turnaround point—Chesapeake City, appropriately, on the C & D Canal at the Bay's tippy-top, where Capt. and Mrs. Adams had their shoreside home—then back south through the fall from Maryland to Virginia and on to Elizabeth City or Wilmington, NC, for either winter lay-up or, if it had been one of those infamous Novembers, for salvage, repair, even reconstruction. The company would thence disperse for three months of vacation and/or pick-up work until rehearsal time the following March.

Given the world's subsequent changes and FLOPCORP's particular charge from Dorset Tradewinds Enterprises, *TOFO II* confines its travels to the Chesapeake, from Havre de Grace, Elkton, and Chesapeake City in the north (where the Canal Museum houses a scale model of our predecessor) to Norfolk/Portsmouth in the south. With Sherry's cadre of Arkade "regulars" and a summer complement of interns like Your Narrator from area colleges, our short history appears to be settling us into a routine of Preview Season (mid-March to mid-May), Main Season (mid- or late May to mid-September), and "Postview" Season (mid-September to mid-November), after which we lay up for the winter months as an "art film" theater in Dorsettown's Snug Harbour—Mort Spindler's not-bad idea, to help defray hibernation expenses. Through Preview Season, Sher's Regulars work southward from the Choptank in one- and two-night stands, perhaps longer in the larger cities, down to Norfolk and then back up as far as Alexandria on the Potomac before closing this shakedown circuit. During the day we run an Educational Video (Yr Narrator's not-bad idea) pitched especially at the school field-trips that we make a point of soliciting; it covers or at least touches upon the Adams showboat (of which we now have our own glass-cased model in the lobby, along with blowups of Black November newsclips and photos), its Ferber/Ziegfeld spinoffs (*Show Boat* posters on the walls, display-cased playbills and first editions), and *TOFO II*'s own evolution, including film-clip previews of the coming evening's live entertainment. That, typically, will be a half-fresh, half-nostalgic menu of comedy skits, vaudeville, and concert numbers—whatever Sher's skeleton-crew Regulars happen to be cooking—and perhaps some previews-within-those-previews of the Main Season's scheduled attractions, *Coming Soon! . . .* That season, too, we most often do two-night stands, augmenting Sher's Cast of Several with both new and veteran Summer Teamies. Although school's out for most of that period, we still draw cut-rate daytime visitors as a floating floating-theater museum before morphing back into a theater proper at afternoon's end. On Night One, as razzle-dazzly a variety show as ATC's full complement can mount, including sample bits from the Feature Production to come; on Night Two, that production itself, our impresarial fingers crossed, for it is here that we've had the most program trouble. The four-month Main Season will fetch us up the northmore rivers of the Eastern Shore—Tred Avon, Miles and Wye, Chester, Sassafras, Bohemia, Elk — then down the Bay's busier northwestern ones, with extended stops at Baltimore, Annapolis, and Washington and routine two-nighters in selected river-towns between. Come Postview Season, it's back to the Regulars, supplemented on weekends by the best available of the Summer Team; on weeknights our stripped-down bill of fare will be the most successful small-cast numbers from the Preview and Main Seasons, on weekends a modified restaging of the Main-Season feature, unless (the case thus far) it has proved a turkey and been scrapped. Insofar as logistics permit, our autumn itinerary will aim for bases missed or skipped in the spring and summer, concluding in what ideally would be a triumphant pre-Thanksgiving homecoming to Dorsettown, but in historical fact has been mainly a chastened resolve to do better next year. In any case a party, not unrelievedly glum, before *T II* reverts to art-film dormancy.

Narrator slips into those clubby *we*'s, *our*'s, and *us*'s because, as You will have divined, he has long since "bonded" with FLOP-CORP's flagging flagship: if not quite from his maiden, unpaid internship itaboard (August–October '93, *T II*'s late-started inaugural season, played mainly in home port while Cap'n. Ad. recruited and commissioned our Propulsion Team and finally deemed us ready for short trial excursions to Cambridge, Oxford, and Easton), then surely from Preview Season '94, when, hooked on showboatery and in hopeless love already with his immediate superior, he cut dangerously many end-of-junior-year college classes to Jeep *TOFO-II*-ward, to our springtime stops on the James and York, Rappahannock and Potomac; and unequivocally from our mid-May Casting Off on that year's Main Season. He it was, begorrah — a salaried, liveaboard hand by then — who organized and named the Pit Bulls (our music thitherto had all been canned); who produced our Pretty Good Educational Video (*Showboat 'Round the Bend!*) as the centerpiece of *T II*'s Floating Floating-Theater Museum mode; who pressed the ATC to go as higher-tech as we could afford in the way of rock-show-worthy sound and light equipment and movie-style special effects to enliven our campy period pieces. Who save he (he kvells on, praying Your indulgence) urged Sher & Co. to exploit the

*Show Boat* connection by punctuating our first-night "Revue" with take-offs from the musical ("Ol' Man Choptank," "Just Plain Bull," "Why I Don't Love You," "Make Me Leave," etc.)? To capitalize, even, upon the Novelist Emeritus's maiden but still-in-print show-boat novel? ("Nah," nixed Sherry and Mort Spindler as one: "Who's read it, 'cept you college types?") These brainstorms receptively received and at least modestly implemented, we wound up our first full season disappointingly in the red but feeling very much a team — indeed, a team of Teams, from the Gee Dash Dee Team calling our shots up in Patmos Tower to the Popcorn-and-Pepsi Sub-Squad of the Galley, Concession & Bar Team in *T II*'s lobby — our teamly routines honed by experience, from Scheduling & Publicity through Docking & Undocking to Galley Provisioning, Holding-Tank Pumpout, and (another aspect of Waste Management, perhaps) Program Adjustment.

This last was, and remains, critical, and by Postview Season '94 it was already in its now-familiar state of near-crisis. A showboat's bottom line is, of course, the Show, and that show must entertain. More specifically — as Sherry's mom, "Bea Golden," made passably clear at the 1994 Main Season Orientation Session — it must attract a sufficient number of end-of-the-century tidewaterfolk (at least half a houseful nightly) to leave their televisioned and VCR'd and desktop-computered homes, haul arse down to their local waterfront, and pay our cheap-as-we-can-make-it-and-still-hope-to-break-even admission fee. It must then entertain those folk sufficiently to induce a sufficiency themof to return, if not next evening then at least next season, and to pass word of their entertainment along to a sufficiency of their friends and neighbors. In the case of our first-night variety show, *Tidewater Follies*, we have found it comparatively easy to mount a brisk-paced mix of not-bad skits and stunts and musical numbers addressed to assorted ages and levels of sophistication (every *TOFO II*ster is required to have more than one string to his/her bow) and then to adjust, rearrange, or scratch individual items as their reception calls for: to rescore Cap'n Harry Kane's virtuoso "straight" trumpet rendition of Rimsky-Korsakov's "Flight of the Bumblebee," for example, into a still-virtuosic but

163

also comic "Flight of the Saltmarsh Mosquito" (he swats at the invisible pest with his left hand while blowing those *presto* runs with his right, etc.), and to try scheduling that showstopper *after* Kit & Kaboodle's "Takes Three to Tango" routine (never mind) instead of before it.

The Feature Production, however, we soon learned to be another and altogether more mattersome matter, since all of our second-night eggs were in a single, high-overhead basket. As a '93 newbie (but we were all, except Ms. "Bea Golden," new to showboat biz back then), Narrator found himself painfully enmeshed in an awkward revival of the 1920s music-melodrama *Smilin' Through*, a tearjerker so successful on the original *Adams Floating Theatre* that, in the aptly mixed metaphor of one old trouper, at the final curtain "there weren't a dry seat in the house," but too outdated nowadays to play straight and not quite outdated enough to play for laughs. Despite Sher's valiant performance in the dual roles of "Kathleen Sheridan" and "Moonyeen Clare"—roles played by Norma Shearer in MGM's 1932 filming of the play and by Jeanette MacDonald in the '41 remake—we bombed, especially with the pre–Social Security set, to whom the mere phenomenon of live theater was a distracting, unconvincing novelty; they applauded the songs politely, but were unmoved by the hokey romance. In Narrator's still-amateur judgment, snazzier **SPECIAL EFFECT!**s for the play's several beyond-the-grave sequences might've saved our butts; but he hadn't muscle enough back then to press his case, and so the only wet seats were in FLOPCORP's accounting office.

Chastened, we opened 1994 with an attempt at comic-nostalgia-cum-topical-satire as our Feature Production: a restaging of the *Original Floating Theater*'s 1939 restaging of the nineteenth-century temperance melodrama *Ten Nights in a Bar Room*. Sher's idea was to "nostalge" the 1930s the way Darl Hulit (Charles Hunter's successor on the *OFT*) had nostalged the Gay Nineties. It didn't fly. Your Narrator's counteridea—actually attempted by mid–Main Season, such was our desperation—was to update the script by changing *Bar Room* to *Crack House* (nixed by the Arkangel Team as too *noir*, and so with a wink at Carson McCullers we settled on

*Salad at the Baaad Café*) and by cross-dressing the Gay 1890s as the Gay/Lesbian 1990s. Didn't fly—except with the Rainbow Pride crowd, of whom there was an insufficiency either to pay our bills on the one hand or to much damage our reputation on the other. We finished that season by abandoning hope for repeat business and doing our *Tidewater Follies* on both nights.

"A floating casino," Sher reported that her mom began muttering that winter: "Only way we're gonna make it's to take out all the orchestra seats and put slots in the back half and tables in the front, with a little arena stage for cabaret stuff while the customers drink and gamble." To effect that particular mighty morph, however, FLOPCORP would need a change both in the state's gambling laws and in the mindset of Patmos Tower, where the Arkangel Team ("Todd Andrews" and Sherry's mom's mom) were determined that *T II* be either a showboat or no boat. We would try another season or two, they decided; if we couldn't come up with a workable program —in particular with a successful Feature Production—we would pack it in, disband the company, decommission and sell the sumbitch *Floating Opera II*.

Narrator was senior-yearing it by then and beginning to begin to consider graduate school, if only *faute de* fucking *mieux*—beginning, even, to begin to envision, as his soon-to-come M.A. thesis, some sort of electronified . . . *showboat novel*?—meanwhile Jeeping Dorsettownward nearly every winter weekend to play onshore gigs with our Pit Bulls band, to help Sher plan our upcoming Preview and Main Seasons—and, Aphrodite willing, to get himself laid.

Sherry! McAndrews! Singer! To type her name is to make these apprentice fingers exclaim upon the keyboard. Front and center, Coach-o'-my-heart, for better-late-than-never Proper Introduction! Only child of June Harrison Singer Bernstein "Bea" Golden—officially by the first of that shrewd though more or less marinated matron's serial husbands, but equivocally middle-named "in honor of" Bea's on-and-off lover, so to speak, Capt. Adam. Andrew. Lake., and her perennial patron "Todd Andrews," of whom inevitably more anon—SMcAS was, when Narrator first beheld her, twenty-seven, he twenty-three and no virgin, but greener than he fancied himself to be in the arts of Eros Incorporated. Had had girls and girlfriends — yea, even a Relationship or three — but was and for better or worse remains a critter of the highflying, shallowrunning U.S. Nineties, and so at an age when his GreatUnc Ennie, e.g. (critter of the pompadoured postwar Fifties), was already married and making books and babies, Yrs T'ly remained an undergrad apprentice, cunt-countrywise, as well as in the realms of art and academe: not quite a bachelor themallof, but nowise their master.

If still an apprentice, though, Lord knows an ardent one, entranced to find in so smalltime a venue as Snug Harbour so bigtime a talent so smashingly packaged. Longmuscled lean is S. McA. Singer, but neither fashion-model anorexic nor bodybuilder freako: just a smooth, fit, fucking-perfect female figure. Hair of frequently changing cut and tint, but most often a curly, wheatstraw-colored cloche. Face . . . Muse help us, where to start? Face . . . oh, makeup-free except when made up for a part, its planes strong and prominent, lips and teeth and nose to die for, and, should You perchance survive 'em, killer eyebrows (darker than her head-hair and borderline bushy: Sher won't pluck) browing . . . well, her eyes.

Those eyes. Sher's eyes. Showstopping, dead-in-your-tracks-stopping eyes. Gladly would one do a chorus each on jointure of tush and thigh, on tuck of navel, ear-sculpt, nip-tip, vulval fold— Ah! — if ever one could close eyes to those eyes. Not a chance. Deep apprentice breath, then, and here we go: *Level*, they are, those eyes, for starters. And gray of iris, yes. *Clear* bright level glistening gray. Fucking luminous-numinous wolf-goddess $n$th-power level gray-irised eyes that make the splendid rest of SMS's incorporation seem the necessary precondition. Large bright clear intense horse-shit-free amused-and-friendly-but-don't-fuck-with-me lively lovely level Athene-gray eyes, one each to left and right of that finely chiseled nosebridge; eyes that at audition-time back in summer '93 called each of us prospective newbies one by one onstage herwith, *them*with—Okay, so it must've been her voice did that: that husky, hormone-rich yet bullshit-free contralto that Sher can range from falsetto through profundo. But it was her eyes that levitated us onto the rehearsal stage and at once inspired and challenged and put us at our ease—to see what we could do.

"Johns Johnson," she read from her list, then raised those eyes itover, usward: "*Johns*?"

Make it *Hop*, okay? (Narrator's so-familiar plea.)

"*Make it hop!*" Sher's delighted voice commanded, eyes invited/dared/encouraged: "A-*one*! A-*two*!"

*A-scooby-dooby-doo!* Narrator came back as if on cue, and although his audition was meant to be and would presently get around to being as drummer, stagehand, and bit-part actor, he found himself improvising with shorts-and-T-shirted Sher an *a cappella* finger-snapping, barefoot-stomping doo-wop dance duet:

> *Make it hop* (two, three)*!*
> *Make it hop* (yessirree)*!*
> *Make 'em flip, make 'em flop,*
> *Make 'em hop* (whoo-pee)*!*

—et cetera, in hair-raising unrehearsed synchrony, concocting new verses and dance steps together:

> NARRATOR: *Feelin' blue?*    SHER: *Boo hoo!*
>
> N: *Here's* TOFO Two*!*    S: *Woo-wooo!*
>
> N: *Comin' soon! Half past noon! Just for you!*    S: *Wa-hoo!*

—joined then spontaneously by the whole crew of auditioning interns, clapping on the afterbeat, dancing in the aisles, and singing with us what had now become the chorus:

> *Make it hop* (doo-wop)*!*
> *Make it hop* (don't stop)*!*
> *Make 'em flip, make 'em flop,*
> *Make 'em hop!*

Which in very sooth she did, our braless boss, and forthwith hired Yrs Truly as drummer/techie/bit-part-actor/Corpse-de-Ballet-dancer/whatever—including spiritual kid brother and spookily insynch random-tandem improviser, an experience altogether new to Johns Hopkins "Make It Hop" Johnson and, so she later declared himto, novel at least in that degree to Sherry McAndrews Singer as well, with happy consequences presently to be set forth.

We could work that bit up as a production number, her new adorer made bold to suggest that same evening, or the next: a Recruitment Scene. It could even be a frame for the whole revue: You're auditioning acts for the showboat's variety show — called *The Tidewater Follies*, maybe? Song-and-dance numbers, comedy routines, whatever. And you ask the audience to help you rank the contestants with their applause. . . .

"You've watched too many old Andy Hardy movies," Sher opined — acknowledging however that the idea might be half feasible if we happened to have a pit band to accompany the tryouts, as Cap'n Harry Kane had many times lamented our lack of. But Narrator hadn't yet met the Kane twins, had he? He blew a wicked trumpet, did Cap'n Harry, and one of the new Galley-and-Bar Teamies was reported to be a mean keyboarder. . . .

*The Pit Bulls*, Narrator on-the-spot proposed: drums, trumpet, and keyboard to begin with; other instruments as they come out of the woodwork. Narrator still had all basic amps and mikes and mixers from his rock-band days stashed in his parents' club basement, and would fetch 'em aboard soonest. Let's post notice: tryouts next Monday A.M.?

"The Pit Bulls," mused Sherry McAndrews Singer, a deliberative look in those eyes those eyes, which then she turned full upon Yours Truly. "I like it! *Tidewater Follies* sounds good, too. You have a way with words."

We'll make 'em hop, euphoric Narrator promised, and in the remaining days and weeks of that inaugural season we busted butt so to do, not without some success. By autumn's equinox we had ourselves both a pit band and the prototype of what would become in '94 the versatile, elastic frame of our successful *Tidewater Follies* variety show: the Auditioning Shtick, with its ever-evolving acts, its comic flops and redemptions (ingenue fails as operatic soprano but blows 'em away with Janis Joplin–style Git-Down lament, or vice versa, etc.), and its periodic all-hands-on-deck numbers, of which the first and longest-lived was "Make It Hop."

"So are we Postmodern, or what?" Sher asked somewhere along the way. For we were using the performers' real names onstage, and directly posing the question to the audience whether a showboat show could be floated successfully in the age of electronic digitality, and if so, whether via the nostalgia route (couple of *Show Boat* take-offs here) or high-tech special effects, as best we could mount them. In short, we were talking and singing about what we were doing as we did it, as well as about the history of our medium, and making that metanarrative and metacommentary part of the entertainment. Was that Postmodern?

*Are we Post-mah-dern?* Narrator crooned back to her, to the tune of "The Party's Over," and at once quick Kit (for such was she beginning already to become in certain of our routines) picked up the melody and improvised a next line:

"*Is this the end-of-the-road?*"

Whereto her proto-Kaboodle, thinking as fast as he could under the uncommonly distracting circumstances, responded

*Or is ree-cycled self-conscious i-ro-ny just one-more-passing-mode?*

"Et cetera, dear Hopsie," sighed sleepy Sher, "and oy, is she tired," for among her several endearing-to-Your-Narrator whims was, in languorous circumstances, to speak of herself in third person.

So was he, he acknowledged, this being indeed the hard day's night after *T II*'s final trial excursion of that maiden season and our most elaborate (and well-received) presentation thus far of the *Tidewater Follies* Audition Routine. Should we put this in the show too, this "Are We Postmod" number?

"Too uptown for the homefolks, I think," thought Sher. And it's time You were told, Readerissimo, that while at this juncture those eyes those eyes of hers were for the nonce closed, those thighs of hers were not; that she lay on her back in full amazing exhausted but welcoming nakedhood upon her berth in her cabin, whereinto, once the postshow end-of-season party was over and the company dispersed, she had wordlessly led Yours Truly by the hand for the first time, to say him a not quite wordless *muchas gracias,* one trouper to another, not only for his several really major contributions to the show but also, whether he realized it or not, for his Not Asking, either directly or indirectly, about her sex life, which was nobody's freaking beeswax but her own, as only he and Cap'n Elva Kane, bless her, seemed to understand. And now, if he had no objection, she would latch her cabin door and remove his clothing item for item as he removed hers, and never mind that we're both still sweatsoaked from that workout of a show and the party-dancing after; let's not even wash up except with each other's tongues on each other's skins, 'cause salt water's our medium, no? And what's this she finds her partner's packing here if not a rarin'-to-go Ain't-We-Postmodren kaboodle, let her kiss it hello, mwah mwah, would it like a tryout too? Hop to it, then, Hopperino mio, 'cause she is truly pooped to the socks, but maybe just maybe not too pooped to Make It Hop.

> KABOODLE: *Make it hop?* (O joy!)
> KIT: *Me on top.* (Down, boy.)

Which we did, she athletic even in her near-exhaustion, he in his scarcely believing his erotic good fortune. For he had in truth begun to wonder, had Narrator, what she did for jollies, this unmarried, evidently unattached, to all appearances prevailingly uninterested embodiment of cheerful American female-sexual fitness. Onstage, as dancer/singer/actress, she worked her considerable sex appeal along the full range from vamp/tramp/siren to ripe-virginal ingenue, though ever most convincingly as good-humored, high-spirited, no-bullshit, been-around-the-block American Beauty. Offstage, she was that very item: an untemperamental, hardworking but easygoing, quick-on-the-comeback regular guy, everybody's buddy —but, so far as Narrator and Company could infer (and You may be sure that among ourselves we male-persuasion newbies discussed the matter at length, if not in depth), not only nobody's girlfriend but nobody's more than occasional "date." Is queer for Cap'n Elva, some of us ventured—for indeed the *Dove*'s skipper and the director of the Arkade Theatre Company were tight pals, and Elva Kane appeared to us if not lesbian then nonsexual. Gets off with a 220-

volt vibrator, some others lewdly speculated. Has built-in dildo with won't-quit Energizer-Bunny batteries, which explains those eyes those eyes those eyes. Is saving it up for New York and Hollywood. Is Cap'n. Ad.'s secret sex-slave in ménage à trois with her gin-soaked mom. Is old "Todd Andrews's" ditto. Is virginal and frigid. Is transsexual.

*Is simply not driven by the mating instinct*, Narrator himself had come by summer '95 to understand. Is almost certainly, though not busily, bisexual: depends on the partner. Prefers for the good of the order to do her main fucking outside the ship's company, since puts high value on group morale and personal privacy, but will fuck only folks she knows, trusts, and admires who are moreover to her knowledge infection-free and not otherwise committed, and so the field of candidate fuckees is limited. Permits herself, however, occasional what-the-fuck exceptions to this prudent principle, as in Yrs Truly's privileged case—making clear more by implication than by ex- that to such vigorous instances no sequel is to be assumed, which is not necessarily to say that none will follow. Happens to enjoy the odd session of sex with an able and qualified partner the way she enjoys . . . oh, the odd full-course gourmet meal, say, or night at the opera, or weekend of scuba-diving in the Cayman Islands, without making a Regular Thing of it. Does in fact routinely Get It Off, she supposes Narrator could say if he insists on that vulgar expression, onstage, whether solo or, better yet, with a really insynch partner like Present Company, and whether in a theater-piece or a comedy skit or a musical routine, and most especially when such a routine is enlivened by some inspired reciprocal improvisation, e.g. our original "Make It Hop" thing, which literally so tickled her clit that she lushed her step-ins. Okay? Unh! *Oh, Hopsie! Unh!*

Ah, Sherry! *Ah*, et cetera. And yes, well: But what about love, chère Sher? Does the big L never come into it? For Narrator himself was heels-over-heading in that direction even before Coach Singer made it hop and hop again (and It her, he adds with some pride; especially at our second such get-together, spring rehearsal-time '94, when, Kit happening to be unabashedly in tampon-stuffed midmenstruation, she directed Kaboodle to Astroglide her rectum and —Eea-sy does it, mate— intromit thereinto to Its heart's content, so to speak: his maiden go at anal copulation, and for her too ouchy for him unreservedly to enjoy, although it sure got his rocks off and hers as well, whom he reached 'roundunder to digitate whilst gently buggering to climax).

"The L word," Sher said, and sighed. In her opinion (she gave Narrator somewhere along that season's way to understand), there're those inclined to hump whom they're currently in love with and those inclined to love whom they happen to be humping. Sher supposed herself more the latter than the former; *nota bene*, however, that "currently" to her meant really *currently*: not this Preview Season or even necessarily this whole weekend, but *tonight* (or this morning, afternoon, whenever we happened to be making it hop) — after which we're back to being pals and workmates, period.

Husband? Family?

"Not her thing."

Lover, though, Sher? Not Fucker, y'understand, but Lover. Mate. *Beloved. . . .*

She closed those those eyes eyes. Reopened them. Compressed a bit her unlipsticked perfect lips. Slightly and shortly shook her head.

To himself, in his apprentice way, Narrator mused A strange upbringing, no doubt: that loopy, stagestruck souse of a mother (with whom, however, Sher seemed to get on well, if with frequent eye-rolls); those serial stepdads and boarding schools (she'd been a pain-in-the-ass kid, she agreed with "Bea Golden"). But green though he was in more fields than novel-writing, he nonetheless allowed for the possibility that S. McA. Singer simply happened to be what she sexually/emotionally was, no armchair psychologizing called for, and that that's being other than the norm did not ipso facto make it anyhow defective. End of Proper Introduction, and let's see now, wherenhell were we?

"Post-welcome-back-coital present time, luv," Coach Sher reminds us: "Preview Season Ninety-five? Scrolling aft to How You and Morty Baited the Hook for Old Whatsisname. Coming Soon?"

Give a chap time, hon; Yrs is Truly two apprentice-years older than he was at our initial It-Hop-Making. Is learning, if hasn't altogether learned, to take things as they narratively come, shall we say?

And is, moreover, in intimate simultaneous double congress, enough to keep any narrator hopping: snug-harbored with "his" fair Sher (nobody's Singer, Y'understand, but her independent own) in her welcome-back sack aboard Snug Harboured *TOFO II*, and at the same time, if You're reading this, still cyberlinked with kinky You. Whom he here invites (and her too, and she too) to CLICK ANY BUTTON:

> **Bait? Hook? Old Whatsisname?**
> **And who's this quote/unquote**
> **"Todd Andrews," s.v.p.?**

> **Enough narrative hopscotch already!**
> **On with "1995.2," after which, one**
> **presumes, there're still '96, '97, and '98**
> **to be narrated before we're done**
> **with this floating "novel"'s MIDDLE,**
> **for Chrissakes! Hop to it!**

> **And while you're at it, big boy, make**
> **US hop, whydontcha?**

Hop You did, thankee, by clicking . . . All of the Above? *That*'ll keep Yours Truly hopping—to address the remaining two and get on with the show.

Bait. Hook. "Todd Andrews." Life imitateth art, here and there, and not always well. Back in mid-century, when at Yrs Truly's present age Old Whatsisname wrote that *FlOp* novel, he chose for the most part to call spades spades, placewise—Cambridge, Maryland, Race and High Streets, the municipal waterfront's Long Wharf, where James Adams's showboat had once upon a time many times tied up—but his plot and characters, he swears, were hundred-proof fictitious. Small towns being what they are, however, it was in retrospect probably to be expected that the juxtaposition of real place-names with imagined people and situations—e.g. the mid-fiftyish eccentric bachelor lawyer Todd Andrews, involved in a decades-old adulterous triangle with the wife of the wealthiest man in town (a complaisant pickle-packing magnate)—would lead some locals to surmise that "Harrison Mack," say, the wittol CEO of "Mack's Pickles," might be a takeoff on the eldest son of old Colonel P_____, of the P_____ Packing Company (a local fruit-and-vegetable cannery, the town's largest industry), and that although by no stretch of imagination could the discreetly adulterous "Jane Mack" have been inspired by that chap's pious and retiring wife, she *was* in some respects reminiscent of the country-club *doyenne* Jane Harrison—which would therefore point intriguingly to the widowed and, yes, somewhat eccentric Howard F_____, the Harrison family's longtime attorney and friend, as the possible original of "Todd Andrews." . . .

Et cetera. Had the novel been, like Ms. Ferber's, a nationwide bestseller made into a Broadway hit and a Hollywood extravaganza or two, such titillative speculation might have caused embarrassment for some innocent bystanders and the author. But as it was a mere *succès d'estime*, whose subsequent half-life in reprint editions went unremarked by Cantabridgeans, all hands were spared such consequences. . . . Until, just in time for the go-go Reagan Eighties, there emerged on the down-home scene a certain senior-citizen mover and shaker yclept Andrew S. "Cap'n Andy" Todd, a.k.a. dot dot dot "Todd Andrews."

It's a common surname hereabouts, is Todd: *TOFO II*'s slender phonebook for the rural mid–Eastern Shore counties lists no fewer than 135 several Todd subscribers—half a dozen themof in a town called Toddville, presumably the tribal seat. But as Narrator's principal informants have it (S. Singer and M. Spindler), Mr. Andrew S. appeared as if out of nowhere in the form of an uncommonly wealthy and energetic retired Something-or-Other from Somewhere who very quickly established himself as a Somebody in the local yacht and country clubs (though himself neither yachtsperson nor golfer) and in the affairs of the town at large.

Which pleasant town, Narrator believes GreatUnc Ennie would agree, has been, if not quite in decline since the *FlOpera* Fifties, not remarkably prospering either. The big cannery closed decades ago, when the region's agribusiness switched from human to nonhuman food crops: instead of tomatoes and lima beans and peaches, feed corn, soybeans, and sorghum. The busy crab-and-oyster packeries that once ringed (and polluted) the town's central creek, like the adjacent shipyard and lumber mill, have been replaced by mid-range condominia and marinas. Suburban plazas have evacuated the former downtown shopping district. While racial integration in the county school system and all public facilities, so bitterly fought over in Cambridge through the incendiary 1960s, is now an accepted fact of life, residential integration there, as in most small southern towns, remains for various reasons near zero, and the black Second Ward is still the city's poorest. Finally, the large-scale gentrification that has made tourists and retirees an economic mainstay of such nearby tidewater municipalities as St. Michaels, Oxford, and Easton has, as of this writing, yet to "catch on," quite, for better or worse, in Cambridge—despite the best efforts, fifteen years since, of Andrew S. Todd.

"What we need's a big resort complex down where the tuna boats used to come in," proposed Cap'n Andy (for some years a national brand of canned tuna took over part of the defunct tomato cannery for processing albacore shipped in from Iceland; but that, too, passed); "plus an upscale retirement community out where the old Oakley Beach Hotel was" (named after the street named after the Annie of *Get Your Gun* fame, who thereon briefly dwelt in the 19-Teens); "plus a convention center down by Long Wharf to anchor the whole shebang, with water-taxi service to our new hotel and restaurants." The town listened politely—even attentively when it appeared that this puzzling mix of elderly down-homer and go-getting "C'mere" (the local term for outsiders who Come Here to retire or build vacation homes) commanded impressive financial resources—but finally backed off from committing itself to such large-scale transformations as Cap'n Andy's visions entailed, and

the tax breaks and other subsidies attendant thereupon. Cantabridgeans inclined to agree that their town's idle waterfront areas were a
potential goldmine, but could not agree that Andrew S. Todd was the
fittest miner-in-chief thereof. Maybe a *five*-story hotel instead of a
ten-? A *fifty*-slip marina, at least for starters, instead of a hundred-?
With perhaps not *quite* so large a municipal bond issue or so long-
term a tax concession? And as for that projected seventy-five-unit
(Phase One) luxury retirement community and adjacent assisted living facility, well . . .

Well hell, said in effect Andrew S. "Cap'n Andy" Todd: no half-
assed half-measures for him and his suddenly-materialized Dorset
Tradewinds Enterprises, Inc. (for he was not without supporters in
the town council and chamber of commerce and among the county
commissioners and the populace at large, especially certain members of the yacht and country clubs). If the town wouldn't let him do
for its benefit what he had in mind, he'd build himself a brand-new
town next door that would! And so he did, not without extended hul-
laballoo and foofaraw in the local press, petitions pro and contra,
narrow-margin referenda, and the like — *et voilà*: the planned (and
gated) community of Dorsettown-on-Choptank: Snug Harbour, Patmos Tower, the whole nine yards, including *The Original Floating
Opera II.*

And precisely what, You reasonably inquire, has all that to do
with "Todd Andrews," and "Todd Andrews" with our story? Coming
soon???

Whatever he'd been back wherever he came from, old Todd (as
let's conveniently call him) was in all likelihood not an avid reader
of "serious" fiction. He was, however, an elderly bachelor or wid-
ower, still fit and not unhandsome in his probable seventies (the fellow's age, like other details of his curriculum vitae, was less than
certain), and among other things at least once upon a time an attor-
ney-at-law. Add to these his phonebook listing — TODD ANDREW
S, comma-free as are all such — and it's not surprising that someone at the yacht or country club would remark to him (folks like to
suppose the remarker to have been Jane Harrison, the aforementioned *doyenne* widow of McCall Harrison and mother of our "Bea
Golden," but it seems to Yrs T as probably to have been the lawyer

Howard F_____, glad to shift winking Rumor away from himself) his several correspondences to the protagonist of a certain "local" novel or two, authored by a once-local boy — as if those fictions had invoked him into fact, or (not the homefolks' words) supplied him with a template for his improvised persona. As with other matters, it is unclear whether Todd happened to be already familiar with the relevant texts at first or second hand, or (more likely) then consulted them or caused some DTE functionary (not Mort Spindler; perhaps Howard F_____, now on Todd's payroll) to research and "background" him themupon; the man has a way, reports Mort, of seeming to have known already what in fact he's learning, as if for him all knowledge, Platowise, is recollection. In any case, it became his pleasure and custom not only to refer to himself, always in written or orally implied quotes, as "Todd Andrews" ("Just call me 'Todd'"), but to imitate that character programmatically. No way the guy's actually in his nineties, for example, but it amuses him to declare that like T. A. he's coeval with the century. Unlikely, though not quite unimaginable, that he did some out-of-town legal work for the Harrisons before moving to Cambridge; improbable indeed, though, that — as he came discreetly to intimate and Mrs. H not to deny, if only because none presumed to confront her therewith — they were not only longtime friends but old former lovers, and June Harrison "Bea Golden" etc. their possible love-child! Call it *folie à deux*, or *trois* (Sher's mom seems woozily complicit in the ongoing masquerade): Just as the fictional Todd Andrews's mistress, Jane Mack, established a Marshyhope Foundation to tax-shelter her late husband's millions, so "Todd Andrews's" Jane Harrison endows The Tidewater Foundation ditto. If it be written that among The Marshyhope Foundation's marshyhopeful philanthropies was an *Original Floating Theatre II*, then let The Tidewater Foundation (like the God whom some Creationists maintain created the world just a few thousand years ago, complete with geological and fossil evidence of a much longer history) bring into being an *Original Floating* Opera *II* — complete with a purported earlier incarnation as that former vessel!

Thus do the wealthy, powerful, whimsical, and crazy-like-a-fox entertain themselves, sometimes: not only with "the contamination of reality by dream," as Jorge Luis Borges puts it, but also vice versa. As the matriarch Jane Harrison moved into her dotage (and into Penthouse Suite 999 of the Patmos Tower Assisted Living Facility, with only DTE's boardroom—"the Gee Dash Dee Room"—herabove), she became "the former Jane Harrison," now Jane Patterson (Mrs. Harrison) Mack, with her geriatric former lover "Todd Andrews" ("the former Andrew S. Todd") ensconced three floors below in #666. In "their" author's other works they reportedly took and take no interest; may even be ignorant that such exist. But his two pertinent texts became for them History and (for the fading *doyenne*, at least) Memory; not only scripture, but script. Does it therein say that the late Harrison Mack, a colonial-history buff, in his dotage came sadly to confuse himself with George III of England? Then so, alas, it must have been with the now doubly former McCall Harrison. That, as his senility advanced, he moved from fancying himself George III sane to fancying himself George III *mad*, who furthermore in his madness sometimes fancied himself Harrison Mack sane, able to recognize family and friends and to manage his affairs with his previous acumen? Then so, alack, for his head-shaking widow, it was.

Et cetera.

"Cap'n Andy," meanwhile—whose Ferberish nickname antedates all this and provides him and his associates with a convenient ontological middle ground between Andrew S. Todd and "Todd Andrews"—had been by virtue of that nickname long since led to Ms. Ferber's *Show Boat* novel/play/film, but had felt no particular identification with the raffish, near-buffoonish skipper of her *Cotton Blossom*. When, however, as "Todd Andrews" he came to learn that *Adam's Original & Unparalleled Floating Opera* in That Other Showboat Novel had been modeled upon James Adams's *Original Floating Theatre*, and that it was thereaboard that Ms. Edna had done her homework, he not only caused into existence *The Original Floating Opera II* but also became among other things an ardent though not disinterested collector of Chesapeake showboat-and-steamboat memorabilia. His plans for Dorsettown's future, Mort Spindler happeneth to know, include a Snug Harbour Museum to "synergize" (Mort's term) with *TOFO II*: Just as the showboat has already its aforementioned floating-theater-museum aspect (our lobby displays, our edupromotional tours and video), so when it's in home port—or if and when it fails altogether as a working showboat—it will become the Snug Harbour Museum's centerpiece.

And here, none too soon, the plot thickens, or at least our story resumes. Preview Season '95! Whaddafug to do for a Feature Production to alternate with our *Tidewater Follies*? "Nothing," had suggested Doctor Spin last fall, when we bagged our parody of *Ten Nights* etc. Back in more media-deprived times, folks had often returned to the Adams showboat three, four, even five nights straight, but Mort's audience questionnaires indicated that repeat customers nowabusydays were the exception: Depending on their tastes and schedules, *T II*'s attendees chose either Follies night or Feature night, but seldom both, and there had been no notable falling off of business in Postview Season '94 when we had done the Faute-de-Mieux Follies *tout court*. Yr Narrator was inclined to agree Mortwith—and in fact, for want of better, we were T-Follying still in spring '95, with the somewhat upgraded effects (Sound, Light, and **SPECIAL!**) that certain of us had long lobbied for in vain and been at last vouchsafed, thanks to the economies of mounting one instead of two productions. Coach Sher, though, together with her ma and, most emphatically, Andrew S. "Cap'n Andy" "Todd Andrews" Todd, was of the opinion that a showboat isn't really a showboat unless it offers updated versions of all the items listed on, e.g., this 1920ish playbill from the James Adams Floating Theatre:

---

**CLEVER ACTORS!**

★ ★ ★

*FUNNY COMEDIANS!*

★ ★ ★

★ **POWERFUL PLAYS!** ★

★ ★ ★

**CORRECT COSTUMES!**

★ ★ ★

*BEAUTIFUL SCENERY!*

---

And so the search went on for a dramatic *chef d'ouevre* to follow the Follies: a search that Narrator right readily joined out of his growing general commitment to *TOFO II* and, more particularly, his ongoing lustful fascinadmiration withof Ms. SMcAS. (What made the woman who Made It Hop *tick*? How could so multitalented and physically striking an all-'round wowser futz her life away in D'town-on-Ch'tank, aboard funky floundering *T II*, and in occasional bed with no better than the likes of Yrs T — and, maybe, Cap'n Elva K?) Whereto — said search — he devoted more than he ought to've of his senior undergrad year but contributed little beyond the wish that we could exploit the Ferber Connection via some *Show Boat* of our own, perhaps concerning the Sophisticated City Girl's involvement with the backwater vaudeville milieu of James Adams & Co.: an involvement rich in comic misunderstandings and *faux pas* but ultimately enlightening to all hands — Ferber wiser in the ways and wiles of Scotch-Irish cracker Methodists who however were also seasoned (indeed, sometimes pickled) showbiz troupers to the bone; the Redneck Regulars discovering that their visiting "nice little Jewish girl from Chicago" was plenty street-smart, tough as nails, nowise patronizing, game for almost anything, and able to give as good as she got.

Et cetera.

"Sounds cool," allowed Mort Spindler: "*Write* the sucker already, and if Sher thinks it'll fly we'll start rehearsals in March."

Can't, replied Narrator: Senior course-work? Graduate-school applications? Weekending with the Pit Bulls? And write a serious musical comedy in my spare time?

As only Sher can urge, "Can't you call it your senior thesis or like that, Hopsie?" Sher urged. "And/or your grad-school project? And make it, like, you know, *hop*?"

But apart from such considerations as that one had never written for the stage before, and had only a middling familiarity with the medium, the material, and the historical period, and could imagine no connection themfrom to one's official interest in Hypertextual Electronic Fiction, one was (unbeknownst to Mort and Sher) already committing one's spare spare time to plugging away at one's projected plugged-in *pièce de résistance*: the Novelist Aspirant's aspiring e-novel, on the strength whereof one had been admitted into the M.A. program at one's namesake university.

*Tant pis*, we three agreed; for unlikely as it was that an utter greenhorn would score first time at bat even if he devoted himself exclusively to the attempt, the story-idea itself was not without appeal, and we were desperate. Among ourselves that winter therefore, while working up new numbers for the '95 Follies and upgrading old ones with newly-enhanced effects, we bandied about that hypothetical, still-nameless **POWERFUL PLAY!** and even improvised musical bits therefrom. E.g.:

—*Too True to Be Good*: Mort Spindler's idea for a half-teasing, half-lamenting number to be sung by the "Edna Ferber" character to or about some married Lothario in the Adams company who comes on to her like Don Juan Tenorio but then "Retreats in a huff / When she calls his bluff," as the song's tentative lyrics put it, pleading devotion to his acting-partner wife. Yr Senior Undergrad Novelist Aspirant saw in Mort's title a promising allegory for Poetry's criticism of History; was outvoted 2-1.

—*That's Entertainment?*: Sher's inspiration for a derisive first-act number to be sung by Miz Big City after her first exposure to the showboat's cornball bill of fare, before she comes to appreciate the fine-tuned rapport between Adams's players and their tidewater audiences; or, "if we want to get into that," expressive of her initial appall at white minstrels in blackface doing Coon routines to biracial but strictly segregated houses — evidently to the amusement of black customers in the balcony as well as whites in the orchestra. To which musical question the "James Adams" character responds, "Anyhow, it's show biz, ma'am." The song to be perhaps reprised tit-for-tat in Act Two (Narrator's suggestion) when Ms. Edna invites the rubes to be her guests at the Ziegfeld Follies, where the **FUNNY COMEDIANS!** incline to rapid-fire risqué *double entendres* and the chorus girls' **COSTUMES** are decidedly not **CORRECT!** by Bible-Belt-Baptist and Meth-Prot-Southern standards. Turning up her palms, "That's show biz," would reply Edna.

—*Takes Three to Tango*: Narrator's modest contribution, somewhere aforementioned. Ostensibly Edna's wannabe/dontwannabe paramour's reply to *Too True to Be Good*, wherein he declares that his flirtations with the likes of herself serve to fuel his ardor for his wife, "the Mary Pickford of the Chesapeake." But Narrator saw in it too a nifty allegory for Hegel's dialectic of Thesis/Antithesis/Synthesis, not to mention old tripartite Gee Dash Dee? and *His* aforenoted analogue to Author/Text/Reader (read Me/This/Thee) — or, in this instance, Singer/Song/Sung-To. All such highfalutin allegories and analogues nixed by Mort and Sher, who however grooved on the literal scenario despite the anachronism of a 1940s pop song's being parodied in the 1920s. Teased Dr. Spin: "History's criticism of Poetry?" Shrugged song's composer, "Show biz."

Et cetera. *That's Entertainment?* we actually worked up during Preview Season into a production number that by Main Season would evolve into a running dramatic frame for Tidewater Follies '95: Program notes and a little prefatory spiel by Sher establish the historical Ferber-Adams connection, whereafter our standard vaudeville routines — spun where spinnable to the non-Roaring Tidewater Twenties — prompt Edna's taunt. After Intermission, per Narrator's recommendation, the tables get turned — Backwater Babes on Broadway, etc. — leading to a heartwarming back-home finale (not to say a Hegelian Synthesis) wherein, if we bring it off, each side of the sociocultural divide is seen to've learned something from the other.

"Now *that's* entertainment!" "Bea Golden" rasped approvingly to her daughter upon previewing our Preview-Season version thisof. "Whose bright idea *was* it, anyhow?"

Song itself by Singer, she was informed. Procrustean fitting of individual numbers to overall scenario mostly by Spindler. Scenario itself, together with most of libretto, orchestration, incidental music, and interstitial action to advance the rudimentary City-Mouse/Country-Mouse story — all by Make-It-Hop Johnson, so his chief teammates generously acknowledged. Whereto he responded, an arm around each, "Takes three to tango."

"Mm-*hm*," hmmed that formidable personage, appraising Yrs T as if through a lorgnette. "Our college boy."

Meet "Bea Golden," Reader: the smashed-up, cautionary After whereto her daughter is the smashing and perhaps overcautioned Before. Née June Harrison and thereafter serially wed and divorced, she borrowed her (terminal-)stage name — at "Todd Andrews's" urging if not actually on his orders — from a similarly stagestruck boozy loser in one of "Cap'n Andy's" sacred texts: the fictional Jane Mack's daughter, officially by her husband but not impossibly by the fictional Todd Andrews. The name-assumption was a condition, 'tis said, of The Boss's appointing her CEO of DTE's New Ark Productions, comprising FLOPCORP and the Arkade Theatre Company (see Big Picture). In any case, if in her "Bea Golden" role the lady can be no small asspain — nudging daughter Sher, for example, whom she is at once ambitious for and jealous of, to consider "more mature" roles, such as *she* long since accepted the inevitability of playing, and to leave ingenueing to the likes of Holly Weil . . . — in her June Harrison aspect she is a fairly formidable businessperson, her own shrewd mother's shrewd daughter even when half sozzled, more interested in the profit-potential of FLOPCORP (read *TOFO II*'s threatened conversion to casino/restaurant) than in the Aht of the Theatah and the shoestring medium of showboatery. Fortunately usfor, her double aspects are self-canceling enough to afford us wiggle-room: June Harrison's conversion of *T II* into Something More Profitable, for instance, might force Sher out of the boonies into the big time, but it would also deprive "Bea Golden" of her own last theatrical hurrahs (sixtyish, she still takes "mature" bit-parts in *T II*'s Powerless Plays) — and so, on with the show, guys, for a few more seasons anyhow, if Our College Boy and his teammates can come up with one.

Yeah, well, OCB admitted: I do college. Yeah.

"Over at John Hopkins, am I right?"

Well . . . Yes'm.

"And Mister Mort tells me you're actually working with Whatsisname — the *Opera* fellow?"

Yeah, well. Not exactly.

"*Fascinating!*"

Modest shrug. Yeah, well.

"Don't you agree, Sherry." Enunced more presumptively than interrogatively, June-Harrisonwise.

"He sure is, Ma," loyal Sher agreed, and bestowed on College Boy's starboard cheek a resounding *mwah!*

"Tease your poor mother all you want," invited or dared "Bea Golden"—and then to all hands' surprise appended "*I* think you've got your next Feature Production there, if you all put your heads together and get Whatsisname to work it up into a professional script. Don't you think so, Ad."

Grunteth Captain. Adam. Lake., beside her at this previewing as oft he is at one thing and another when not actively engaged in captaining, "[*Grunt*, pitched and inflected to convey possibility that his longtime moreorless mistress may well be On To Something]."

Yes, well. *Forget it*, Narrator advised his Theatre Teammates, once safely out of Angel Team earshot: The guy is not one's coach. Is no more a playwright than oneself is. Is anyhow presumably as busy as he wants to be with his own projects. And who knows him all *that* well, for crying out loud? Plus what's in it for *him*, to futz around with the likes of us?

"A nice lobby display?" Mort wondered aloud, his professional wheels already a-spin. "His books for sale at the concession stand? Surprise cameo appearance as Cap'n James Adams for the hometown audience? A pitch to his roots, maybe?"

Forget it, guys. Whereafter good Sherry maybe did, but not Doctor Spin, whose job after all it is to check out all likely publicity-ops. And not, evidently, Angel-in-Chief June "Bea Golden" Harrison, who must with Mort have floated her Great Idea forthwith up to the Arkangel Team. For not long therefollowing—We're talking maybe late April now?—comes a call to Narrator's Charles Village digs in Baltimore. "'Sfor you," his apartment-mate let him know—D'You remember friend Sybil, Reader? The right cool Practicing Lesbian doctoral candidate?—who'd been expecting a call from a sapphic fellow-practicer in Classics specializing in, in fact, Ms. Sappho of Lesbos: "Morton Spindler?"

Greetings from Charm City, Mort. What can one do for you?

"Roger that, man, and hey: Can you hop right over here, mañana latest? Cap'n Andy himself has something big that he wants to show you in person!"

How big? For one had learned the magnifying effects of Doctor Spin's professional enthusiasm. Was Andrew S. "Todd 'Cap'n Andy' Andrews'" Todd's Big Something set in ironic caps/lowercase, like "Bea Golden's" Swell Idea of recruiting GreatUnc Ennie for *T II*'s Theatre Team?

"All caps and no irony," Mort swore. "Cross my heart!"

Cross your heart? You've converted!

"No ethnic teases, College Boy! This is uppercase B-I-G, okay?"

Mm-hm. And had Brother Mort personally viewed this upper-case item with his very own unaided eyes?

"C'mon, Hops. I didn't have a chance to read chapter and verse, but the guy had the thing out on his desk and in his hand while he told me all about it. He *waved* it at me, man! BIG-BIG-BIG!"

Valued teammate: Are you summoning your junior colleague away from his senior-year studies and clear across the Bay to Arkangelville for the purpose of inspecting a half-demented but thus far harmless old rich guy's shlong?

"Would I do that? And please, lad: no ageism! No economic classism! No old-fart jokes! *T II*'s a whole-family entertainment boat, right? Plus no Yiddish east of the Bay, *farshteyst*? Remember Bertolt Brecht's donkey!" Whereof the Marxist playwright was said to keep a picture near his writing-table with the caption EVEN I MUST UNDERSTAND IT.

No donkey jokes too, Mort, okay? Every thing that breatheth ith among our brethren. Breathren?

"Breathren and sistren, Johnzo: no sexism on thissere showboat, s.v.p.! Correct Costumes and Politics! Coming soon?"

Please: no premature-ejaculation jokes. Whatcha got, Mort, seriously?

"The thing wherewith to catch the conscience of the king, College Boy! The bait to bait the hook to hook your Not-Really Coach and haul him aboard *TOFO II*!"

Forget it.

But "How's this?" went on Mort: "a long-lost playscript from the *original Original Floating Theatre!*"

Come again, please?

"No serial-orgasm jokes! Djever hear of Charles Hunter? Husband of Beulah Adams Hunter, your Mary Pickford of your Chesapeake and your sister of your Cap'n James Adams himself?"

Who's your Cap'n James Adams himself?

"C'mon, Hop: *Sufficient unto the day is the bullshit thereof,* as your Christers say. Whoops, sorry: no religio-ethnic teases! Here's the poop, man:"

Et cetera, the de-exclamationized and joke-free gist whereof was that our *That's Entertainment?* scenario, as recounted approvingly by "Bea Golden" to "Todd Andrews," had put our eccentric and increasingly reclusive Arkangel-in-Chief in mind of a curious item that he'd happened to note among some Adams-family papers recently acquired for his growing showboat-memorabilia collection: A draft playscript, it was, entitled *Show Barge,* evidently written in the late 1930s by the former longtime artistic director of the Adams Floating Theatre after that vessel had changed hands and the author-director had left the company. Which playscript had to do, as by remarkable coincidence did our new *Tidewater Follies* frame-gimmick, with Ms. Edna Ferber's time aboard the Adams showboat and —"Get this, College Boy!"— her romantic involvement with the Mary Pickford of the Chesapeake's husband, the playwright himself!, pardon Mort's exclamation.

"You gotta see the thing, Hop! It's spooky! Plus terrific! Your guy'll flip!"

Leave My Guy out of it, *por favor.* He's not My Guy. But there was no denying that the coincidence was arresting and that the playscript, if authentic, was probably not without some regional-historical interest.

"*Regional-historical interest? Prob'ly not without?* Gimme a *break,* man! This is exactly precisely what we've all been looking for! Getcherass over here and see! This is HUGE!"

Well: Promise the old fart won't wave it at me?

"All right already! No waving!"

And no more of this My Guy stuff, okay? The guy's *not my guy*.

"That I can't promise, Johns. We'd be doing your guy a disservice not to bring such a relevant item to his attention! But I will promise this: We'll do nothing in the hook-baiting way till you've seen this treasure in the flesh — *if* you'll getcherass et cetera! Done?"

Coming soon's I can, Mort.

"Like eleven A.M. tomorrow, Patmos Tower Suite Six Nine Six? Meet me in my office ten-thirty and we'll go up together."

Yeah, well: That's an early start from over here for a college boy.

"So ten forty-five. But *be* here, man! This is BIG!"

Yeah, well. Bear in mind, Readie — May one deploy, now and then, that affectionate diminutive? — that we're talking, like, April '95 here: pre–Solomons Island Chance Encounter with Erstwhile Sort-Of Mentor; pre–Ontological Lunchbreak, Novelists Only; pre–Battle of the Works-in-the-Works, e-fiction versus p- contest to see whose *COMING SOON!!!* cometh sooner, and like that? Narrator's own (what You're reading, Readie, if etc.), while far from certain of its course, destination, and ETA, had long since cast off and made headway enough to serve as his Writing Sample (on disk, natch) for application to two graduate fictioneering programs and admission to the safety backup one thereof. His curiosity re this alleged play-script *trouvé* was therefore innocent, is what he's saying: the amusing coincidence of its material and that of our improvised Follies frame-situation; its possible "background" relevance to the opus that You're currently Scrollin' Through, bless You — perhaps even its possible incorporation thereinto, should Author/Narrator ever get his shit together, storylinewise. As for its possible development into a Feature Production, however, to alternate with the *Follies* . . . doubtful, on the face of it: Narrator happeneth to know, from his own showboat homework and *TOFO*'s edupromotional video, that Charlie Hunter had been a versatile fellow — musician, character actor, stage director, unofficial historian of his father-in-law's showboat, and husband of its leading lady — but no more a playwright than Yrs T or GreatUnc E. Anyhow, let's have a look, shall we?

We did: hauled out of the rack at 0700, stuffed down a bowlful of granola wetted with orange juice instead of milk (a two-bird stone picked up from housemate Syb, and — just as she predicted about our apartment-sharing — not bad at all, once one gets used to it), hit the 0800 rush hour in the old pre-graduation Cherokee from heavy-metal days, and managed to nudge therethrough and zip down the interstate and over the Bay Bridge and down et cetera in time to check into Mort Spindler's office ten minutes early. And not incurious, one might add, to meet up close and personal the quirky personage at or near the tippy-top of our Big Picture: *T II*'s Arkangel-in-Chief, if not our Gee Dash Dee? Himself.

But hey, You haven't really yet met Mort, have You: the man behind the voice before the exclamation marks? Meet Morton Spindler, Pal Morty, Doctor Spin: black-curled and -mustachioed, twinklefaced, plump and graceful, surprisingly strong, agile, supple, light on his feet, is Mort, and hirsute head to toe; one of the few Otherwise Normals in our ship's company (married, two young daughters, Nice House in nearby East Cambridge, wife an obstetrician/gynecologist there) and one of the even fewer offspring of that town's half-dozen Jewish families — second-generation Americans, most of them, owners of the local clothing and furniture emporia until the suburban plaza chain-stores killed the town's downtown — who after "going off" to college actually returned to their hometown, their affection for the place outweighing its parochialism and limited economic opportunities. A fellow Hopkinsian now in his thirties (whose wife had done her ob/gyn residency at the *other* Johns Hopkins and was therefrom acquainted with Narrator's med-faculty parents), Mort could no doubt have made bigger bucks doing PR and ad-copywriting "over in the city," where too his wife's practice would unquestionably have been more lucrative; or they could have established themselves across the Choptank in more affluent Talbot County, the Gold Coast of Maryland's Eastern Shore. But Mort is happily bonded with raw, funky, ungentrified Cambridge, where (by his own testimony) his childhood had been all but free of anti-Semitism — in part because his dad was a much-respected civic leader as well as a prominent businessman, and Mort's two elder brothers had been star athletes at the old all-white Cam-

bridge High; in part because, even after World War II and the Holo-
caust, so few of his WASP schoolmates and neighbors knew quite
what Jews *were*. Something like Italians? In those early years of
forced racial integration in the Dorchester County public schools,
any differences of religion or ethnicity among white students must
have paled, so to speak, beside their collective difference from their
new Second Ward classmates. Even in the communal boys' gym
showers at the new North Dorchester High, testifieth Mort, thanks to
the general popularity of infant male circumcision in the Spock generation he was spared the anatomical teasing that he'd surely have
been subjected to a generation earlier. And so while most of his
high-school classmates who crossed the Bay to do their baccalaure-
ates — and nearly every one of the few non-*goyim* themamong —
came back thereafter only to visit, Mort and Rachel Spindler (she a
Pittsburgher, to whom smalltown Delmarva must have seemed as
much another world as to the Cuban and Indian medical émigrés
who've established their North American practices hereabouts) not
only returned but settled in for keeps, involved themselves busily in
the affairs of the community, and have even — not without acknowledged misgivings — enrolled their children in the county grade-
schools, supplemented with large doses of home education. High
school, they allow, may be another story, despite Mort's mainly-
fond memories of North Dorchester: Like Yrs Truly, Dr. Rachel was
herself privileged with a first-rate prep school, and she wants no less
for their girls — not least because her medical practice and her
volunteer Sex Ed presentations at the county's two high schools
have given her a fair glimpse of contemporary American smalltown
public-school adolescent girlhood: less scarifying by far than its
inner-city counterpart, but *oy gevalt*. . . .

   That Yiddish ejaculation is Rachel's. Both husband and wife are
the secular, assimilated offspring of more or less secular and assimilated parents, like Narrator's Doctor Mom; their own children, Mort
guesses, are about as aware of being "Jewish" as a third-generation
Irish- or German-American is aware of being "Irish" or "German"
— or they would so be except for the occasional grandparental
noodge, mainly reflexive in Rachel's opinion, to get them bat mitz-

vah'd when the time comes ("If you ever happen to forget you're Jewish," Mort likes to paraphrase Bernard Malamud, "some *bubbeh* or *zayde* will remind you"), and except further for the incontrovertible fact that "Oh dear!" and "My my!" just don't cut it like *Oy vay!* And so Doc Rachel, especially, finds that while she can manage readily without Friday-night candles and with only token acknowledgment even of High Holidays, and can be at least as critical of Israeli politics as is your average Israeli, she cannot dispense (once home from the office) with her lexicon of household Yiddish, in particular its arsenal of finely calibrated disparagements. Their American counterparts — *dork, wonk, nerd, geek, airhead* — are not without pungency, but they suffer the limitation of being slang and, ipso facto, like many things American, style-driven and evanescent: A teenager today who used such dated put-downs as *drip* and *square* would be branded forthwith as a [*supply appropriate current term*], but *nebbish, putz, shmuck, shmendrick, shlemiel, shlimazl,* and *shmeggege* are forever. Even Mort — whomto and to whose office we now return, and who likes to swear that his vocabulary was, excuse the expression, *Judenfrei* until he went off to college and allowed himself to be tapped by the Jewish social fraternity Alpha Epsilon Pi — finds the bounty irresistible, as do Yr Narrator and various other of the ship's company, once exposed it-to. "Bea Golden," to be sure, has run through several Jewish husbands and was moreover once upon a time in show biz, sort of, which-all accounts for her *gonifs* and *momsers, shnorrers* and *shtunks*; Sherry S. is her mother's daughter in this respect if not in most others, and thus seasons her talk with the odd *shlump, shmo,* and *shnook.* But one has heard even so intensely local-*goyishe* an item as our Capt. Adam. Andrew. Lake. exhorting our tugboat-skippers in mid-docking to give *T II* "just one more little noodge astern," VHFing the vowel not as in "fudge" but as in *nudnik* — which term in turn one has heard from perhaps the unlikeliest lips of all: a certain gender-ambiguous marsh-creature from the Maintenance & Engineering Team by the name of Ditsy, whom never You mind, just yet. In Morton Spindler's headshaking opinion, it may be that just as all that remains these days of the Chesapeake's once-abundant native Indians are their musical place-names, so too when American Jewry has been altogether assimilated, its onliving monument will be in the likes of *dreck* and *shmatte*, *futz* and *potske*—"And won't *that*," tisks Mort, "be a *farshtinkener* kettle of gefiltefish!"

So meet our valued-indeed teammate Doctor Spin already, if You haven't already: so denominated not alone for the dexterity wherewith, in his capacity as ship's publicist, he spins bad news into not-so-bad and not-so-bad into pretty-good-all-things-considered, but as well for his terpsichorean agility. Remarkably—indeed, almost incredibly for a boy brought up in a semi-rural, semi-southern small town—our plump and perky, even borderline-beefy Mort has since childhood been unabashedly enamored of *dancing*: not just the traditional ballroom steps and the pop dances of every recent decade, from Cakewalk and Charleston through Jitterbug and Bunny Hop and Frug and Electric Slide to whatever they're doing on MTV as one types this sentence, although Mort's a whiz at every one of those; not just assorted folk-dances, from the country-fiddlin' Square to the round *shtetl*-fiddlin' Hora, although he's a whiz at those as well—but also, first among equals . . . classical ballet!

It all started, declareth Mort, when one set of his grandparents, the last of the immigrant generation, at Chanukah-time bestowed upon Mort's older sister, then maybe ten, an intricate music-box, under the lid whereof, when the thing was wound and set a-tinkling, inch-high figures twirled, levitated, and intercircled to Chopin's *Polonaise*. Our boy, then five or six, happily imitated them until decked by vertigo, while his grandpa clapped and exhorted "Put pep, Morty! Put pep!" Either his mom or that same sister had observed that professional dancers and ice-skaters avoid vertigo when spinning by facing in a fixed direction for as long as possible while their bodies turn and then whipping the head around in one quick motion. Child Morton learned that trick in no time and thereafter spun and leaped and circled, while all hands clapped and all feet stomped and old Zayde called *"Put pep!"*

Pep he put, did undiscourageable Mort, right through the county public-school system and off to university and beyond. The inevitable redneck-macho taunts of sissification if not faggotry — taunts aggravated by his being the brightest boy in class — he countered with his prowess on the North Dorchester varsity wrestling team, his athletic energy as captain of the NDHS cheerleading squad, and his showstopping agility on the school-dance floor: a middleweight Michael Jackson before that fellow's time. He was even able, in his school's senior-year Christmastime production, to bring down the house with the Tarantella from the finale of Tchaikovsky's *Nutcracker*, danced perfectly straight except for a "put-pep" proto-moonwalk at the very end. And pep he puts still in our *Tidewater Follies* productions, as coach-choreographer and primo ballerino of our by-him-named Corpse de Ballet. Even at his office desk Mort seldom sits for more than a few minutes before whipping his head to one side, e.g., as if on cue; firing one arm out in that direction while curving the other *en haut*; then perhaps springing from his swivel-chair to strike some Balanchinish attitude and pirouetting around front to greet e.g. Yrs T, chanting as he springs ". . . -and-*two*, and-*spin*, and-*bow!*" Ending with knees *plié*, head low, left hand daintily aflutter behind, right hand proffering *"Le manuscrit, monsieur:* Show Barge, *par le grand Charles Un-tair,* courtesy of Gee Dash Dee's vicar in Dorsettown, Cap'n Andy et cetera!"

This is it? For 'twas no more than a single, evidently vintage typewritten title-page: *SHOW BARGE. A play in three acts.*

On his feet now in Position Whatever, "Makes Beckett look windy, no? I told you the guy's proto-Postmod! Top o' the mornin' t'ye, Johns!"

We did a high-five, Mort's customary greeting, whereafter "The rest's upstairs," he declared, *"chez le* Boss. All set?"

What we sought, however, he added en route to and in the Patmos Tower lift, was not to be found in fabled Suite 666, nor yet in comparably fabled 999, but in one of DTE's two conference rooms, #696—the other being (You guessed it) . . .

"And the difference *between* them being, I must now explain," Mort now explained as we rose through the high-rise and he did ballet exercises, using the elevator's handrail as a *barre*, "that whereas in Nine Six Nine one converses with the Word made flesh, in Six Nine Six—" he tapped on door of same, just across from the elevator; was answered by a breezy *"C'mon in, boys!"* and opened—"'tis vice versa. *Allons! Voilà!* Put pep!"

With a sweeping balletic After You he ushered Narrator into a handsomely paneled chamber overlooking Snug Harbour: subdued overhead lighting, oval conference table with three leather-upholstered chairs down each side, in its center the presumable playscript flanked by a brace of table-mikes, and at its head . . .

*"Make yourselves comfortable, Morty, Mister Hopkins. May I call you John?"*

Well . . .

"We call him Hop, sir," Mort informed the senior-citizenly face on the large closed-circuit, camera-topped television screen at the table's head end: a face lean and seamed, shrewd but not unkindly, pale-blue-eyed and white-wispy-haired, clean-shaven and eyeglass-free but sporting either a small earphone or a hearing aid in one Ross Perot–size ear. The wiry chap whose phiz it is was blue-double-breasted-suited, white-shirted, and red-bowtied, at ease in a chair like ours except with arms, at the end of a table like ours in a room like ours, presumably #969, where presumably he faced a TV screen with us-all on it.

Well.

*"Hop it is, then. Coffee and water on the sideboard, fellas; make yourselves to home."*

Thanks, but no; just fine, sir, Cap'n. Mort gestured Narrator to take the seat beside him, but on an impulse of experiment or mischief that fellow went 'round the table-end, even over to the sideboard, before seating himself across from Dr. Spin. Sure enough, with a little servomotor-whir the camera tracked him.

*"Checking things out, eh? Smart young fella!"*

One shrugged. Mort made a what-can-I-do-with-the-kid? gesture from his eloquent inventory.

*"We knew we had talent on our hands, and your new Follies routine proves it. What's its name again?"*

Hard to resist saying *Hop Johnson, sir,* but Mort got there first with *"That's Entertainment?* Ends with a question mark?"

*"Rightrightright: ve-ry clever! My compliments!"*

Actually a collaboration, one modestly protested: but G-D? wasn't interested in self-effacement. *"I look forward to shaking your hand in person someday soon, Hop Johnson. Meanwhile, I've told Miz Golden to tell Miz Singer full speed ahead on that production and damn the torpedoes! If she needs extra funding, she'll have it."*

"Thank you, sir!" thanked Mort, and flashed a *Thank-the-sumbitch* grin cross-table. The minicam whirred oneward; one nodded one's gratification for Arkangelical support.

*"That routine's gonna be your Number One of a One-Two punch that's gonna make TOFO Two the talk of tidewaterland!"* spake He. *"And your Number Two's right there in front of you! Mort's told y'all about it, right?"*

He hath, one almost responded, but managed Yup instead and reached for the script, atop which Mort had replaced the title page.

*"Handle with care, lad,"* warned He: *"Mort'll give you a copy to work with, but I wanted you to see the capital-O Original, 'cause the coincidence is almost too good to be true!"*

Or vice versa, one merely murmured under Himself's enthusing *"If y'all ever doubted the Almighty's got His eye on us, there's your proof, right? First the coincidence of that Edna-Ferber/Charlie-Hunter business in your Follies routine and Hunter's old playscript on the same subject that's been gathering dust in our Archives since we acquired the family papers in Ninety-three. And then the clincher that you just happen to be over to John Hopkins studying with [Etc.], who I'd give an eyetooth to have him write something specially for us! And they say God's dead?"*

Mort smiled Narratorward his ball's-in-your-court smile.

Actually, sir—

*"I know! Mort says you like to claim you're not really working with the guy, don't want to impose on him, blah blah blah. I respect that! But the fact remains that you* know *him and have access* to him *and we don't, and we're not likely to get a Yes if Mort just phones him out of the blue. Busybusybusy, right, like who isn't? But if one of his own students, that he knows and works with, shows him a gen-you-wine never-produced lost playscript from Adams's* Original Floating Theater, *that tells the untold story of its author's romance with Edna Ferber that led to* Show Boat, *and on top of that the script's unfinished and if he himself'll just give it a few final touches so we can produce it on TOFO Two, he'll be closing the circle on his*

*own life's work and Charlie Hunter's and Edna Ferber's and mine, all in one stroke! How's* that *grab you, John Hopkins Johnson?"*

"You can imagine the publicity tie-ins," earnestly put in Mort. "Especially with the big new *Show Boat* revival on Broadway. All the wire services, network news, Sunday-magazine features in the *Sun* and the *Post*, maybe even the *Times*. Maybe one of those *American Experience* documentaries on PBS about the showboat era, leading up to TOFO Two and our production of *Show Barge!*"

*"Terrific idea!"* seconded 969.

Waitwaitwaitwaitwait, Narrator felt obliged here to protest: Neither Mort nor I've even *read* the thing yet. Assuming it's authentic, how do we know it's not a bomb? A bonafide, authentic vintage turkey?

*"Not my department, gentlemen,"* quoth the unruffled apparition of Andrew S. "Todd 'Cap'n Andy' Andrews" Todd. *"Once you've satisfied yourself that the thing's authentic, Mort'll put it back in the vault and supply you with an authorized copy—not to leave the premises or be recopied, please, for obvious reasons. I happen to think you're gonna agree it's just exactly what we need to turn this showboat of ours around, if we can persuade* [Mm-Hm] *to sign on. If it looks to you like a bomb or a turkey, so what? Our job up here's to give you-all a showboat and at least the makings of a show; down there it's your and Mort's and* [That Other One]*'s job to turn bombs into fireworks and make turkeys fly! Am I right?"*

"Amen, sir!" actually cheered teammate Morton Spindler.

End of séance, virtual theophany, whatever. Pleased to've met me, Gee Dash Dee? declared Himself, and clicked off. Likewise, Narrator supposed to the fading dot on the now-dark tube, and then pointed interrogatively at the table-mikes by way of asking Mort whether we were still wired for sound. Eloquent Who-knows? shrug himfrom, and so one declared stagily Well now let's just see what we have here and, reserving one's pithier comments for later, riffled through the half-ream of more-than-half-century-old typescript.

"No reason to doubt it's the real McCoy," in Mort's opinion. Out of his chair now, he pepped about Conference Room 696 in assorted muscle-stretching attitudes. "You can look through the box of crapola it turned up in, 'fyou want to, and you're to offer your guy access to all such materials in our archives. D'you know who The Real McCoy was, by the way? And-*two!* And-*three!* Kid McCoy, turn-of-the-century American boxer, real name Selby Something-or-Other or Something-or-Other Selby. Or *Shelby*, maybe. Something or other. And-*four!*"

Mm. For one's eye had chanced upon a specimen exchange from the apparently only half-dramatized scenario of *Show Barge*'s second act—

CHARLES [*appalled, to* BEULAH]: *You* did it! You scuttled the Ark to keep us from accepting Edna's invitation to the Broadway premiere of *Show Boat*!

BEULAH: No! No! [*Then, weeping*] But I *wanted* to! [*Then, angrily*] And I *should've*, after what you and she did! And I *will*, by golly, if you don't cash that doggone *check* of hers and get her out of our life completely!

—and this directorial note toward the close of Act Three: *Audience to choose by voice or show of hands either Ending #1 (straight theater), Ending #2 (straight film), or Ending #3 (Cinestage).*

Cinestage? Back in . . . no date on typescript, but Mort had mentioned "late 1930s," and internal evidence—German U-boats off Chesapeake Bay in Ending #2, references to the Floating Theatre's self-advertised Final Season but none to its actual destruction in November 1941—suggested a date as late as but no later than 1940/41 for this anticipation of what, forty years later, would be called Intermedia Art. One was hooked—this one, anyhow—even before one arrived at the One Drop and Mingling of Essences themes, the Jewish Gaylord Ravenal, "Beulah Hunter's" leaping from the *OFT*'s upper deck like Puccini's Tosca from the battlements, and the playwright's playing himself playing himself. Copy shmoppy, one told good Mort: Let's you'n me read the sumbitch right through right here right now. For quite apart from its possible utility as bait for the Novelist Emeritus and POWERFUL PLAY for *TOFO II*, "Charles Hunter's" *Show Barge* (as it certainly appeared to be) struck Yr Novelist Aspirant as Just What He Maybe Needed for the centerpiece of his aspiring e-novel, *COMING SOON!!!*: the story-with-in-the-story that is also the story *of* the story, or story *in utero*.

And so read it we did, till lunchtime and beyond, there in 696 in 4/95, whisking page after dog-eared, pencil-edited page cross-table from Yrs T to Teammate Spindler, who punctuated our critical ejaculations — Hey, wow, get *this*! Cheap shot, Charlie! Good move here, though! K-I-M means *K*oshered *I*n *M*aryland? Come *on*, Charlie-babe! — with cell-phonecalls to his secretary and a pizza delivery to see us through.

'T's a piece of crap, one was obliged in all candor to conclude at the conclusion of Ending #3 of Act III. But an *extraordinary* piece of crap, no? — by a smalltime, smalltown, unsophisticated and ultimately unsuccessful old tent-show and vaudeville hack thirty years ahead of his time. *Show Barge* was precocious not only in its means and its metaphysics — the audacious mixing of fact and fiction, or life and art (one pointed out to Mort the likelihood that Hunter meant the thing to be played during the *OFT*'s provisionally advertised Final Season, just as the script declares in Act III, so that the audience's choice of endings would literally influence, if not determine, the showboat's future), as well as live theater and film — but equally in its themes. Imagine dramatizing, in the racially segregated, more-or-less-redneck tidewaterland of 1940, the cruelties of racial bigotry and anti-Semitism!

"Talk about bringing down the house," Mort marveled: "Fifty-five years ago they'd've sunk the showboat and lynched the author-character! But in Nineteen Ninety-five — *dynamite*!" That was exactly, in his professional opinion, the angle to promote: Make the homefolks proud of how far they've come since the Bad Old Days! "It oughta help hook your guy, too, right? He may not remember the last lynching in Cambridge, back in his childhood, but he took a stand on the Sixties riots" — when black civil-rights activists in the town's Second Ward, stirred by the incendiary H. "Rap" Brown, set fire to a number of neighborhood buildings and had to be restrained by the National Guard from marching on the downtown business district when the chief of police forbade the all-white volunteer fire company to enter the Second Ward. ("You [bastards] brought Rap Brown here," he was reported to have told black businessmen pleading with him to save their burning establishments: "Put out your own damn fires.")

Valued teammate, it was time to tell one's valued teammate: One is more than happy to've neglected one's academic responsibilities in order to shlep over here, converse with the televised Arkangel-in-Chief, and peruse this presumably authentic and, in its way, really quite remarkable proto-Postmodernist wacko turkey-bomb of a playscript—all the more appealing to Yrs T in its quote-unquote *unfinished* condition, whole stretches of it summarized instead of dramatized, in effect mixing prose narrative with theater as well as theater with film, et cetera—

"Heyhey, you're right!" Mort cheered, fifth-positioning in the down-bound elevator. "More mingling of essences!"

For the afore-established Reasons A, B, and C, however, one will not not *not* disturb itwith the presumably creative peace of Not-My-Guy—he being, damn it, *not my guy*. So sue me, Mort. Fire me. Excommunicate me. Won't do it.

Allowed spinning Dr. Spin, "I'll tell Cap'n Andy you've gotta think it over. You *should*, too, man! The guy can say No, for Chrissakes!" *Entrechat* in hallway, between elevator and office door. "So suppose he *does* say No: You'll've done your bit, and we're off the hook with Gee Dash Dee! Wouldja wanna take a crack at it then yourself?"

Forget it, man! One has a novel to compute! Grad-school comin' soon! . . .

Undeterred, "So you use it in your novel while we use it on-stage!" Mort argued—and then, feet *croisée* and eyes alight, "*Interaction*, right? Like Charlie's pick-an-ending shtick interacts with both the audience and the real-life situation, you let your user-interactive e-novel interact with Charlie's interactive *Show Barge*!"

Yeah, sure, right, one scoffed reflexively—but then bethought oneself: Hey, Mort! Like, wow?

"You're welcome!" *Glissade* through office doorway. "And-*four!*"


"Can we, like, mingle essences right now?" Sherry Singer wondered toward that afternoon's end, when I stopped by her Snug Harbour apartment to touch base and more before hauling back to Baltimore (the woman rolls her astonishing eyes at the idea of living in a gated retirement community, but her rent-free pad is among the Arkade Theatre Company's directorial perks), and wound up rehearsing to her in detail the story-line of *Show Barge*. "I mean, like, make it hop before you run?"

Sigh, Reader: Such is the tidal pull of Narrative—upon us tidewater apprentice narrators, anyhow—and its consequent eddies, vortexes, and countercurrents, that one finds oneself pants-down and cock-up with Ms. S. McA. S. for the severaleth time in this extended chapter (this time a full month earlier than the "present," when we commenced her introduction) without having really "done" her yet, despite one's serial approaches theretodoing, in the way one finally "did" Doctor Spin. Why it is, e.g., that if, while dressing or undressing, one thoughtlessly yanks one's belt from its belt-loops, thupthupthup*thup*, that deliciously tough-but-not-invulnerable woman flinches at the sound—as does one's heart at the sight thereof? Time once again, maybe, in the spirit of Act III ("Show Barge") of Chas. Hunter's *Show Barge*, to offer our virtual audience (You, luv), three options:

> **On with Introduction.**

> **Hold Introduction;**
> **On with Story already.**

> **Hell with Introduction;**
> **Hell with Story;**
> **Let's fuck.**

On with Story it is, then, O Model of Narrative Discipline and Venereal Restraint: "I'm with you," Sher declared, as indeed she postcoitally still was (back in mid-springtime, we mean, in her Snug

Harbour apartment, and again "now" in her candlelit cabin aboard *TOFO II* in the cast-off narrative present, if we ever hop our way therebackto), and Yrs Truly with her, hauling back he into his jeans and she her sweatpants. "With or without Your Guy on board, we're talking next season earliest for this *Show Barge* thing, right? By when you'll be all but done with school and ready to get cracking fulltime on whatever."

You should see Ms. Sherry Singer slip postcoitally into her clothes. To see Ms. Sherry Singer slip postcoitally into her clothes is to re-crave the sight of her slipping precoitally out themof. "So *this* season let's see what we can do with *That's Entertainment?* — maybe work some bits from Hunter's script into our new frame for the *Follies*? And if you can make use of it in your school project [as Sher was pleased to call the opus-in-hand, as if it were an eighth-grade social studies research paper], so much the better: two birds with one stone." Bra hooked on backward, below the bubbyline, then spun 'round to cup its perfect cargo. "Put the whole fucking *Follies* on disk, if it floats your boat! This time next year you'll be out from under GreatUnc Whatsisname; maybe *then* you can pitch the guy to lend us a hand, if we're still in business and still want his help. If Mort wants him pitched before then, let Mort pitch him."

All this while slipping et cetera, her every agile motion whereof rebestirring Narrator's just-expended male essences. But Nope, one found oneself saying: Grateful as one was for one's immediate superior's postcoital support, one had come, so to speak, to an altered perspective on the matter of "pitching" C. Hunter's *Show Barge* at one's sort-of-mentor. Even in mid-essence-mingling (discreetly passed over this time through) one had found one's imagination a-hop with *Show Barge*'s possibilities as an anticipatory paradigm, shall we say, of *TOFO II*'s present plight and, by extension, of one's hypertextual COMING SOON!!! And even as one came (sooner, in these hopped-up circumstances, than one would otherwise have wished), one understood that it was no longer for one's GreatUnc Ennie's sake that one wished him unaware of *Show Barge*'s very existence, but rather for one's apprentice own.

*Now*, then, darling Interactor: Push Button Three, begorrah, or one'll push the little rascal Youfor:

```
┌─────────────────────────────┐
│        D'you mean,          │
│          at last,           │
│        Let's us . . . ?     │
└─────────────────────────────┘
```

No no no, Cybercomrade! Be ye neither alarmed nor on the other hand overhopeful! Of J. Hop Johnson, after all this chatter, one daresays You have some idea; but what does JayHop know of You, beyond Your admirable willing-to-give-it-a-gohood thus far, wherefor he's truly grateful? You may be, e.g., of the male persuasion; JHJ's 100-proof hetero, and so for better or worse there goes that. Or You may be female but Not His Type — No offense intended; *de gustibus* etc.! — although Your obliging persistence in this cybertale most certainly speaks well for You. Or You may be the companion of his dreams, sexually as well as narratively — his Aristophanic other half, we each the other's perfect fit, body-and-soulmates — and be clicking that momentous button, moreover, while Yr Narrator's still alive and more or less able (he is, let's remember, freshly come from two flashback Singer-sessions already and has another to reprise ere this chapter's impending close). But even in that case — Sigh! — we recall that it doth indeed Take Three to Tango: Not You/Hop/Sher — piquant as that kinky notion might for all one knows strike You (and even, in certain humors, her) — but Teller/Tale/Told. And bee-busy as You've been in that T$^{3rd}$ capacity, clicking Your course through T$^{2nd}$ as't pleaseth You via the menus provided by T$^{1st}$, nowhere themamong will You find Literal Sexual Congress twixt T's 1 & 3, as was the case e.g. twixt Ms. Scheherazade and King Shahryar, her imperious auditor. *That* sort of thing went out, more's pity, with, shall we say, the oral tradition.

Just thought we ought to get that straight, Luv, be You thereby relieved or vexed. But lookee: Here in formal form's yet another me'n'u option — one that, to be sure, has been from the first Yours to exercise at any moment, any word, but which one hopes You'll forbear from opting before this chapter's end (COMING SOON!!!):

```
┌─────────────────────────────┐
│    Buzz off, wiseass.       │
└─────────────────────────────┘
```

Roger that. Hopped back to Hopkins, did Yrs T (we mean last April), and, at risk of displeasing G-D?'s virtual Arkangel-in-Chief, did *not* straightaway bait that institution's Novelist Emeritus with tidings of C. Hunter's lostandfound *Show Barge* script, but right busily, through Preview Season, cannibalized bits and pieces therefrom both for our *Tidewater Follies '95* and for the cybernovel at Yr presumable present fingertips. "He's feeling the situation out," spun good Dr. Spin to "Bea Golden" and Co.; "he'll let us know when the time's right to make our pitch." And to Yrs T, "They're getting nudgy, Hop. . . ." Wound up the old baccalaureate in May as aforenarrated; bye-byed one's lez-lit roomie Sybil and patient parents; Cherrykeed *TOFO-II*ward, Main Seasonward, Sherry Singerward —with but one detour, to check out the Solomons Island Competition. Checked out and checked off same as Coming No Time Soon, not to worry—and there encountered, by most-improbable-though-not-impossible coincidence, the real, the surely formidable, the unanticipated-even-by-himself Competition: Unofficial GreatUncular Mentor v. More-or-Less Mentee; Emeritus *Grise* v. Green Apprentice; p-medium v. e-; our suddenly-declared Battle of the Showboat-sagas; our race to the millennial wire! . . .

What one's saying, Readie, even as per orders one buzzes off (aboard *TOFO II* now, under way from Snug Harbour down the Choptank to commence our 1995 Main Season at Oxford, Easton, and St. Michaels), is that that Ontological, Novelists-Only Lunchbreak back there back then appears to've had the side-effect of one-eightying Yr Narrator like *T II*'s tugs in tight quarters and inspiring him with the following hastily improvised Grand Strategy: So far from insulating oneself (along with one's showboat and showboat-story and *Show Barge* turkeybombscript) from one's Competition, and him likewise from them, one would set about to enmesh One's Guy hilt-deep themin; to distract the bejesus himoutofthemwith on pretext of offering him — *him*, the least Edna-Ferberish, the least go-immerse-oneself-in-one's-materialish of novelists — what must surely strike him as all but irresistible Material. Let Mort spin him the *Show Barge* spiel and entreat him aboard as Playdoctor-in-Residence, with the added come-on not only that our *Original Floating*

*Opera II* was after all by him inspired, sort of, but that we've a mini-zoo of 'ministrators—"Todd Andrews," "Bea Golden"—more or less modeling themselves upon characters of his presumable invention. Aye and aye!: Involve him to the Plimsoll and beyond, we would, with Saving Our Ship in expectation of cargoing his own, while Yours Truly's cyberversion scrolleth ahead like *T II* at warp-speed behind full-throttled *Dove* and *Raven*—Coming Soon! Sooner!! Soonest!!!—itself now both cargoed with and powered by the downloading tale of GreatUnc's enmeshment, our novelistic head-to-headhood, and the eventual, *inevitable* triumph of Apprentice- over Emeritusship, Green over Gray!

Not that one wished the old gent ill, mind—one respected, one duly admired, one even sort of *liked* the guy?—but that's show biz, Ace, and lit biz too. And okay, we're not talking *War and Peace* or *Moby-Dick* here, but what the hey, it's 1995.5 these days: Cold War thawed (perhaps by global warming?); our astro- and their cosmonauts mating in orbit; local loonies bombing federal buildings in Oklahoma; CTV and the Internet replacing Real Life even as one clicks. . . . We work with what's left.

Such as? Ah, well: Such as . . . the thing speeding ustoward from 4.5 years down the road and rendering every "teen"-date, from 1300 through 1999, already quaint (that these nineteen-hundreds are called the twentieth century is mere numerical perversity, although no doubt it lubricates the transition, like being already in one's twentieth year at age nineteen). Such as . . . the millennial-apocalyptic foofaraw that that arbitrary time-mark, a mere cultural-historical convention, is provoking already and will inevitably up-ratchet as the countdown downcounts. Such as (Narrator had already begun a-musing well before that Ontological Lunchbreak, and found himself increasingly possessed by thereafter) . . . a NEW SHOW for *TOFO II* and for one's e-novel thereabout: a NEW SHOW to make Chas. Hunter's (and soon GreatUnc Ennie's) creakyleaky old *Show Barge* seem the nineteen-hundredy affair it is; an apocalyptic fooferall of a NEW SHOW for the new century and millennium—Yours Truly's century and millennium!—having to do with the end of the old,

*COMING SOON!!!*

Which, come to think of it, would do nicely for its title, or perhaps subtitle: *End Time (Coming Soon!)*. A winner: All that remained was to *write* the thing, or two, thus titled. And so "He's ready," had opined Hop Johnson to Mort Spindler back there in Dorsettown-on-Choptank back in this chapter's early pages — meaning, really, that oneself was ready for Doctor Spin to bait the hook, pay out his line, snag Big Fish Emeritus, and reel the sucker in, while oneself got down to more pressing business with the muse and Sherry Singer.

So off I buzz, Sport; You should be so lucky. Play with Your little buttons now, there's a good lad.

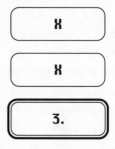

# 1995.3

*"Let your guard down,"*
had advised Mr. Morton Spindler of Dorset Tradewinds Enterprises
Inc. This by way of inviting the "Novelist Emeritus Character" —
luring him, daring him, whatever — to "come out of [his] shell" and
down to Dorsettown-on-Choptank to view firsthand *The Original
Floating Opera II*, meet its principal functionaries, and inspect that
playscript allegedly left unfinished by the late Charles Hunter of
James Adams's old showboat company, with an eye to "developing"
it for production by the Arkade Theatre Company. Indeed, picking
up unwittingly and fortuitously on our Engine Trouble theme from a
previous episode, that ebullient fellow had gone on to say "Maybe
just toss that sumbitch guard overside and *full speed ahead*, you follow me?!"

Yes, well, I had replied — which turned out to mean Yes and No:
One understood his recommendation, all right, but would by no
means necessarily act upon it. A large (and vulnerable) receptiveness to novelty in general and new experience in particular is natural
and proper for the young; by one's mid-seventh decade, however
(*this* one's, anyhow), habit and experience — including the habit of
succeeding, or at least not failing, and the experience of seeing others fail, or at least not succeed — make one indeed more guarded, although one endeavors not to ossify altogether. "Old oyster!"
Spindler had gone so far as to tease me, and I'd bade him shuck off.
For us seniors, Zeno's tortoise is an apter image: We move cir-

cumspectly and carry our shells with us, understanding that the race is not always to the swift, less often yet to the reckless and impulsive. *Audacity*, to be sure, is another matter, as are Spontaneity and Intuitiveness: Virtues all, and so at the end of the day my totem of choice is the hermit crab, who fares forth upon his life-business with his vulnerabilities safely housed in his (carefully chosen) carapace until such time as he finds he has outgrown it, whereupon with (deliberate) audacity and (programmed) discernment he exchanges it for one more suitable.

In the event, what got "tossed overside" meby was neither "guard" nor "shell," but those clunky metaphors, and with them that unwieldy artifice of a fake third-person narrative viewpoint—"your Narrator," "the Novelist 'Emeritus,'" etc. *C'est moi moi-même*, Reader: first-person singular, whose guardshell henceforward will be that pronoun only. Ample wiggle-room therein, I trust, for its antecedent.

That baggage tossed, I didn't after all take Spindler up on his invitation. Through the rest of June and a record-breaking hot July that killed eight-hundred-plus Americans, I pursued my usual and regular pursuits: among them, making further notes toward a possible Next Last Book, that maybe-novel suggested by the conjunction of the approaching millennium, my happening upon the derelict COMING SOON! in Solomons Harbor, and my chance encounter there with the bodacious J. H. Johnson. Indeed, I even drafted a couple of trial starts thereto—e.g., a hedged letter of recommendation from an unnamed "Novelist Emeritus" for a maverick "Novelist Aspirant"—as one does sometimes in search of the right narrative approach to a large and still unclear new project while exploring its salient images (chiefly, in this instance, the dubious-but-hopeful vessel itself) and projecting characters and main lines of action.

Thus the mornings, your working fictionist's year-round Usual and Regular, interspersed (as is our waterfront summer season's usual and regular) by welcome visits from our farflung family. The afternoons, as is also our U&R, my wife and I spent on routine chores and errands and subtropical summer diversions, keeping a weather eye on the busy Atlantic hurricane season, which would run that summer from Allison through Opal but mercifully spare the Chesapeake. No follow-up phonecalls from Spindler, to my relief. Jiffy-bagged in the early-July mail, however, there arrived from Dorset Tradewinds Enterprises Inc. (*Dorsettown-on-Choptank MD 21614*) a photocopy of *Show Barge: A Play in Three Acts*. Authentic on the face of it as to period—old manual-typewriter fonts, the uneven inking from overused fabric ribbons, the penciled emendations and revisions in clear though crabbed longhand, without the copy-editing symbols and other manuscript conventions of the professional—it bore on its title page a Day-Glo chartreuse Post-It inscribed *When Mohammed wouldn't go to the mountain . . .* and, below that truncated proverb, *Still hopefully, M.S.*

Yes, well. The mountain, I assumed, was the playscript; I took its sending as a last-ditch (anyhow *next*-ditch) teasing come-on, and while I had no interest in developing it for production, I looked through it during that same torrid, air-conditioned afternoon both out of general curiosity and to see whether any aspects or details of it might be usable for my own project-not-quite-in-the-works. It was, I found, altogether as Spindler had described and summarized it at length by telephone: a curious combination of smalltime theatrical savvy and authorial inexperience, if not ineptitude; the work of one more familiar with producing and acting in stageplays (typically melodramas and broad comedies) than with scripting them. One, moreover, well acquainted with the Adams showboat and Edna Ferber's connection thereto, and with enough formal imagination and cinema-experience (however narrow) to conceive of those alternative endings done in varying media—a sort of down-home proto-Postmodernism after all. If, as alleged, the thing had surfaced among the late Charles Hunter's effects, then (absent proof to the contrary by handwriting and typescript analysis) it seemed reasonable to suppose that he was indeed its author, and not at all impossible that something like Morton Spindler's scenario for its composition was correct: a belated effort on Hunter's part to mend fences with the new owners of *The Original Floating Theater* and join forces themwith to keep the operation afloat.

So? So I would drop the sender a note of thanks, reaffirming my opinion that *Show Barge* was a not-unfascinating specimen of less-than-professional playwriting and a worthy item of Chesapeakia—showboatiana, whatever—for DTE's archives. Want to have a look? I asked my mate, to whom I had reported that earlier phone-talk and described the script.

"Not unless you tell me I should. You know what I think." Which was (and I agreed) that I would probably do well "not to get involved" with Hop Johnson & Co.—she hadn't *disliked* the young man, but had found his breezy chutzpah a touch unsettling—although of course such decisions were ultimately mine to make as my professional judgment inclined.

Amen.

"The thing seems to be real, by the way," she added—meaning not *Show Barge* but the vessel Johnson referred to as *TOFO II*. "You know how once your attention's been called to a thing you start noticing it where you didn't before?"

Indeed.

"Well, I noticed in last week's paper that it's coming to Chestertown."

Really. You didn't mention it. . . .

"Guess I figured you'd see it."

Ah. Coming when? For that week's issue of the county newspaper, along with two weeksworth of the daily Baltimore *Sun* and the Sunday *New York Times*, had been recycled already.

My wife—best friend, companion and lover, editor of first resort, indispensable helpmeet etc. etc., whose role in this story will hereforward (at her urging) be minimized if not altogether outedited, as for that matter she much wishes her husband's could be—shrugged: "Soon?"

An unexpected new dimension to Spindler's Post-It proverb. Sure enough, in next day's mail or the day after's came a similarly return-addressed envelope containing a pair of complimentary tickets for each night of *The Original Floating Opera II*'s upcoming two-night stand at the old steamboat landing at the foot of High Street in Chestertown, where it would be featuring (both nights) TIDEWATER FOLLIES '95. *Afternoon tours of historic showboat available at no extra charge*, the tickets declared—fudging the adjective "historic," it seemed to me, who reflected as well that James Adams's original *Floating Theatre* had not regarded itself as historic; it simply and unselfconsciously *was*, until, Ferberized, it became *The Original Show Boat*, *The Original Floating Theater*, et seq. The tickets were paperclipped together with another Post-It, Day-Glo cerise this time:

SHOWBOAT 'ROUND YOUR BEND!

Mm-hm. Before it rounds that bend, a bit of geographical scene-setting may be in order: Our modest Eastern Shore establishment fronts, as aforementioned, one wide fork of a tidal creek, with a long view south down the even wider confluence of that creek's twin forks and the wider-yet Chester River beyond, some fifteen tranquilly winding miles below Chestertown. From the workroom where I draft this tranquilly winding sentence (mid-September '98, the global economy in precarious pass, the Republican majority in the U.S. House of Representatives making political hay of Independent Prosecutor Kenneth Starr's titillatingly detailed report of President Clinton's *liaisons amoureuses* with a young White House intern), the water-view extends some eight miles south, past Island Point, Drum Point, and Piney Point down to Hail Point, where the river hooks west under Eastern Neck Island and up to meet the Chesapeake. Hail Point takes its name from the circumstance that eighteenth-century sailing vessels bound for the colonial customs port of Chestertown were routinely "hailed" there, so that news of their names, home ports, cargoes, and approach could precede their arrival. The distant point itself, low-lying and treeless, can't be seen from where I sit a-scribbling, but any large-enough vessel rounding it can, on a clear day. It is not unusual for me, between sentences or sentence-members, to look up and out while the next words phrase themselves for scription; it *is* unusual—even rare these days, when virtually none but crabbers, clammers, oysterers, and pleasure-boaters ply the Chester—to glance up from some dash or semicolon and see something large enough to be seen turning the (invisible) green can-buoy down there that marks the Hail Point shoal and heading ponderously upriver.

Usward. Meward.

At that distance, even a large vessel is little more than a speck; in this case a mainly white speck, perhaps boxy, with perhaps a black speck or two before or beside it — the ensemble set off by a gray-green line of trees along Blackbeard's Reach (named for the notorious pirate, who frequented these waters) on the far shore of the river-bend. Deep into the trial episode under my pen — "Same Old Story," about an aging novelist, temporarily stymied, who sets sail down that same river-stretch half in search of inspiration — I didn't immediately think to wonder . . . And then I did, and fetched a pair of 7 x 50 marine binoculars that we keep handy for stargazing and waterfowl-identification. My workroom windowscreen fuzzed the image. I stepped out into the humid yard; refocused. Big-boxy indeed, black-barge-mounted, twin-tug-towed — it could be nothing other, and though still miles off, it looked to be aiming directly our way.

As, to be sure, it would need to do for some while yet, whatever its upstream destination, in order to follow the river-channel north until, off the mouth of our creek, that channel turns northeast for Chestertown. I called my mate from *her* workroom, across and down the hallway from mine, to come see.

"Well, now." She handed back the binoculars. "Let me know if it rams us. Otherwise" — her tone went italic — "*leave me out of this*, okay?"

Okay. I too returned to work, anyhow tried to, drafting Narrator's and Mate's first sight of the would-be *James Adams II* in Solomons Harbor, COMING SOON! But yonder Relative Reality lumbering upstream was the very antidote to concentration; phrase by phrase and clause by clause I watched it draw nearer. Off Piney Point (by my estimate) it could be seen that while one of the towboats pulled straight forward, the other was offset at a bit of an angle, whether as a corrective or to commence the turn to starboard that the river, the channel, and the vessel should be making soon, if not quite yet. On it came, its tugs maintaining that odd angle. Must be some sort of corrective, then. Now, surely, I judged, the turning maneuver could be expected — but onward the thing continued, straight up our pipe, white bow-wave visible now at the barge's squared-off front end and strings of decorative pennants a-flutter along its superstructure. While it would doubtless be dwarfed by the mighty containerships and bulk carriers that ply the Bay, a mighty mother it was to see advancing up the placid Chester, where almost nothing its size had ventured since the days of steamships and, well, showboats. *Now*, I said to myself, it must surely begin its turn, and we'll see its full broadside length as it heads for the red-and-green mid-channel buoy out there somewhere and proceeds upriver.

But on it came, and on.

Bye-bye, Muse. I capped my pen and stepped outside again with the binoculars. Our creek, though broad, is shallow, like much of tidewaterland; its channel — unmarked except for a trio of green can-buoys down near its mouth — shoals rapidly from perhaps two dozen feet to more like a dozen at mean low water, and winds among unmarked sandbars that extend from those aforenamed wooded points farther than one might suppose. Indeed, one of our summer diversions is to watch unwary weekend sailors misjudge the extent of Island Point Shoal, just across from us, and to predict the moment when they'll run rudely but harmlessly aground and have either to back off or to hail a passing motorboat for assistance before renegotiating their passage. This with drafts in the range of four to six feet. Flat-bottomed barges like the one (still!) massively approaching might for all their bulk draw no more than that, but surely those tugboats would. Moreover, although the creek is easily half a mile wide where it forks at Cacaway Island, and no less than a third of a mile still where it passes our house, its channel is considerably narrower. No way a floating theater and its towboats could pay us a visit.

Yet on they came, as if bent upon doing precisely that: up past Cans "3" and "5," out of the river, into the creek-mouth proper, and up toward "7," the last of the markers, where the channel narrows and swings close to the creek's east bank before forking at Cacaway. The tugs, I noted, were snugged now port and starboard at the barge's bows to squeeze between that mark and the shore; clearly, their skippers knew their trade and had a watchful eye on chart and depthsounder. Thenceforward, however, navigating our creek would be a matter of what mariners call "local knowledge": just how far one needs to swing to port *right now* in order to avoid the shallows on the southwest quarter of Cacaway, and how hard an S-turn one must then make to clear the Island Point shoal.

I don't believe it, I told my wife, who had joined me on our dock to watch.

"I don't *want* to believe it."

Now we could hear the tugboats' rumbling engines; I imagined their mighty propellers churning up the creek-bottom not far below their keels. And soon after—as, by golly, they turned Can "7" and in tight unison swung themselves and their huge tow smartly north-westward, not straight our way but, properly, toward Island Point itself—there blared usward an amplified calliope playing "Sailing Down Chesapeake Bay." At that angle we could now see THE ORIGINAL FLOATING OPERA II lettered along the showboat's starboard side, then along its port side when it made the almost 90-degree turn northeastward, the center of the S (more correctly, the Ƨ), to clear Island Point Shoal. Astonished crabbers paused on their trotlines; pleasure-boaters getting an early start on the week-end swung clear, properly yielding right of way to a vessel "constrained by its draft" (as the Coast Guard's Collision Regulations phrase it) if ever there was one, and then tagging along behind to see what in the world was afoot.

> *Come on, Nancy, put your best dress on!*
> *Come on, Nancy, 'fore the steamboat's gone!*
> *Everything's lovely on the Chesapeake Bay —*
> *All aboard for Baltimore!*
> *If we're late we'll all be sore. . . .*

Now they turned hard a-port once more to round the shoal and headed hugely westward, straight up our fork. Whistles blew. Crab-bers, water-skiers, and neighbors waved; seagulls circled, ospreys wheeled, a great blue heron squawked and flapped off toward some-where quieter—as we, too, rather felt like doing. Now several fig-ures appeared on the showboat's roof-deck, facing our way and waving usward. In mid-channel exactly before our property, the tugs hard-reversed and stopped still, broadside to us just a couple hundred yards off our dock. The fivesome — three men and two women, all in shorts and tank tops — lined up in alternating gender, linked arms, and high-kicked to the music:

> *Banjos ringing a good old tune,*
> *And up on deck there's a place to spoon. . . .*
> *Sailing down the Chesapeake,*
> *All aboard for Chesapeake!*
> *Sailing down Chesapeake Ba-a-ay!*

The short, skinny, bespectacled central male I recognized even without binocular assistance as Hop Johnson, flanked by two trim young white women, a muscular young black man, and a plumpish, less young, but equally limber white man. As the tugboats (*Raven* and *Dove*, I could read now on their bows) spun THE ORIGINAL FLOATING OPERA II in a tight counterclockwise circle, the chorus line danced its way astern and around from starboard to port side, facing always usward. More whistle-blasts signaled Forward; the ensemble got ponderously under way to retrace its tricky entrance; the amplified music cut from Dixie jazz to hard rock, the dance from high-kick chorus to do-your-own-thing boogie. The only words clearly intelligible across our increasing distance were *Make it hop!* . . . until, after Island Point, the music stopped and the chorus waved good-bye.

Remarkably, the enormous three-in-one threaded its way back out of the creek and into the river without grounding: an extraordinary bit of piloting. At the farthest green can, it hung a left and headed on upriver.

*"Well, now,"*
my wife said — like her husband, more impressed than delighted by the spectacle: "That was a come-on, we gather?"

We do.

"And do we come on, I hope not? You, I mean?" Her general feeling, which I quite shared, was that, other things equal, a novelist probably does better to find fresh material than to recycle his/her past work, tempting as that notion demonstrably is to many a fictioneer from Homer onward, not to mention moviemakers, TV programmers, and authors of bestselling self-help books. Moreover, I had recycled already my showboat theme and characters nearly twenty years ago, which was twenty-plus years after their debut. Did I mean to recycle them cyclically?

Not a bad idea, I teased, now that you mention it. Then at age ninety I'll recycle 'em again, the way Sophocles did with Oedipus.

Just kidding. But shall we catch the show, at least, now that they have our attention? How often do we get live entertainment out here in the boonies?

"How often do we want it?"

Point taken. But we went after all, a touch warily, to have a look at *Tidewater Follies '95* — choosing seats near the rear of the house instead of the front-row ones that our tickets indicated, in order to keep open the option of an unobtrusive exit if, as was not infrequently the case with us and Theater, we decided early on that we'd had enough. We went, and we rather admired the sight of *TOFO II* at the foot of Chestertown's old High Street: A larger, handsomer vessel it was than James Adams's rough-and-ready Floating Theatre, but, like the original, pleasingly free of the steamboat-gothic furbelows of its Mississippi counterparts and their latter-day replicas, and quite at-home-looking in that eighteenth-century neighborhood. A fair crowd (but only half a house-full, it would turn out) flowed itward through the balmy evening from nearby parking lots and the little town's business district, two blocks away, greeting friends and neighbors, as did we, en route to the box office — an agreeable smalltown summer-evening sight. I had wondered whether our sizable black community would show at all or perhaps shun the thing out of discomfort at the traditional association of showboats with blackface minstrelsy; in fact not many turned out, but their scarcity we decided was owing less likely to unpleasant historical memory than to admission prices fairly steep (adults $10, children under twelve $5) for a predominantly bluecollar community. We went, and chose our easy-ejection seats as noted, and approved the theater's spacious, simple, gingerbread-free interior, and scanned our programs, which provided a capsule history of *TOFO II*, its avatars in fact and fiction, Ms. Edna Ferber's acknowledged debt to the James Adams Floating Theatre, the tantalizing possibility of some extramarital romantic attachment between her and Adams's artistic director Charles Hunter, and the recent discovery of an unfinished play on that subject "apparently by the late Mr. Hunter himself," which the Arkade Theatre Company "hopes to produce someday for *TOFO II*." Et cetera. We duly applauded the Pit Bulls' appearance in the pit (I saw Hop Johnson scan the house before taking his place behind the drums) and their spirited rendition of the same tune that they'd loudspeakered usward earlier in the day. And then we came near to auto-ejecting when, just after, a somewhat stiffstern fellow in captainly uniform welcomed us-all aboard, introduced himself (one word at a time, as if putting a period after each) as Captain. Adam. Lake., and expressed his gratification at being back in beautiful Chestertown. And at having as special guests in tonight's audience Mr. and Mrs. [us]. The Mister of whom he had reason to believe was currently writing something expressly for The Original Floating Opera Two! "But let's not embarrass him and his good wife further than that [*Chuckles from audience, looking around as we cover our faces with our programs and shrink down in our seats*]. Let's go *on. With the show!*" But we stayed put after all, if only because rising and exiting at that point would have made us even more conspicuous. We merely shook our heads as the house lights welcomely dimmed and the music rose (recorded now rather than live, for the Pit Bulls had other things to do) and the curtain opened on a setting evocative both of *Show Boat* and of the scene outside: wharf-piles, a lookalike of the Adams Floating Theatre painted hugely on the backdrop and tidewater-clapboard buildings on each side, along with an actual vintage wooden-sided Ford station wagon to establish the period. On the building-front Stage Left, the set designer had cleverly hung a sign reading CHESTERTOWN, presumably changed for each port of call.

The show? Not bad, actually, although at least some measure of the audience's receptiveness was no doubt akin to that at a community theater or high-school production: Those are *our* pretty-talented kids/neighbors/whatever up there, imitating genuine actors and singers and dancers more ably than we guess we had expected them to: Bravo! More impressive to this particular spectator than the performances themselves (which I judged in general to be at best Not Bad At All, Considering) were the overall conception and the imaginativeness of several incidental numbers. Instead of being a straightforward variety show, the *Follies* had a rudimentary but effective story-line, obviously borrowed from Hunter's *Show Barge*: Roaring Twenties Big-City woman novelist (not explicitly Jewish in this version, but played by a black-haired ingenue identified in the program as Holly Weil) comes to smalltime tidewater showboat in search of Material; is at first amused and a bit dismayed by contrast between sophisticated Broadway stuff she's used to and cornball Floating Theatre fare, as showboat troupe in turn is at first suspicious of being patronized by fancy uptowner. But she learns to respect their dedication, versatility, unpretentiousness, and shrewdly-calibrated rapport with local audiences, while they in turn come to see that she's tough, affectation-free, genuinely friendly, and uncondescendingly helpful. More than a hint of romantic attraction between "Edna" and "Charlie" (played by Morton Spindler), and of jealousy on part of latter's wife ("Beulah," played by the company's director, Sherry Singer). Et cetera — a conceit that allowed the company to pitch to both kinds of audience, or both aspects of the same audience. There were occasional echoes and parodies of the Kern/Hammerstein *Show Boat* score as well as those aforenoted Not Bad At All original numbers, some of them directly related to the "story" (e.g., *That's Entertainment?*, contrasting naughty-flashy Broadway with demurely sentimental Hicksville; *Too True to Be Good*, "Charlie's" wistful complaint about marital fidelity; *Takes Three to Tango*, suggestive of a truce, if not a reconciliation, between "Beulah" and her rival "Edna"), others less so or not at all (*Casting Off*, in which the showboat's departure is cleverly simulated by a line of dancers "onshore" moving slowly back from another line "aboard ship"; *One Long Laugh*, its title taken from old showboat playbills and its "lyrics" consisting simply of laughter by the cast onstage, commencing with half-stifled titters and giggles and building to a raucous, thigh-slapping, floor-rolling hilarity that spreads to the pit musicians, the stagehands, and of course the audience; and *Make It Hop*, a sexy, high-energy "breakdown" version of the number we'd heard that afternoon as the showboat exited our creek)—these latter presented as if being staged aboard the showboat represented on the backdrop.

"So what do we think?" we asked each other at intermission time. The barge's limited space permitted only a small enclosed lobby area behind the box office, with concession stand, restrooms, and showboat memorabilia—including, we noted, first editions of those novels mentioned in the program. As the Pit Bulls reconvened to entertain the customers who remained in their seats, we leg-stretchers overflowed onto the deck areas fore and aft, the narrow promenades along both sides, and ashore, where two portable toilets and a second concession stand (labeled CHESTERTOWN to echo the scene onstage) had been set up under multicolored strings of lights. The showboat too, now that night had fallen, was festively lit, and a gibbous moon framed by bright-edged cumulus clouds hung over the river and the town.

We think it's better than I for one expected, was my opinion—once they got past the Welcoming Remarks.

"Oy, that." We were among those who elected to stroll *T II*'s outboard walkway to its afterdeck, facing downriver toward a small marina and a waterfront park beyond. We had passed up the lobby displays, in which I had some interest, in order to avoid being buttonholed by strangers and/or teased by acquaintances for having been singled out by Captain Lake. "So have we seen enough, or do we want more?"

"*More more more!*" mock-pleaded a voice behind us that I recognized. Busy Hop Johnson, on break from his intermission gig and still in costume from the *Casting Off* number that had closed the *Follies'* first half ("Edna's" farewell to "Charlie" as she returns to New York to write her showboat novel: Will the lovers remeet, and did they consummate the adulterous mutual attraction that they had equally resisted and ratcheted up between numbers?), pushed his wire-rims up on his nose and invited us to meet the four also-costumed comrades standing behind and beside him, whom we recognized from the program. In order of rank and self-introduction ("Gotta get back to the Bull-pit," said Hop: "Great to see you again, Miz B. . . .") — which we couldn't graciously decline, much as we winced at further public attention in a venue where for some sixteen years we'd been keeping a comfortably low profile — these were the aforementioned Sherry Singer, strikingly attractive and of unquestionably professional talent; Morton Spindler, still sweating from the closing dance-number and ebullient as he'd been on the telephone, but more immediately likable in person; an athletic and handsome black fellow self-identified merely as "Obie" but named in the program as Jay Brown, whom we'd seen dancing with the others on *T II*'s rooftop that afternoon and who in Part One of the *Follies*, in the role of the cook Jo in Ferber's *Show Boat*, had sung a satirical version of Stephen Foster's *Old Black Joe*, politically corrected to "Senior African-American Citizen Joseph"; and finally the sexy-bumptious ingenue Holly Weil. Pleased to meet you all, we allowed, wishing our fellow townsfolk were absent from this little scene.

"We have to hustle backstage and get changed," Sherry Singer said — What eyes that woman had! — "but we wanted you to know how pleased we all are that you paid us a visit."

"*Honored!*" Mort Spindler amended, and wiped his forehead with his sleeve, and made a balletic mock-curtsy.

"Pleased and honored," Ms. Singer went on — addressing herself, I was gratified to note, to the two of us equally — "and how much we hope you'll help Save Our Ship."

"It *needs* help, for sure," dourly commented Holly Weil, whereat Mort Spindler put a finger theatrically to her lips and said "*Shh!* Our audience is listening!" Ms. Weil pretended to bite his admonitory finger.

"We're all fans," Jay Brown declared: "Even Holly, who hasn't read a word of you."

"I loved the movie, though," that young woman protested. Sherry Singer rolled her splendid eyes; Jay Brown groaned and said

"That was the *other* showboat, Holl!" "Well, I *loved* it," Ms. Weil insisted, and elbowed her colleague's ribs, whereupon he whisked her lightly up onto his shoulder. "Gotta run, guys; enjoy the rest of the show."

"Oh help help help," his fetching trophy declaimed, kicking her bare legs and striking an operatic attitude of distress: "I am being abducted by a Person of Color!"

Bystanders chuckled and made way for them.

"We *do* have to run," Ms. Singer affirmed. We complimented her singing, dancing, and acting; Spindler's dancing and choreography; the stage set; and the resourceful adaptation of elements from *Show Barge*'s story-line as a thread on which to string the several Really Quite Good individual numbers — most of them credited to Hop Johnson, to whom our regards.

"He did the adaptation, too," Sherry Singer informed us. "A really talented guy. *But . . .*"

"It's pretty good," Mort Spindler declared, "but not good enough, as Hop would be the first to agree. That's where *you* come in, we hope."

Please don't count on it.

Pitching cannily to my wife rather than to me directly, "You see how we-all have to be doing fourteen things at once," Ms. Singer said. "And on top of everything else, poor Hop's trying to get a *novel* written!"

As are some of the rest of us, I reminded her. To the both of them then: Look, guys, I intend to take a look at that script, if only out of curiosity. But I wish you well, and I promise to keep your proposal in mind.

Just here there came by way of end-of-intermission signal a ringing solo trumpet fanfare from *TOFO II*'s forward deck: Mouret's *Rondo*, the theme of *Masterpiece Theatre*.

"*That*, believe it or not," Mort Spindler said, "is one of our tugboat captains!"

"Versatility everywhere," my wife acknowledged. The pair shook our hands again, hoped we'd enjoy the remainder of the show, urged us to tour the showboat with them tomorrow afternoon and to catch the *Follies* again tomorrow evening if we were so inclined (we'd see, we allowed), and then ducked into a backstage entrance as the audience began moving to retake their seats.

"Well, now," my wife said.

*Part II?*

We guessed so, tempted though we were to jump ship instead and head homeward for a normal bedtime. We did not often "go out for the evening" even in the city, where there was considerably more to go out for; even less often from the Eastern Shore place. But we reminded ourselves that we were academically retired these days, with more free time than formerly; that the *Follies* thus far had been at least passable live entertainment, and that I had some professional interest in the material (and in my "competitor's" handling of it) as well as historical. So we filed back inside with the others, applauded the Pit Bulls' musical interlude, and cheered again when the curtain opened on essentially the same set as before, but cleverly relighted in the manner of the scene outside: nighttime; colored lights on what was now the CHESTERTOWN concession stand (complete with flanking portable toilets) and the festive showboat; the company strolling about under a gibbous moon as the audience had been doing, while the Pit Bulls' intermission-music finale came in muffled reprise from behind the backdrop as if from inside the painted *Original Floating Theater*—until a swarthy fellow with a trumpet stepped onstage from "inside" and rallied the "audience" with Mouret's *Rondo*. A quite effective *coup de théâtre*.

Followed, alas, by a comparatively lackluster second half. The love-triangle story borrowed from *Show Barge* was more or less lost sight of except in a couple of not particularly effective reprises: *That's Entertainment?* this time showing Charlie and Beulah in the audience at Ziegfeld's *Show Boat* musical, impressed by the glitzy production but critical of the vessel's misrepresentation as a fancy sternwheeler; *Casting Off* this time vaguely implying that North is North and South South, so to speak, and never the twain shall meet again—without clarifying (as Hunter's playscript did) what exactly has been at stake, or climaxing and resolving the extramarital affair.

Instead, we were diverted with more incidental skits, Not Bad At All, by "Kit & Kaboodle" (Singer and Johnson as a comedy duo on the Adams showboat) and song-and-dance routines by them, Spindler, Brown, and Weil in assorted combinations—including a clever variation on the earlier *Old Black Joe* parody, in which "Senior African-American Citizen Joseph" reappears as Mark Twain's Nigger Jim ("African-American James") steering his raft down "Ol' Man Chester," the river-name no doubt changed from landing to landing along with the port-sign and perhaps the phase of the moon as well.

The *story*, however, such as it was, got lost; not surprising in something hastily cobbled up (so Spindler had acknowledged) by a busy company of not really professional scriptors. Among my own feelings as we applauded the finale and the curtain calls, and Hop Johnson made an ambiguous raised-fist salute in our direction (Did it mean "Top *that* if you can, Great-Uncle Ennie!"?), was a near-certainty that I could, if I had a mind to, do considerably more with the *Show Barge* script—even as a frame for the *Follies*, not to mention as a freestanding drama—than the "Novelist Aspirant" had thus far done. Indeed, as we drove home through the cricket- and cicada-rich country night, watching out for deer on the county road and comparing impressions of the show, it was not difficult for me to imagine, in a general way at least, a second-night sequel to the *Follies* in which the proportions of dramatic action and incidental numbers would be reversed, Hunter's story-line occupying center stage, as it were.

But why get involved? That unfinished playscript was truly no more than a minor historical curiosity, and I had no ambitions or pretensions in the playwriting way. Edna Ferber herself, a competent and deservedly successful popular novelist of my parents' generation, had in my judgment been no more than that (these seventy years later, who reads even her Pulitzer-prizewinning first novel, *So Big*?): a writer remembered much more for Kern and Hammerstein's perennially popular adaptation of one of her bestsellers than for any of the novels themselves. In short, no Edith Wharton or Willa Cather here, much less a Virginia Woolf or Gertrude Stein

checking out the Chesapeake and just possibly (but not very proba-
bly) indulging in a bit of crosscultural flirtation with her material.
*There* would be a story, maybe, given resonance by the stature of the
Interloper. But Charlie Hunter and Edna Ferber (and Hop Johnson,
Mort Spindler, and Sherry Singer)? Why get involved?

"A little crosscultural flirtation with your own material?"
my wife wondered when I shared these sentiments with her and
announced over breakfast next morning my inclination to tour
*TOFO II* that afternoon, after my usual morning's work. Not to
worry, I assured her: For better or worse, I was no Edna Ferber. Just
want to have another look, if only to remind myself that there *is* no
reason to Get Involved.

"Your call," she affirmed—but I should count her out, please, as
she had appointments and errands over in Baltimore that day.
Through the forenoon, then, I made further notes upon and drafted
another trial page or two of what looked to be Coming No Time
Soon and then reread the *Show Barge* script as well: by turns fascinating, risible, touching, and preposterous. Full of possibilities? Not
impossibly, though a likelier candidate for a recurrent minor motif
in a novel about . . . well, showboats.

But what *about* showboats? Notwithstanding the old musical's
triumphant new Broadway revival, who at the end of the twentieth
century cared a fart about showboats, other than as a colorful detail
of American social history? Why get involved?

*"I'll tell him why,"*
Hop Johnson volunteered to Mort Spindler that afternoon, after I'd
been toured through *TOFO II* from top to bottom and stem to stern
and urged to watch from backstage, "for perspective," their impending rehearsal. It had been, unquestionably, an entertaining and illu-
minating excursion thus far. At *T II*'s gangplank I'd been ushered
aboard along with a dozen other curious Chestertonians by a forty-
ish woman whose black braids, dark eyes and sunbrowned skin,
bare feet, bright headband, tie-dyed muumuu, and beaucoup beads
and bracelets gave her the aspect of a New Age Native American.
Stroking a half-grown black cat cradled in her left arm, she intro-

duced herself as Elva Kane, skipper of the towboat *Dove*, moored aft of brother Harry's larger *Raven* on our outboard side. If we would please step with her into the lobby, we'd see a short video about the original Chesapeake showboat and its modern-day counterpart as well as a display of related historical items, after which she would be happy to answer questions before showing us the theater itself.

"And remember what the proverb says," she added cryptically: "*If you cut your toenails on a Friday, you'll never have a toothache.* Follow me, please?"

Sort-of-chuckling, we did as bidden, myself pleased to remain this time anonymous: viewed Hop Johnson's quite effective educational/promotional *Showboat 'Round the Bend!*, inspected old playbills and programs and Authentic Scale Models, and put our questions (but I reserved mine: Why get involved?). In the forty years since doing my novelist-aspirant homework on the Adams Floating Theatre, I had forgotten most of its specifications; it was agreeable to be reminded themof and, by extension, of the greenly ambitious two-dozen-year-old who had scouted that info at mid-century for his purposes. As I compared the models and associated spec-sheets of *TOFO II* and its predecessor, Cap'n Elva (as she bade us call her) explained to a questioner that while the automobile had indeed made it profitless for showboats to pause at every river-landing as in days gone by — Kern and Hammerstein, she reminded us, had visited the Adams Floating Theatre during its stop at the tiny village of Crumpton, only a few miles upriver from Chestertown but a separate show-stand in those days — it was not altogether bad news: Anyone in the town of Rock Hall, for example (*T II*'s next scheduled stop), could of course easily drive twenty minutes and catch the show in Chestertown instead, but on the other hand, anyone in Chestertown who happened to miss the show here or wanted to see it again could just as easily pop over to Rock Hall two days hence and catch it there. What goes around comes around, right? And *the left hind foot of a rabbit shot in a graveyard at midnight in the dark of the moon with a bullet made out of quarter found in a horse's track will bring good luck.* More questions?

*"If so, ask us,"* Mort Spindler stage-whispered behind me, and put a friendly plump hand on my shoulder. "Welcome back aboard, sir!" With him was Ms. Singer, terrific-looking in denim short-shorts and halter top and flashing silvergray eyes. With a tandem balletic bow they voiced their joint hope that I would let them give me the grand tour. "Minus Elva's PR and proverbs," the young woman said behind her hand: "We want you to hear it straight."

And so while the others, glancing back at us over their shoulders, filed into the theater proper (we would catch *that* later, at rehearsal-time, Sherry promised; I was to call her Sherry, please. "Short for Scheherazade," Mort added with a wink; I was to call him Mort, please), we three detoured through the rest of the vessel, and my amiable guides—mainly Spindler, as knowledgeable and forthright as he was light on his feet—gave me a running commentary on the differences between, let's say, *T*'s *I* and *II*, with their associated pluses and minuses.

"We're bigger but smaller," was how Mort summed it up. The Adams barge, 128 feet long and 34 wide, had had seats for 850 customers ("Five hundred whiteys in the orchestra," Sherry added with a sigh—not knowing, I presume, that that had been my late father's nickname—"three hundred fifty coloreds in the balcony. You should hear Obie Brown's takeoff on *that*!"). *TOFO II*, some thirty feet longer and ten wider, had only 400 orchestra seats—no balcony, no boxes—"And we'd jump for joy," Mort confided with an illustrative leap, "to fill three hundred of 'em." The extra space—not needed for customers in any case, as there weren't that many—was required for or anyhow devoted to such things as air conditioning ("Adams was proud to have *electric fans*; we've got compressors, condensers, ductwork . . ."), sprinkler systems and other fire precautions not required in Adams's day; restrooms for the public (handicapped included) and bath facilities for cast and crew, together with holding tanks and related sanitation facilities (the Original Floating Theater had provided but a single, "dry" toilet, emptying straight overboard, for its company of twenty-five); water-making machinery instead of the washwater cisterns and drinkwater barrels of *Show Boat* and *Show Barge* fame; laundry facilities; a spotless dining room under the stage, and a galley formidably equipped with restaurant-size freezers, ranges, microwave ovens, dishwashers, and ventilators. There was, moreover, a combination accounting office and high-tech communications center (dubbed Spindler's Retreat), replete with fax machine, intercom, computer, and color printer, from which Mort and Captain Lake kept in touch with their Dorsettown base, their upcoming ports of call, and *T II*'s box-office receipts; also a well-equipped projection booth and sound-and-light-control center high on the theater's rear wall. All this in addition to modest accommodations for the company (who numbered sixteen or so, compared to Adams's two-dozen-plus) in two tiers of double rooms backstage, small but luxurious by Adams's standards, each with washbasin, toilet, and shower, not to mention telephone and small TV, as well as somewhat larger "state-rooms" for Captain Lake, Sherry, and Mort above the forward box and accounting offices (the Kane twins, with one crewmember each, slept aboard their respective vessels, and on mild nights the younger folks often hauled sleeping bags out onto *T II*'s small "balcony" decks and huge flat roof, where two large lifeboats rested in chocks beneath their davits). In the barge's bowels, under the lobby area—which, in order to meet the elevated rear of the theater's forward-sloping floor, was actually at the same height as the proscenium stage—I was shown the mighty diesel-fired generators that powered all this equipment plus the theater-vessel's stage-, house-, cabin-, and running lights and its high-tech sound system, together with a well-equipped maintenance-and-repair shop to keep things up and running.

My particular Virgil through these latter petroleum-smelling, brightly lit but darkly rumbling depths was neither Call-Me-Sherry nor Ditto Mort, but a coveralled, bill-capped, lank-limbed personage, face ridged like an English walnut and as brown, long of nicotine-stained tooth, red-rimmed eye-"whites" (but their pupils sparkled: lively schoolkids in a drear playfield), voice raspy as the rat-tail file wherewith its wielder was smoothing some aperture in a metal something clamped in a bench-vise in the creature's lair— and, incongruously, fiddling with a grease-smudged desktop computer between rasps — when Mort called out, "Got comp'ny, Dits!"

Reader will have noted that but for the allusion to Dante's tour-guide in the netherworld, my description of *T II*'s maintainer-in-chief is indeterminate as to gender. At first I took her for a him — the job and outfit, together with a grizzledness beside which *Dove*'s Captain Elva, for example, was as thoroughly female as she was unfeminine. The name was no clue: *Dits*? But something vestigially womanish in the yellow-toothed smile, the body-carriage (touching one hand to thin gray ponytail behind bill-cap and smoothing cover-all-front with the other while stepping to greet the visitors), even the register of that iron-filinged voice, gave me to wonder whether he mightn't after all be a she. The inevitable machine-shop calendar art was no help: photos of bikini'd bodybuilders both male and female.

"Call me Ditsy," she/he invited, and wiped hand on coverall for shaking, with questionable results: "Right pleased ta meetcha." To my considerable surprise then, "'Fn I'd a known you were comin' I'd a baked a cake and brought a book for signin'. Me'n my partner EARL were fans a yours. Afternoon Miz Sherry, Mister Mort."

As they returned the greeting (Singer with buss on seamèd cheek and Spindler with mere cordial nod, I noted inconclusively), I could not resist pressing: "*Were* fans? Where'd I lose you?"

Bill-cap off; rueful shake of head (gold stud in starboard ear-lobe, I noted inconclusively). "You never lost *us*, Cap'n. *I* lost m'EARL, is what happened. Show ya 'round?"

A de-sexed, tough-as-leather widow, then, I reckoned, but al-though something familiar about this character teased my errant memory, I pressed no further. Declared Ditsy of the power-genera-tors, with some pride, "Cain't do nothin' upstairs without these dudes down here," and then added, surprisingly: "Like *inspiration*, right? Where the juice comes from!" And more surprisingly yet — removing bill-cap and scratching thin gray hair — "Fact is, though, the juice that runs *these* babies is Arabian oil, same's Aladdin's lamp." With a wink: "Cain't carry no thousand and one nightsworth, but I reckon we're good for 'bout a month." At our short inspec-tion's end, she/he requested almost shyly that, in default of "their" copies of my books, I inscribe "for EARL" the grease-stained bill of "their" cap, which only then — as its current owner went to fetch marking-pen from workbench — I saw bore on it the initials E.A.R.L.

"Estuarine Aquacultural Research Lab," Ditsy explained, with equal rasps of pride, rue, and indignation. "Down to Backwater? Use to be my fella's operation, till the fuckin' Pentagon scrubbed it, 'scuse my French."

I see, I said, although I didn't. But as I duly Magic-Markered *for EARL* (all uppercase, at requester's request) and my signature on the bill-cap — which Ditsy then kissed and set atop the computer monitor, out of reverence clearly less for present signer than for absent signee — there came back to me that eccentric opening passage of Hop Johnson's protean "writing sample," no doubt long since scrapped by its author: A bisexual old Chesapeake "progger" scavenges from the marsh a computer disk labeled COMING SOON!!! ... What was she/he doing aboard the showboat — which, if I remembered correctly . . . ?

But I didn't, and was given no chance to ask, for "We're running late," Sherry here observed to Mort, who agreed, bade the maintenance-chief hasta la vista ("*Es mas tarde que pensáis*," Ditsy replied in clear though enigmatic Castilian), and politely hustled the three of us out of there.

Well, now, wow, I said, looking forward to some illumination. But my tour-guide-in-chief was eager to get back to our pre-Ditsy agenda. Once we were out of there, "Jim Adams prob'ly thought he had it tough," Mort Spindler declared; "but he didn't even carry *lifeboats*, much less casualty insurance and liability coverage. You wouldn't *believe* our premiums! Plus access for the disabled — can you imagine Edna Ferber's people bothering with that? Plus Social Security payments, health insurance, *pension plans!*" He did a ballet spin, presumably for emphasis. "Fortunately, we can put FLOP-CORP under DTE's umbrella — the Floating Opera Corporation? — so we get a decent large-group rate. But a hundred paying customers just about cover the day's operating costs *before salaries*, and it takes two hundred to break even."

"Which we don't," sighed Sherry Singer, "as a rule. Two hundred is a *good night*." We had, evidently, completed our tour of the Support Facilities—whereof the high point for me had been that low point, so to speak, down in Ditsyville, but which in general I'd found worthwhile as grist for the mill of a still-nebulous project—and were climbing a steep metal two-stage staircase up into the theater's wings, from where I'd been invited to watch the company rehearse numbers for that evening's performance. Ms. Sherry led the way, and between the steepness of the stairs and Mr. Mort's following immediately behind me, I found my face on a level with, and disconcertingly scant inches from, her compactly working buns as we climbed. Halfway up, at the stair-landing, having delivered herself of the above, to my startlement the young woman turned and gave me a sudden hug—which, given our relative positions, meant pressing my face briefly into her bare midriff and my pate into her haltered breasts while she added, "But you'll come to our rescue! Right?"

Reader of these lines: Their author is a happily decades-married fellow no longer young, altogether in love with his lawful mate and temperamentally content with monogamous fidelity. Even as he makes these affirmations, however, he reconjures with helpless male pleasure the feel of his nose in Sherry McAndrews Singer's navel and of his scalp sweetly by her beboobed.

Ah.

As she unembraced me (with a light kiss on the forehead when I promised to Think About It but recautioned both her and Spindler not to count on my involvement) and we resumed our stair-climb, Hop Johnson's voice sang out above us: *"Life u-pon the wick-ed stage!"*

He was waiting for us up at stage-level. "See how we theater-types carry on, Dad? Welcome to the bunny-hutch!"

Taking his cue, Sherry Singer exaggerated the twitch of her butt before my face on the remaining few steps. Upon what lucky chap, I couldn't help wondering, does she bestow the whole scrumptious package? Surely not Mort Spindler, a busy and devoted husband/parent who had mentioned in course of our tour that he commutes almost daily between home and showboat, regardless of the hour, to be with his family. Perhaps—her physical match, certainly—Jay

"Obie" Brown? Perhaps (and why my twinge of displeasure at the notion?) J. Hopkins Johnson? More probably some shoreside lover, not of the ship's company.

Who cared?

With a stagey shrug, "Did my best," she reported to her upstairs colleague.

And your best is good indeed, I assured her: onstage and off. Much obliged for the tour, guys, and the extras too.

"More extras where those came from, man!" Hop assured me, and gave his ear-ornament a twiddle (left-lobe ring, we remember, as against "Ditsy's" right-lobe stud. Not for the first time, Is there a code?, I wondered. And, speaking of that *Ditsy* character . . .). "Right, Holl?"

The *zaftig* Ms. Weil had slipped up behind him from onstage and tickled his ribs; he deftly seized her wrists, drew her tight against his back, and clamped both of her hands atop his trouserfly. Echoing her mock-protest of the previous evening, "Oh help help help," she declaimed again: "I am being sexually harassed in the workplace by a Colorless Person!"

"So color me Horny," her harasser invited, and released her, pushed up his eyeglasses, and extended a hand to greet me.

"Color you Insatiable," Sherry Singer reproved him — whether teasingly or half seriously, I couldn't judge.

"Color us Talented but Desperate," Mort Spindler suggested to me, now that we were all upstairs in the Stage Right wing of the theater: "Pretty damn good, but not good enough to compete with *Seinfeld* and the cineplexes."

Linking one arm with Hop Johnson's and striking a Kit-&-Kaboodle attitude, "He's not sure he wants to get *involved*," Sherry Singer reported of me to her partner. They did a step as if to launch into *Takes Three to Tango*.

"Why *should* he get involved?" Mort rhetorically asked all hands except Holly Weil, who had skipped back onstage to rejoin Jay Brown in some tandem routine that they'd been working out. "Just because we're going under? Why should that concern *him*?"

I made to protest, uncomfortably: Really, guys . . .

* * *

*"I'll tell him why,"*
volunteered Ms. Kit's Kaboodle, and forthwith delivered himself, with her kinetic assistance, of an argument impossible to reproduce in written words, because — whether by virtuoso improvisation or after prior rehearsal (as, for all I knew, my "impulsive" embracement on the stair-landing might have been planned) — the pair *danced* it round about me as he chanted, with interstitial comments by his partner/boss(/lover?) and Morton Spindler:

*Strophe:* Although (unlike Edna Ferber's) it was not my habitual practice as a novelist to "go out and get the story," but rather to abide in my workroom, confining my "fieldwork" to university libraries when my own fell short, until the story came and got me . . .

*Antistrophe:* It was to be remarked that that comparatively passive and sedentary M.O. had no doubt evolved in part from the constraints of fulltime teaching and busy parenting over the earlier decades of my career: constraints whereby I was, these emeritus and grandparental days, no longer constrained. . . .

*Strophe:* To break with such by-and-large-productive work habits is no doubt difficult (for older chaps especially) and perhaps imprudent as well, *so long as those habits remain productive.* . . .

*Antistrophe:* Should the time come when they fail me, however, dot dot dot

*Apostrophe?* I might do worse than to recall my early creature Todd Whatsisname, of *The Floating Whatsitsname*, whose habit it was now and then to break and even discard his longstanding habits, so as not to become altogether their slave.

(And look what happened to *him*, I couldn't resist inserting here — although in fact I was less than confident that I quite remembered, at that remove, in what pass I had last left that imaginary fellow.)

Affecting ghettospeak as he joined the dance at this point, "We good," declared Obie Brown, "but we not good 'nuff, you dig?" They *had* rehearsed this elaborate pitch, then — or else were even abler improvisers than I had supposed.

"Got the right stuff," Holly Weil strutted in, as if doing the "Tits and Ass" number from *Chorus Line*, "but not the right *stuff.*"

"But what's that to *him*?" Kit Singer rhetorically asked them all.

*En pointe* in his deck moccasins, "In the immortal words of our own dear Ditsy," Morton Spindler orated: "*Every boat starts a-sinking from the day she's launched, but constant maintenance can postpone that eventuality. A little first-rate material wouldn't hurt, either.*"

"Some Black November down the road," Call-Me-Sherry speechified next, "we're bound to go under—"

"Ho, mon!" interrupted Jay Brown, and struck a hulking-monster pose: "Heah come muhfuckin' Black November!"

"—but we're determined to put that sad day off till the new millennium at least, if we possibly can."

Parodying now a number from the 1960s musical *Hair*, Hop Johnson falsetto'd "*We-would-just-like to say, that-it-is OUR CONVICTION*," and lapsing then into speech, "that some chemistry of the right material, the right presentation, and the right promotion can successfully move back our expiration date." Back to declamation: "'Tis the same with printed fiction as a robust medium of art and entertainment, is't not, my friends?"

"*'Tis! 'Tis!*" the chorus affirmed, and then its members individually, in series:

—or the Dow Jones Industrial Average . . .

—or this nation's preeminence as a world power . . .

—or the Chesapeake Bay as a healthy and gracious eco-entity . . .

—or Civilization As We Motherfucking Know It . . .

—not to mention one's own continuing health and flourishment, especially as one groweth older? . . .

"So okay," Call-Me-Mort concluded, more straightforwardly but still in performance mode, "we're small potatoes compared to those biggies . . ."

"But we're what we happen to be committed to," declared then of all people Captain. Adam. Lake. himself, appearing as if on cue and flanked by Captains Elva and Harry Kane, like *TOFO II* by its tugs. "And've worked mighty hard on behalf of. And'll be sorry to see go down."

We rather stiffly shook hands.

"So help?" entreated then quietly Captain Elva, squeezing my other hand in both of hers (while her black cat rubbed itself against her ankles) and glancing to cue her uncomfortable-looking twin brother. Which worthy thereupon frowned, focused somewhere in the neighborhood of my forehead, and recited,

"*Let down yer guard?*"

*Not likely, friends,*

I was obliged to tell them, after most hearty congratulations on their so-elaborate and entertaining double pitch: first that audacious side-trip up our creek, and now this. I re-agreed to re-review the *Show Barge* script with an eye to perhaps making suggestions along the lines of those I'd made impromptu in my initial phone-talk with Morton Spindler—in case the ATC's obviously talented Hop Johnson, for example, might want to rescript the thing for production or incorporate more of it into *Tidewater Follies*. . . .

"*Keep the kid busy,*" Kaboodle cracked to Kit behind his hand: "That's his way of sandbagging my *COMING SOON!* novel, so his'll come sooner."

Behind *her* hand, "Oldest trick in the book," his partner agreed.

The truth was, however (I told myself, but saw no point in telling them), I had altogether more enjoyed being ignorant of *TOFO II*'s material existence, and unrestrainedly *imagining* a fin-de-millennial Chesapeake showboat inspired into reality by the old Adams Floating Theater and that unpromising derelict in Solomons Harbor. The larger the Real Thing's presence—on the Bay generally, and particularly in my life—the less usable it became for my purposes. ("Hooray!" I imagined J. Hopkins Johnson cheering at this, and therefore silently appended *No problem for untried Novelists Aspirant, maybe, but at least some of us elder specimens still honor the useful distinction between fact and fiction, art and life.*)

As if reading my thoughts, "What he really wishes," Kaboodle said on, "is that we'd quietly disappear, so he can get on with his story."

On the contrary, I assured them, not in entire good faith: I wished them success, and would either find some way for Life and Art to coexist—perhaps even to cohabit?—or else tell some other story.

Back in her mock-come-hither aspect, "Let's cohabit!" Sherry Singer urged. "Come be in our story, and you can put us all in yours!"

Glancing at his watch, "Quite seriously," Captain. Adam. Lake. said quite seriously, "you're welcome aboard any time. In any capacity. 'Fyou want to, you could even *live* aboard for a spell—"

"We'll find a bunk for you *somewhere*," vamped Holly Weil, fluttering her mega-mascara'd lashes.

"Or you could follow us by car. The way Mort here does."

"*Whatever it takes*," Sherry Singer said, patting my cheek and actually winking one of those resplendent gray eyes.

"I'm sure Cap'n Andy Andrews will approve of our covering your expenses," Mort Spindler added, putting the nickname (and the surname too, I hoped) between finger-quotes. "I wish he were here in person to invite you, but Cap'n Ad and I can speak for him."

Enough, really, I insisted: Your generosity embarrasses me. I'm going to slink back to my den now and chew on Charlie Hunter's script.

The Kane twins, their parts played, were exiting already (Captain Elva blew me a little kiss, held up one forefinger, and declared "*Snakes are blind in August*"), and Holly Weil was nudging Jay "Obie" Brown stageward to resume their workout. Sherry Singer whispered something to Hop Johnson, to which the Novelist Aspirant responded with a facial shrug, as if to say It's Your Call.

"Shall I phone you in a week or two?" Mort Spindler asked. "See how it's going?"

As I think they say in show biz, *I'll call you*, I demurred—but not Unless and Until. I shook hands all around. Meanwhile, it's *Break a leg*, right?

"Or, as I believe they say in Spain," Sherry Singer said sweetly, "*Eat shit*, mister."

I was startled, even a bit shocked. But "*Come mierda*," Hop Johnson back-translated with a grin: "It really *is* what Spanish performers say for good luck." Ms. Singer made a *mwah* to confirm her benevolent intent and hoped she'd see me in that night's audience, she said. All the same, I doubted that the Spanish routinely add *señor* to their imprecative blessing; and I never did find out what it was that Kit had whispered in Kaboodle's ear, for by the time I spoke with them-all again (the following spring) I had quite forgotten about it. Once home, to my mate's evident relief I decided after all not to attend that evening's repeat of *Tidewater Follies '95* (Mort Spindler would report to me later, grimly, that the Saturday night's turnout was smaller than the Friday's: "Scarcely enough to cover Utilities"). Nor did I make the short trip over to Rock Hall in the days following, or the slightly longer ones thereafter up to Chesapeake City and Havre de Grace, to see firsthand how show and scenery were adjusted from port to port.

Indeed, once I had watched from my workroom windows *The Original Floating Opera II* returning Bayward down the Chester behind its eccentric tandem tugs (no side trip up our creek this time; no whistle salutes from the river-bend), I found myself attempting, if not to purge the *Coming Soon!!!* project altogether from my imagination, at least to keep its real-life counterpart at arm's length. No easy task, that: Now that the showboat's real existence had invaded and contaminated my imagination of it, I was reminded of the thing repeatedly by notices and news items that must formerly have escaped my attention—*Chesapeake showboat to be featured at Defenders Day festival*; or *Biggest boat at Annapolis Boat Show not for sale*; or *Last of the old or first of the new? Chesapeake showboat is one of a kind (for now)*—so that ignoring it was rather like ignoring the sign IGNORE THIS SIGN. Nevertheless, through the rest of summer '95 and the autumn following I did my best to ignore the sign that had so signaled me in Solomons Harbor: I set aside ("to ripen," I told myself) both my focus-resisting opus-in-embryo and—with telephoned apologies to a much-disappointed Morton Spindler—Charles Hunter's *Show Barge*, and turned my attention as completely as I could to alternative projects and pleasures: miscellaneous short stories and essays; the odd lecture/reading junket, for a change of professional pace and scene; our usual property chores and other family business; and—now that we were academic re-tirees—a bit more pure pleasure-travel than had been our custom.

But again and again these routine activities, among other things, brought *T II* back to mind. The serial Atlantic hurricane threats, for example, set me to wondering what it must be like to ride one out aboard a floating theater, as James Adams's crew had done in August 1933 (nowadays, to be sure, one has sufficient advance warning never to be caught in mid-Bay; but What If . . . ?). A fall end-of-season sailing cruise—unprecedented calendrical luxury!—led us inexorably into the Patuxent, where in Solomons Harbor we found old COMING SOON! as evidently unadvanced since our first sight of her as was . . . *Ignore that sign.* Hauling and decommissioning our boat at season's end, I imagined *T II* preparing to lay up in its off-season museum/art-moviehouse mode down in Dorsettown's Snug Harbour, but resisted the impulse to go check it out. As the geese moved down from Canada and the weather chilled and the world's more newsworthy events duly made news—the "Dayton Accords," signed by the Serbs, Bosnians, and Croatians to stop the fighting in what had once been Yugoslavia, the criminal trial and acquittal of O. J. Simpson on double-murder charges—I met with a group of student writers at the small liberal-arts college in nearby Chestertown and spent most of the hour talking showboat history with them instead of the craft of fiction (for the sake of experiment, I avoided any mention of *TOFO II*, to see whether they would bring up its name, and was oddly comforted when none did). An October appearance on a public-television series about the Book of Genesis set me to busy note-taking on the Ark and the Flood, although my official subject ("The First Murder") was Cain and Abel. In November, the state of Maryland repealed its 55 mph speed limit, in place since the more energy-prudent 1970s, and that same week the Dow Jones Industrial Average topped 5000: *Full speed ahead!* those otherwise unrelated items whispered to me. *Let down your guard!* But I chose otherwise and plodded on: another short story; another essay. In December, my wife and I celebrated our silver wedding anniversary on the beaches and snorkeling-reefs of Tobago, where we had honeymooned a quarter-century before but hadn't happened to return to since. Closing that circle and toasting the presumable next's commencement, I found myself reflecting, inappropriately, that a Last Book dealing with a resurrected tidewater showboat really would close the circle neatly on my first, whether or not at my age another circle followed. Whereas for a certain Novelist Aspirant, *TOFO II* was just material-at-hand: *my* material (and Edna Ferber's, to be sure, and Ziegfeld/Kern/Hammerstein's, and Charles Hunter's), in his indifferently deserving hands. Toward the end of that wintrier-than-usual month, while the unresolved feud between a Republican Congress and a Democratic administration shut down much of our federal government, we shut down our Chesapeake base of operations, loaded our old station wagon to capacity, and, with mixed feelings indeed, drove south like tens of thousands of our fellow aging North American "snowbirds" to try our first, experimental, retirement winter in rented lodgings on the southwestern coast of Florida.

Once upon a time, Reader, when those occasional lecture-visits to campuses other than my own happened to fetch me to the City University of New York, I opened an informal session with a street-smart group of apprentice writers there by asking them, innocently, what in their opinion was the single most useful service that older, more established writers could render younger, less established ones. No novice at such sessions, I did not expect them to say, on the one hand, "Set an inspiring example of literary artistry, sir, for us to follow," or, on the other, "Let us in on your trade-tricks, dude." Something like "Read our stuff, show us what needs fixing, and find us a good agent" was probably what I thought I'd hear. In any case, I was scarcely prepared for the smiling but not unserious response (from a fellow dressed head to foot in *de rigueur* NYC black), "*Die*." He pushed up his eyeglasses, Hop-Johnson style, while his classmates chuckled. "*Die*, man, and get out of our way. Okay?"

I promised to do so—no time soon. And I mention that little exchange now perhaps to account for my having omitted a relevant item or two from this catalogue of IGNORE THIS SIGN diversions. My young self-designated competitor was, I knew, presently enrolled in what for two decades had been "my" graduate-level fiction-writing workshop, now presided over by the excellent writer/ teacher and amiable longtime colleague who was my more than able successor in that seminar room. So how's Johnson's e-novel coming along?, I had asked that friend sometime that fall. And is he doing it online, or what? For I knew my colleague himself to be a bit of a Luddite who declined to work even on an electric typewriter, much less a word processor, and to whom "electronic fiction" was as alien a medium as laser holography or performance art. Indeed, it had afforded me some unsporting amusement to imagine J. H. Johnson's laboring under so masterly but probably ill-matched a master. But "Oh, he's Full Speed Ahead," my successor had reported, and explained that while he understood there to be a computerized version of the project circulating among the plugged-in seminarians— What did *he* know or care about *that*, who took no interest in any writing-instrument fancier than his brace of trusty Hermes manual portables?—the version being distributed and critiqued in seminarial instalments was in workaday printed pages, conventionally formatted except for occasional, not-unclever imitations of those whatchacallems—option buttons?—and suchlike computerish gizmos here and there in the text. These were duly explained to him when necessary by his more with-it wife and children or the other writers in the room; he judged them to be, on the whole, more of an amusing enhancement of the narrative than a distraction from it— reminiscent of some of the early Modernists' linear simulations of nonlinear effects. "The guy's bright, talented, and hardworking," my friend summed up, "and hell-bent on going head to head with you on that showboat business. He's even got a You-character in the story, doing a novel about a Him-type apprentice novelist. Sounds like a real turn-off," he acknowledged, "but it sort of works, actually." And he urged me, if not to have a look for myself (he was sure Johnson would be pleased, but he would clear it with him first, of course), then at least to guest-visit one of the seminar sessions before I left town for the winter. Any Thursday afternoon?

Yes, well. I did incline, nostalgically, to another look at that jim-dandy seminar room, where for so many years I had coached so many and variously talented apprentices: the most elevated room on campus, up in Gilman Hall's clock tower, with great windows on three of its sides overlooking the university, and on the fourth a restricted-access stairway up into the clockworks proper. And I was not uninterested in seeing a specimen of . . . What's Johnson calling the thing?, I asked my friend disingenuously.

"*COMING SOON!!!* Like on movie ads and stuff? All caps and three exclamation marks."

Ah, right. Because in fact I, too (I explained), in a few trial starts of *my* new showboat opus, had experimented with pseudo-mouse-click options and faux-hypertextual effects. . . . But no: Never mind his manuscript, disk, whatever. I'll come visit the seminar, but let's make it a time when Johnson's not on deck. I'll add my two centsworth to whatever's being workshopped that day and then chat a bit after.

"Done." And so I did, just before the university's Thanksgiving break, and an agreeable though unsettling experience it was to reclimb those much-climbed stairs and sit at the long seminar table among the usual dozen gifted men and women from all over the USA and elsewhere, ranging in age from just-out-of-undergraduate-college to somewhere-in-their-thirties (inasmuch as fiction-writers, and novelists especially — unlike mathematicians, chess-players, and lyric poets — often don't discover their vocation early on), and, inevitably, to feel them measuring me against the probable caricature in their classmate's work-in-progress. Before we took our seats there were introductions and handshakes; Hop Johnson, who as I entered had winked and waggled his fingers cordially from across the room, now twiddled his earring and stood back like a grinning cricket in order to be the last hand shaken and to press upon me a pair of tickets for *TOFO II*'s postseason wind-up, down at Baltimore's historic Fells Point over Thanksgiving weekend.

"The whole gang's coming," he said, and added "Better catch us while you can, before one or the other of us goes *around the corner*."

That locution struck me as a touch off — "around the corner"? — until my colleague-friend pointed out with some embarrassment a new addition to the seminar room. High in one corner, in a horizontal row, hung framed photoportraits of half a dozen writer-coaches who had once upon a time held forth in our department: on the right-hand wall, those who had since died, in the order of their deaths, beginning with the most recently deceased and ending with the poet-scholar who had founded the university's then-pioneering writing program (only the second such in the nation) immediately after World War II, and had been among my own former teachers in those bygone days. And on the wall adjacent, a couple of us still-living emeritus types, of whose mug-shots mine was nearest the corner.

Oy, I said, and my colleague—a publicity-shunner himself—turned up his palms: not *his* idea. But "When you kick," Hop Johnson cheerfully explained, "we just shift you 'round the corner. No hurry, man!"

*Don't hold your breath,*
I recommended. And to the amused room at large, Shall we get to work?

We did, and although the ensuing two hours of manuscript analysis were both enjoyable to me and, I trust, useful to the seminarians, I felt those photos (which have since been quietly removed) ever at my back. Having made his point, I suppose, Hop Johnson behaved himself thereafter: He offered his share of reasonably astute and wittily phrased suggestions to the two pieces under discussion —one of them an ably conceived and fairly finished short story, no doubt publishable after minor revision, the other a problem-fraught middle chapter of "a longer work," the more difficult to assess for its having neither synopsis nor prospectus. My impression from the subsequent general conversation was that My Rival was regarded by the group as neither more nor less than a peer (spirited critical exchanges based on reciprocal respect and an undogmatic plurality of aesthetic tastes are a happy tradition in that room), and that his peers considered his "e-novel"-in-progress to be a commendable experiment without necessarily sharing his messianic attitude toward the medium. Indeed (so one of their number remarked to me at intermission time), they were more critically troubled by the project's "ontological status" (her term, I swear, sans prompting from me)—how much of it was fictive invention and how much a mere record of the showboat's travails as a viable enterprise and the author's as a fledgling novelist—than by the pros and cons of electronic narrative.

"But the sumbitch is surfing right along," Johnson himself let me know as the group dispersed at our session's end. "I'll be winding up Chap. Ninety-five by the end of this semester and turning the corner on Ninety-six—under budget and ahead of schedule!"

To his clear satisfaction, Ninety-five chapters already!, I couldn't help exclaiming. "No no no," his coach and my colleague-friend explained: "He's naming his chapters for successive years of the showboat's history."

"Last time you looked, anyhow," the young author teased, and good-humoredly complained that so frequently had he reconceived his novel's whole plot and structure—in response to terrific new ideas from his muse, his coach, and his fellow seminarians, not to mention from things actually happening aboardship—he'd been obliged to pledge no further remakes of The Story Thus Far until he was safely out of the program: too much for his coach and classmates to keep up with!

"So how's yours?" he then cheerily or as-if-cheerily inquired. "Coming soon? I bet *you've* turned the corner on the millennium already!"

His repetitions of that phrase did not escape me. As Elva Kane might say (I told him), Bad luck to count narrative chickens before they hatch.

"Aha!" Up with the eyeglasses. "So *that's* why you guys make us do it all the time in the workshop: Plot outlines! Prospectuses! But chickens shmickens," he added, "let's talk turkey": All kidding aside, he hoped to see my wife and me in the audience at *T II*'s last stand of the season, down at Fells Point at TG time. Talk about turkeys! He'd invited the whole seminar to be his guests—America's Next Great Novelist Makes Public Fool of Self for a Living! —promising all hands a walk-on part in Chapter 1995's wrap-up, and he'd be in Seventh Heaven if I took that bait along with them.

"Whaddafuck's Seventh Heaven," he concluded, "anyhow?"

Muslim eschatology, I happened to know, and said. "Also the Cabala," my friend believed. But neither of us could say whether the Muslims had borrowed the conceit of graduated paradises from the Jews or vice versa, inasmuch as both traditions trace themselves back to Abraham, and although Judaism is much the older faith, the Judaic formalization of Cabalism happened several centuries after the establishment of Islam.

"You guys," Johns Hopkins Johnson sighed. "One day *I'll* know a shitload, too, instead of being just a whippersnapper genius novelist. See you at the show?"

*Don't hold your breath,*

said I to myself; but to him, We'll see. In the event, my wife and I spent Thanksgiving quietly with extended-family members on the Eastern Shore; the show, if there really was one, went on without us (we saw no notice of it in the Baltimore *Sun*, although truth to tell, I more or less avoided looking for any; and because we shifted south not long thereafter, I had no occasion to ask my colleague whether he'd attended and how it went. But there were those printed tickets that Johnson had pressed upon me, surely not fake, and he had extended his invitation more or less publicly. . . . See how my uneasy fancies ran!), and *TOFO II*, having survived its predecessor's November Curse, was then presumably laid up for the winter. As for your narrator: Prepping for our own cold-weather retreat, I found that the seminar encounter in general and Johnson's "around the corner" teasing in particular, together with the dismayingly confident progress of his M.A. thesis, inspired me to a not especially creditable (and, I hope, uncharacteristic) resolve, perhaps at bottom no more than a muse-ruse to get my imagination up and running. Once settled in sunny Geezerville, I would after all direct my whole or at least my main professional attention to Charles Hunter's odd *Show Barge* script, with a triple aim: (1) To revise, redraft, and all but "complete" it for the Arkade Theatre Company, to the point where someone more experienced in the medium than I — perhaps J. Hopkins Johnson? — could set his other priorities aside, heh heh, and work the thing up for summer production on *TOFO II*. (2) In doing so, to get a better handle on my own still-elusive ground-plan for a millennium-turning (I had almost said "corner-turning") *FlOp II* novel, in the hope that once its narrative course was clear, my advantages of professional experience and established trade-publishing connections might yet fetch me first to the finish line despite my young rival's impressive head start. And (3) in any case, to purge my fancy of its late preoccupation—nay, obsession—by writing it out of my system, as I had fruitfully purged or anyhow exhausted other of its obsessions in decades past: the story of many an artist's professional life.

After a week of concentrated review and busy annotation of Hunter's script, in early December I telephoned the first of these intentions to an overjoyed Morton Spindler. In the faux–Yiddish accent that he enjoyed sometimes affecting, "I'm dencink!" he cried, and it was not difficult to envision that light-footed fellow's literally spinning, phone in hand. In his normal Eastern-Shore-of-Maryland-ese then, "Wait till Sher hears this! Wait'll *Cap'n Andy* hears! All hands on deck! Rescue's a-*coming soon!*"

For pity's sake don't *count* on it, I reminded him. I'm giving the thing my best shot, is all. Don't hold your breath.

In faux-Yiddish again, "I'm holdink already! Whole femily's holdink! Liddle Moishe, liddle Velvel, liddle Shmuel—all hold-ink!" And in straight Tidewater, "Thanks two million, Mister B! Full speed ahead! And remember: *Put pep!*"

Excuse me?

# The Millennium Bug

READER: On or about the winter solstice of 1998, Your aging author of Your aging narrative COMING SOON!!! came belatedly to understand that he and it had a "Y2K Problem" of their very own. As the closing days ran of that Hottest Year Thus Far on Record (U.S. launches Operation Desert Fox against Iraq; Israeli/Palestinian "Wye Plantation" peace accords unravel; President Clinton impeached by House Republicans; M/M Narrator take up again their winter tenancy in southwest Florida), and as the calendar by which most of the world these days dates time approached what most of the world regarded, correctly or not, as the final year of the final century of the second millennium of the Common Era, and as concerns about the Millennium Bug, or Y2K Problem, in the world's computer-software programs ranged from shrug-shouldered to TEOTWAWKI-apocalyptic (The End Of The World As We Know It), what presented itself to Your "Novelist Emeritus" Character was the following:

- That this project-in-the-works, by him conceived in Gemini-time '95 (see Chapter 2.3, "Ontological Lunchbreak," above), was, by Capricorn-time '98, 3.5 years old and nearly 300 draft pages long.

- That he had devoted professionally the entire year called 1998 (see "1998," below)—from, say, the first revelation of *l'affaire* Clinton/Lewinsky in January through the President's impeachment eleven months later — to the planning, drafting, revising, and editing of the first segment of Part II: i.e., "1995" — a single year of the story's action.

- That at that rate of composition — one "year" per year, so to speak — this tale of novelists Aspirant and "Emeritus," of Unoriginal Floating Operas, and of the possible End et cetera would never reach the present in time for its grand finale "next year": the climactic *fin de siècle*, COMING SOON! In short, that the swift Achilles of his pen would never overtake the tortoise Time. Indeed, inasmuch as "1995," a year in the writing, actually covers only the months from late May to December, he could expect Chapters "1996," "1997," and "1998" to require rather more than a year's chronicling apiece: the tortoise pen in even vainer pursuit of Time's fleet Achilles.

What to do?

This Y2K problem, moreover, was by then alas not the fellow's only; he was bugged, if not altogether buggered, by insectae over and above the mere Millennium. Indeed, as the Judiciary Committee of the U.S. House of Representatives wound up its acrimonious hearings and voted (along strict party lines) to send four articles of presidential impeachment to the full House, and as that scarcely less partisan assembly passed two of them on to the Senate for trial, Your N.E. Character felt that the year that had opened so positively ("1998," below) was closing as negatively himfor as it was for the American President. For just as Mr. Clinton, despite undiminished and even growing support from at least two-thirds of the national electorate, was by their congressional "representatives" nevertheless impeached, so Your Protagonist *pro tem* — despite his fruitful year's scribbling of "1995" and publication of half a dozen earlier-written short stories and essays (see "1998," below) — appeared and felt himself to be defeated on a number of fronts: not only to have failed in his earnest attempt at showboatery (the *pro bono* renovation of "Charles Hunter's" *Show Barge* cinestageplay and its featured billing on *TOFO II*, which had come to matter much himto), but also to have lost, in order of increasing seriousness, (1) his contest with a certain young Novelist Aspirant for, believe it or not, the amorous favors of . . . Ms. Scheherazade McAndrews Singer ("Say *what*?!" You exclaim: See "1998," below); (2) his ditto for successful completion-before-deadline of a *COMING-SOON!!!* novel; and, very possibly, (3)—*Miserabile dictu!* (See "1998," below.)

!

While his rival, contrariwise, by that year's end appeared on every front victorious: His maybe-not-so-wacko-after-all "New Show," *End Time*, was scheduled to replace his "GreatUnc Ennie's" flagging *Show Barge* as *T II*'s last-ditch Feature Production for '99; he was once again the enjoyer-in-chief of Ms. Kit's toothsome Whole Kaboodle; and his maybe-not-so-wacko-after-all cybernovel (*COMING SOON!!!* THE NOVEL?) was, by his own grinning Thanks-giving-time declaration, "off to the publishers, man, just under the wire for Y-Two-K! How's yours?"—just as said GreatUnc was put-ting the closing period (closing "option button," actually) to his own Chapter "1995."

In sum: Youth + Strength + Cunning really did appear to have defeated Age + Experience + (Could it be?) Fatigue. . . . *Hate to be the one to say this, sir,* Mort Spindler e-mailed him as Mr. and Ms. Us made our way south in mid-December—a cyberletter not re-ceived until the aforementioned solstitial P.M., when the couple were sufficiently unloaded, unpacked, and settled into their rented digs to get their laptop-cum-peripherals up and running—*but maybe it really is time to, uh (you shd excuse the expression), Pass the Torch? :-)*

What a fall from the spring of that year ("1998," below), when, barreling along on his draft of "1995," the old chap had successfully prevailed upon "Doctor Spin" and Newly-Special Friend S. Singer (over the objections of one Johns Hopkins Johnson) to mount *Show Barge* as *TOFO II*'s sole Main Season feature—magnanimously incorporating thereinto, as a sort of show-within-the-show, a few of the brighter bits of Johnson's less-than-successful *End Time* (includ-ing Kit & Kaboodle's not-unclever "Passing the Torch" routine: See below). Impatient with compromises and half-measures, rejuvenated in spirit by the experience of writing "1995" from the "Novelist Aspirant's" point of view as if reliving his own apprenticeship (a rejuvenation that, even at the time, he saw might ultimately leave him feeling older yet, the way taking a much younger lover at his present age and stage would likely do), Let it be make or break, Narrator had told the Arkade Theatre Company in *T II*'s fifth and his own sixty-eighth spring season: If the turkey doesn't fly this time, I'll pass the torch and jump ship for good.

This was in that year's April: Court dismisses Paula Jones sexual-harassment suit against President Clinton; Dow Jones Industrial Average tops 9K; Serbs attack ethnic Albanians in Kosovo, etc: See "1998." M/M Us were back north from Geezerville and reestablished on the Chesapeake, where, against Her better judgment, He had reengaged himself with the fortunes of FLOPCORP's faltering flagship. "His" *Show Barge* and Hop Johnson's *End Time* skits and parodies having alternated as the vessel's main feature through the preceding season (see "1997") and fared neither badly nor well enough, their rival authors had each done a bit of script-tinkering through the winter along with more considerable adjustments to their respective *COMINGS SOON!!!*, and in Preview Season '98 the ATC had tentatively resumed that alternation. But in the elder's general oats-feeling rejuvenation (for this was the springtime after the winter when, having decided that his version of this narrative was getting too autobiographical for comfort, he had all but eliminated the "Novelist Emeritus" character except as a minor foil and had redone the thing entirely as the story of an ambitious and not-untalented young writer's first feeling his professional oats) he became convinced that his rival's production was siphoning the company's limited resources from his own; that "we" would do better to put all our eggs of talent, rehearsal time, and production budget into one basket: *Show Barge*, "by Charles Hunter and friends," as it was being billed, with a modest little program note of explanation. Thus his make-or-break, turkey-fly-or-pass-the-torch proposal to the ATC.

"Don't pass your torch," had directed that company's amazing-eyed director, dropping to her bluejeaned knees astonishingly before astonished old "N.E." in her *T II* cabin like thong-pantied Ms. Lewinsky before the nation's Commander-in-Chief (as all hands would learn *ad nauseam* some months hence from the infamous Starr Report: See "1998") in that now-famous hallway off the Oval Office, "until I've lit it. *Then* we'll do the Flying Turkey."

Yes, well: I ought to tell you ("N.E." told his fetching gobbler presently, when he had, let's say, collected himself) that I toyed for a while with the idea of having the Hop Johnson character in my novel arrange for his old-fart rival to be seduced by the You character—

"Mm?"

—with the object of apparently rejuvenating him for a spell but ultimately distracting him from his projects-in-progress, wrecking his marriage, and leaving him an older, exhausted man: a burned-out has-been.

She raised those eyes those eyes from her own project-in-the-works. "And?"

Sitting on that bed-edge then, shaking his head at himself even as, appalled, he buried his fingers in her wheatstubble hair, And I bagged the idea, he told her. Too potentially embarrassing for all hands.

Shame on him for that, she paused to scold: In her humble opinion, *nothing* should have priority over capital-A Art. "So?"

So—Ah! Sherry!—I invented instead a much *older* lover for the Hop Johnson character, to confuse and distract *him* from *his* projects: a bedmate the age and stage of our Miz Bea Golden, excuse me. . . .

Flash of Eyes. "What's to excuse?" Zipping then out of her jeans but not yet her shortsleeve sweatshirt and her fetching though non-thong underpants, she returned to torch-ignition. "The bastard *has* been humping Mom now and then," she presently explained to the not yet technically adulterous but already guilt-stricken "N.E.," "in order to quote *enlarge the range of his experience*? And so he can *project into the Emerital point of view*, unquote—whatever *that* is? —in his crazy novel." Which, she went on to declare, was by its author's report not going well at all. In fact, she now felt justified in confiding, behind his cocky façade her Novelist-Aspirant pal Kaboodle was so shit-scared of losing out to his more experienced rival that "Get this: He pitches his girlfriend — the quote *Sherry Singer character*, that he supposedly really loves? — to go fuck the quote *Novelist Emeritus character* in order to distract and morally confuse him, et cetera. Now, I *ask* you!"

Mm-*hm*. And does she do it?

"Of course not!" Giving the torch-in-hand a reproving finger-snap: "What kind of tramp does he think she is? She throws the creep out for even *proposing* such a thing! Which is why he took up with Ma, to get back at me? I'll show *him*!"

How, exactly? By now shucking, Reader will of course have anticipated, her aforeadmired (black) sweatshirt and (robin's-egg-blue) undies; by energetically bestriding and all too soon snuffing the torch that she had most Kitfully lit; by shmooshing her new lover's old phiz the while so entirely into her et ceterae that he could scarcely breathe, let alone narrate. In short — and short it was, but hot, delicious, and unequivocable — by not only flapping that turkey's wings but making him fly.

Whereafter — the pair of them an offstage team now — over her mother's and ex-lover's objections, the shrugged shoulders of Holly Weil and Jay Brown, and Mort Spindler's worried-but-abstential "You're the boss, Sher," Director Singer and Friend put on Hold for the Main Season both *Tidewater Follies '98* and Hop Johnson's never-the-same-twice *End Time*, as problematically Protean as his alleged e-novel *COMING SOON!!!* — excerpting themfrom only the aforementioned brightest bits ("Passing the Torch," e.g., and a global-warming, fire-next-time allegory called "The Heat Is On," and the peppy "Y2K? Hip Hip Hooray!") for incorporation as incidental numbers in *Show Barge,* "by Charles Hunter and friends."

It was a much-improved script, all hands agreed, even those opposed on principle to this new eggs-in-one-basket policy or unhappy with the chosen basket: a script improved not only over Hunter's original, unfinished version (which Hop Johnson enjoyed maintaining was perhaps not unfinished at all, but rather "strategically incomplete," like the torso sculptures, "broken" columns, freestanding "preludes," and artful literary "fragments" dear to the Romantic period), but over "N.E.'s" earlier redoings of it as well: See "1996" and "1997," below. Truman Capote once remarked that he wouldn't do filmscripts because he had no taste for "team sports," and like many another novelist, ours had shared that bias. Dependent as one may be upon the advice of trusted editors (in his own case, principally though not exclusively his keen-eyed, keen-eared wife), the savvy of one's agents, and the sundry skills of designers, graphicists, publicists, and sales reps, novelizing remains nonetheless an essentially solitary art, by contrast whereto the arts of stage and screen are intensely, vitally collaborative. To his own surprise—for a dizzy while in that dizzy season, anyhow—our chap found this contrast refreshing. It is not simply that poor direction or inept performance can kill an effectively scripted scene and that, contrariwise, inspired stagecraft may redeem a merely adequate one: In the ongoing interplay between and among script, director, actors, and audience, the production *evolves* over the course of its rehearsals and even its run: Strengths are exploited, weaknesses strengthened, minimized, or eliminated; better line-deliveries and bits of business occur to actors or director after six performances or sixty, before audiences whose reactions are monitored nightly line by line, effect by effect. All very fascinating, for a season at least, to temporarily high-flying Novelists Emeriti.

Fascinating and (for a season, at least) *rejuvenating*—like drafting "1995" full blast from the point of view of a ballsy young Novelist Aspirant such as The N.E. Character had once been, while that character's rival struggled to imagine being *him*. Like observing, on that year's June sailing cruise down-Bay, that the *Chesapeake Floating Theatre James Adams II* (whose fading banner COMING SOON! had disappeared by June '96, and its entire crumbling superstructure by June '97, whether preparatory to reconstruction or to abandonment one couldn't then determine: See "1996" and "1997," below) had vanished altogether from Solomons Harbor, as had Hop Johnson's *End Time* from the active repertory of *TOFO II*. Like enjoying—however infrequently, furtively, and guilt-rivenly—a certain Kit's kaboodle. Nineteen Ninety-eight, Reader may recall, was the year that Pfizer Pharmaceuticals' Viagra offered to re-lead, at seven dollars a pop, the world's dysfunctional pencils. Mounting his re-revised *Show Barge*, like mounting and being mounted by Et Cetera, was for Your conflicted-to-the-marrow N.E. Character a Viagra of the spirit.

[*Horny "Star's Report" details discreetly excised.*]

"I should bloody think so!" You protest—no more indignantly than Yrs T: "What's this *guilt-riven, conflicted-to-the-marrow* crapola? For the first time in a nearly-three-decades-old and extraordinarily blest connection, the bloke betrays irrevocably the love and trust of the person most important to him on the planet—his other more-than-half, his sinequanon—with a woman of no emotional importance to him whatever, a mere (to him) young *piece*, simply out of some preening, unadmirable, and altogether uncharacteristic old-turkeycock sense of a rejuvenation based upon or anyhow involving the defeat of a less experienced rival. This is what a long and honorable career of coaching and otherwise aiding aspirant young writers comes to? This is the fruit of a union as dear to him as, indeed dearer than, his life? O Very Prince of Assholes he! Scumbag Emeritus!"

Yes, well. Patience, Reader: He'll get the bill.

"None too soon."

Yes, well. We are speaking, pray remember, of a season only: the spring and early summer of a year ("1998," below) by the winter solstice whereof all seemed, to Your Very P of A's, Your Et Cetera Emeritus, lost. Justice done. The old turkey plucked, his bill rendered and unpayable, his spring chickens come home to roost. . . .

"No more'n 'e deserved."

. . . E.g., his make-or-break *Show Barge* production unmade and broken—not impossibly sabotaged by his frustrated young rival, who put such pep into those incidental numbers from his own failed show (so generously incorporated into its successor) that critics and audiences alike applauded the Thing Contained above its Container, so to speak—some even suggesting that that show-within-the-show could do without the show-*without*-the show, if You follow me. . . .

"Hmp and ha."

. . . With the result that our N.E.'s postseason ultimatum to the ATC—to purge those *End Time* bits and do *Show Barge* straight on its merits in '99 or else scratch altogether both it and its renovator-emeritus—led to Mort Spindler's e-mailed winter-solstice response himto aforequoted: *Hate to be the one to say this, but* et cet. . . . :-)

"Tough titty for 'im! 'E 'ad it comin', mate."

. . . While strategic leakage of the quote *Phantom*'s quote *Star's Report*, replete with those guilt-riven et cetera but nonetheless horny details excised above, threatened to sink a union that the old bloke would kill to save. . . .

"So 'e says now. 'E should off 'imself already, sez we: Resign or be impeached!"

Yes, well. And on top of all this, that last solstitial straw: his aforeforeshadowed Y2K Problem, or Millennium Bug. . . .

"Up 'is bloomin' arse with it!" crudely suggests impatient Reader: "'Tis bloody tired We are o' this *See below* crapola, 'nall them quote-unquote *Nineteen Ninety* whatevers. On with the story or off with yer 'ead!"

Yes, well. *Voilà*:

"Wot the bleedin' 'ell?"

Click where Thou wilt, Mate.

"Will not!"

Amen. Allow me, then. [*Narrator "clicks" on "1996," where-upon there materializes "onscreen" a tricolumnar Virtual Chron-omenu:*]

# 1996

| | THE NEWS | THE NOVELIST EMERITUS | THE NOVELIST ASPIRANT |
|---|---|---|---|
| WINTER | Dow Jones up 33% in '95. Budget deadlock shuts down U.S. gov't. _TOFO II_ in hibernation until ATC Preview Season cast rehearses Tidewater Follies '96 for its 4th season. | At winter HQ, attempts to "put pep" into _Show Barge_ script while accumulating notes for "narrative" _COMING SOON!!!_ When _CS_ project stalls, shifts full attention to _SB_ script rewrite. Other usual winter work & pleasures. | @ Johns Hopkins U, shifts M.A. thesis topic from _CS_ e-novel to e-novel-in-form-of-postmod-showboat-show _End Time_. With S. Singer, helps ATC develop _Tidewater Follies '96_. All this plus weekend gigs with Pit Bulls. Whew. |
| SPRING | "Unabomber" suspect arrested. _T II_ launches Preview Season. Ex–CIA chief Wm. Colby disappears while canoeing near home on Chesapeake (heart attack). | Returns to Maryland; finishes _SB_ script renovation. No progress on _CS_ narrative. Edits proofs of forthcoming short-story series, etc. Lectures & vacations here & there; usual spring chores & pleasures. Is not displeased to hear that N.A.'s version of _CS_ seems to have morphed into something else entirely. Sets _CS_ narrative aside; turns 66. . . . On spring sailing cruise, notes removal of COMING SOON! banner from James Adams II in Solomons Harbor, MD. | All of above, plus commuting between Baltimore & Dorsettown for _T II_ rehearsals, etc., @ some cost to academic coursework. Oy. Submits M.A. thesis to advisor, who calls it "a scattered but lively allegorical mishmash." Oy$^2$. Degree awarded despite dept'l reservations abt "digital Postmodernism." Happily flees to _T II_, S. Singer, & other tidewater follies. Ah! + Oy! = _Ahoy!_ |
| SUMMER | _T II_ begins Main Season: _TF '96_, expanded w bits from J. H. Johnson's _End Time: Coming Soon!_ Hurricane Bertha threatens but misses Chesapeake. NASA launches Mars Pathfinder. Sheep-clone "Dolly" born. TWA 800 crashes. In "spare time," | Short-story book published. Drafts new stories & essays, _faute de mieux_. Usual summer chores & pleasures, between hurricane threats (see News, wch now & then elbows into one's personal affairs). . . . | See News. @ summer solstice, turns 26! Usual summer rat-race: Ah, joy! All juices surging, returns to e-novel _COMING SOON!!!_, not displeased to hear that N.E.'s version is stalled—perhaps abandoned? . . . ! In "spare time," nibbles S. Singer's |

| THE NEWS | THE NOVELIST EMERITUS | THE NOVELIST ASPIRANT |
|---|---|---|
| **SUMMER [CONT.]** ATC begins rehearsing *Show Barge* for Postview Season tryout. President *Clinton* renominated. Hurricanes Edouard & Fran threaten but miss Chesapeake. | | ear etc. & rehearses Great-Unc Ennie's not-bad overhaul of "C. Hunter's" *Show Barge.* |
| **FALL** *Show Barge* opens *T II*'s Postview Season. Dow Jones cracks 6000. Clinton reelected for 2nd term. *T II* is spared November Curse, except for even worse than usual deficit. Shining Path guerrillas seize hostages @ Japanese embassy in Lima. Jon-Benet Ramsey murdered. DJIA closes @ 6448. | Same as above, *f.d.m.*, plus apprehensive monitoring of *SB* opening. Inclines to blame self for play's shortcomings, but shrugs shoulders: not his dep't. Off on extended lecture/vacation tour of Australia & New Zealand. Usual fall chores & pleasures. Wonders whether Novelist Aspirant might be sandbagging *Show Barge* production. Shrugs shoulders; returns to SW FL HQ for usual winter work & pleasures. Against better judgment, agrees to re-revise "C. Hunter's" *SB* script. | Notes w some pleasure that *TF '96* plays better than *SB*, thanks to interpolated bits from *End Time* M.A. project, heh heh. Usual Postview Season rat-race. In "spare time," proceeds w state-of-the-art e-novel COMING SOON!!! (or, *End Time* or whatever). At close of (poor) 4th Season, accepts winter job as assistant to Mort Spindler. Lots of spare time. Collaborates w S. Singer on *The New Show: End Time* plus other hot stuff. "Loves" but fails to "understand" Ms. S.S. |

There You go, Mate. All underscored items hypertexted; click on any for amplification.

"Bloody will not!"

No? Perhaps "1997," then: *[Clicks same.]*

# 1997

| | THE NEWS | THE NOVELIST EMERITUS | THE NOVELIST ASPIRANT |
|---|---|---|---|
| WINTER | Clinton inaugurated. Peru hostage crisis continues. J-B Ramsey case fills tabloids. O. J. Simpson convicted by civil court. Hale-Bopp comet & "Heaven's Gate" mass suicides. ATC rehearses "new" *Show Barge.* | At SW FL HQ, hopefully reviews *CS* project & tinkers w *SB* re-renovation. Sends re-re-revised *SB* script to ATC for spring rehearsal; sets aside *CS* project (again) and returns to essay & short-story writing, *f.d.m.* | Busybusybusy! *Tidewater Follies* to be replaced by The New Show, *End Time: Coming Soon!!!* Show & novel each morphing into other: So what? Is sorry to hear ATC will remount N.E.'s leaky *Show Barge* in Preview Season :-(. Busy busybusy rehearsing same while tuning up show version of *End Time.* "Loves" but despairs of "understanding" S.S. . . . |
| SPRING | Massive flooding in U.S. Midwest. TV's "Ellen" comes out as lesbian. Peru hostages rescued. *SB* opens *T II* Preview Season. Killer tornadoes in TX. "Deep Blue" computer program defeats Garry Kasparov. T. Mc-Veigh convicted in OK bombing case. *Mir* supply rocket collides w space station. Boxer M. Tyson bites opponent's ear. *T II* opens 5th Main Season w *Show Barge & End Time* on alternate nights. | Returns to MD; bears down once again on *CS* project notes. Lectures & visits here & there. Actual progress on *CS* project! Turns 67 :-(. On spring sailing cruise, sees that *James Adams II*'s entire superstructure has been removed. May do same w *CS*'s. . . . | Business as usual. Promises to "give old N.E.'s new *Show Barge* our best shot," heh heh heh. Is tempted to sandbag the sucker; wonders whether N.E. is somehow sandbagging *End Time* by remote control? Resists such unworthy speculations & temptations, mostly. |
| SUMMER | Hong Kong ceded to China. *Pathfinder* lands on Mars, deploys *Sojourner*. DJIA cracks 8K. Princess Di killed in Paris car crash. Mother Teresa dies. Islamic fundamentalists massacre Algerian civilians. | Usual summer chores & pleasures. *CS* dragging again; shrugs shoulders, works on other projects, *f.d.m.* Hears "his" "new" *SB* is less than successful; again shrugs shoulders. *CS* project slogs along. Family visits, vacation in "spare time." | Turns 27. Is obliged to admit that neither *SB* nor *ET* is doing either badly or well enough. "Put more pep!" advises Dr. Spin. . . . Dum dee dum dum. In "spare time," slogs on w mf-ing e-novel: dum dee dum dummer. Understands will never "understand women." Needs vacation, but can't spare time. |

254

| | THE NEWS | THE NOVELIST EMERITUS | THE NOVELIST ASPIRANT |
|---|---|---|---|
| FALL | ATC drops both _SB_ & _ET_ in Postview Season; improvises _Tidewater Follies '97_ from wreckage. No news noted; world evidently on Hold. _T II_ flounders through Postview Season; is spared November Curse, but Can't Go On Like This. Ends 5th Season in deep doo-doo, per usual. | Usual fall chores & pleasures. Attends 50th high-school class reunion (!) in Cambridge, MD. Hiking/touring vacation in Arizona. _CS_ project stalls again; maybe needs major reconstruction, like _James Adams II_? Vacations in Dutch Antilles while considering major changes to _CS_ project. Readings & lectures here & there before shifting to SW FL HQ for usual winter work & pleasures. Decides _CS_ project is "too close to home"; will eliminate "N.E. Character" except as minor foil & redo story entirely from N.A.'s viewpoint: young writer's 1st novel, etc. On w story! | Decides his _CS_ e-project lacks "center," just as N.E. warned back in '95. . . . Too busy w _T II_'s problems (see News) to address his own. Attends 6th high-school class reunion in Baltimore. Works arse off on _T II_. Decides whole _CS_ project needs major reconstruction. . . . Decides to redo it entirely as faux–electronic novel from N.E.'s point of view: senior novelist's last hurrah before e-fiction & EVR supplant p-fiction altogether! YOUTH + STRENGTH + CUNNING OMNIA VINCIT! On w story! |

The "mouse" is Yours, Mate, virtually: Click away!

". . . ! Tricolumnal Chronomishmash me bloomin' arse!"

Mm-hm. Surely "1998," then—already to some extent reviewed usby, but its hypertextual details here now at Your virtual fingertips. Click _ce que Voudrais!_

# 1998

| | THE NEWS | THE NOVELIST EMERITUS | THE NOVELIST ASPIRANT |
|---|---|---|---|
| WINTER | Mild & wet El Niño winter in U.S. Pfizer markets Viagra. Clinton/Lewinsky scandal exposed by K. Starr & Co. UN/Iraq standoff, again. "Asteroid may strike Earth @ 1:30 P.M. Th 10/26/28." Arkansas school murders. *T II* rehearses *SB, ET, & TF '98, f.d.m.* | In SW FL HQ, replans *CS* from N.A.'s point of view. Lectures here & there on History v. Fiction. | In D-o-C, MD, assists Mort Spindler & replans *CS* from N.E.'s point of view. Will maybe give Old Fart a young lover & then expose him, heh heh? Also cobbles up *Tidewater Follies '98* for poor dear *T II*. Not easy to project into N.E.'s POV; proposes SS seduce Old Fart, *pour l' art*, heh heh heh. ;-) Stay tuned. . . . |
| SPRING | Paula Jones v. Bill Clinton dismissed. DJIA tops 9K; spring tornadoes rip Midwest. Serbs attack Albanians in Kosovo. *T II* launches 6th Preview Season w modified *Show Barge + Tidewater Follies '98.* Irish peace accord; India/Pakistan A-bomb tests. ATC decides to drop *TF '98* for Main Season; will do *Show Barge* only. | Returns to MD; full speed ahead on *CS* Ch. "1995," from N.A.'s POV (maybe give Young Twerp a much older lover, heh heh heh?) To CA for daughter's wedding + here & there for misc. lectures. Presses ATC to drop N.A.'s *End Time* & concentrate on *Show Barge* (w a few bits from *ET*, to pacify N.A., heh). Feels rejuvenated: Ch. "1995" chugs along, from N.A.'s spunky POV. Spring chores & pleasures! Turns 68. . . . On spring cruise, sees no trace of *James Adams II* in Solomons Harbor. *Sic semper* competition! Full speed ahead! | Arranges pretense of SS's shucking Yrs T in favor of N.E., heh heh heh. Pretends to go along w ATC's misguided new agenda, heh. . . . |
| SUMMER | Clinton/Lewinsky case heats up; ditto global warming. Kosovo battles continue. DJIA sets record (9338). U.S. embassies bombed in Kenya & Sudan. Clinton "apolo- | Hears *SB* show is flagging after good start; suspects sabotage. "1995" chugs on; ditto summer chores & pleasures. But annual beach vacation is scrubbed by Hurricane | Turns 28, w trick or 2 left up sleeve, heh heh. Lets it be known that *his CS* novel is "about finished," heh heh. Has yet other cards sleeved. YOUTH + STRENGTH + CUNNING RULE! |

| THE NEWS | THE NOVELIST EMERITUS | THE NOVELIST ASPIRANT |
|---|---|---|
| **SUMMER [CONT.]** gizes" re Lewinsky. Hurricanes Bonnie & Danielle miss MD but strike elsewhere. DJIA plunges to 7600s; Swiss-Air 111 crashes; K. Starr's dirty-laundry list released to Congress (& to public). M. McGwire breaks baseball HR record. Hurricane Georges misses MD, but etc. Republicans call for Clinton to resign. | Bonnie, and the news from _T II_ (& elsewhere) nags. . . . | |
| **FALL** ATC drops _Show Barge_, limps into Postview Season on _TF '98_. Netanyahu/Arafat conference @ Wye Plantation, MD, amid record heat & drought. DJ back up to 8700. Milosevic "retreats" from Kosovo. Chile's Pinochet detained in U.K. Iraq blocks U.N. inspectors again. Democrats gain in off-year elections despite Clinton scandal. Hurricane Mitch kills 1000s in Central America. DJIA back to record highs. _T II_ is spared November Curse, except for etc. Wye Plantation Accords unravel; Clinton impeached in House; DJIA closes @ 9481. ATC rejects N.E.'s ultimatum re _Show Barge_; may stage "all new" _End Time_ instead, by Novelist Apparently Triumphant JHJ :-( | Bad news from ATC re _SB_, from FL re Hurricane Georges, from DC re Starr Report, from N.A. re his _CS_ e-novel ("About done, Dad!"). Despite all which, "1995" chugs along. 1995? Lectures & tours in Spain. "1995" still chugs on & on & on. One begins to wonder. . . . Then finishes "1995" at last: a whole year's work! Ultimatum to ATC: Do _SB_ in "pure form" next season or drop it altogether. To SW FL for winter, but funerals & other setbacks impede usual pleasures of the season. @ winter solstice, reviews year's work on _CS_ project & sees perhaps fatal Y2K Problem therein. Bad news from Dorsettown-on-Choptank, too. . . . | Heh heh heh. Maybe time for a "Star's Report" from the Phantom?

(Heh.)

Lets it be known that _his CS_ e-novel is "off to publishers"! N.A. to N.E.: May be time to pass torch, heh heh heh? _Sic semper emeriti!_ |

Clicquez-Vous, s.V.p.?

"In a pig's arse We will! Who's in charge here, you or Us?"

Now You're talking.

"Yours to navigate and steer, says We! Ours to enjoy the ride or jump ship!"

Aye aye, Mate.

"Fish or cut bait, resign or be impeached, et cet! Can't help noticing, though, that yer cockamamie quote *Chronomenu* there makes no mention of Old Turkeycock's floating hankypank; nor are We offered hypertextual horny details of that Phantom chap's quote *Star's Report*, heh heh. Miz Editor at work again?"

Nope: Yours Truly at work: Novelist Emeritus back in saddle, unpassed torch in left hand, virtual mouse in right, with which latter he now "clicks," without so much as a By Your Leave,

$$\boxed{1999}$$

" 'Ow's that?"

## 1999

| | THE NEWS | THE NOVELIST EMERITUS | THE NOVELIST ASPIRANT |
|---|---|---|---|
| JAN. | La Niña blizzards blanket U.S. Midwest. Iraq/U.S. air skirmishes continue. Clinton impeachment trial opens in Senate. DJIA sets new record highs until Brazil crisis pulls plug. ATC drops N.A.'s *End Time*, too: Any suggestions for *T II*'s Final Season? | In SW FL, down but not out, deletes fictitious "SS affair" (a crude ploy of N.A.'s) from novel; solves *CS*'s Y2K Problem w stroke of virtual mouse! Back to drawing board w *CS* project: re-designs it from alternat-ing N.E./N.A. viewpts, a p-novel w some aspects of e-fiction. Will have it both ways, & to hell w Millennium deadline: AGE + STRENGTH + CUNNING + PATIENCE OMNIA VINCIT, or al-most *omnia*. . . . ;-) | Learns hard way that "off to publishers" ≠ accepted for publication: His e-novel can't find agent, much less publisher. Deletes "elderly lover" from novel & life (crude ploy of N.E.'s). Down but not out, con-ceives for *T II*'s Final Sea-son a haveitbothways show called *Show Barge II* in wch best large chunks of *End Time* replace *Show Boat* bits as show-within-show. . . :-(? |

"More bloomin' Chronoblather! Spare Us the rest, luv — but 'ow come it's naught but Jan'ry this time up?"

Since You ask: Because 1/99 is *where we are.* More exactly, 'tis where Narrator was in his literal life-story's chronomenu when, with a click of his muse's virtual mouse first on <u>CS's Y2K Problem</u> . . . [*"Clicks" same on same, whereupon appears "onscreen" the hypertexted amplification* "If it continues to require at least a year of Real Time to inscribe a year of Narrative Time, then the telling will never overtake the tale in time for their projected convergence aboard *TOFO II* on 9/9/99, *coming soon!"*] and then on <u>solves</u> . . . [*"Clicks" on same, whereupon appears "onscreen" the hypertexted amplification* "By conception and deployment of Virtually Hypertexted Tricolumnar Chronomenus to dispense with '1996,' '1997,' and '1998' in one fell swoop, or three, thereby leaping, in January 1999, to 'January 1999'"], he not only solved his *COMING SOON!!!* novel's Y2K problem but, while he was at it, purged therefrom that altogether fanciful "affair" with "Sherry Singer" as well as "the Phantom's" lubriciously detailed "Star's Report" thereof: crude stratagems of his young competitor's to undo his competition, as Ms. Singer herself acknowledged when she dumped the sly sumbitch for even proposing such a thing or things, not to mention for his shacking up on the side with her aging-but-still-occasionally-horny mom. Thus with one *coup de maître* or two did AGE + STRENGTH + CUNNING + PATIENCE + PERSISTENCE, with a little help from INSPIRATION, carry the day over mere callow YOUTH + TALENT + TRICKSINESS + AMBITION and clear the narrative decks for our going

On
with
the
story
!

# 1999

*Push that button,*

and You get this spiel. The world onspins, but Narrator finds himself
with a leg up, temporarily, on Time. Both in our story and in fact,
it's just now latter January 1999: Ugly goings-on between Serbs and
ethnic-Albanian separatists in "the former Yugoslavia," which "the
community of nations" seems unable to ameliorate; ditto in Iraq,
where Saddam Hussein, in defiance of the not-so-United Nations,
presumably continues to rebuild his arsenal of mass destruction
while his people suffer and die from the economic sanctions meant
to punish him. Here in the US of A, President Clinton delivers an
upbeat State-of-the-Union message to the Congress deliberating his
removal from office; his ever-higher ratings in the polls remain as
impervious to his personal derelictions and the clamoring of his political enemies as is our booming stock market to the economic
woes of Asia and Brazil.

Et cetera, per 1/99's Virtually Hypertexted Tricolumnar Chronomenu, while—at his rented desk in his rented digs in sunny southwest Florida—Yours Truly writes the words *Yours Truly writes the
words* and contemplates his odd new vantage-point. Thanks to that
smoke-and-mirrors "Y2K Breakthrough" aforefloated and to the
narrative Great Leap Forward thereby vouchsafed him, instead of
vainly pursuing Time's Tortoise he finds himself (temporarily)
astride the creature's carapace: in synch! Nay, more: The Arkade
Theatre Company having finally and no doubt wisely abandoned his

*Show Barge* play "by Charles Hunter and friends," he is suddenly, unexpectedly free to dismount and (barring Real Life's unforeseen setbacks, distractions, interruptions) even to run on ahead of said Tortoise; to imaginarrate Chapter "1999" of *COMING SOON!!! A Narrative* before that plodding beast (he means T's T) sprouts wings, as is its notorious wont, and once more leaves him scribbling in its wake.

The prospect is daunting, to be sure. Another balmy Gulfcoast-winter day has run already since I began this chapter; yet another runs as I add *yet another runs*. It's 1/99 still, but for not much longer; the world and I persist and function yet, as does the Clinton presidency—but one day closer to who knows what? What if this morning I should write, e.g., that *on St. Patrick's Day '99, going on with our story, Mr. & Ms. Us returned north per schedule to tidewaterland and our Usual Spring Chores and Pleasures,* and then a month from now—i.e., a month before "then"—on St. Valentine's Day we're creamed in a car crash on the Tamiami Trail, two blocks from where I pen this hypothetical scenario? *Old(er) fart suffers fatal coronary @ 55 mph behind wheel of white Lincoln Town Car southbound on Rt 41 N; vehicle crosses median and collides head-on with aging Buick Century station wagon, killing snowbird novelist driver of same. . . .* Or what if we get word that, even earlier, the furnace in our Chesapeake creekside base, unattended in our absence, developed a propane leak that ignited at 7:02 A.M. on Groundhog Day, house and contents a total loss in the ensuing explosion and fire despite best efforts of good neighbors and Kent County Fire & Rescue Squad? What if today I launch the fictive *"TOFO II"* on its "Final Season" this coming "April," only to have it happen that agents of the Islamic terrorist Osama bin Laden—taking advantage of our national distraction by the Clinton trial's Quite Unforeseen Latest Development or Aftermath—manage on the ides of March to devastate the whole Washington-to-Philadelphia corridor, including the entire Chesapeake estuarine system, with a fiendishly coordinated array of biological Doomsday devices? This while we mere novelers are addressing such loose ends and cannons in our story's plot as the unquestionably gifted though heh heh as yet unsuccessful aspirant novelist J. Hopkins Johnson and his on-again-off-again-on-again partner and lover Sherry Singer (she of those eyes those eyes, etc.); the twin tugboat captains Harry and Elva Kane and their stillborn triplet brother — Abie, was it?; peppy Morton "Dr. Spin" Spindler; supple Jay "Obie" Brown; Holly Weil; and even that category-eluding belowdecks entity self-denominated "Ditsy" — of whomall, I confess, I grew quite fond, my young competitor most certainly included, in course of my professional involvement themwith in "1996," "1997," and "1998." Yea, even of Ms. "Bea Golden" and her stalwart Captain Period Adam Period Lake. And that reclusive oddball Arkangel-in-Chief, Andrew S. (Todd [Cap'n Andy] Andrews) Todd? Even he, forsooth, insofar as one can feel fondness through so many filters. All of those folks dedicated, more or less and more or less ably, to the quixotic enterprise of keeping "our" sinking ship afloat.

As am I.

*In June of that year,* I might write now in its January, *on their customary good-bye-springtime/hello-summer sail down-Chesapeake in their venerable but still eminently Bayworthy cruising cutter, upon entering Solomons Harbor for their customary pit-stop and Competition check, M/M Us were* [dismayed/astonished/delighted/relieved/intrigued] *to behold, where the* Chesapeake Floating Theatre James Adams II *had once bravely advertised itself to be* COMING SOON!, [etc.] . . . But what if, as Narrator's sixty-ninth-birthday surprise, The World As We Know It should end in May '99, seven months ahead of the millennium-crazies' timetable?

What if, what if, what if: incantation at once soothing and stimulating to us talesters, whose stock-in-trade is *what if*s, *what next*s, and *and then one day*s. No sooner do I inscribe that proposition than, sure enough, Real Life intrudes as is its habit, and suddenly it's no longer January: Distractions of concern to me but not to our story have kept me from it for nearly a fortnight, while the Tortoise step by step gained ground. It's now 2/2/99 already, Groundhog Day: six more weeks of winter weather ahead for the mid-Atlantic states if the creature sees his shadow today. Our house, I note with relief, did not explode this morning as aforewhatiffed; Capt. Elva Kane, though a firm affirmer of folk wisdom and its associated proverbs, allows that global warming and La Niña winters may weaken the predictive value of Pennsylvania's Punxsutawney Phil, the most looked-to weather groundhog. Here in relentlessly sunny Florida it is only we expatriate snowbirds who take note, half nostalgically, of the 2/2 tradition, remembering when it mattered to us whether spring arrived early or late; when, as children, we hoped for cloudy weather today so that the critter venturing out of his hibernation-hole would not be frightened by his shadow back into it, and our snow-and-ice season be thus prolonged.

Johns Hopkins Johnson, I confidently imagine, while no doubt disappointed by his novel manuscript-or-disk's unsuccess thus far with the New York literary agencies and trade publishers, will not have languished in discouraged hibernation back home in Maryland. Rare indeed in our profession are instant recognition and success, regardless of the newcomer's talent. So more usual is initial rejection that back in my coaching days I advised my most promising apprentices to hope for everything but expect nothing, inasmuch as their fortunes would likely lie somewhere between; to develop if they could a tunnel-visioned imperviousness to discouragement.

As has, I'm sure, our Dorsettown-on-Choptank Novelist Aspirant. Even should he know, as he cannot yet, of the sudden "Y2K" advantage that positions me on 2/2/99 to speed our story toward its September climax COMING SOON!, I can nowise imagine his giving up the ship. On the contrary: I see him waking at dawn this Tuesday morning — 7:10 A.M. and clear-skied down here in florid FL, some minutes later and raw and rainy up there in Dorsettown, although he's snug enough snugged naked front-to-back with Sherry McAndrews Singer (his lucky front, her perfect back) in the Snug Harbour apartment that those lovers have shared since *T II*'s last-Thanksgiving lay-up. *There never was any proposal by him that she attempt to seduce Yours Truly* in order to disrupt my life and, in presumable consequence, my progress on this novel: That business, like "the Phantom's" tattling *Star's Report*, was an unworthy invention of Hop Johnson's, for which I'm accepting his apology. Neither was there any "experience-widening liaison" between him and Sher's mother, June "Bea Golden" Harrison: an unworthy invention of mine, for which I offer him my apology. No: The ever-less-young couple—he's twenty-eight these days, she thirty-four—have been partners for several years now offstage as well as on [*For details, click appropriate hypertexted items in "1996" et seq.*], the only unresolved issues of substance in their relation being (1) a persisting semi-sexual voltage between Ms. Singer and Capt. E. Kane, which pair Hop knows to have had at least occasional connection in seasons past but, they swear, not since Singer went straight in, oh, 1997?, plus (2) a confessed lapse or two of Hop's with Holly Weil in '96 [*Click around in "1996"; it's in there somewhere*], pretty much past history since Holly's engagement to Mort Spindler's elder brother Mark, an orthodontist in nearby Salisbury, MD. 'Twas oral sex anyhow—two-way oral, unlike Clinton/Lewinsky's, and to that extent less deniable as "sexual relations," not that anybody's counting such distinctions except Holly and her new fiancé, both of whom have busy erotic histories but share an old-fashioned inclination to come to their marriage bed technically virginal, if scarcely innocent. Their business, surely; let's leave them to it while Hop and Sherry get to theirs.

He wakes, stiffpricked as usual at that hour—Ah, youth!—from mere young-male vigor plus the need to urinate. His colleague and wintertime boss, Mort Spindler, has explained to him that the traditional Orthodox-Jewish-male awakening cry—"Thank G-D I'm not a woman!"—far from being misogynous, is a grateful salute to these morning erections, to be uttered as one turns lovingly to one's wife. Be that as may, finding his boner poked between those sweet nether hemispheres, heathen Hop thanks Aphrodite not that he's a man but that his bedmate is a woman—and such a woman! She's still a-snooze and, he happens to know, in mid-menstruation, but not so out of action on either front, so to speak, that she fails to register the hand on her upper breast (they're lying left-sided) and the urgency at her hinder cleft. Without even opening those eyes those eyes she fishes from her nightstand the Astroglide, presses it into his tit-hand, whispers "Go easy," and then herself obligingly handspreads those cheeks those cheeks for readier rectal access while he, covering her shoulderblades with kisses, greasejobs their respective anatomical equipment and gently effects penetration. The unaccustomedness though not-quite-novelty thereof—such *bite* in his fit friend's sphincter! — brings him quickly to ejaculation. "I love you," he does not forget to whisper, the fact being that he does. "Me too you," she murmurs back, hoping and pretty much believing that she does; half wishing she were a normal wife and mother already at her age as well as a real professional, like say Mort's ob/gyn wife Rachel (who has cautioned her that too vigorous or frequent anal intercourse can lead to hemorrhoids, infibulation, and other unpleasantnesses, but gentle and occasional, not to worry); half relieved that she isn't, given her mom's less-than-inspiring example. Still spooned, the pair re-drowse, but as the morning infiltrates their bedroom she finds herself mentally reviewing the day's schedule—postbreakfast exercise run; then office phonecalls and e-mails to Preview Season ATCers, to work out March rehearsal logistics; 10:30 brunch with her mother in hopes of divining how seriously the Angel Team intends their billing of 1999 as *T II*'s Final Season; then a trial workout with maybe just Hop and Mort of the number "Fire Next Time," or, "The Heat Is On," salvaged from their *End Time* show and surely adaptable for *Tidewater Follies '99*.

Her lover, meanwhile—his face buried in her neck-nape and his penis flaccidly ejecting from her butt like, um, toothpaste from a tube? Not quite right; hell with it—finds his imagination already engaged, unromantically, with Next Lines for that old "Are We Postmodern?" bit from back in *Tidewater Follies '95* or thereabouts, of which the first eight bars (with a wink at "GreatUnc Ennie") went

> *Are we Postmodern?*
> *Is this the end of the road?*
> *Or is recycled self-conscious irony*
> *just one more passing mode?*

The *Follies* takeoff had been set to the melody of "The Party's Over," and while its taker-offer has recalled or invented the next two lines—

> *If we're Postmodern,*
> *How come I feel so passé?*

—he can't for the life of him come up with where the lyrics went or ought to go from there—something-something *at the end of the day*? *life's just a cliché*?—and he thinks he sees a spot for that number in the script of *Show Barge II* that's been his front-burner project since *CS!!!:* THE NOVEL? disappeared into the trackless wilds of Manhattan.

Youth, youth. Juice/bagel/coffee and morning newspaper with friend Sher, who's less confident than he that FLOPCORP's "Final Season" billing for *TOFO II* is mainly that: an ironic, self-conscious recycling of *The Original Floating Theatre*'s half-serious gimmick in 1940, already recycled in Charlie Hunter's *Show Barge* play and readily supersedable, should they get lucky for a change this year, by the old Back By Popular Demand! routine in Spring Zero-Zero. And if this season really turns out to be *T II*'s last, in the showboat mode? He already has more ideas for a twenty-first-century Floating EVRkade than Mort & Company will sit still for. Large initial capital outlay required for all the requisite high-techery, he grants, and the stuff has to *stay* front edge or it's nowhere. Done right, however, it could be the hottest thing on the watershed: Tidewater timewarps! Digitized nostalgia! Wraparound holography! You are *there*, baby: front and center in the Virtual Big Picture! Maybe some input from Ms. **SPECIAL EFFECT!**? He'll just see.

"So *come mierda*," his patient partner sighs for good luck, and checks her watch. "Meanwhile, we're four weeks from rehearsals with *nada* to rehearse. What do I tell Ma?"

Her friend looks to be reading the sports and op-ed pages simultaneously, as if somehow correlating them. For openers, he suggests without raising his head, how 'bout *At the end of the day, life's just a cliché*?

Doing a few fetching stretchies in her sweatsuit before she takes off for track and office, "My power brunch with her is set for half past ten," she reminds him. "Put that line in the show somewhere and give me two capital-I Ideas to fool Ma into thinking we're thinking."

Two uppercase Ideas coming up, dum dee dum dum. . . .

She has grown fond of the Jiminy-Cricket look he gets when

he's Really Thinking, as indeed he really knows how to do on demand: pushes his eyglasses up, puts on his mock-heavy Let's-See-Now expression, and likely as not comes up pronto with something bright. So okay, his *End Time* show (*theirs*, really) was over the locals' heads (Sher's convinced it would've played well off-off-Broadway); and with his "Great-Uncle Ennie's" *Show Barge* remake there was all that crazy Novel-Competition baggage dragging them down. Lord knows whether they've a capital-F Future together, but their three-year-now association has convinced Ms. Kit that her pal Kaboodle is more than merely many-talented; she has come pretty much to believe that he's . . . let's not say a *genius*, but a virtual wizard for sure, take that "virtual" anyhow one chooses. He *knows* stuff — a shitload more than she does — about everything from medicine (his parents) through art history and politics and philosophy and quantum physics and poetry (his prep school and namesake university) to Baltimore Orioles batting averages. The guy is clever, agile, sympathetic, serious but never solemn about his work, and prevailingly good-charactered: Those lapses with Holly Weil were one-third running joke ("Holly Weil says Holly won't, but Hollywood says Holly will," etc.), one-third a leveling of the sexual playfield after Sher's experimental dalliance with Elva Kane, and one-third mere Clintonesque priapism, for which he Sincerely Apologizes. Above all, he's imaginatively resourceful. E.g.:

Two uppercase Ideas, he says again, coffee cup in right hand, left forefinger already raised. *Uno:* We add a big *Arke*-and-*Dove*/ Lord-Baltimore/Maryland-Day shtick to the New Show. When's Maryland Day? September the somethingth? We schedule a major-league production for Maryland Day on Saint Whatsisname's Island — Clements (like Solomons, no apostrophe), where the first colonists landed — and/or in Saint Mary's City, where that working replica of the original *Dove* is already in place. Our Noah's Ark in the *End Time* show does double duty as Lord Baltimore's A-R-K-E; Elva's *Dove* plays Noah's dove, and Cap'n Harry's *Raven* gets to stand for both Noah's raven and Edgar Poe's, with Baltimore's new football Ravens thrown in for good measure. Big publicity shmeer for Maryland's Whatevereth Anniversary, see, and we ride it all season by way of buildup to the Saint Clements landing on Maryland Day. *Then*—Get this! [*holds up left-hand index finger beside ditto forefinger, indicating both Victory and Uppercase Idea Two*]—as our Ninety-nine season runs, we funnel in more and more Y2K crapola, so that *End Time Coming Soon!* starts attracting national media attention as light topical filler on the network news shows; and after pumping things up to our Maryland Day blowout on the Potomac, we make our triumphal grand-finale procession up to Baltimore—fireboats, clipper ships, newscopters, all flags a-flying—and we blow our lid off in the Inner Harbor on guess when: Eleven Eleven! Which is Veterans Day, but never mind that: What we'll be selling is *TOFO*'s legendary November Curse combined with the millennial Eleventh Hour and the Y2K hysteria. Final Season! End Time Coming Soon! Nine Nine Ninety-nine followed by Eleven Eleven!

She leans over him to kiss his head. "Maryland Day is like next month: March the Twenty-somethingth. We think you're thinking Defenders Day, mid-September: Fort McHenry and the Star-Spangled Banner and all? Anyhow, you're my wizard."

He shmoozles his shnoz happily side to side in her shirtfront, never mind how it smears his specs. So we call it Maryland Defenders Day at Saint Clements in September. Want a better Uppercase Idea yet?

"Gotta run. Anyhow, you lowercased me once already this morning."

*Youth. Energy. Mile-a-minute inspiration,*
even if it's nine parts chaff to one of wheat. Here in Florida USA, where one sits in shortsleeved sunny February imagining this tidewater breakfast scene and drafting its paragraphs between one's own breakfast and lunch, Time's advance and mortal course are everywhere apparent: in the age and stage that permit us snowbirds to escape our northern winters if we so choose (Key West, a few hours farther south, crawls with writers this time of year like Martha's Vineyard or the Hamptons in summer); in the preponderance of silverhaired citizens, their Cadillacs and Lincolns with midwestern li-

cense-plates filling the abundant Handicapped Parking slots in every mall and plaza; in the motorized grocery-carts standing by in supermarkets, the daily full-page ads for estate-tax-beating seminars, the rapid turnover of retirement real estate as advancing age and/or spouse-death moves the golf-and-gardening set in their gated communities from landscaped full-fledged houses to lower-maintenance "villas" and "coach homes," thence to even-lower-maintenance condominiums, and anon to assisted-living units or extended-care facilities (*Be kind to your children*, reads a popular local T-shirt: *They may choose your nursing home*). For one approaching age seventy in good health, there is comfort, to be sure, in seeing so many vigorous octogenarians on the scene along with the variously impaired to whose ranks fate may well consign him before his next birthday. And there are of course *young* bodies on the beach as well as old; young faces in the streets and stores; even cheery yellow schoolbuses chugging down the Tamiami Trail. But Time's human vector is more ubiquitously apparent down here than it is Back North, even in communities like Dorsettown-on-Choptank (its Patmos Tower facility excepted—but those folks remain largely indoors and out of sight this time of year, save for group excursions to market and movieplex). From his own past experience of twenty-somethinghood, Narrator understands that to people of the age and stage of Johns Hopkins Johnson—unless personal circumstance has rubbed their noses in decrepitude and death, as it has not yet his—mortality is little more than a notion. They know better, of course: have perhaps lost grandparents, have surely heard parents speak of their own youth, and've seen family photos of those unimaginably distant decades—the 1960s! the 1950s! not to mention the virtually prehistoric decade thembefore, when World War II hit History like the meteorite that ended the Cretaceous period, its massive extinctions, migrations, and landscape-rearrangements making way for the birth of the world that gave birth to them. All the same, they can't help feeling that the aged and even the infirm have somehow *elected* that condition, Lord knows why, or have as it were been assigned those roles the way ATC members may be assigned to play Foxy Grandpa, Querulous Aunt Bessie, or Heavy but Goodhearted Old Dad, so that *they*, the Leads and Ingenues—the Sherry Singers and Hop Johnsons, Holly Weils and Jay "Obie" Browns—can play their youthful-energetic, all but immutable selves. *We* enter a new decade knowing that it will zip past in nearly no time and hoping we'll survive it more or less intact; to them, the 1980s spun on forever as they themselves crept all the way from prepubescence through adolescence to voting age, and these 1990s, like their young-adult twenties or thirties, have lasted a long, long time already—the way summer vacations used to stretch out between second and third grades, and then third grade went on interminably before the next summer vacation. . . .

Well. By when anyone reads these lines in print, whatever's going to happen Y2Kwise (next to nothing alarming, Narrator bets) will already have happened, perhaps long since. But on this brilliant subtropical Floridian February morn, already a day after the preceding paragraph's—Jordan's King Hussein having in the interim died of non-Hodgkins lymphoma, four U.S. Presidents past and present en route aboard Air Force One to Amman and his funeral as I pen this—none of us here-and-nowers knows what the millennicentury's sooncoming wind-up will bring with it: not worldwise, not uswise, and most certainly not *TOFO-II*wise. In that last category, however, Author acknowledges a few cards up his sleeve and does not doubt that his erstwhile rival, his once-and-future competitor, the Novelist Aspirant in Temporary Remission, has a few of his own tucked here and there about his busy person.

Such as? Without presuming to speak for one's still-possible successor-of-sorts, one can readily imagine even from this distance that Morton Spindler, when his associate lays out his grand *plan du jour* for *T II*'s Final Season, will promptly nix the September "Maryland Defenders Day" whizbangery on St. Clements Island in the Potomac as "*Meshugge*, man! Never mind the fudged dates: The place is an *island*, for Chrissake: a state park in mid-river without even a ferry service! Six yachties and four crabbers we'd have for an audience! Fuhgeddaboudit already!" The rest of the proposal, on the other hand, excites him more and more as they review it (in truth, it was not born at that morning's breakfast like Athene from the head of Zeus; Mort and Hop and Sherry too have been mulling something of the sort since fall '98 lay-up time): St. Mary's City, where Lord B's colonists established their capital shortly after the St. Clements landing on March 25, 1634, looks to be an ideal September MD-Day destination: All the colonial dreck in place like a mini-Williamsburg; their *Dove* next to ours; nice mid-size college there that'll be just starting its fall semester, and so a potentially large student-discount audience. Plus good wharfage smack in front of the place, just up the St. Mary's River off the Potomac, with potential draw from the gentry of St. Mary's County and environs. The conflation of Y2K mania and *T II*'s advertised "Final Season," like the conflation of Noah's Ark and Lord Baltimore's *Arke*, might be exactly the kind of CPR to Put Pep into a revamped *End Time* show —

"End Time Show *Barge*," Hop interrupts, aiming both forefingers at his colleague as he sometimes does to make as it were a point: "We're stealing the Final Season bit from GreatUnc Ennie, who stole it from Charlie Hunter, who anticipated Life's imitation of Art in Nineteen Forty/Forty-one."

"*Are we Postmodern?*" Mort can't help happily rising from his desk-chair to sing. "And do we need your guy's okay to steal his stolen goods?"

Not in Hop's opinion: The idea was indeed Charles Hunter's, borrowed from *The Original Floating Theatre*'s half-seriously proclaimed Final Season for use in his unfinished (and uncopyrighted) *Show Barge* playscript fifty-plus years ago, and so for all intents and purposes it's public domain. Anyhow, the war seems to be over between Aspirant and Emeritus: One of Hop's fiction coaches over at JHU, who's in e-mail contact with both her senior ex-colleague and her former coachee, has let the latter know that the former reports having solved a certain (unspecified) nagging problem with his project-in-the-works and is currently steaming full speed ahead on it down there in Alligator Alley, whereas Hop's own "P/E" novel *COMING SOON!!!* (part Print, part Electronic, but its author sometimes suspects those initials of standing for Premature Ejaculation) has yet to find an agent willing to bother with it. He'll be lucky to land it on some software outfit's list for a ten-dollar advance on royalties, no advertising except on the house's website (speaking of which, Hop's working on a snazzy new homepage for *T II*'s website; remind him to call it up for Mort's approval when we're done here), and no "readers" except the online e-fiction crowd, excuse the overstatement.

"What you're saying?" Mort Spindler prompts.

"Is that old GreatUnc isn't likely to mind our recycling a couple of his recyclings, though I s'pose we should ask permission." In fact, given what looks to be their current détente (he even got a holiday card from the old gent, congratulating him on his novel's completion and wishing it good luck in New York), Hop has in mind asking him to consider a guest appearance or two toward season's end — maybe at the Maryland Defenders Day bash and the Inner Harbor finale; maybe as a guest of honor on *T II*'s procession up the Bay from St. Mary's to Baltimore, along with the governor and a congressman or two: *Honoring the Free State's historic contributions to American entertainment* blah blah, especially showboatery but including pop music and movies and even poor shitkicking *literature*. Think, like, Barry Levinson and John Waters and Tom Clancy and Anne Tyler, all waving from *TOFO*'s top deck along with blowups of Poe and Mencken and Scott Fitzgerald as we chug past Fort McHenry. . . .

Mort's sold. What's more, he has reason to believe that the Arkangel-in-Chief'll be receptive too; more than receptive, "'Cause, get this: The word from Six Six Six [*Mort points toward the upper reaches of Patmos Tower*] is that Cap'n Andy Et Cetera has Bought the Farm on that Why-Two-Kay TEOTWAWKI crapola — The End Of The World As We Know It? The guy claims to be ninety-fucking-nine years old, though he can't be a day past eighty, and he has no family that anybody knows of, so he'd probably get a toot out of seeing the world end along with quote *Todd Andrews* unquote. Anyhow, Captain Period Adam Period Lake Period tells me that despite our regular deficits, old FLOPCORP's been given virtual *carte blanche* this year, 'cause Cap'n Andy intends Tee Two to be his ark for riding out the Y2K crunch!"

The old fellow's remarkable plan-in-the-works, Mort explains — not all that extraordinary in view of the Christian cultists flocking to Jerusalem, and the TEOTWAWKIs holing up in New Mexico and Montana with their rifles and canned beans and power generators — is to bring the showboat back to Snug Harbour this November per usual at Postview Season's end, but instead of shifting it into museum/art-moviehouse mode, to stock and refit it as a Y2K refuge for himself and his entourage: Jane and June "Bea Golden" Harrison; June's daughter Sherry Singer and quote *any friend of her choosing*; also Captain. Adam. Lake. and the Kane twins, the Spindler family if they're inclined (better an ob/gyn on board than no M.D. at all, Mort reckons his boss reckons); Obie Brown and at least one Asian-American for Mix; maybe even Mr. and Mrs. Emeritus if *they're* interested; a couple other crewmembers maybe, and Present Company if he hasn't already qualified above.

Mort goes on to his eye-rolling colleague, "Ready for more? The plan is to extend the quote *Secure Zone* to the community of Dorset-town in general and Patmos Tower in particular. They'll beef up security at the gate, maybe raise the perimeter fencing by a foot or two, stockpile supplies, the works, with the Ark all set to put to sea on short notice if things get nasty ashore. I was so plotzed at what I was hearing on closed circuit up there in Six Nine Six that all I could think to ask him, believe it or not, was 'Suppose the creek's frozen on New Year's Eve?' To which Gee Dash Dee replieth, 'Global warming's in our corner, Doc; we've had no outdoor ice-skating since Seventy-three.' The guy even *winked* at me! At the camera, anyhow."

And if nothing happens on the big day? wonders aloud Johns Hopkins Johnson.

Mort replies with a balletic whole-body shrug. "We pop the champagne and go on with our stories! Butty-but-*but*" — Big Happy-Face grin — "what a fucking form-*fit* we have here with our *End Time Show Barge* Final Season plan! Made for each other! It's you-should-excuse-the-expression *huge!*"

It doth have a certain dimension it-to, JHJ allows: great fit, great Final Season plan, great media angles everywhere, great show-title. Now all we need's a show.

Echoing the song from MGM's *Wizard of Oz*, "*If we on-ly had a show!*" Mort Spindler gleefully pretends to lament. "That, my friend, is *your* department, and your girlfriend's. You're the spinner; I'm the Spindler." He taps his watch. "But Preview Season rehearsals'll be on us in no time, so let's have a script by Saint Veesday latest, okay?"

It being February 11 already as I write this, and not much earlier in Mort's Patmos Tower FLOPCORP office (where, a few days ago, I envisioned this scene's taking place, if You can parse those adverbs, so let's grant them the time-difference), Hop has to hope that his boss's "Veesday" reference is to the third-century Christian child martyr Vitus—canonized 1621 and patron of the neurological dysfunction called St. Vitus's Dance—and that the poor kid's saintsday is farther down the road than San Valentino's of the hearts and flowers, or Mort's gotta be joking.

Joking or not, the dancer in Doctor Spin is so quickened by mention of St. Vitus that he's out of his desk chair again and improvising a spasmodic jig while explaining to his office-mate (who knows it already from his M.D. parents) that the medical name for St. Vitus's Dance is chorea—

"From Greek *choros*," Hop is able to add from his university education, "meaning dance, as in *choreography*?" and then they're at it in jerky tandem all about the office, agreeing that something like this *has* to go into the new New Show as a whole-chorus number, though not of course anything so politically incorrect as making fun of a serious neurological disorder. They're at a loss as to how to cleanse it of that association until Sherry Singer happens to pop in, takes one look at their quasi-spastic highjinking, thinks she gets the idea (she's fresh from her mother's brunchtime revelation of Cap'n Andy's Y2K Plan), and asks as she joins the dance, "So what're we, bitten by the Millennium Bug?"

*Et voilà*: "The Millennium Bug Boogie, or, Swing Your Way Through Y2K," a showstopper for sure if they only had a show for it to stop. When *they* stop, winded and laughing, Sher confirms her mother's confirmation of Mort's account of Andrew S. Todd Cap'n Andy Andrews Todd's "666/999 Plan" (as that gentleman and Sher's grandma are calling it, after their respective condominium-numbers in Patmos Tower) for T(Possible)EOTWAWKI, with the additional infobit that that canny brace of Arkangels may be being less loony than they seem: "Bea Golden," at least, reads the whole project as a scheme to jack up Dorsettown property values, which have lagged behind D-o-C's initial projections, by billing the place as a Y2K-proof community, complete with its very own Ark of Last Resort.

"The way Ma sees it," she explains, draping her gray-leotarded person over an office chair, "it's a win-winner: If the world crashes on schedule, they're more or less ready. If it doesn't, they figure the Final Season shtick is good for another year, since the millennium doesn't *really* start till Oh One Oh One Oh One. So what do we do for a show?"

Hop Johnson's already improvising:

> "*O One O One O One,*
> *You're the one, O One, O One!*
> *Our romance has just begun!*
> *Shall we dance, O One, O One?*"

No more song-and-dancing, the three then agree (tempting as is the invitation, and surely usable down the road), till they've a show to sing and dance in. Given the date — Presidents Day weekend already, Incumbent Clinton about to be acquitted by the Senate on the House's articles of impeachment, Valentine's Day all but upon them and Preview Season rehearsals a mere fortnight thereafter! — any really *new* show is out of the question. The best they can do —

"*You*," Mort corrects. "I've got my hands full scheduling and promoting."

Sherry Singer corrects that correction: "*We*. Hop can't do it alone."

*We we we we all the way home*, JHJ affirms. It takes three to tango, if he remembers correctly — but he acknowledges the chief responsibility to be his. As we were saying, he then resumes: The best they-all can hope to do in the time available is a truly jazzed-up makeover of whatever's salvageable from their almost-successful *Show Barge* and *End Time* productions, bridging the two story-lines

275

with the Final-Season/Millennium-Bug theme—leave that to him, now that his so-called novel's out of the house—and maybe calling the whole shebang, uh, *Coming Soon!!!*?

"*Yes!*" Sherry cries at once, and "*Zingo!*" Mort Spindler: "Coming soon to a showboat near you! Final Season! *Coming Soon!!!*"

Final Season, Curtain Time, Final Curtain, The End—it's mainly a matter of jiggering all that stuff into synergy, right? 'Scuse him now, friends; he hears the muse a-calling: *Show Barge III*, *End Time Redux*, *The New New Show*, whatever—

"*Coming Soon!!!*" with one voice his two associates triply exclaim.

—he'll set aside everything else and get its main action-line blocked out by next week latest, so's the three of them and every damn soul else in the ATC can start working up the bits and routines. Preview Season's going to have to be Stitch-It-Together season even more than usually; sets and props we'll try to mix and match from what's on hand. *The Original Floating Theatre* standing in for Noah's Ark we already have, and we can add what it takes to make it Baltimore's A-R-K-E too. Adam and Eve in the Garden we conflate with Charlie and Beulah on the Adams showboat before Edna the Serpent shows up from the Big Apple, get it?, or with Charlie and Edna before S-E-X joins their party (couple of Bill/Hillary/Monica jokes if anybody still remembers that mess by Main Season). Global Warming and the Flood we've got already from the old New Show; maybe add a Chesapeake Hurricane with Ferber aboard the *OFT* if we can manage the special effects, and let it echo Shakespeare's Tempest and/or segue into *Tempest and Sunshine*, which'll also stand for Flood versus Fire; and our "Fire Next Time" number becomes The Doomsday Factor, old Y2K. *Oy gevalt*, it's the thirteenth already! Gotta get cracking!

"Did I hear *oy gevalt*?" Mort Spindler pretends to ask of Sherry Singer.

"*Be my valentine* is what *I* heard," Sher declares, and gives her really quite impressively resourceful lover/colleague a kiss-and-squeeze, he her an appreciative though distracted *potch in tuchis*, she then Mort an affectionate *geshmechte* kiss on cheek—

The Israelites!, all this office-Yiddishing inspires either Hop or Mort to exclaim: Kern/Hammerstein/Ziegfeld in Hunter's *Show Barge* equals the Israelites after the Deluge equals Lord Baltimore's colonists arriving in the promised land. . . .

"Milk and honey transubstantiate into oysters and tobacco?" either Mort or Sherry wonders, and the other "Saint Clements Island as a low-level Ararat?"

Palms to his temples, Ararat/Arafat, *Two weeks till March!* Hop groans—then grins: Don't count on it, guys. But don't count it out, either.

"*Don't* count *on* us," Dr. Spin starts in, counting off the rhythm on his fingers.

"But don't *count* us *out*," Sher adds, snapping hers on the back-beat—and there's the makings of yet another number: maybe Noah's sons being prodded by their dad to get their big damn boat finished *soon*; or maybe young Cain and Abel responding to their parents' orders to play more *nicely* together, for God's sake; or maybe the cast of the new musical COMING SOON!!! assessing in song the odds on their reappearing for a Final Season II in Y2K itself.

*"By next week latest"*
was the lad's rash pledge of a page or so past. So fleetly plods Time's Tortoise, Next Week is now already This, and'll soon be Last. The acquitted-though-not-exonerated President goes about his and presumably the nation's business; Iraqi and American warplanes daily rattle at each other their lethal sabers; the "peace process" makes no apparent headway either in the Middle East (where last October's Wye Plantation Accords are like last autumn's leaves on the oaks and maples of that handsome seat) or in Kosovo and environs, where a good day remains one with only a few new atrocities. Yet such is the improvisatory energy, let's call it, of our indefatigable young Novelist Aspirant now turned show-maker-over-in-a-hurry, in little more than the time it takes us careful veterans to form the sentences reporting his progress or lack thereof, he has in hand the promised armature for a new New Show, duly mating or miscegenating *Show Barge* ("by Charles Hunter and friends")

with his apocalyptic-allegorical *End Time* romp and bravely re-titled *Coming Soon!!!* A mere summary can't do the thing justice, he warns Mort and Sherry—and me as well, by e-mail, he having hacked his way who knows how to my cyberaddress. For all hands' sake we must hope he's right, for that summary strikes this reader as little more than a radical synopsis of a certain novel thus far, with alternative scenarios for or prospectuses of what lies ahead:

"Charles Hunter's" (and Yours Truly's) *Show Barge*—the story of a possible shipboard romance between the city-wise novelist Edna Ferber and the country-shrewd artistic director of James Adams's old Floating Theatre—deployed bits and pieces of Kern/Hammerstein/Ziegfeld's *Show Boat* as an implicit play-within-the-play, by way of anticipating Ferber's novel-to-come and its famous spinoffs. In *TOFO II*'s recent seasons (see, e.g., "1997" and "1998"), those bits were replaced by numbers from Johnson's *End Time*, and for at least a part of one season this relation was virtually inverted, so that snippets from *Show Barge* were framed by the *End Time* story.

Which was? Not easy to summarize so fluid and morph-prone a production! Enough perhaps to remark that in its amalgamation of themes from the first and last books of the Bible, *End Time* centered on the Flood and the Ark but included St. John at work on the Book of Revelation; it turned upon the conflation of Noah's Mount Ararat with John's Mount Patmos, not to mention the conflation of John the gospel-writer ("In the beginning was the Word," etc.) with John the predictor of Armageddon *et seq*. In Johnson's play, Noah & Sons build not the conventionally depicted menagerie-vessel, but a show-boat, *The Original Floating Opera* ("The world's ending?" one of Noah's sons exclaims: "Let's put on a show!"), with the intention of sailing it to Patmos, finding the "Author of the Apocalypse" and persuading him to "change the story's ending": to rewrite Revelation such that (to quote a speech by another of Noah's sons at the play's climax) "the world won't be ended *in* time, sir, by any special-effects stuff like flood or fire; instead, let it be ended *by* time, okay?" In short (and by the terms of "Saint John's" shrug-shouldered concession to the desperately merry showboat troupe), the Apocalypse will be "deferred" because it is ongoing. "The world is ending already, guys," declareth John: "It's been ending ever since the beginning. Amen?"

Thus *End Time*, in bare-bones synopsis. As for the prospective musical *COMING SOON!!!*: Aspiring young First Novelist and aging Possibly-Last Novelist share an interest not only in their chosen medium (whether e- or p-), but specifically in the Chesapeake Bay showboat that happened to inspire a certain 1920s bestseller—the youngster because he currently works aboard a replica of the original and is writing a novel based on that experience, the oldster for literary-proprietary reasons involving his own bibliography—and that shared interest extends to each other as well: first as unofficial mentor and mentee, then as comrades-in-arms (reluctantly, on the elder's part) in their effort to sustain the very vessel aboard which the show-in-progress is in progress, and anon as rivals for authorial top billing in the showboat's "end time," or Final Seasons, as well as for the favors of the troupe's female lead: a First Really Serious Relationship for the "First Novelist," a guiltful Last Hurrah for the Last. Their competing script-entries, needless to say (from which excerpts are staged here and there through the drama), are the shows *Show Barge* and *End Time*, whichabout nothing further need be said here except that by Act One's curtain the term "First Novelist" has acquired correspondences to the author of the Book of Genesis, and "Last Novelist" to John of Patmos, scribbling away about the Number of the Beast, the advent of Antichrist, and other colorful matters "coming soon!"

In Act Two (of two), although the rivals reach an apparent détente by collaborating on a show called *COMING SOON!!!* for "the old Ark's final season"—a show that, it goes without saying, hybridizes their competing efforts and is in fact the play-in-progress—each remains half on the lookout to gain final ascendancy over the other ("Age and Cunning," chants the chorus, "versus Youth and Strength," etc.) until a conveniently climactic storm-at-bay puts vessel and all hands—including both novelist-playwrights, who happen to be aboard—in such peril as to bid indeed to be their End Time. Borrowing then from Yours Truly's borrowing from Charles

Hunter's planned conclusion of *Show Barge*, the prospectus of COM-
ING SOON!!! offers the audience its choice of alternative endings
(though not, like Hunter's, in alternative media, since they all involve what Hunter called "cinestage" combinations of live actors
and film-projected effects). . . .

*The details of wch we'll work out in Preview Season,* concludes
Hop's e-letter — *not to mention the "wch" of wch those details'll be
the details. Any suggestions, Unc? How d'you* think Our Story
oughta end? ;-)

*Yrs in Christ,*
*M. le Fantôme*

*Successfully,*
I sooner or later e-mail him back. *Which is not to say "happily ever
after,"* but rather — as Scheherazade knew and frequently appended
to *her* stories — until Time, "The Destroyer of Delights and Sun-
derer of Societies," does its inexorable work upon all hands, all
scenes and scenarios, all connections. Busy as I want to be with my
own projects (chief among them this chapter of the book-in-
progress, now that its Millennium Bug seems to have been swatted),
I thank Mr. Phantom for his invitation but decline to offer more
specific suggestions. It's late February already, both in Tortoise-
time and in the chronology of this story — wherein, still sunnily
Florida'd, Narrator imagines and proceeds to narrate the commencement of the Arkade Theatre Company's Pre–"Final Season"
rehearsals up in rainybleak Dorsettown-on-Choptank, Maryland:
skits and numbers from their brace of insufficiently successful recent productions, plus foretastes ("The Millennium Bug," "O One O
One," etc.) of the still-embryonic COMING SOON!!!, already subtitled
THE MUSICAL as if to distinguish it before the fact from my A
NARRATIVE and Hop Johnson's THE NOVEL?

Quite as Mort Spindler predicted, Arkangel-in-Chief "Todd Andrews" applauds the Johnson/Spindler/Singer proposal aforeset-
forth; he gives the ATC, if not quite a blank check, at least a very
considerable budget increase and authority to hire extra staff to help
Dr. Spin with the promotion of both *TOFO II*'s Final Season and the

"Y2K-proofed" Dorsettown. Such news items as the U.S. Federal Emergency Management Administration's Y2K advisory of 22 Feb., recommending that all households stock a weeksworth of bottled water and canned foods along with adequate flashlights, batteries, and candles, Cap'n Andy welcomes as part of his ad campaign. Such an interest does he take in the forthcoming production that he proposes, with some evident seriousness, to do a quad-cane-assisted walk-on bit himself therein, perhaps as "G-D?'s" emissary alerting Noah to the impending deluge. "Folks'll get the message," he reckons with a closed-circuit wink.

Says Mort to his wife and close colleagues, "Oy." But to his boss's image, "Zingo, sir!"

The publicity program, however, goes better than the scripting of the Main Season feature. The regional media take a half-amused but attention-getting interest in the interlinked projects, the showboat-as-Ark in both, and the "background" releases from Mort's office about the Original Flóating Theatre's declared "Final Season" before its truly final burning on 14 November 1941, almost as if in omen of America's plunge just three weeks later into World War II. More e-mailed appeals come down from the Novelist Aspirant to the Ditto "Emeritus" (or, as Hop Johnson now calls them, "The N.A. Character" and "The N.E. Character") for his coachly reaction to, e.g., escalating the Ferber/Hunter "One Drop" theme from *Show Barge* (where, You will recall, it had to do first with ethnic interbreeding and later with "Edna's" impregnation) into a chemical/biological doomsday threat—"one drop of *this* in their water supply," etc.—from the aforementioned terrorist Osama bin Laden, whose whereabouts are as of this writing unknown to the world at large. And couldn't the Ferber character's "Whatever It Takes" theme (originally her resolve to seduce Charlie, if necessary, to "get her story") become, say, Noah's daughter's selfless resolve to fuck St. John on Patmos, if need be, in order to persuade him to defer the Apocalypse by "changing the story's ending"?

*C'mon, man!* exclaims another of Hop's cybernotes: *Jupiter & Venus spooned in the sky last month* [his reference is to the extraordinary conjunction of those two planets within one degree of arc on

Feb. 23, their bright proximity observed with pleasure just after dusk over the broad Choptank by Hop and Sherry and over the Gulf of Mexico by M/M Narrator]; *can't you & I declare our very own Wye Plantation Accord and make this baby together?* E.g., he e-mails on: By way of climaxing the show's "N.A./N.E. Rivalry theme," he has in mind a Transfer of Authority scene [*"Authority" derives from* Author, *right, Dad?*] in which the elder scribbler, "victorious," gracefully yields the field to his bettered former rival [*BETTER former rival? Just kidding . . . ;-)*] — but he has as yet no clear notion how such a scene might most effectively be staged. *Suggestions?*

Not really, I reply: It's your ship, lad; I've a book to finish. Noah had a daughter?

*So okay, we'll make Holly Weil his daughter-in-law. And seriously, if you get any Stellar Ideas . . .*

I'll pass them along. But you mustn't feel obliged even to acknowledge, much less to use them.

*Don't worry, Unc.*

In fact, as the year's briefest month speeds to its close, my fancy races ahead, my pen hard on its heels, and that fell swift Tortoise never far behind. The ATC, I imagine, spurred by the new-New Show concept and fired by the ambient Final Season/Y2K fever, not to mention by their newly-fattened budget, pull together as never before. They come up with almost more material than Hop can handle, with the happy result that toward March's close and the actual Maryland Day, when we snowbirds re-migrate to the Chesapeake and its Canada geese take off for home, *T II*'s Preview Season revue — *Final Follies!* — is almost ready to roll, and it seems no longer unthinkable that, given most of April and May for the company to work things up, by Main Season there'll be something like a COMING SOON!!! THE MUSICAL after all.

Captain Elva Kane, for example — knitting her brows while unknitting her morning's macramé during one of the company's late-afternoon brainstorming sessions, opines that the absence of any finally coherent story-line in the show thus far may be a nonproblem. When she first heard the LP recordings of the musical *Hair* back in the late Sixties, she remembers, she and her girlfriends ("I mean *girl friends*," she adds smartly to, of all people, Ditsy from Maintenance, smiling beside his/her new More or Less Significant Other: Jay "Obie" Brown of all people) tried in vain to imagine the story-context that they assumed must meaningfully link those famous numbers: "Good Morning Starshine," "Donna," "Abie Baby" (Elva's personal favorite), and the rest. Not until she saw the show in D.C. some years later did she learn that there *was* no story-line to speak of; that what sounded like "situation" songs — the flower-child's plaintive search for her rough-trade heartthrob Frank Mills in the tune of that title, the brash Brit-boy's apostrophe to "Manchester England, England," etc. — were in fact freestanding whatchacallums. . . .

"Palimpsests?" offers uncertainly Mort Spindler, pleased to've come up with the highfalutin word but unsure of its application.

"Maybe not palimpsests," mildly corrects Johns Hopkins Johnson: "A palimpsest has to've had something else written on it first and then erased and written over?" What Elv means, he ventures, is more like *deliberate fragments*: the lyrical/narrative equivalent of those Romantic-period torso sculptures and freestanding musical "preludes" that somebody already mentioned earlier on in this story — "and it's a *terrific* idea, Elv!" Why lose sleep trying to link the Genesis/Revelation theme to the Young-Fart/Old-Fart Novelist theme to the *Show Barge* Mingling-of-Essences theme to Lord Baltimore's *Arke* and *Dove* and the rest in some meaningful, you should excuse the expression, Ur-Narrative? Let the sumbitches just, you know, *reciprocally resonate* within the general sequence of (he counts off on his fingers) Prepping for the Final Season, Casting Off, Searching for the Author, Trouble on the Ark, Tempest and Sunshine, and Apocalypse Deferred! *"The fragment is the only form I trust,"* he quotes Donald Barthelme; "you've saved our ass, Cap'n!"

*"If the fog lifts late,"* declares Elva Kane, unstitching the last of her macramé, *"the day'll be clear. But if the cat turns on its back with its nose up, there'll be rain."* Her contribution and proverbious wisdom earn her a hug and kiss from Sherry Singer, monitored by

Hop Johnson inconclusively. Captain Harry Kane then gruffly allows as how his Gabriel's Last Trumpet bit from the old New Show *End Time* — a comic/virtuosic sequence that, like his Rimsky-Korsakovian *Flight of the Saltmarsh Mosquito*, never failed to bring down the house — ought to be an easy fit with the Y2K theme, which by the way (the Y2K Problem in general) he personally isn't worried a fiddler's fart about.

*"Bringing Down the House!"* cries Hop, pointing happily at *Raven*'s skipper with both forefingers. "End Time a-comin' soon!" June "Bea Golden" Harrison, a more-or-less Methodist before and after her serial Jewish husbands, sings Captain Harry's phrase to the old Protestant tune "Bringing in the Sheaves." Which. Come to think of it. Methodically. Remembers. Captain. Adam. Lake. Beside her. Is a sort of a End Time hymn itself. Wouldn't they-all say?

"Zingo, Cap'n Ad!" cheers Mort. "Into the show it goes!"

*"Show it goes,"* shrugs smilingly Jay "Obie" Brown, turning up his palms. His new friend Ditsy gives the nearer themof a smart smack, that poor pun's punishment; but quick Jay turns the reproof into a congratulatory high-five, grins his broadest fake blackface-minstrel grin, and adds, "Just shows to go you."

"I ain't *pushin'* the idea," Harry Kane wants it understood, although the company has perpended his Gabe's Last Trump suggestion and moved several steps on already. "Just thought I'd mention it."

"Cap'n. Harry. Don't. Push." Gravely. Affirms. Captain. Ad.

Winking at her fraternal twin, "That there's a Christ fact," Elva Kane agrees, and begins reknotting in a different pattern. All hands (including Elva's nose-up cat) wait for a proverb to follow. When none does, Hop Johnson makes to supply one from his inventory of Elva-isms — *Cut your toenails on a Friday and you'll never have a toothache*, perhaps, or the simple, nonadvisory *Hogs can see the wind*, or the more baroque *Put a coal on a snake's belly while it's waiting to die at sundown and it'll sprout legs and walk* — but before he can deliver, Holly Weil, in Perennial-Ingenue mode, inquires "Why *is* that?"

Meaning Why will Captain Harry, in his capacity as *Raven*'s skipper, find a way to manage even the tightest docking or turning maneuvers by artful tugging while his sister's *Dove* does any necessary pushing? With a private-looking smile, "Thereby hangs a tale," Captain Elva acknowledges to cover her brother's frowning silence. "But *Raven* herself couldn't tug it out of us."

To get off that subject, "*Raven*'s a girl?" Sherry Singer wonders aloud. "I guess I never knew that till now."

Wagging a finger as if the Elva-proverb applies, "*Hens won't lay in a potato-field*," Hop sagely reminds his lover—and after a better-than-usual Preview Season, sparked both by the unaccustomed media interest and by the clearly promising promotional theme that's attracting that interest, the Arkade Theatre Company find Main Season upon them: still mere last-day-of-February as I begin this paragraph Down South, early March already by its end, almost time for its writer to head Back North. But so advanced is the narrative calendar up in Storyville that what gets written is

## Late May!

Late May up there in tidewaterland, *TOFO-II* land, whereto Narrator and mate will have returned toward March's close from their winter base, reestablished themselves on Maryland's Eastern Shore, and taken up their customary back-home works and pleasures. Up *here*, then, now, in present-tense Storyland—where, on the late-May Friday evening of the first weekend of Narrator's (gulp) seventieth year, *The Original Floating Opera II* opens its Last Main Season to a not-bad turnout in Dorsettown's Snug Harbour with an expanded, full-company version of the variety "revue" *Final Follies!*, followed on the Saturday by a Special Home-Port Sneak Preview, to an almost-capacity house, of . . . Ta-da! . . . *COMING SOON!!! THE MUSICAL. "Freely adapted in advance from forthcoming novels by* [Yours Truly] *and by our own J. Hopkins Johnson*," declare the playbill and publicity releases; Narrator's permission for same begged both by the Novelist Still Hopefully Aspirant Despite No Good News Yet From NYC and by Ms. Singer of the so-persuasive eyes, "in the name of our now locally notorious rivalry and its happy evolution into comrades-in-armshood and even limited cordial cooperation, if not (yet) outright collaboration," as they put it in their e-mailed and telephoned appeals and even, one spring afternoon, an unannounced drive-by visit.

"Drive-by shooting, more like," one of us will remark thereafter, for Mort Spindler accompanies the couple in Johnson's cherry-red Cherokee to the end of photographing, "for DTE's archives only," what he himself acknowledges to be "this really unpardonable but really *really* important intrusion on your privacy, folks, and I swear we're out of here in five minutes! Don't even *think* of inviting us in [*click click*]! Just pretty pretty please stand there for one second between Hop and Sherry, sir, and you on Hop's other side, Miz B please—Perfecto! [*Click click*, all five of us in workaday jeans and tees.] And please *please* be a great sport and let us use that 'Freely adapted in advance' line in our promos. Please?"

M/M Us consult each other with a glance. Permission granted, we shrug and suppose. But change *forthcoming novels by me and him* (for so went the credit-line as initially proposed) to *forthcoming novels by me and by him*, okay? Cooperation maybe; collaboration no. And promise us these photos'll stay in your archives, yes?

"Trust us, sir!" And JHJ winks and gives the emendation two thumbs up, and Sherry Singer hugs us drive-by shootees—both of us at the same time, tactfully, given that troublesome fabrication in her boyfriend's novel (later expunged) of Emerital hanky-panky herwith. *Click click click.* I *swear*, we swear, but not ill-humoredly, when they are indeed out of there after ten minutes tops, having duly declined our what-the-hell invitation to come sit on our creekside porch for a spell, and having urged urged *urged* us to be their Special Guests at the May 29 Snug Harbour Sneak Preview of the miraculously finished musical *Coming Soon!!!* Likewise at its June 1 Gala Premiere at Annapolis Town Dock, where they fully expect the governor and other dignitaries to be in attendance—even Bill and Hill just might pop over from D.C.! And at any other showing any time any place throughout the season, but especially *especially* at the Maryland Defenders Day bash in St. Mary's City on September 14 and the grand procession in early November from Annapolis up under the Bay Bridge to open their final Final Performances in Baltimore's Inner Harbor. But firstfirstfirst: Snug Harbour! Saturday, May Twenty-nine! *Coming soon!*

As do all days, soon or otherwise that day comes. Do we go? We'll just see, we decide. A touch discomfited by the Final Season hoopla, we nonetheless wish the FLOPCORP company well. Their Annapolis Grand Opening we'll definitely steer clear of, but at least half of us wouldn't mind checking out what Hop & Friends have cobbled up out of his imaginings and mine (and, allegedly, the late Charles Hunter's), if we could see without being seen, so to speak, at that Snug Harbour preview. On the other hand, we feel we've maybe had enough already of *showboats*, except in this narrative of mine tortoise-racing toward its climax. And there is the matter of Yrs Truly's birthday, just a couple of days therebefore: It is our house tradition to mark that milestone quietly afloat, May being prime weekend-cruising weather on the Chesapeake. Perhaps we'll set out on a bit of a sail on the Thursday, pop a birthday-champagne cork over our vessel's taffrail at anchor somewhere that evening, make our way down Choptankward next day if wind and weather conduce thereto, and, should we find ourselves convenient to Dorsettown on the Saturday . . . ? Indeed, not to have our craft recognized by The N.A. Character (who, remember, first reconnoitered it over at Solomons early in our story and saw it again at least once since, when *TOFO II* invaded our creek back in '95), we could even anchor downriver in Cambridge Creek and hire a cab to and from Snug Harbour, the better to preserve our anonymity at the show. . . .

Yes, well: Not likely, we suppose; let's just go sailing. Life, however, abounds in unlikelihoods—Real Life especially (wherein, e.g., NATO "smart bombs" manage embarrassingly to strike the Chinese embassy in Belgrade), but the lives of characters in fiction as well, with the difference that whereas Real Life may merely shake its head thereat, in a proper fiction everything that happens *matters*, even the apparently meaningless or accidental, and the most unlikely happenstances turn out to be, if not inevitable, anyhow plausible and significant. Whatever the actual, factual, real-life M/M Us happen to do with ourselves on the late-May weekend in question, therefore—and who can say what that will be, since I'm writing this in March? — The N.E. Character in our story and his companion decide "in fact" (You know what we mean) to cast off from their dock on that aforeproposed Thursday for their traditional His-Birthday Sail. Not really a replay, this, of their somewise similar embarkation back in spring '95, as recounted long since in Episode 1.2, "Same Old Story": Back then his muse was mum, the couple's float-plan deliberately aimless — whither the wind listeth, etc. — and the voyage open-ended for a fortnight or more. This time, Ms. Muse is merrily a-chirp, sensing Climax soon to come; and while nothing's definite itinerariwise, the crew have Cambridge/ Dorsettown-on-Choptank as their provisional aim, whether or not they sneak into *T II*'s Sneak Preview, as they suppose they'll just maybe take a shot at doing. And they intend to be back in their respective home offices on the Monday morning, or Tuesday latest should the currently fair forecast fail and hold them for a day somewhere in harbor.

It doesn't. A sweet afternoon westerly fetches us out of our beloved creek under all plain sail and down the gracious-spacious Chester; three hours later we drop sails to motor through Kent Island Narrows, under and through its pair of highway bridges, and into Prospect Bay. Just enough breeze and afternoon left then for a slow reach down to the mouth of the Wye, where we furl sail for the day and power upriver to anchor for the night off the briefly famous Wye Plantation. There last October's Middle East Peace Accord, presided over by our sexually compromised President Clinton and Jordan's dying King Hussein, was reluctantly arrived at, duly signed by Israel's Benjamin Netanyahu and Palestine's Yasser Arafat, and promptly consigned to the populous Limbo of such hopeful gestures; and there at sunset we pop the ritual three-quarter liter of Codorniù Brut and toast, in order, (1) that failed accord and troubled land, may its peoples somehow find peace at last; (2) the welcome late accord, at least apparent, between Novelists Aspirant and "Emeritus," long may both wave; (3) the so-blessed three-decade accord between this anchored brace of toasters, may it never waver — and (4), to be sure, one's birthday anniversary. A light night's sleep then for Yrs T, par for the course in any cruise's first-night anchorage: His drowsy senses register every airshift, the lap of wavelets against our hull when we swing side-to a bit on our anchor line, the occasional soft bump of the dinghy when breeze or tide fetch it up to our transom, the hum in our standing rigging toward dawn, when the wind freshens.

That same breeze, by breakfast a brisk southwesterly, gives us a fine Friday's sail. No matter that it's piping straight up Eastern Bay, our aisle to the Chesapeake proper, and is thus squarely on our bow: That aisle is wide; there's tacking room aplenty plus an ebbing tide behind us to compensate for leeway, and we've neither timetable nor fixed destination for the day. Like a story whose digressions are part of its pleasure as well as part of its point, our course for the morning's first half is back and forth across Eastern Bay, south and west and south and west from tack to tack but always incrementally southwestward, past Tilghman Point to port and Bloody Point to starboard, past what little remains of the fast-eroding Poplar Islands, and out into the Chesapeake. Lunch in the cockpit, while under closehauled main and genoa we beat right across to its western shore (never capitalized like its Eastern, as it's not properly a *place*); then a splendid long starboard tack straight south through container-ships and bulk carriers, watermen's workboats, sport-fishing craft and other pleasure-vessels, to the Shore's next river-system down: the broad Choptank, my birthwaters. Into it we turn, right ready by now to exchange heeled-over windward work for more relaxed and vertical offwind sailing. We ease main and jib to a medium-broad reach; consider setting the spinnaker but decide we're doing just fine as is (six knots plus, in eight to ten of apparent wind over our starboard quarter); peel out of our shirts and lotion up to enjoy the mid-afternoon Maryland sunshine on our skin; fetch up the ship's boombox and find a bit of Bach on a D.C. public radio station to en-hance our upriver easting. Past Cooks and Todds and Castlehaven Points to starboard, Broad Creek and the handsome Tred Avon River to port; then — as the river narrows to half its four-mile mouth-width and approaches Cambridge, the Route 50 bridge, and the end of its best sailing grounds — we turn north into Trappe Creek (*La* Trappe Creek on the chart, but no Eastern Shorester gets his/her tongue around the French article), glide thereup in the failing air to Sawmill Cove, feel our way thereinto under power with a watchful eye on the depthsounder, and anchor in a scant five feet (but our cutter draws only three with its centerboard raised) in as snug, unspoiled, and spring-lovely a spot as any sailor could desire, just in time for a short exercise swim in the nettle-free but still-chilly water before Happy Hour.

Happy hour indeed, of a happy late-May day (here riskily imagined in advance from the disadvantage-point of the March before) — anyhow a fine one of Chesapeake sailing to initiate the close-out year of Narrator's seventh decade; a day shadowed only by the misfortunes of the world's less fortunate and the preoccupational hazard of entering one's seventieth year. To wit: the inevitable, double-edged reflection that should this prove to be for one reason or another one's last such sail from Chester down to Choptank — as who dares say it couldn't possibly be at one's now age, despite one's thus-far-robust health? — then it was, as folks say hereabouts, a right good one.

*On the Saturday, then,*
its morning air warming fast but too cool for swimming and (as best we can judge from the surrounding treetops) too light yet for sailing, in no hurry we take a postbreakfast dinghy-row around Sawmill Cove, poking into its crannied covelets and oak-hung bowers in vain search of the eponymous long-gone mill before weighing anchor and motoring back out into the river. Plan A, we suppose, is to sail up under the highway bridge, past Cambridge on its hither side and Dorsettown on its yonder, as far up the ever-narrower and more-winding channel as wind, tide, and interest conduce, then make our way back downriver as far as D-o-C's Snug Harbour in time to shower and change, do dinner ashore (no doubt there's a restaurant somewhere in that complex), and sneak into *TOFO II*'s Sneak Preview. . . .

"Some sneak," half of us remarks. "With our boat in full view?"

Who knows us by our boat? the other half questions — he having scrupulously withheld the vessel's name, e.g., throughout this narrative. But of course, he then answers himself, J. Hopkins Johnson had a good look at it in Solomons Harbor back in spring '95, both before and after our Ontological Lunchbreak, and again at our dock a few months later when *T II* boldly trespassed into our creek. 'Tis four years since, to be sure, but one doubts that that sharp-eyed chap will have forgotten, feign though he might to know not cutter from ketch. So what, however, if our cover's blown, so long as we're left alone and not embarrassed publicly?

"Which history teacheth us not to count upon."

Yes, well. Plan B, in the absence of sailing-breeze, is to diesel up and across to Cambridge; tie up somewhere in the municipal creek that divides my old East Cambridge neighborhood from the rest of the town; stroll again those childhood haunts that I so seldom have occasion these days to revisit; lunch ashore in some creekside crab-cakery, and then, *s'il nous plaît*, proceed upriver a bit by power or sail, depending, back down to Dorsettown, and on with the show.

"Whatever. You're the birthday boy."

In other words, my call, and when in fact we find that morning's Choptank air too light and variable for sailing, I elect Plan B: details irrelevant until afternoon's end, which finds us back aboard, my home bases duly retouched and our walking muscles exercised, up-river from the Cambridge bridge, motoring exploratorily through the branch-channel markers into Dorsettown-on-Choptank's Snug Harbour.

Whatever one's general feeling re residential "developments" and gated communities, D-o-C is, we agree, a not-unimpressive midscale spread for this neck of the Eastern Shore woods. Its (wid-ened and straightened) entrance channel leads us into a snug harbor indeed, ringed by waterfront condos, by the Tradewinds Park mid-rise motel-cum-conference-center and full-service, amply slipped marina whereat we find transient dockage for the night, and by the nine-story Patmos Tower Assisted Living Facility. Beyond these—so the marina's handout map indicates and its thoughtfully provided bicycles permit us to check out firsthand—are sundry small, indi-vidually named and tidily landscaped subcommunities ranging from detached one- and two-story houses (some quite expensive-looking, others down-county modest, but all impeccably maintained) through lookalike duplex "villas," in realtors' lingo, and over-and-under "carriage" and "coach homes." We see the offices of Dorset Tradewinds Enterprises, the parent organization. We see not one but two restaurants, the larger associated with the motel, the smaller and more casual — quite sufficient for our dinner purposes — with the marina. We see . . . what else?

Ah, well, to be sure: *The Original Floating Opera II*, visible already from back in mid-Choptank not long after we pass under the bridge. The showboat and Patmos Tower flank the harbor entrance and dominate the scene: the massive-for-these-parts vertical of the curtainwall high-rise to starboard as we enter, the big-boxy white horizontal of the theater-barge to port, fresh-painted and flag-festooned, her tugs lashed trimly alongside. An excursion boat rigged out like a smallscale Mississippi sternwheeler (our Chesapeake steamboats were all either sidewheelers or propeller-driven) shuttles tourists between Dorsettown and Cambridge; it passes us outbound as we enter, its passengers waving usward as boat passengers will. Other pleasure-craft come and go: The harbor is busy as well as snug this weekend afternoon. Aboard *T II* itself, evidently in its floating-theater-museum mode till showtime, we see a tour group being shown around; can't tell by whom. And spread high across the vessel's squared-off, inboard-facing bow, when we're far enough into Snug Harbour, we see two banners, one atop the other, the upper exclaiming FINAL SEASON! and the lower — as if full-circling the one that launched this book —

*COMING SOON!!!*

Through our little bike-tour, our cocktails-in-the-cockpit time, our shave-shower-and-change in the marina's facilities, and our unremarkable but quite okay blackened-rockfish dinner on the restaurant deck, we keep half an eye out for familiar faces, preferring to see none but prepared to greet any amiably and make a polite pitch for privacy. We see none. Across the harbor usfrom as we dine, the lowering sun handsomely sidelights *TOFO II*, its own multicolored light-strings already switched on. Of Heather, our short-shorted and tight-T-topped but nonetheless pleasingly prep-school-looking server, we ask idly whether she'll be off duty in time to catch the Sneak Preview. She beams and replies "I sure hope so," emphasis not on the *hope* but on the *so*, and accent pure lower Eastern Shore despite the cultivated look of her face, hair, and general bearing: "I'm *in* that sucker!"

Aha. Then we guess we shouldn't ask you whether we're going to enjoy it?

Equivocally but good-humoredly, "J'all enjoy your Cajun rock-fish?" Heather parries. Over another round of house chablis we ponder in vain that question's bearing, then settle our bill and tip the asker generously: an efficient, non-phony waitress who moreover looks to be a summer-jobbing student and, to our unsurprised mild relief, doesn't pick up on the credit-card-imprinted name. On Heather's recommendation we'll stroll showboatward early to present our Special Guest passes at the box office, as a good house is anticipated.

"So break a leg," my wife cheerily encourages her, and Heather with a grin inquires whether we've ever heard the Spanish equivalent of that expression.

In fact we have, I acknowledge. It then occurs to me to ask in turn whether *she* happens to know the Chinese equivalent.

"*Chinese*?!" My mate, too, regards me skeptically. "What is it?"

Haven't the faintest, I confess. Thought maybe *you* might know, being in show biz? Our compliments to the rockfish chef.

As we amble then *T-II*ward, "Now, was that nice?" I'm asked. Wasn't meant otherwise, I insist: One enigmatic non sequitur deserves another, is all. Does it by the way look a touch woozy to you over yonder? For the northwest evening sky out over the Choptank does to me, and although the forecast admits only a 20-percent chance of an evening thundershower, and our boat is buttoned up securely anyhow, we decide I'll go fetch our slickers, just in case, while she does the box-office transaction. We'll re-meet halfway between, in front of the marina restaurant, and do a bit more strolling; there's time to kill yet, and we prefer not to hang out where Spindler, Johnson, or Singer might happen to espy us.

"As if they haven't seen our boat already," with its conspicuous hardwood ratlines laddering the portside shrouds (for climbing up to the mast spreaders to watch, so we tell our grandkids, for Chesapeake icebergs, coral heads, and whales).

My guess is that all hands are too busy just now to monitor transient marina traffic. When we rendezvous shortly thereafter, I learn that the box office is being manned, if that's the right word, by an odd-looking grizzled entity unknown to my wife but whom I infer from her description (and soon after confirm) to be the genderfree or ambigendered "Ditsy" from Maintenance, who I'm told inspected our Special Guest passes so skeptically that one feared he/she was going to check with Mort Spindler or whomever for verification— but who then shrugged and gave us two orchestra seats front row center, which my wife swapped, presuming my consent, for others safely to the rear. And waitress Heather's advice turns out to've been sound, for—"*Ditsy*, was it? As in ditsy?" Yup—has seconded her expectation of a large turnout. People are lining up already; nothing like The End Of The World As We Know It, we suppose, to get folks' attention.

We recall Henry David Thoreau's remark that he, for one, wouldn't trouble himself to walk around the corner to see the world blow up, and agree that inasmuch as we needn't now stand in line for our tickets, we'll contemplate the scene from outside until shortly before curtain time.

A pleasing spectacle it is, as it was upon our first beholding it four years past at the foot of old High Street up in Chestertown: the balmy tidewater evening; the brightly lighted harbor and now resplendently floodlit showboat, its faux–steam calliope alternating with amplified cuts from the new Pit Bulls CD (also for sale at the souvenir/refreshment concession set up onshore between *T II*'s gangways); the Cantabridgean and out-of-town couples and families moving aboard now to claim their seats for the show. Anon we do likewise, choosing the sternmore gangway because the ticket-taker there turns out to be our Heather, recostumed in what looks like a generically biblical or monastic light brown robe, whereas the similarly got-up official at the bowmore gangway is Captain Elva Kane, who would likely recognize us.

"Oh, hi!" Heather greets us, and takes and tears our tickets. "I, like, asked everybody backstage how Chinese theater-people say 'Break a leg' or 'Eat shit'?" She returns our stubs. "But nobody knew. Y'all enjoy, now!"

That's it! I pretend: *Ya-len choy nao!* Means "Eat my leg" in Mandarin or "Break wind" in Cantonese, I forget which. Maybe both.

"The inscrutable Orient," adds my wife, and nudges us along before I carry the riff too far. But Heather understands it's a joke — "Oh, you!" — and promises to pass it along "to Hop and Sherry and all."

Uh-oh. But what's done's done; my expectation anyhow (anyhow my hope) is that "Hop and Sherry and all," even if aware of our presence in the audience, will diplomatically preserve our cover, if only to encourage our support and even — but Perish the thought! — my participation later in the Final Season. Another monk-robed junior trouper at the rear entrance-door hands out programs and ushers us to our row. What's with the robes? we ask him. He grins and shrugs: "Like, *repent*?"

Hoping we don't have to, we take our seats in the sure-enough nearly full house, admire *TOFO II*'s admirably freshened interior — wisely kept clean and simple, as in Shipshape, rather than theatrically decorated — and peruse the program. FINAL SEASON!, it reminds us lest we've forgotten, and goes on to declare Dorset Tradewinds Enterprises', The Floating Opera Corporation's, and The Arkade Theatre Company's pride in bringing us, for "the final season of an Ark for All Seasons (see p. 2)," COMING SOON!!! THE MUSICAL, "freely adapted by J. Hopkins Johnson and friends from forthcoming novels by same, or some of same, with particular nods to the late Edna Ferber of *Show Boat* fame, to the late Charles Hunter of *Show Barge* not-quite-fame, to the thankfully not-yet-late [author] of *The Floating Opera* and the forthcoming COMING SOON!!! A NARRATIVE fame—"

Ever loyally sensitive in these matters, "What about the-dozen-books-between fame, you turkeys?" my wife wants to know.

"— also to the authors of Genesis and Revelation, without whose inspiration et cetera."

I like that.

"The et cetera or the whole acknowledgment?"

Both, I guess. Yeah, both.

"*De gustibus*, et cet."

*Ya-len choy nao*, et cet.

At a certain point, as we're scanning on p. 2 a much-condensed history of the James Adams Floating Theatre and its present successor — "to be retired from active theatre service in November 1999 after seven exhilarating seasons of carrying on the Chesapeake showboat tradition, but by no means about to disappear from the tidewater scene (see *Y2K?*, below)" — the Pit Bulls, monk-robed, file into their pit (scattered applause) while their recording of "Sailing Down Chesapeake Bay" plays on the theater's sound system. One by one they begin mugging on their instruments in synch with their recorded selves, until all hands are faking in high-spirited ensemble; gradually then they supplant the fading canned rendition with a lively live, to now-vigorous and well-deserved applause: an effective effect. At the number's wind-up, Sherry Singer and Holly Weil appear onstage in front of the curtain from opposite wings, their monk-robes opened down the front to give us glimpses of net-stockinged legs, chorus-girl tights, and cleavage. After bowing to us and to each other, they meet stage center and draw the curtain-edges back a few feet, revealing a home-theater-size television screen from which a much-enlarged and shrewdly beaming old white male phiz — Mr. Andrew-S.-Et-Cetera Todd's, would be our guess — nods appreciatively at each young woman in turn (they acknowledge his greeting and stand primly by, their robes persistently falling open despite their mock-modest attempts to close them with their free hand) before winking hugely at the audience and declaring *Good evening, friends and neighbors! Thissere's Cap'n Andy Todd Andrews Todd speaking to y'all live from Patmos Tower, just across Snug Harbour. 'S my pleasure to welcome y'all to this Special Preview of The Original Floating Opera Two's Final Season feature:* COMING SOON!!! The Musical, *coming to the theater nearest you —which is the one y'all're a-settin' in right now, am I right?—just as soon's I've said my say 'bout* Why-Two-Kay. *The long and the short of which is this:*

Et cetera: a brief and mildly amusing pitch in exaggerated red-neck style about the soon-coming possible End Of The Goshdurn World As We-all Know It, which more'n likely won't happen atall, 'f we should up'n ask *him*, but who wants to be caught with their pants down if'n it does, 'scuse his French. So just take a dadblame minute 'fore tonight's fun starts and cock an eye at the inside back cover of our program—*Why Y2K?*—where we'll read all about the best-bet gol-durn Millennium-proof deal in these or any other parts: namely, the New Improved Dorsettown-on-Choptank, with its on-site power substation and its private auxiliary water and sanitation systems and what-all, including its very own Ark of Last Resort, no pets allowed on board unless spayed or neutered, just kidding! Watching his blown-up image spiel on, I think So okay, the old guy's not ninety-nine, as he affects to be, any more than he's my "Todd Andrews" character from that long-ago maiden novel; but he is unquestionably in his mid-eighties, economically well off indeed and his mental faculties apparently intact. My question therefore, asked from the threshold of my own seventies, is, What keeps him interested enough in the world to launch and oversee such considerable new projects as this, when one would expect, in the words of Shakespeare's Prospero, his every third thought to be the grave?

Whereto I reply (while "Cap'n Andy" tips the brim of the yachtsman's cap that I forgot to mention and commands "On with the show!," and the curtain-girls let fall the curtain, draw back their robes, and high-kick their way offstage to the Pit Bulls' peppy "There's No Business like Show[boat] Business," and the curtain now reopens upon a scene familiar to us from earlier productions: a painted *TOFO II* on the backdrop, moored at a landing now labeled DORSETTOWN, where presumable townsfolk assemble while the vessel's company, played by a contingent of themselves, choruses the appropriately altered lyrics of the old Irving Berlin tune) that even when thirty-three point three three three percent of one's thoughts become ineluctably so fixed, there remains the other sixty-six point six six seven percent, which might still attach sufficiently to the world—if one be not plagued and consumed by physical or emotional distress—to initiate projects therein: a Y2K-proof community, e.g., whether or not oneself survives to that overhyped date; a *COMING SOON!!!* narrative, coming rather later than one had at its inception hoped.

Et cetera.

*A right good show,*
we agree two hours later, making our way ashore and back around to our marina'd boat: not bad at all, considering with what haste it was reportedly cobbled together and the newly-assembled company rehearsed. Some rough edges to be smoothed out, of course, and weak spots to be strengthened, but really: an ingenious, one could even say *inspired* dramatic-allegorical marble-cake of a show— potpourri, ragout, whatever....

"Mishmash?"

Okay, mishmash. But a high-energy, let-the-chips-fall-et-cetera mishmash: a Rube Goldberg mishmash of a production that improbably took off and flew, excuse the mishmashed metaphor. And all the more admirable (the show, we mean, not the metaphor) to those of us familiar with where the thing's coming from: the old *Show Barge* and *End Time* ingredients effectively if sometimes zanily recombined and admixed with new themes. To have *TOFO II* stand in simultaneously for the James Adams Floating Theatre and for Noah's Ark (with "Charlie" and "Edna" at their famous water-barrel echoing Adam and Eve in the Garden) is no small feat in itself; what chutzpah, to superimpose on this conceit Ms. Sherry-as-Scheherazade Singer, magically transported by a Genie Emeritus from medieval Baghdad to Lord Baltimore's *Arke*-and-*Dove*-full of weary English Catholic refugees approaching the Chesapeake in 1634, and to have her reinspire their colonial project with the tale of Noah's Ark and its good-news-bearing dove (dramatized by the company in their Genesis-robes even as she recounts it) and then *fore*telling a Chesapeake three centuries later—plied by *The Original Floating Opera II*, overflown by Hercules transports carrying relief supplies from Dover Air Force Base to Kosovar refugees in Albania, and polluted by chicken farmers and real-estate developers fretting about Y2K. And actually to bring the thing off, more or less!

"Some of us thought the Emeritus/Aspirant business was just a tad sticky. . . ."

For sure. And some of us never quite figured out what Pocahontas and Captain John Smith, a.k.a. Edna and Charlie, were doing on Prospero's island, a.k.a. Saint Clements, which isn't even in Virginia waters. But it *worked*, yes?

"It sort of worked. And we liked *You're the one, O One, O One*."

They really got their shit together, as the Chinese say. Even the faux-Fort-McHenry fireworks and "The Star-Spangled Banner" as we stepped ashore! Are they postmodern, or what?

"*That* one worked." She even sings one of that plaintive number's late stanzas, as put to The Novelist Aspirant Character by his partner and lover ("Noah's Eldest Daughter, Scheherazade") and several times reprised:

> *What good's Postmodern,*
> *If at the end of the day*
> *Life seems just a cliché?*

"Was that some kind of dig at you, do we think?"

A tease, maybe; not a dig. Like that Transfer of Authority scene at the show's climax — wherein the Ark's "Skipper Emeritus," at the vessel's helm when the dove returns aboard with its olive-branch, declares to the young Skipper Aspirant, "I've brought you this far, son, first as a passenger and then as my apprentice captain," and a dialogue ensues, the old skipper still stubbornly gripping the wheel as his eager replacement stands by —

"Thanks a bunch, Dad!"

"Now the ship's yours. Godspeed, boy."

"Thanks a million, sir!" [*Waits expectantly for the old gent to step aside.*]

"See whether you can do as well, lad. Maybe even better."

"Not a problem, Dad! Now, then, uh, sir: Would you mind, um, leaving the pilothouse? Like, *immediately*?"

"Not quite yet, son."

"*Let go the wheel*, then, okay, if you insist on hanging around? Sir?"

"Not quite yet."

"At least *take your left hand off*, for pity's sake!" [*Tries in vain to pry the oldster's fingers from the ship's wheel.*]

"Not just yet."

—et cetera, more effective in live performance than retold.

"Anyhow, a better Evening of Theater than we feared and expected."

*Much* better. Plus they left us alone. Remind me to pass along our compliments once we're home.

"Along with our conviction that they need no further assistance from The N.E. Character, especially since Zeus is clearly in their corner"—her reference being to the brief but noisy thundershower that flashbanged through Snug Harbour just as, onstage, Skipper Emeritus Noah/Prospero/James Adams and his Successor Aspirant left off competing for control of the helm and together wrestled their many-aspected vessel through an all-purpose "cinestaged" Storm at Sea.

Yes, well. That storm's real-life counterpart being now well to eastward, we find the night sky over Dorsettown star-bright, the damp air cooled and freshened. At risk of being spotted after all— but who cared about that, really, at this point?—we wipe rain-puddles from our cockpit cushions and enjoy a nightcap under the marina-dock lights before turning in. *"You're the one, O One, O One,"* my mate's still humming as we kiss goodnight—whereafter, in the cutter's forward berth, for some time I find myself unable to clear my head of Scheherazade's Complaint:

> *If it's Postmodern,*
> *Why does it feel so passé?*
> *What good's Postmodern,*
> *If at the end of the day* [etc.] . . . ?

*Those questions happen to be answerable,*
I e-mail Johns Hopkins Johnson on the Monday following, once we-all are back at our creekside desks. By which questions I mean both the brace above-put by "Noah's Eldest Daughter" (who never looked to me more beguilingly Scheherazadish, her radiant yet teas-

ing smile suggesting as she sang that she knows something other than stories that we do not, which something she may or may not share with us on some tidewater Arabian Night to come) and the one on the unsigned card on the bouquet of Brandy roses that we found on our vessel's helmsman's seat the morning after Sneak Preview Night:

> *So, guys: Are we Postmod?*
> *Anyhow, here's a dozen thanks*
> *for yr advice & assistance*
> *throughout our voyage together.*

No signature(s), but sender(s) obvious.

*However,* I assure my erstwhile rival and competitor in that cybernote's continuation, *you-all can answer them for yourselves, w' out my hand on yr wheel. The more important question, always, is "Does it fly?" And our house opinion, in this instance, is that it does.* Compliments au chef; *thanks for the Brandies; on with your show, man, and I'll with mine.*

Whereto I postscribe a question that only belatedly occurred to me: *Just curious: What happened to those multiple/optional/alternative endings?* Not that, in my judgment, they were as novel and interesting an idea this late in the day as they had seemed in the original *Show Barge* script-outline of circa 1940. And the production-mechanics of alternative "cinestage" denouements, all on standby for instant deployment at the audience's behest, must be particularly daunting within the constraints of a floating theater, even with its Y2K-enhanced budget. Moreover, the ending that we-all sneak-previewed a few nights past, while no doubt fine-tunable down the road, struck us as adequate and fitting, in the main: Dawn's-Early-Light Sunshine after Tempest; a more amicable Transfer of Authority scene after the Skippers Aspirant and Emeritus jointly bring their Ark to Ararat/Patmos/St. Clements/Snug Harbour (this last, I presume, changeable to whatever port *T II* happens to be playing on a given night, so that the audience is truly "brought home" at the show's end, and their subsequent disembarkation from the theater becomes in effect the play's final action); and Apocalypse duly Postponed by the relenting Author after some offstage special pleading by Noah's daughter Scheherazade — "postponed at least till y'all-know-when," says the mischievously winking projected phiz of "Cap'n Andy" as the curtain closes.

On second thought, however — lest my multiple-ending question be mistaken for a critical suggestion, one Skipper-Emerital finger still on the wheel — I scrap that postscript and transmit my mere good wishes: *Ya-len choy nao*, so to speak.

For one does indeed have one's own show to get on with as best one can, lest that fell aforefeared Tortoise — the *real* 1999 — overtake this fictive projection and juggernaut it flat. As I pen this apprehension, May turns to June in *TOFO-II* land: The Grand Opening in Annapolis Harbor grand-opens, suitably attended by dignitaries but not by us and amply covered by the regional media (the Baltimore *Sun*'s drama critic is particularly charmed by the Ark's making its way safely after the Tempest to "Annapolis Harbor" at the play's end, "just in time for us storm-tossed passengers to come ashore"). The company's Final Season is auspiciously under way. In Real Time, on the other hand, April just now turns to May on the Chester River: Azaleas, lilacs, crabapples, and cherries are in full bee-bumbled flower outside the penman's window, with dogwood and rhododendron ready in the wings for their star turn. Like most of the world, he who pens *he who pens* etc. is horrified by the Serbs' atrocious "ethnic cleansing" of Kosovo and the wretched plight of Albanian refugees therefrom; appalled by the recent Columbine High School massacre in Colorado and the immeasurably larger cataclysm that its teenage perpetrators had elaborately prepared. What is his gun-nutsy, Internet-addicted, family- and community-weakened country coming to, he wonders along with everybody else who cares, and isn't there *some* way to forestall the next Rwandan/Kosovar disaster? And yet one spends one's mortal mornings imagining Floating Operas II and COMING SOON!!! THE MUSICALS making their late-spring way from port to Chesapeake port, while the interval between their dreamed-up movements and this pen's real ones inexorably diminishes: a mere month now, in short (and shorter), between fictive time and real. Talk about Final Follies!

\* \* \*

*All right: some things heretofore unmentioned,*
but perhaps glance-attable while Reality crowds Fiction's muse:

- Captain. Adam. Andrew. Lake's stiffness of speech and bearing, though characteristic, has a recent additional justification — if that's the right word and if any is needed — unappreciated by his fellow FLOPCORPers and the Arkade Theatre Company: A prostatectomy last December, while successfully eliminating his cancer of the relevant gland, has left him in his late fifties both impotent and occasionally incontinent for the remainder of his life. This burden he bears more stoically than does the only other soul aware of it besides his doctors: his sometime paramour June "Bea Golden" Harrison, whom her friend's affliction would drive to half-sympathetic, half-self-pitying drink, had she not already arrived at that destination.

- That lady is, in fact (as only I and now You know, until *her* doctor joins us and so informs her after her upcoming routine physical examination), no longer borderline liver-cirrhotic, she having alas crossed that border in the year since her previous checkup. A bone-density scan will further reveal to him, and he to her, that for lack of estrogen, sufficient calcium intake, and low-impact exercise, her bones are turning seriously osteoporotic. Nasty times ahead for this Angel Team leader, who inclines to meet them by adding Valium to her booze. Do not stay tuned.

- One of Jay "Obie" Brown's half-brothers was fatally gunned down in deepest inner Baltimore between some early paragraphs of this Chapter "1999." A "drug-related homicide," the police report surmises. Jay has other semi-siblings, elder and younger, by yet other fathers, but of this one, Dontay, he was especially fond and protective, determined to guide him out of the black-urban-American Pit as by luck and pluck he has guided himself. What particularly salts this wound for Jay is its reinforcement of egregious racial stereotypes that his own life thus far has endeavored to transcend. In his bereavement he is much tempted to abandon the stage — another stereotype, after all, the Nimble Black Entertainer — and to become . . . oh, a public-high-school drama coach, maybe, if he can muster the credentials, or maybe a sales clerk in the Toys "Я" Us store where he worked parttime while studying at UMES, the mainly black Eastern Shore branch of the University of Maryland. Jay's new friend Ditsy swears that she(?) wouldn't be caught dead in one of them there Inner Cities. You sure would be, Jay grimly teases, without me to walk you through the 'hood.

- Although Sherry McAndrews Singer's serial stepfathers (June "Bea Golden" Harrison's second and third husbands, Mel Bernstein and Louis Golden) were and remain invariably affectionate hertoward, her biological dad (June's first husband, Barry Singer) used to whip her roundly and often with his belt throughout her childhood for "talking back" to him or her mother, while that distracted lady would merely murmur "Not so *hard*, hon." This painful history accounts for Sher's involuntary flinch and shudder, aforenoted, at sight or sound of her present consort's absentmindedly whipping off his trouser-belt — snapsnapsnap through the belt-loops — as she has begged him not to do, but he forgets. Likewise her early self-promise, in the memorable words of the poet Philip Larkin, to

> *Get out as early as you can,*
> *And don't have any kids yourself.*

Likewise, it may or may not be, both her passionate vocation for the stage and her hyper-self-critical reluctance to Go For It beyond tidewaterland. Her tough-loving if not merely sadistic father having "got out early," Sher hangs around still, more or less looking after a mother whom she has never loved. Such welts as Dad raised on her outlast their visibility, and different fleshes are scarred differently themby.

- Mort and Dr. Rachel Spindler's (adopted) elder child, whose oddly obstreperous behavior since babyhood they've tried simultaneously to ignore, accept, ameliorate, and investigate, they have lately discovered to be the son of a chronically institutionalized paranoid-schizophrenic birthmother by an unidentified rapist in one of the former's several "residential situations" —an infobit withheld from the adoptive parents by the placing agency until a recent *New York Times Magazine* piece on the subject prompted Rachel and Mort to threaten litigation if the relevant records were not produced. They love troubled Benjamin, they swear, "every bit as much as his kid sister" (biologically theirs), but live now in quiet dread that the malady will strike full force down the road—and that their fear itself will taint their bond to him, somehow aggravating his disturbancy.

- Hop Johnson's parents—gifted and dedicated physicians both, as well as loving and indulgent parents who have programmatically resisted disappointment in their only child's career-track and have loyally taken pride in his "theater projects"—will alas not survive Parts III of this narrative: plane-crash into the Atlantic en route to a well-earned Thanksgiving holiday at Caneel Bay, St. John, USVI. Cause undetermined, but Bermuda Triangle nut-theories rife. They thus will never have the pleasure of seeing . . . never mind, for a while yet, what.

- And then there are the Kane twins, are there not: neither ever married nor, it seems, even party to a "relationship" of any considerable duration. We bet there's a story there, not likely a cheery one. Let's let that bet go uncalled.

- And there's Holly Weil, isn't there, and **SPECIAL EFFECT!**, and the rest of our Cast of Several. And there's You, Reader of this paused fiction, burdened who knows how; and there's I, its fictor, and all the other passengers-in-transit aboard this joy- and beauty-spangled wretched bloody ark the world. Going on; going under.

Must the show, too, go on?

*"We'll just see,"*
allows the televised face of Andrew S. Etc. Todd in Patmos Tower 696 shortly after the July Fourth holiday weekend, in closed-circuit

conference with Mort Spindler, Hop Johnson, Sherry Singer, Capt. Adam. Lake., and a not-at-all-well-looking "Bea Golden"— *"after Y2K. But your news is good news, and I congratulate all hands."* That news being, in more or less chronological order,

1.  that despite the admittedly weak-link role of The N.E. Character in *CS!!!*TM—an all-purpose "G-string" part, as the showbiz term used to be, doubling in this instance as Noah, Lord Baltimore, Prospero, Scheherazade's imperious Sultan Shahryar, Author John of Patmos, and, lately, some blend of Francis Scott Key (setting "The Star-Spangled Banner" to the old drinking-tune "To Anacreon in Heaven" while the Brits bombard Fort McHenry in September 1814) and his descendant F. Scott Fitzgerald (drunkenly singing that anthem in Baltimore in 1936 while writing *The Crack-Up* in an apartment just across North Charles Street from Johns Hopkins University's Homewood campus), and played by ever-shifting "cinestage" combinations of Capt. Ad. and "Cap'n Andy" himself—that despite this and some other minor but nagging problems, *TOFO II*'s Main Season is going so well thus far as to excite speculation among the company and even "ashore" that it mightn't be, or at least needn't be, Final after all. The old troupers and new hands are in unprecedented synergy; so too are the Final Follies and the Main Feature, each continually evolving and improving the other. *T II* groupies have taken to following the showboat from port to port, comparing notes on that evolution and talking it up in their Internet chat-room, which like FLOPCORP's own new website is registering a respectable number of daily hits. Each of ATC's principals, indeed, now has his/her small but loyal claque of fans, as do several of the supporting cast, including Holly Weil ("Miranda," "Pocahontas," "Noah's Youngest Daughter," "Scheherazade's Kid Sister," etc.), Jay Brown ("Ariel," "Abel," "Pocahontas's Big Bro," "Scher's Kid Sister's Boyfriend," etc. — not to mention "Senior African-American Citizen Joe" singing "Ol' Man River" as Flood sweeps Ark down Chesassippi), Captain Harry "Cain" and Elva "Eve's Aunt" Kane, even Ditsy as a polymorphous "Caliban." The more vertiginously multireferential

the production becomes (incoherent, some would say), the live-lier its audience response, thanks surely to that last-lap, now-or-never spirit among the company. Mort, Sherry, and Hop are pushing the envelope's edge so hard that just now they're not at all sure they *want* a Final Season II in the year 2000; but "We'll just see," they agree with the Arkangel-in-Chief.

2. that a fortnight since, on the summer solstice, the young princi-pal author of *CS!!!* TM and Novelist Still Quietly Aspirant (de-spite zero good news from NYC re his disketted e-fictive proto-version of *T II*'s unexpectedly successful musical) turned twenty-nine — forty years this present penman's junior! *Seventy* years the junior of Andrew S. Todd, who celebrates his birthday on the solstice whether it falls on June 21 or June 22. At the little postshow cast party in their joint honor (attended televisionally by the senior celebrant), the junior proudly announced

3. that among their show's ongoing mutations will be certain small story-line accommodations to the circumstance that [*puts arm around blushing friend Eve/Noah's-#1-Daughter/Scheherazade*] "We're *preggers*, guys!" Two and a half months so as of that party-time announcement, end of first trimester as of this con-ference-in-progress, the progenitors having successfully "taken a crack" (so Dad indelicately puts it) at conceiving on Friday, April 9, the optimum start-up date for Y2K natality. This despite Sher's no-kids credo, aforephrased by poet Larkin, which some-thing has evidently superseded: Shall we call it love? At the news, Captain Elva bestowed an I-*knew*-it smile upon her knit-ting-in-progress. Mom's been having some problems with morn-ing sickness, aggravated by *mal de mer* in bumpy weather, when that oil-smell rises from the showboat's bilge; but Doc Rachel Spindler has been a godsend, as has the kid-in-the-works's medical grandparents-not-yet-in-law and its "Auntie Elva," who makes gut-settling herbal teas and has since early May ceased unraveling the little things she knits ("Our first clue," Sher de-clared to the party-attenders, whereto Capt. E. replied "*Plant your seeds by moonlight and the crop'll be good*," and Holly

Weil couldn't help adding "But the moon wasn't full till, like, last day of April, right?"). Imagine the script possibilities, Hop invites them now at the semi-teleconference: Eve literally pregnant with the world's first child! Noah's daughter throwing up over the Ark's lee rail! Scheherazade's ace in the hole, so to speak, if her narrative powers fail her! "Bea Golden" is, let's say, much affected: "So shall we have a shipboard wedding," she asks straight out, "while the bride can still fit in my old gown?" Reply Expectant Ma and Pa as one, after a consulting glance: "We'll just see."

Because while Hop feels they should take the plunge despite their precarious economic and professional status (and while his parents, though careful not to push their agenda, encourage the match in hopes that marriage and parenthood will lead their son at last into "a real profession"), Sher is even warier of matrimony than of motherhood. She much loves her fetus's sire (*"Our* fetus's sire," Hop corrects her, and she lets the correction stand), but can't help feeling that to officialize their bond might be somehow to *verhex* it. "Let's just see."

*"Your grandma's going to be one happy lady,"* Cap'n Andy's pixeled face assured her back there at the solstitial announcement-party: *"I'll get the news up to Nine Ninety-nine right now"* —where the aged Jane Harrison has for some time—Did this get mentioned? —been under heavy sedation and round-the-clock nursing care for advanced senile dementia and general physical decline.

So the show goes on, and while The N.E. Character remains its weakest link despite all efforts at reinforcement, the cast's performances improve with experience, and attendance holds at a gratifyingly high average. But as if Cap'n Andy's *"We'll just see"* were an invitation to the gods of adversity, before July's end the first of several setbacks sets things back. Not two weeks after this conference, "Bea Golden's" failing liver fetches her to Dorchester General Hospital in Cambridge, where she decides to ride out her serious condition with the homefolks despite Hop's parents' recommendation that she be transferred to their renal-specialist colleagues in Baltimore. "Don't you worry," she tells the daughter who much cares about the mother she cannot love: "I'm going nowhere till I've kissed my first grandchild."

She will, alas, not have that satisfaction, despite her lingering on in Extended Care past this novel's end. Her several bit parts in *CS!!!* TM — as Noah's wife, Grandma Eve, Edna Ferber Old, even The N.E. Character's Grayhaired Muse — are filled more or less convincingly by the ex-techie **SPECIAL EFFECT!**, whose talents have extended over the seasons to *maquillage* and character-acting. But Capt. Ad.'s concern for his longtime ladyfriend takes a toll on his effectiveness both as walk-on player (Capt. John Smith, Capt. Andy Hawks of Ferber's *Cotton Blossom*, etc.) and, it must be said and will soon be shown, as skipper of *TOFO II*. Harry Kane and Mort Spindler overextend themselves to fill those roles in addition to their many own; Hop edits a few such out of the "script," and even Ditsy — though most comfortable as a grumping and galumphing Caliban — finds himherself pressed into service for some of the others.

Then, in early August, "Bea Golden's" also-ailing mom is smitten by a fatal though perhaps merciful coronary up in PT 999. Although her consort's legal and other aides make all the funeral arrangements and address the matron's very considerable estate (*"Don't you worry 'bout a thing, young lady,"* Cap'n Andy assures Sherry Singer. "Won't be long till she never *has* to worry 'bout a thing," agree Jay Brown and Holly Weil, enviously but not unsympathetically), Sher and Hop find themselves running from showboat to hospital to funeral home to Patmos Tower to obstetrician's office and back aboard by curtain time. Their performances, too, might be expected to show the strain; but they share the artists' saving knack — *some* artists', anyhow — of translating stress into even more inspired performance, at least for a time.

To these adversities add the unusually active La Niña Atlantic hurricane season this year (I write this in May, too early to tell, but the experts agree it'll soon be hunker-down time on our eastern seaboard), which by mid-August I imagine to be racing through the storm-alphabet and serially threatening when not actually disrupting the showboat's itinerary. Add to that the late-August defection —while *T II* is in Snug Harbour for mid-season maintenance and a bit of R&R for the weary company before heading down to Solomons Island, the Potomac, and its much-touted "Maryland Defenders Day" at St. Mary's City—of, of all people, Ditsy. "Said she didn't like the *smell* of things downstairs," reports sad Jay Brown, who prefers the feminine pronoun for his lately significant other. "Something different about that oil-stink?"

"Don't talk about it," pleads Sherry Singer (whose morning sickness has, however, by this time largely passed), but comforts her sorrowing colleague with a cheek-kiss.

"Plus this crazy storm-season," Jay goes on, and Captain Elva reminds all hands that *every rainy day in August means a day of snow come winter.*

"Oh, *can* it, Elv," Hop Johnson frets, but kisses his friend's friend's head to show he's not angry with her, just distressed.

"Plus she still pines for that E-A-R-L character," glooms Jay, "whoever *that* mother is."

"Estuarine Aquacultural Research Lab," Hop reminds them-all and You, "down near Ditsy's old stomping grounds on Hick Fen Island. All-caps EARL was the guy that ran the place till the Navy reclaimed it for target practice in Operation Desert Storm. Dits wanted me to work that into the show somehow, but I couldn't make it fit."

"Fit shmit." Mort Spindler turns up his palms. "Now we've lost our Caliban."

"Caliban . . . shmaliban," surprisingly echoes Captain. Adam. Lake.: "We've lost our main maintenance man. Is what we've lost. Nobody better at keeping our bilge pumps up. And running."

"Main *maintainer*," Holly Weil politically corrects him.

Glum Jay concludes his report: "Says she's going back to progging till the weather clears."

Of Elva, Sher requests "No proverbs, please." But her friend can't help mouthing one silently to the baby-garment-in-progress: *Eagles may soar, but weasels don't get sucked into jet engines.*

"I'll bite," says **SPECIAL EFFECT!**: "What's *progging*?"

Her comrade Heather—Remember down-home waitress

Heather from Sneak Preview night, now a rapidly rising ingenue who has moved into several of Holly Weil's former roles as Holly moved into several of Sherry's as Sherry grew pregnanter and pregnanter?—elucidates: Her granddaddy used to take her a-progging down to Hoopers Island when she was little. "You know: *progging*."

"Oh."

Add to all these the perhaps unkindest cut of all: that on the same end-of-August eve as the conversation abovereported (which is to say, just past the halfway point of her pregnancy), Sherry Singer finds herself seized by cramps and contractions alarming enough to warrant a Jeep-dash from Dorsettown to Cambridge, where Rachel Spindler meets her and Hop at Dorchester General just in time to oversee the couple's miscarriage. A 4.5-month baby girl, it was, whose parents, had she lived to term, might have named her Dunya: short for Scheherazade's kid sister and accomplice, Dunyazade. Mother physically okay and soon discharged from hospital, empty-wombed and empty-armed. News withheld for a time from ill maternal grandma, who however not only divines or otherwise gets word of it but contrives somehow to lay hold of consolatory liquor—*verboten* generally in the extended-care facility and most particularly in her liver-damaged case, as she well knows but no longer cares.

"Pack it up?" the company ask themselves and one another. "Pack it in?" They had earlier agreed, after all, to "just see," and it would sure seem that they've seen. So fallen is their fortune from the heights of just a few pages back that not only does a Final Season II appear out of the question now, but equally the finale of FS I. Given the circumstances, it's to Hop and Sherry that they leave the call. He's inclined, uncharacteristically, to bag the whole thing; has never felt so set down in his nine-and-twenty years: first the failed e-novel, now all this. But he up-pushes his specs and looks to her, as do Mort Spindler, the captains Kane and Lake., Jay, Holly—all the usuals plus selected newbies.

*"On with the show,"*
declares sadpale Sher. On to Solomons, St. Mary's, and the Inner Harbor. "That's what we're *for*, right? It's who we fucking *are*!"

Now that she's de-pregnanted, she can resume a wider range of parts to relieve overburdened Holly and Heather, not that they were complaining; and fewer script-accommodations will need to be made to her condition. Best way to handle torpedoes is full speed ahead.

Even before Hop can, Mort asks "You sure, Sher?" and that amazing-eyed woman answers "Of course I'm not." Then adds, "Let's do it."

"Yo!" "Right on!" "You go, girl!" "Aye. Aye. Ma'am." "Do it do it do it!" "Swim or sink!" "Yes, well."

This last from "the original of The N.E. Character" when, on Thursday, September 2, he gets by telephone, telefax, and e-mail a cross-their-heart-final last-ditch appeal from SpindlerJohnson-Singer setting forth their several recent settings-back, their unanimous determination to see the Final Season through despite all, and their urgent *urgent* request for his "final assistance" therewith. What manner of assistance, pray? Well: What they have in mind is a series of In-Person Guest Appearances as The Novelist Emeritus Character, presently being "cinestaged" no more than adequately as afore-described. As if old Charlie Hunter *in propria persona* could appear in the role of "Charlie" (which, remember, he allegedly had planned to do in his "proto-Postmodern" draft of *Show Barge*), or E. Ferber herself as "Edna"!

I'm not Edna Ferber, Narrator reminds them — meaning no disparagement either way, only that the audience-thrill value of a live appearance by the bestselling author of *Show Boat* in the role of herself cannot be expected to be approached by present company, even if present company were willing to give it a go. . . .

"Granted," Hop Johnson mischievously grants. One imagines him upping his wire-rims, twiddling his lobe-ring, and grinning his bright-cricket grin.

"*Not* granted!" protest Singer and Spindler. Leave everything to them: All Narrator need do is take a few days off from his daily routine to join *T II* at Solomons Island, say, after its upcoming Labor Day weekend stand there. A couple of rehearsals should put him at ease in the role — He will, after all, be playing versions of himself, and any fumblings will be part of the fun! — in time to open at St. Mary's City on "Maryland Defenders Day" weekend (September 10–12, actually, although the semipseudohistorical date is Tuesday, September 14), maybe in D.C./Alexandria the following weekend, maybe again in Annapolis first weekend in November, after *T II* has toured its way back north from the Potomac to the Severn — and then the grand float-parade up to Baltimore for 11/11 in the Inner Harbor! Between those dates they'll make shift as presently, and Narrator can return to his narrative — for which a little stint of hands-on showboat-performing could be inspiring, no?

"Do it do it do it!" Ms. Singer pleads.

"Our last best hope, sir!" exclaims Mort Spindler.

E-mails Hop Johnson, *A proper captain stays with his ship.*

Yes, well, one reminds him: But your ship is not mine these days, lad. *My* ship is my ship, and may neither go down.

"Ours will, I fear," Mort fears by phone, in a tone more grave than one had theretofore heard from him. "On the scale of human misfortunes, no big deal for sure. But we-all've worked so *hard* ! . . ."

Yes. Well. I myself, Reader, for better or worse could never be tempted by such a proposal. But with Time's Tortoise breathing down my narrative neck (mid-May now here already! Azaleas finished, roses and rhododendrons abloom, and the world fucked up even more than usually, what with NATO's misguided missile-strikes in Belgrade and impeachment proceedings proceeding against Russia's loose-cannon President Yeltsin), I here reluctantly permit The N.E. Character — *my* N.E. Character, in *my* p-fictive *COMING SOON!!!* — not only to be tempted but, against his mate's sensible better judgment, to consent, and then that'll be that, he swears to her, *TOFO-II*wise. It's Ms. Singer's miscarriage, I believe, that tips the chap's balance from sympathetic arm's-length encouragement to sympathetic in-person assistance: He had enjoyed the image of his Scheherazade pregnant literally as well as figuratively, spinning out her ark-tales as her belly grew, prolonging both her own life and her womb-child's by nightly entertaining that true life-or-death King Shahryar, the audience. (Had he himself happened to be Hop Johnson's script-coach, he'd've urged clarification of that theme at the play's conclusion, when the S.O.S. pitch is made to "John of Patmos" to "change our story's ending" from Armageddon to Apocalypse Deferred: That Author-figure might draft alternative denouements till the cows come home, but only the Audience, Shahryar-like, by their nightly approval and call for encore, can defer the apocalypse.) Such a pity that what had seemed so happily on its way to due fruition came prematurely, with mortal consequences.

"Like my e-novel, yes?" Hop Johnson proposes when I express these sentiments soon after, at our talk-it-over meeting aboardship in Snug Harbour just before *T II*'s casting off for Solomons. "Another miscarried preemie, out of the shop before term." Eyeglasses up. "Coming *too* soon's the name of our game, I guess."

"*Not!*" protests his partner, a drawn but very determined-eyed Sherry Singer. "That project's not dead yet, and neither is ours."

"*In the family way by Y2K,*" Jay Brown jives lightly, and Holly Weil high-fives him in salute.

It feels, this time, less like a business meeting than like an extended-family ingathering. Four years I've known these characters now (Hop Johnson for even longer), engaging them almost daily in my imagination and now and then in person, monitoring and sometimes influencing, in my way, their ups and downs. I commiserate with Sherry and Hop; with Captain. Ad. Lake. as well, normally a stiff upper lip from head to toe, but lately so shaken by "Bea Golden's" precipitous decline that among themselves (so Hop confides to me) they've taken to calling him Captain Addled. I'm welcomed by Jay and Holly, by the Kane twins (Elva's back to undoing her macramé, but leaves the finished baby-garments intact), by Heather and **SPECIAL EFFECT!** and the others; perhaps most relievedly by Mort Spindler, whom I find noticeably aged since our last path-crossing: Those aforementioned worries re the adopted son and attendant legal hassles with the adoption agency, I presume, together with *T II*'s basketful of new difficulties, have sapped his characteristic pep, though not his resolve. Time's short, we all agree (without my needing to invoke that Tortoise on the verge of juggernauting me): No way I'm going to turn self-performer, I make clear from the outset, to anything like the extent proposed; won't play that N.E. Character right through the script for even one performance. Against my better half's better judgment, however (by which I mean my muse's as well as my mate's), I'll go so far as to make two-maybe-three Guest Appearances as that John-the-Author character in the closing scene — Patmos John, shall we call him? — to pronounce the Floating Apocalypse postponed at least till tomorrow night if Their Majesty the Audience consents. *How many for Apocalypse Now? How many for Apocalypse Deferred?* Et cetera.

"How many for GreatUnc Ennie's scaled-down proposal?" Hop asks the company, and every hand cries "Aye!"

"The ayes have it," Sherry Singer declares, her own a-shine. Hop brims already with ideas for modifying the play's ending along the lines proposed—"The audience as King Shahryar!" Mort Spindler enthuses, almost with his old ebullience: *"That'*ll put pep! Zingo!" — and for planting foreshadows thereof in Act One and the early scenes of Act Two.

Cheers perky Heather, *"Ya-len choy nao!"* and the company choruses what has evidently become a mantra themamong: *Ya-len choy nao!*

"Well," sigh Muse and Mate as one, not unskeptically, when I report this meeting's outcome: "If that's what you want, dot dot dot." Whereto The N.E. Character replies that that's what he wants, I guess. After which, showboats good-bye.

"We'll just see. You checked those dates on our calendar?"

All clear, or easily clearable. The plan becomes for us to drive across the Bay Bridge and down to Solomons Island on Tuesday, September 7, after the Labor Day weekend traffic crunch from the ocean resorts: down to Solomons, where on our spring sailing-cruise four years past, the spectacle of a certain bravely bannered hulk launched this enterprise now approaching climax, if not closure. I will there join the company and rehearse themwith my much-reduced curtain-closing bit as "Patmos John." For the sport of it, I propose we leave our car at Solomons and ride aboard *T II* down-Bay and up-Potomac to the St. Mary's River and ditto City on

315

Thursday, 9/9 — though if it better pleaseth Ms. Mate not to watch her husband exhibit himself as a version of Himself, she can simply drop him off at Solomons on the Tuesday, drive back home, and then haul over to St. Mary's for the Friday opening of *TOFO*'s "Maryland Defenders Day." Or not.

"Whatever."

We could even, it occurs to me, set out earlier — like immediately? — in our own vessel; *sail* down to Solomons instead of driving, and truly close the narrative circle by anchoring again in that Special Solomons Cove of ours, in full view this time not of the projected *James Adams II* (long gone who knows where, may it rust in peace), but of *The Original Floating Opera II*, long may it wave, *ya-len choy nao*. Leave our boat there while we ride the showboat down to my gig, then hop a lift back and resume our regular September cruise. Good idea?

Maybe, maybe not, given the superactive hurricane season — but that's her mate's department. He is, in fact, the family weather-watcher, and her reservation is, as usual, well taken: A check of the National Storm Center's hurricane advisory website (www.storm99.com) shows Tropical Storm Zulu — *Zulu?* — tracking northward up the Gulf Stream from the Bahamas toward Cape Hatteras. Computer models predict a turn northeastward after it grazes the Cape, a course that should keep TSZ safely offshore — but one never knows.

So okay: We'll postpone sailing until the coast literally clears. On the aforespecified postholiday Tuesday we pack our seabags (though we'll be sleeping in motels; no room in the ark) and drive over and down, Narrator already beginning to feel more than a little . . . he won't say *foolish*, just out of character; uncomfortable with what he has agreed to do and not at all convinced that his doing it will even minimally affect the showboat's fortunes or prove of any use whatever to the composition of this tale. But a promise is a promise.

Reader will excuse me, please, from detailing my preparations for that walk-on curtain-closer as "Patmos John" beyond the whitening of my already-gray beard by **SPECIAL EFFECT!**; my outfitting in a cowled robe meant to evoke simultaneously a monk's habit and a silk dressing gown such as might be worn by some 1930s Hollywood version of A Writer (there is, in fact, an extant photograph from that era of Charles Hunter in comparable attire, sitting at his typewriter aboard the *James Adams Floating Theatre*); my equipage with both quill pen and laptop computer; my memorization of such deathless lines as *At this point, just as the writer of this story was inscribing the words* At this point, *the writer of this story was interrupted by an urgent knocking at the door of his isolated retreat. With the words* He put down his pen *he put down his pen, closed his laptop, and went to meet Noah's youngest daughter, Joan of the Ark, who he knew was coming to plead with him to change the ending of this story, for he himself had written this episode even as she slipped unseen from her father's vessel and climbed the rocky path up Mount Patmos to his den* — lines that, in the event, were never by me delivered except in rehearsal and on this page. For in the course of that same Tuesday, Tropical Storm Zulu gained strength and speed, barreling straight for the Outer Banks and threatening to upgrade itself to a hurricane. By Wednesday morning, the Weather Service had extended the warning zone as far north as Kitty Hawk and the watch zone all the way to Cape May, New Jersey.

Not good, we say to each other and to the company. Captain. Ad. Lake. poofs and declares they've weathered past storms aplenty. And will weather this one too. If it actually comes our way. Though more'n likely it'll either bounce off Hatteras and head for New England. Or else fizzle inland as nothing more than a rainy day. But we neglected to make our creekside place storm-ready before we set out, knowing we'd be after all but a few hours' drive itfrom: We ought to have doubled up our boat's docklines and battened its hatches, just in case; shut off the dock water- and power-lines, stowed the lawn furniture — our usual and regular hurricane preps. No great matter, though it means good-bye to my inclination to ride the showboat down to St. Mary's: We'll just zip home after today's rehearsal, do those precautionary chores tomorrow while *T II* is in transit, and on Friday drive back to rendezvous with the company at St. Mary's, in plenty of time for another run-through before the evening show. Okay, guys? *Hasta la vista*, then; *bon voyage*, et cet.

Sherry Singer hugs us both. Hop Johnson grins — at exactly what, one isn't sure. Captain. Ad. shrugs his eyebrows. Harry Kane, Jay Brown, Holly Weil, and **SPECIAL EFFECT!** are busy elsewhere. Warns Captain Elva, stroking her cat, "*When you see a centipede, be sure to keep your mouth shut, 'cause if a centipede counts your teeth, you'll die.*"

Gotcha, Cap'n — though experience teaches that most folks die anyhow.

Bids Heather, as is her tendency, "*Ya-len choy nao.*"

You, too.

*9/9/99,*

therefore, finds us at home, much relieved that we neither sailed our own boat to Solomons Harbor earlier in the week nor set out therefrom this morning aboard *TOFO II* for the Potomac and St. Mary's; hoping, indeed, that Capt. Ad. changed his mind last night and has kept the showboat safely in port. For in the course of that night, while we finished our busy storm-preps and went to bed exhausted, our fingers crossed that those preparations will suffice, Tropical Storm Zulu once again defied predictions, gained strength and speed, and roared straight up the coast of Virginia and lower Delmarva. By this morning's dull light (so Narrator imagines as, astride Time's Tortoise in the preceding May, he writes this sentence) it is presently pummeling both the peninsula's Atlantic beaches and the Chesapeake with torrential rain, sustained sixty-knot winds, and abnormally high and low tides as those winds change direction with the storm's passage. Trees and power-lines down, flash flooding on some upriver stretches in the higher elevations of Maryland's western shore, tidal flooding here and there on our Eastern, our own dock at one point a full foot under water! In a mid-morning break from his composition (nothing more we can do outdoors; might as well make sentences as we watch and wait), the man of us tries to place a shore-to-ship call to Mort Spindler's showboat office. The call goes through, but there's no response. At lunchtime he phones the Calvert Marine Museum (see Chapters 2.1 and 2.2 of *Its tripartite second chapter*), where *T II* had docked for its Solomons Island performances, and is told by a voice not unlike that Nice Infolady's of four years back that indeed the showboat set out early this morning — was, anyhow, gone when she arrived to open the museum, which Lord knows why she bothered to do, as nobody in his/her right mind is likely to go museuming in weather like this! On a hunch he then rings up that neighboring marina whose associated restaurant was the venue, once upon a time, of a certain Ontological Lunchbreak, Novelists Only (Chap. 2.3), and which, he happens to know, monitors VHF Channel 16, the maritime "calling frequency," as do many marina offices. Busy as their people are with the overseeing of their storm-hassled boat-slips, they not only confirm that *Raven* and *Dove* towed the showbarge past their docks and out into the Patuxent by dawn's blustery half-light, but add that they overheard just a while ago a "Security" call (pronounced French-style, *Sécurité*, the nautical lingua franca for a distress-alert less urgent than a "Mayday") from the showboat's skipper to the Coast Guard, reporting that the tugs and their tow were "experiencing storm-related difficulties." But while there was scuttlebutt aplenty around the harbor — that the showboat had broken free of its tugs; that one or more of the three were taking on water, etc., etc. — all that was known with any certainty was that there had been a "Sécurité" and that the USCG was either standing by or had already dispatched either a cutter or a helicopter to the scene. Concerned indeed now, our man next calls the offices of FLOPCORP, down in Dorsettown: Busy. He redials: Busy, and yet again Busy (Looking at the word just written, How did that *u* come to sound like *i*? he wonders now, and in his mind's ear hears the impish Phantom chuckle at that punning question). Busybusybusy — until toward mid-afternoon he finally gets through to some secretary who, although she doesn't doubt the caller's identity and concern, is at liberty to say no more at present than that out in the Bay, off Point No Point (i.e., a bit more than halfway down from Drum Point at the mouth of the Patuxent to Point Lookout at the mouth of the Potomac), *T II* & Co. did indeed experience storm-related difficulties. Now that the worst of said storm has passed, however, the situation appears to be in hand, and the crew and vessels are reportedly in no danger.

They're on their way to St. Mary's, then, in time for tomorrow's opening?

She's really really sorry, but is not at liberty to say. An updated report is expected shortly.

He doesn't like the sound of that; on a hunch calls Rachel Spindler's office in Cambridge and asks *her* secretary whether she happens to have heard what's what. Secretary can't or won't say, but will relay query to Doctor Spindler—who promptly phones back, although we scarcely know her from our occasional connection with her husband. The woman of us happens to take the call; she and Doc Rachel are in immediate rapport; Narrator is invited to listen in on his desk-phone, and we get both the news and its eloquent reporter's handle thereupon:

That *meshugge* Adam-period-Lake-period! Has he lost it altogether, the doctor asks us, to leave port in a storm like this? But they're all *meshuggenehs,* if we should ask her, her husband included and maybe especially, bless his too-big heart. Plus she appreciates that Captain Ad's been around the bend with worry about Sherry's poor mother (who's a goner, if we want to know the truth, poor thing, and no wonder), so he maybe isn't captaining with a full deck these days. And Sherry and Hop and Bless-his-heart-Mort have been working *so* hard to get things in shape for Maryland Big-Tsimmes Day, whatever, so no doubt they were noodging full speed ahead and damn the torpedoes. . . . So what happens? They hit Zulu head-on in mid-Bay, is what happens, with wind and tide both against them, and one or both tugboats lose power or are maybe overpowered by conditions, but do they turn their tushies around and head back to safe harbor? They do not, 'cause Captain-period-Shmendrick-period figures if they can just get around Point Lookout, the south wind and incoming tide'll fetch them right up the Potomac into Saint Whatsername's, and there they'll be! But before they can turn that corner the wind switches from south to west, wouldn't you know it, and they're actually *losing* ground, losing water, whatever, and going backwards full speed ahead! Even *then,*

Captain Elva (Isn't *she* a study? But a sweetheart, really) figures they've still got a fighting chance to make headway if Brother Harry'll move *Raven* behind the showboat and push from back there while she pulls from up front. Something to do with windage? Don't ask Doc Rachel; she just works here. So Captain-period-Einstein-period gives his okay to that, but aha! *Cap'n Harry won't push*, as the whole world knows, although nobody knows why except him and Sister Elva and Yours Truly, who can't tell the story without violating doctor/patient confidentiality even though Elva wasn't this doctor's patient, properly speaking, when she broke down and spilled her story; they two just happened to be discussing poor Sher's miscarriage, which led to the subject of Problem Deliveries, which just happens to be Yours Truly's specialty. *Anyhow*, the whole megillah will no doubt come out in the official inquiry, which we can bet there's going to be! So meanwhile, back at the cuckoo-nest they're not only losing headway on account of *Dove*'s engine is overheating from too many rpms and has to be throttled down, but Tee Two is beginning to take on a bit of water 'cause her bilge pumps haven't been what they ought to be since that Ditsy person flew the coop a while back, right? So at this point Cap'n-period-Shmegegge-period radios the Coast Guard station that they're in no immediate danger but et cetera et cetera and are being carried Eastern Shoreward out of the main channel toward shoal water off Bloodsworth and South Marsh Islands, and you can just imagine what fun and games the Arkade Players are having by this time! Anyhow it's tail-first across the Bay they go, and the water-depth drops from sixty-feet-plus through the fifties and forties to the thirties and twenties and down to the high teens — still enough to float Tee Two, but mighty dicey for the tugboats, *Raven* especially. And by this time the Coast Guard's on hand, but of course they're in the Search-and-Rescue business, not the tugboat and salvage trade. So as a last resort *Dove* and *Raven* drop anchor just in time to keep the whole show from going aground; but mind you, they've got four- and five-foot waves on the bow in less than twenty feet of water! And the climax of this sinking opera, excuse the expression, comes when Cap'n Harry backs *Raven* down hard in reverse to set his bow anchor, and the deckhand who's supposed to keep the towline to the showboat taut somehow manages not to, and the slack line either fouls in *Raven*'s propeller or looks about to do so, and so gets cut either by said propeller or by Cap'n Harry himself, which is what those of us suspect who know Cap'n Elva's Why-Harry-Won't-Push story, but never mind *that*. No reason to doubt the guy did what had to be done under the circumstances, but it leaves *Raven* hobbyhorsing at anchor all by its lonesome while Tee Two drags Elva's *Dove* backward on *her* anchor into shallower and shallower water until they both hit bottom at about the same time, Tee Two in three feet and Cap'n Elva in five. So what's a girl to do in a fix like that? Elv's all for standing pat with her anchor set and her towline taut, hard aground or not, to keep *Dove* and *TOFO* bow-on to the waves for as long as possible; but Captain-period-Nudnik's afraid they'll have *two* boats to salvage instead of one if *Dove* drags any farther aground. So at this point in the story Brother Harry redeems himself by upping his anchor and hitching a towline from *Raven* to *Dove*, to see whether a straight-line pull by the pair of them might get all hands refloated? So they get themselves all lined up, which no doubt took a bit of doing in all that weather, but the problem is that each tug is normally hitched to one front corner of the barge, as the whole world knows, and so when the folks on Tee Two slack off Elva's towline in order to center its thingamajig for a straight pull—Its bridle? Bridle shmidle, whatever—the wave action pushes them even farther up on the shoal, which kiboshes things altogether. Captain-Period-Period-Period then orders Elva's line cast off so *Raven* can rescue *Dove*, which it does, and our story ends with the showboat high if not dry on a mudflat off Bloodsworth Island and the tugboats standing by at anchor some distance off Just In Case, even though they couldn't get close enough to rescue anybody if they needed to, which they don't 'cause all hands are okay. Now, then: I *ask* you!

But in fact it's we who ask her, after much thanks for her account, what exactly is meant by "okay." The last *she* heard, replies Doc Rachel—from her husband Captain Courageous, who's been calling her every half hour by cell phone while her patients have conniptions in the waiting room—is that the Coast Guard has airlifted them a spare bilge pump to supplement their own, and the weather has subsided enough so they're not getting pounded to pieces, and an industrial-strength tugboat is coming down from Baltimore to try whether et cetera. No *way* they'll get to Saint Mary's City on time, in her opinion, 'cause who knows what repairs'll be needed if they ever get loose at all? But don't tell her Put-Pep husband that! Bless his heart. Meanwhile, all hands are safe and sound and would you believe it rehearsing a New Improved Version of that *meshugge* Transfer-of-Authority scene — the one with the storm? Nobody's hurt; they've got food and water and power and beer and a limited selection of jug wines to complement the dinner menu, and unless the weather turns worse again they're all staying aboard except Doctor-Spin-Bless-His-Heart-Spindler, who sure *wants* to hang in there with the team but has been directed by Cap'n-Andy-Shmandy-Whatsisface-Todd to commute back and forth by helicopter between home and Snug Harbour and Bloodsworth Island (which did we know is a U.S. Navy *aerial bombing target*, God help us? But they've kindly promised to hold their fire, bless their laser-guided little hearts) so's he can handle the postponement-slash-cancellation of their Maryland Shnook Day gala if necessary, plus act as liaison among DTE and FLOPCORP and Tee Two while they manage this mess, plus milk it for publicity whether or not they make their Saint Whoozits date, plus get Benjamin to his soccer practice and Judith to her ballet class while Doc Rachel hands out tranquilizers to all hands.

We thank the good doctor again for her report, and praise her and her husband for coping on so many fronts at once.

"We should only," cheerily replies Dr. Rachel — and promises to let Mort know we called, and asks come to think of it whether we'd mind if he gave *us* a call sometime soon, to review a couple of related matters, as he mentioned in one of his thousand-and-two recent cell-phone chats herwith that he'd like to do.

Well, no. [*Nudge from mate.*] Yeah, well, sure. Narrator won't mind at all; will in fact be much obliged if that busy fellow can spare a minute. Narrator has, after all, a certain narrative in the works, for which what's happening here might be mill-grist indeed. E.g. (he tells Doctor Spin himself not half an hour later, when sure enough the call comes from Dorsettown), the Nine Nine Ninety-nine angle, so fortuitously on the cusp of Y2K: You'll get media kilometrage out of that, yes?

"*Zingo*, man! Been almost too busy to notice it, and it's pure gold! The whole show freeze-framed just when the odometer's ready to turn up goose-eggs! We owe you one!"

And that shoal you're stuck on, off Bloodsworth: Does it have a name?

"Between Bloodsworth and South Marsh, actually, and no name that we know of. Why?"

Maybe call it Ararat Shoal?

"Hey, *zingerino!* Watch us run with *that* ball!"

Et cetera. By six o'clock TV newstime there's impressive aerial footage of the wave-pounded showboat being inched ever farther up onto what by ten o'clock newstime has already been nicknamed Ararat Shoal, with explanatory references to the biblical Ark, to the Noah-business in *T II*'s Main Feature, to FLOPCORP's "Final Season" publicity gimmick and DTE's Y2K-proof community-in-the-works "complete with Ark of Last Resort," and to the portentous date of the showboat's grounding. At six, newscopter shots of the Cast of Several in their Genesis get-up, waving bravely through the weather from the flat roof of *TOFO II*; by ten (the rain having paused and the wind somewhat abated), floodlit views of same, high-kicking with linked arms now as they once did just off our dock. Plus videotaped interview with Dorset Tradewinds Enterprises spokesperson Morton Spindler, assuring viewers from his Snug Harbour office that the Historic Vessel is in no apparent danger; that with the help of a major-league tugboat from Baltimore "plus our Ark's own *Raven* and *Dove*," they expect to get off on tomorrow morning's high tide, conditions permitting, and to open in St. Mary's City on Friday as scheduled, or Saturday latest; that the Arkade Players ("As in A-R-K, right?" prompts the spiffy on-the-scene TV journalady; "You got it," affirms Doctor Spin) are in high spirits and rehearsing overtime for Maryland Defenders Day. Channel Whatever's anchor team—dapper black male and dewy-eyed white female, who report the news antiphonally sentence by sentence, each looking admiringly at the other as he/she speaks—then announce that their intrepid (and cute-as-a-button male Asian-American) reporter Greg Kim has been landed onto the showboat's roof by helicopter for exclusive on-the-spot coverage of this still-developing story. By the end of the hour they hope to establish video transmission; meanwhile, this live audio report direct from *The Original Floating Opera II*!

In which, against a freeze-framed background shot of the storm-beleaguered showboat, the voices of Theatre-Team leaders Johns Hopkins Johnson ("That's really your name?" "Better believe it, Greg!") and Sherry McAndrews Singer animatedly assure us all that they're having a ball—"Hey, Sher! Let's put that in the show! Like, *We assure you all / We're just havin' a ball! . . .*" "Gotcha, Hop! *Doin' just fine / On Nine Nine Ninety-nine! . . .*" "*Here on A-ra-rat / Is where it's at! . . .*" et cetera.

"And what happens, Greg," the anchorlady asks, as anchorfolk routinely do to demonstrate live connection with their farflung lieutenants, "if tomorrow's rescue-attempt doesn't work?"

"I asked these folks that, Marcie, and they reminded me that when Mohammed wouldn't go to the mountain, as the saying goes, the mountain came to Mohammed! In other words, if they can't get unstuck in time to reach their opening-night audience in Saint Mary's City, they hope to bring the audience to Ararat Shoal via some sort of television hookup and go on with the show! This is Greg Kim, reporting live from the Ark! Back to you, Jim and Marcie, and *stay tuned, folks*!"

Next morning's Baltimore *Sun* is full of the same, plus official expressions of DTE's confidence in the judgment of *T II*'s Captain Adam Lake, although there will of course be a full-dress inquiry into the accident. The paper goes to press too early, however, to report that the combined efforts of *Raven*, *Dove*, and the tug *Helicon* from Fells Point have failed to dislodge or even budge *T II* on the 3 A.M. high tide in Holland Straits, off South Marsh Island. According to news accounts on the Johns Hopkins National Public Radio station, a second attempt is scheduled for the mid-afternoon high, but the difficulty is that the showboat went aground on the abnormal surge from Tropical Storm Zulu, and there is some question whether any normal high tide will be sufficient to unground it from Ararat Shoal. "Only time will tell," concludes Greg Kim at noon in his additional new capacity as Fox News's stringer for CNN, "whether the Unsinkable Floating Opera can be refloated!" And that taletelling time might prove limited, for according to the network's weather team, Tropical Storm Zulu, after moving over Cape May and out into the Atlantic, has stalled off the coast of New Jersey and intensified. Indeed, some computer projections anticipate that it could even make a U-turn (virtually unprecedented, but then so are two-dozen-plus named storms in a single season) and restrike the Delaware and Chesapeake Bays.

"So tell us, Greg," requests the concerned CNN anchorlady in Atlanta: "Are the theater troupe's spirits still high? Are there standby plans to abandon ship if they don't get free this afternoon?"

"No plans that we know of, Angela," Greg informs her and us. "As for the Arkade Players' morale, just let me say that if the tide was as high as their spirits, this showboat would be sailing down the Chesapeake! Directors Singer and Johnson tell me they've already worked an Ararat Grounding scene into their show, but when I asked them how it all turns out, they said we'll just have to wait and see!"

"And so we will! That was Greg Kim live from *The Original Floating Opera Two* on Ararat Shoal," Angela reminds us. "In other news this Friday . . ."

Uh-oh, we say at six that evening, when — after a soundbite from Captain Elva Kane of the tugboat *Dove* concerning the failed second attempt to free the showbarge ("Nine Nine Ninety-nine was the dark of the moon, right? So if'n we shake our empty purses at tonight's *new* moon, they'll be full by the time the Harvest Moon is") — DTE spokesperson Morton Spindler spins that proverb into a prediction of the Arkade Theatre Company's imminent success. There's even talk, he confides to Greg, that the author of the novel that inspired FLOPCORP's showboat project (he does not mean the late great Edna Ferber, of course, although to her, too, they are forever indebted) might be airlifted aboard over the weekend to play the role of Himself, standing by the Ark of his inspiration whether it sinks or floats or flies — not that there's any danger of the first, mind! Explains grinning Director Johns Hopkins Johnson, "It's what we call *Postmodern!*" In close harmony then with Spokesperson Spindler and Director Singer: "*Are we Postmodern? Is this the end of the road?*"

"You betcher britches it isn't!" fingersnapping Jay Brown assures us newsviewers.

Urges Hop Johnson "Check out our new website!" He then cues Jay, Holly Weil, Heather, and **SPECIAL EFFECT!** to chorus in sassy unison "*Doubleyou-doubleyou-doubleyou dot tofo-two dot org!*"

Get us *out* of here, chorus we — for busy Mort had cell-phoned us in the early afternoon (from the chopper shuttling him between Dorsettown and Holland Straits in preparation for Rescue Attempt #2) in order to float, so to speak, that very idea: that if — as he did not anticipate! — it should turn out that *TOFO II* really is stuck for the long haul, and if — as they were already contingency-planning for! — they do a live telecast of *COMING SOON!!* THE MUSICAL from Ararat Shoal on Maryland Defenders Day Sunday, say, then nothing could more Put Pep into that Special Performance than the Novelist Emeritus's in-person appearance in the role of The Novelist Emeritus Character. Would Narrator-*san* pleasepleaseplease say yes? Chopper could airlift him and Missus direct from front yard to Ararat! Piece of Cake!

No way, friend, was our firm though half-regretful reply: We'll be pulling for you, along with *Raven, Dove,* and . . . *Helicon,* is it? Helicon on Ararat? Anyhow, success to all hands! But we're in midst of a Climax Scene ourselves here, you should excuse the expression, that has to get itself written before Time's Tortoise gobbles Nine Nine Ninety-nine altogether, excuse the family code.

Over the helicopter-rotor racket, "At least let us float rumors?" begged Mort. "No harm in that."

Float *ce que voulez,* bade we, and our regards to Doc Rachel. But ess vee pee, count us out.

We do however click up *http//www.tofo2.org* that evening on our vintage, tortoise-paced Macintosh, just to have a look, and in time's fullness find a not-badly-put-together homepage—Who aboard the Ark had found leisure to design and build the thing?—featuring side-by-side photos of the showboat (*L*) snug in Snug Harbour in calmer days, and (*R*) bashed by Zulu-waves on Ararat Shoal. Beneath them, exclamatory hot-links to such topics as

> —*The News from Ararat!*
> —*Chesapeake Showboats: A Historical Overview!*
> —*COMING SOON!!! The Musical (CS!!!TM)*

and

> —*From 9/9/99 to Y2K—and Beyond!*

Scrolling down, we find at the page's foot the enigmatic credit line *Homepage by Ditsy@BigBitsy.HFI.* Don't ask us; we understood that entity to have jumped ship earlier in this chapter. Experimentally, we click on *CS!!!TM* and, as is the way with websites, are offered more menu-menus (*Previews. Postviews. Reviews. Over& Underviews*).

Enough already. Another look next morning, however—after radio news reports of Unsuccessful Rescue Attempt #3 on the overnight tide and of T. S. Zulu's sure enough drifting now southwestward, back toward Cape May, and gaining strength—reveals that webmasters Johnson (Who can doubt his e-knowledgeable hand in all this?) and Ditsy@Bitsy have not been aslumber: A click on *CS!!!TM*'s submenu item *What's New?* discloses not only that the Ark's grounding and the serial failed rescue attempts have been incorporated into the show, but also (one imagines old Charlie Hunter smilin' through from some snug harbor beyond the end of the road) that there are in preparation Alternative Electronic Endings to the shambling saga of *The Original Floating Opera II*. More specifically, behind the hot-link END TIME one will find "if not now, then *soon!*" a menu of denouement-scenarios-in-progress, including but by no means necessarily limited to

## The "Emerital" Version

—which, we are vertiginously reminded, may actually be the handiwork of that bumptious "N.A. Character," heh heh, as for that matter (Muse spare us!) may be this entire long Chapter "1999" —and

## The Aspirant Version

—which, conversely, et cetera: the sort of thing that, in Narrator's opinion, gives a bad name to the honorably-arrived-at aesthetics of literary Postmodernism.

All the same, those options—Let's limit them to the pair above —await Reader's possible pleasure. *Cliquetez-Vous*, then, *s.V.p.*, ignoring insofar as possible any 'tween-the-lines heavy respiration of

*(The Phantom ;-)*

# *Parts III*
## *The Ends*

# A: THE "EMERITAL" VERSION

*—Or, better, "The Emerital Version,"*
which is to suggest, a *version* of The N.E. Character's Version of the
denouement of *COMING SOON!!! A NARRATIVE* — conceives
of itself as being written in December 1999, no doubt at its author's
winter base Down South, whereto he & Mrs. will have removed per
custom at October's end, there to wind up his outspinning of this extended narrative and to await, with no more than mild curiosity, the
arrival of Y2K. Assuming that neither The World As They Know It
nor they themselves will by some mischance have been terminated
ahead of schedule (for in Real-Life Time I'm writing this back in
the June/July before: Dow Jones crowding 11,000; Kosovar refugees flooding home to their ruined but liberated land; Yrs Truly
outpacing still, by that half-year margin, the Tortoise destined inevitably to win our race), they will have topped off their aging au-
to's fuel tank and laid in a few daysworth of standby provisions and
spare cash, Just In Case. Otherwise, no special plans *chez* They for
either apocalypse or party, beyond spectating the millennium's
close-out sunset over the Gulf of Mexico. If visiting family-mem-
bers are on hand, they'll no doubt wait up to toast the midnight together with champagne; otherwise, the couple may well turn in as
usual after the ten o'clock TV headlines, kiss goodnight, and sleep
through the whole hyperhyped brouhaha — unless awakened, rudely
and briefly, by The End.

  As I see him seeing it, *The Original Floating Opera II* will have been spared after all by that rebounding tropical-storm-turned-hurricane-turned-tropical-storm-again, which rebattered the coastal barrier islands from Atlantic City to Cape May but then broke up over the pine barrens and cranberry bogs of south Jersey and was swept back out to sea by an advancing cold front from the Ohio Valley: *Adieu*, Zulu II, and good riddance! The showboat remained, however, hard aground on "Ararat Shoal" despite several further high-tide attempts at its reflotation; anon the expensively hired maxi-tug *Helicon* was dispatched back to Baltimore until further notice while FLOPCORP and Dorset Tradewinds Enterprises scratched their corporate heads and considered Next Steps. *Raven* and *Dove* took turns standing by and shuttling supplies and personnel between Ararat and Crisfield, the nearest port-town, from where a Snug Harbour minivan made the sixty-mile run up to Dorsettown: inconvenient and time-taking, but considerably less costly than the leased helicopter. More exactly, since the tugboats couldn't approach the barge closely without going aground themselves, an additional transfer was required to one of *T II*'s lifeboats or to any of the numerous shallow-draft visitors — crabbers and clammers, small to mid-size sport fishermen, the merely curious in their runabouts and outboard skiffs — and thence to tug or barge etc.: a bother, but no help for it.

Needless to say, between Zulus I and II Maryland Defenders Day weekend came and went, uncelebrated. The St. Mary's City gig had finally to be canceled and advance ticket sales refunded; likewise the lucrative next scheduled stop thereafter, in Alexandria, and then, after *Helicon*'s return to Fells Point, the next several after that. Sometime in mid-month, however, the company managed, with the aid of Maryland Public Television, to bring mountain to Mohammed in the form of a telecast Special Performance of COMING SOON!!! THE MUSICAL, for which Mr. N.E. was respectfully invited, yea urged, to play Himself. He politely declined, but permitted Mort Spindler to disseminate to the media a statement of his continuing warm support for *TOFO II*, his heartfelt hope that a way might yet be found to refloat it, and his praise for the Feature Production, particularly its clever incorporation of events as they occurred: e.g., the newly revised Tempest scene, wherein Captain Harry Kane's dispute with Captain. Adam. Lake. (over whether to cut *Raven*'s towline or risk fouling it and going aground along with the showboat) was made to echo the Cain/Abel story in Genesis. (This part of the Emerital Statement Mort tactfully omitted in view of DTE's then-pending Official Inquiry into the grounding; no complaint thatabout from "GreatUnc Ennie," who in fact hadn't found the biblical analogy especially apt, but was endeavoring to put the best face on it.)

Thereafter, the Arkade Players, as the ATC seemed to be calling themselves in the press, gradually dispersed, their Main Season effectively over and their Postview Season at best questionable: By small boat/tugboat/minivan they made their way back to Dorsettown and thence to wherever — college, pick-up jobs, their shoreside lives — most declaring their readiness to return on short notice if and when *T II* was refloated and its fall schedule resumed. Their general expectation, however, was that DTE would cut its losses by declaring the barge unrescuable and auctioning it off for salvage, a move seriously considered up in Patmos Tower but deferred "until all other options have been explored and our formal inquiry completed."

One notes the change of adjectives, from "the official" to "our formal" inquiry: What eventuated in fact is a couple of not particularly formal semi-teleconferences in PT 696 with Capt. Ad., the Capts. Kane, the virtual "Cap'n Andy," and selected other conferees ("witnesses" would be too formal/official a term) — including, at one point, Dr. Rachel Spindler, for reasons undisclosed. Her husband's press release on the matter reported "the panel of inquiry's" conclusions to be that while Captain Lake's decision to set out from Solomons Harbor on 9/9/99 despite the grim weather forecast proved regrettable, it was not indefensible in view of his considerable experience, the error-margin of such forecasts, and the importance of *T II*'s reaching St. Mary's City on time. Capt. Ad. thereafter retired from the directorship of FLOPCORP (effective immediately and no great matter, inasmuch as absent *TOFO II* there'd be no reason for that corporation's continued existence). He was retained, however, in his captaincy of the showboat until and unless DTE should dispose of the vessel one way or another. Once the inquiry was closed, he paid a last hospital visit to his sinking friend "Bea Golden" and then returned to the stricken barge, vowing to remain aboard "until her last page. Is turned." As for Capt. Harry Kane: While his precipitate axing (as it turns out) of *Raven*'s towline to *T II* might be argued to have blown the last fair chance to save the day, it might also be argued to have kept the not-quite-anchored tugboat from joining its tow aground on Ararat. Besides which, there were reportedly unreported Extenuating Circumstances. Case dismissed—although none had been formally brought nor would any likely be, inasmuch as no insurance claim pended. Future of *Dove* and *Raven* contingent, obviously, on future of *TOFO II*; tugs, captains, and crew to stand by meanwhile as directed by Elva Kane, the new acting director of The Floating Opera Corporation and a favorite with Greg Kim and the other media people, whom she reminded with a wink to *burn* [their] *eggshells every morning after breakfast,' cause witches go to sea in'em.*

Captain. Adam. Lake. was by no means alone on *TOFO II* upon his return thereto. That M-D-Day telecast of *CS!!!* TM attracted enough viewers to the MPT channels and enough national media attention to the showboat—which attention in turn attracted enough investor interest in the "Y2K-proofed" Dorsettown-on-Choptank despite what one would have thought to be the cautionary example of its Ark of Last Resort's going hard aground—that DTE affirmed its budgetary support of the Johnson/Singer/Spindler proposal to Go On With the Show. That is, to maintain the now-indefinitely-grounded showboat in otherwise operating condition with a skeleton crew and postseason cast aboard (some, like Hop and Sherry, had never left; others returned after what was being considered a fortnight's salaried R&R), to the end of developing and rehearsing pared-down versions of both *Final Follies '99* and *CS!!!* TM for a (Final!) fall season beginning "as soon as we're refloated" and culminating in the still-officially-scheduled Final Performances in Baltimore's Inner Harbor on 11/11. To maintain some presence on the media radar screens, they then produced a series of single-number video spots for regional public television stations to run as fillers between their prime-time offerings: "The Millennium Bug," "Ararat Is Where It's At," "You're the one, One-One, One-One" (the former "O One, O One," modified to anticipate the November date), etc. And the press was given to understand that in its current metamorphosis the *CS!!!* musical would actually open with the Ark's grounding — as if Lord Baltimore's colonists, having successfully crossed the Atlantic, had run their *Arke* aground on the threshold of the promised land instead of reaching St. Clements Island; or as if the story of Scheherazade commenced with her thousand-and-first "Once upon a time" and then reviewed its predecessors; or as if John on Patmos had embedded the Deluge-story as a flashback in midst of his Revelation. "So we're stuck," the new version would essentially begin by acknowledging (in a duet by The N.E./Noah Character and The N.A./Noah's-Son Character, each of whose "log-books-in-progress" is similarly "on Pause"): "So now what?" Whereat The Muse/Noah's-Daughter Character exclaims, *"Let's put on a show!"*

Et cetera. Inasmuch as NATO's air war on Serbia had ended some months before, the U.S. Navy considerately agreed to suspend its use of Bloodsworth Island as a practice aerial-bombing target until the showboat was either removed or abandoned. Reports that FlopCorp had agreed in turn to donate the vessel itself as a target (and a tax write-off) if salvage efforts failed — But had they not already? — were neither confirmed nor denied by either party. In the wake of these reports, toward September's close there emerged one morning from neighboring South Marsh Island and/or its similarly uninhabited low-lying environs a small white crabbing-skiff piquantly named *Nameless* and manned, if that term will serve, by none other than the erstwhile defector Ditsy. "His" Hick Fen Island home, it seems, lay not far hence, and he (let's drop the fussy quote-marks) took as a Sign the showboat's grounding practically in his backyard. From his stilt-mounted cabin's improbable computing facility ("Big Bitsy") he had established covert laptop contact, so to speak, with both his ex-lover Jay "Obie" Brown and Hop Johnson; with the former he had arrived at some sort of understanding, and for the latter, by way of atonement for his defection, had helped design *T II*'s snazzy new website. Ditsy's August apprehensions re the showboat's welfare having been vindicated (and the windfalls from Tropical Storm Zulu thoroughly progged himby), he now put himself and the skiff altogether at Captain. Ad.'s service along with the burly and taciturn, arguably male associate who, in the days and weeks following, sometimes accompanied him in the skiff and was as elusive of name as it.

"You must be the famous E-A-R-L?" Sherry Singer asked that fellow welcomingly upon the pair's first appearance from the marshy mists.

"Oncet upon a time, I s'pose, ma'am, you might say" was the extent of his acknowledgment, delivered with a scowl not at the asker but at unexploded-ordnance-rich Bloodsworth Island.

Taciturn or not, the pair made themselves useful indeed. The barge's bilge pumps were soon up and running again to capacity, and its ubiquitous oil-smell subsided to normal levels. Sturdy *Nameless* became the principal shuttler of supplies and passengers between showboat and tugboats or other vessels bound to or from "Crassfield," as her skipper liked to call the busy seafood port just across Tangier Sound from Ararat Shoal. And in the stripped-down but ever-evolving Main Feature, Ditsy even resumed the Protean "heavy" role of Caliban/"666"/Etc. — which now included "T. S. Zulu" played as a tempestuous drag queen, to his stalwart colleague's grunting amusement.

*Thus until the ides of October,*
when Elva's proverbs, *TOFO II*'s bilge-aromatics, Ditsy's meteorological gut feelings, and *www.storm99.com* all agreed that Hurricane Aaron, currently losing strength off Hatteras — the record-setting twenty-seventh Atlantic tropical storm of the season and the first ever to necessitate a double-lettered return to Square One of the alphabet — would more than likely "impact" the Chesapeake with Zulu-force winds even if, as currently predicted, its eye remained some miles off the Delmarva coast. Taking no chances, a chastened Capt. Ad., with full support from the Arkangel Team in Patmos Tower, ordered all hands ashore over the mid-October weekend, lest

conditions get too hairy for the small-boat transfer. Only the Captain himself, the still-penitent Ditsy, and Ditsy's presumable "EARL" remained aboard the barge, while the Captains Kane stood by with one deckhand each on anchored *Raven* and *Dove*—the former towlined to the latter and the latter to *The Original Floating Opera II.*

*Thought you might be interested to know* [The Novelist Aspirant e-mailed his emerital counterpart upon rearriving with his fellow evacuees in Dorsettown] *that I've w'drawn frm the fiction biz altogether. Not my medium (nor, in me 'umble opinion, anyone else's who wants a bit o' the Real Action in Century 21—no offense intended, Dad ;-).* His disked e-novel, he averred, had been returned from Manhattan to Dorsettown in September by his "virtual agent," who'd had no success whatever with it, and forwarded thence via minivan, *Dove,* and *T II*'s lifeboat-shuttle to Crisfield, Ararat Shoal, and its till-then-still-aspiring author. Taking his cue from the bottled manuscript in one of "GreatUnc Ennie's" *opera magna* (Hop affected not to recall which one), he had thereupon bagged the disk in a Ziploc™ sandwich baggie, that inside another and the second inside a third—this last with just enough air sealed in it for buoyancy —and had ceremonially floated the package off from the showboat's stern at the full Harvest Moon of September 25, to the accompaniment of "Taps," played by Captain Harry: *solemnly on the 1st chorus, up-tempo Dixie on the 2nd & 3rd et seq. Didja ever cut it that way back in yr musician-days, Pops? That sucker* swings!

> *Da-a-ay is done (two-three-four! One! Two!),*
> *Gone the sun (two-three-four!* Hit it now!*),*
> *From the lake (*Hey!*),*
> *From the hills (*Ho!*),*
> *From the sky (Diddly-iddly-iddly* bop! *Etc.)*

*Anyhow* [the e-missive continued], *where shd the sumbitch float if not through Holland Straits (betw B'worth & S. Marsh I's) & thence into the wetland purlieus of "Hick Fen" (sp?), whence 'twas progged a few days later by the sole or near-sole denizen thereof: our own defecting-but-nowise-defective . . . DITSY!(!!)*

*Who* [the writer would have me understand] *was conscience-*

*smitten enough by this fortuitous* objet trouvé —*or nostalgia-smit-ten, JayObieBrown-smitten, whatever —straightway to make cyber-contact w Yrs Truly frm the Serious Computing Facility that his/her marsh-lair happens to be equipped with: the gift of some former Significant Other, whomof we think we've heard? And the rest is history.* I.e., Ditsy's subsequent appearance in *Nameless* along with his long-lost lover, the former director of the former Estuarine Aquacul-tural Research Laboratory in the former Backwater Estuarine Wet-lands Area Reserve (East), a.k.a. B.E.W.A.R.(E.), *"just 1 hoot + 2 hollers frm Ararat Shoal"*; his triumphant re-presentation to its au-thor of the thrice-bagged and still-bone-dry *COMING SOON!!! THE NOVEL?*, and that opus's prompt reflotation himby ("T II *shd be so lucky!*") —this time on an outgoing tide and easterly wind, which carried it forth into the Chesapeake proper.

*Thence, one hopeth, to drift forever & aye among Earth's conve-niently interconnected oceans. Sound familiar, Unc?*

Well, yes—but then, so too did The N.A. Character's ploy of declaring himself done with that e-project in particular if not with the medium of fiction altogether, in hopes of lulling his Competition into easing off while he covertly forges, so to speak, ahead. I ac-knowledged his communication; expressed my mild hope that the author had a backup copy of his "text" in the event of a mind-change down the road; let him know that my own (p-)version of *COMING SOON!!!*, while progressing steadily though slowly, was still very much in the works (in fact it was approaching its present home stretch, but he needn't know that); hoped further that the oncoming hurricane would spare us all; and wondered, in postscript, where on earth the Weather Service would find appropriate double-lettered names for Aaron's successors, should any yet materialize. "B. B. King"? "C. C. Rider"? But then there would go their Politically Correct gender-alternation. . . .

*No problem, Dad* [my graciously field-yielding young counter-part would reply when next he found time]*: PC + Poetic License will permit "Bébé," "Cecil," & "DeeDee," if need be. But Cap'n Elva & MrMs Ditsy are betting that H. Aaron—whom we've al-ready worked into the show!—rang down the curtain on this crazy* *season. Off to B'more we go now, to ring down ours: Care for a final walk-on?*

For what had happened in the space between these cybernotes, Reader (*mirabile dictu*), was that on Tuesday, October 19, the fortieth day after *T II*'s grounding, the storm-surge from Hurricane Aaron—whose weakened eye remained mercifully offshore—pumped enough extra water up into the Chesapeake to submerge our dock (not for the first time) and to give FLOPCORP a new lease on life by doing what mighty *Helicon* & Co. could not: On that abnormal high water, *TOFO II* unmucked herself from Ararat Shoal sufficiently to enable *Dove* and *Raven*, aided this time by easterly winds and following seas off Tangier Sound, to tow her free at last. Adroitly shifting then from their in-line position to their customary not-quite-parallel side-by-siding, they whistled jubilantly back up-Bay *à trois*, past the Little and into the Great Choptank, and (with faux–steam calliope ablast and newscopters clattering overhead) to Dorset Shipyard for damage surveys and repair. Of the latter, next to none were found necessary; by month's end the showboat was home-berthed in nearby Snug Harbour, its sundry "teams" reassembled or replaced, the ATC's Postview Season "core corps," as they dubbed themselves, regathered, rerehearsed in the (New!) *CS!!!* TM "as evolved on Ararat," and raring to go.

*Go where?*

Why, across and up the Bay to Baltimore's Inner Harbor, to be sure, just in time for those long-scheduled, all-but-abandoned, and now triumphantly republicized Final Performances on Veterans Day (Thursday, November 11) and the ensuing holiday weekend. A grand procession it was, especially the twenty-mile leg from the Bay Bridge up to the Patapsco and past Fort McHenry to the downtown harbor. Unsurprisingly, not all of the hoped-for celebrities were aboard for the ride, their busy schedules having been regretfully changed during the showboat's twoscore days aground. But a sufficiency themof lustered the scene with smiles and handwaves from the barge's foredeck, where champagne and fingerfood were served by the Galley, Concession & Bar Team while busy Greg Kim and his teletechies scrambled for soundbites and striking camera angles. The Navy's Blue Angel aerobats, on hand for the national holiday, added to their official schedule a flyover salute as the flotilla passed under the bridge's twin spans (back at Patuxent Naval Air Station, meanwhile, the powers that be declared Bloodsworth Island online again for regular bombing practice). And at the Francis Scott Key Bridge over the lower Patapsco, the ever-accumulating parade of escort-vessels official and unofficial was joined by an armada of pleasure-craft, tourist excursion-boats, harbor tugs (including *Helicon* and her sister-tug *Parnassus*, unavailable back when most needed) and fireboats in full fount for the final few miles to the Inner Harbor.

In short, a proper spectacle — which Yrs Truly & spouse will have witnessed, if at all, only in newsphotos and teleclips from a thousand and a half miles south, they having thereto shifted not a fortnight prior and being still too busy setting up winter housekeeping to consider flying back for a "final walk-on" even if they had been thus inclined. Which however they were not, among other reasons because the he of them had this ending of this story to get written, or to revise and polish if it happen to have been already first-drafted earlier — back in drought-dry Maryland back in June/July, say, from Author's temporary vantage-point astride Time's Tortoise.

All the same, he was gratified to gather that the gala float-parade went off with due galaity, and that *COMING SOON!!!* THE MU-SICAL played to full houses the first two nights of its Baltimore stand and to near-full houses on the third and fourth — thus materially reducing, though by no means eliminating, the deficit accumulated by the showboat's forty days *hors de combat* and attendant expenses. Likewise, that the show earned genuinely warm notices in the Baltimore *Sun* and Washington *Post*. Their drama critics, Sherry Singer was pleased to report to us in some detail, were particularly impressed by the versatility of the "core corps" Cast of Several, every one of whom played multiple roles ("and not only serially," declared the *Sun*'s reviewer, "but even *simultaneously*"), and by the ingenuity of "what the showboaters call their Script Team" at incorporating the Ark's ongoing tribulations and triumphs into the multilayered story. "Which, as of Thursday's opening-night performance," said the *Post*'s reviewer, "concluded with a reconciliation-scene between old 'Noah' and his renegade last-born son 'Aaron' (our notorious recent hurricane personified!) and the Ark's ensuing triumphal procession from 'Ararat' to 'The Promised Land' —but which by showtime Friday had already been amended to close with the successful *opening* of the show in fact then just ending, if you follow me. . . . "

Yes, well: One had, in truth, followed long enough the fortunes of that ever-morphing production, its slippery scriptor (of whom more presently), and the whole refloated *mise en scène*. As to the first themof: It did not surprise us to hear from Singer/Johnson that their enforced month's leisure for revision and rehearsal on Ararat Shoal had honed to a keen edge both play and players, whomto we e-mailed heartfelt congratulation; nor that at Thanksgiving lay-up time, when DTE's accountants totted up FLOPCORP's balance-sheet for 1999, they reckoned their net loss to be after all absorbable enough (thanks to the Inner Harbor gig, which had been "extended by popular demand" for an additional two days) to render entertainable the possibility of a Final Season II in Year 2000—although in our opinion that is a gimmick which, like announcing one's Last Novel, cannot be honorably redeployed. The company would cross their corporate fingers (so Mort Spindler reported to us after a pixelated session in Patmos Tower 696) until they had clearly cleared both the original *Original*'s November Curse and the Y2K Crunch; they would then "just see."

As for Johns Hopkins Johnson, one could not finally quarrel with his e-mailed mid-November self-assessment: that while he was endowed with ambition, flair, resourcefulness, talent, intelligence, and energy to spare, he lacked the long-haul vision, patience, and singleminded—even doggedly blinkered—sticktoitiveness of the congenital novelist. Nor did he any longer bemoan that lack, inasmuch as he regarded the genre as anyhow moribund. *Faute de mieux*, he reckoned ("and what could be *mieux*," he asked us rhetorically, "than Ms S McA S of those eyes those eyes?"), he'd be staying with *TOFO II* as long as that vessel remained literally and figuratively afloat. His muse had already half a dozen new projects in the hopper—the Final Season II thing, the EVRkade thing, the this-that&theother thing—three or four of which he meant to get cracking on once he and friend Sherry returned from the Caribbean Thanksgiving holiday that his parents had generously invited them to share. We would just see.

*So keep yr old Torch, Dad,* his cybernote concluded, *and bring yr version of our story to port w my blessing. Can't wait to read how you'll wrap us-all up!*

*;-)*

*And that I here do:*
my last such wrap, I fancy, and well past its hoped-for deadline (Y2K having surely been long since Tortoise-trampled by when this text sees print), but done done done, as best Yrs T can do it. Or, rather—like century, like millennium, like career and soon enough life itself, anyhow the able span thereof—*all but* done, whenafter let Authority be Transferred, Torch Passed, to whoever merits same. *Adieu* showboats, which've served this talester well at both ends of his career, and here and there in its middle too! *Adieu*, noble genre of the Novel, by whom I hope to have done no less well than you by me! Born a-dying, like all of us, and dying on in fullthroated vigor ever since, may your Final Season outspan that of all your practitioners currently aspirant, not to mention "emeritus"!

So: There remains but to pen this closing sentence of (my) Part III of *COMING SOON!!!* A Narrative and then to bid *adios* for good and all to my trusty pen.

Sentence done.

Trusty pen!

Faithful pen, I say! Unfailing instrument!

*Yo, pen! . . .*

Pen?

**THE END**

*(Unless* [here winketh parenthetically The Phantom] *one seeeth fit to click*

> ## The Aspirant Version!

;-)

# B!

## The Aspirant Version!

;-)

*Whoa! Scratch that, Mate:*

No **SPECIAL EFFECT!**s, please, this late in the day; no faux-cheery *Readerino mio*s and cutesy-winking Who's-*Really*-Writing-This?s. Scrap the crap, sez I, and cut to the chase, ere THE END cuts&scraps us all. A simple

### B: THE ASPIRANT VERSION

will do the trick-free trick for this older and maybe even wiser youngster, Your Novelist Once-Upon-a-Time- and Once-Again-Aspirant Character. Excuse his now-and-then relapses into exclamation, over-hyphenation, and other of his apprentice tics: Time, responsibility, disappointments, and uppercase Experience in general have duly chastened but not yet altogether stifled the guy; he's feeling his way into a presumably maturer voice for Act Last of his little spiel, after too long an intermission.

*J. H. Johnson here!,*

as Muse and Reader will have gathered: at the former's service, the latter's pleasure. Remember him? Last heard from *beaucoup* pages back, in 1995.2 or thereabouts, casting off from Dorsettown-on-Choptank for another not-good-enough Main Season after (a) humping my *sine qua* next-to-*non* playmate (not yet then soulmates, Sher & I, but vectoring theretoward); (b) conceiving herwith our

346

not-good-enough New Show *End Time: COMING SOON!!!*; and (c) greenlighting Mort Spindler to lure "GreatUnc Ennie" into our gently foundering enterprise with the bait of "Charlie Hunter's" unfinished *Show Barge* script—my earlier scruples in that regard having been deep-sixed after our head-to-head Ontological Lunchbreak in Solomons Harbor.

All comes back to You now, does it? Anyhow (as I once heard an old Chesapeake crab-and-oysterman remark), we've passed a lot of water since then, mates. During which interval—Four mortal years! A hundred-plus no-doubt-mortal pages!—our N.E. Character must have seemed to You to've hogged the mike, no? Scarcely letting us Aspirants get an aspiring word in edgewise, beyond the odd e-pistle or passing dialogue-line in his account.

But believe me, or anyhow suspend for a spell Your disbelief: JHJ has not been sitting on his hands since June '95. Even "The Emerital Version," I trust, attests to that. Indeed, while the ups and downs of *TOFO II* and its Cast of Several from then to "now" would doubtless be sung in a different key and with different chord progressions if Yours Truly were its singer (and he shall be yet, Muse willing, ere the *real* Y2K hits History's fan), for efficiency's sake let's let the old guy's chapters stand, up to and including 9/9/99: I mean that off-and-on *mano a mano* between us novelist-types, with its concomitant *Gotcha!*s real and fancied; the serial *Tidewater Follies* and Main Features (*End Time*, *Show Barge*, and the not-bad-if-I-do-say-so-myself *COMING SOON!!! THE MUSICAL*); FLOPCORP's grand plan for a Final Season, off to so promising a start and then beset by miscarriages figurative and literal. Likewise our departure from Solomons on that portentous date into the teeth of Tropical Storm Zulu, the fateful Cutting of the Cord, and the Ark's sub/consequent grounding on Ararat Shoal—'twill serve, 'twill serve, Unc Ennie's rendering themof, till I can recount my counteraccount.

For what happened thereafter, though—specifically, from 9/*twelve*/99 up to the Neverlasting (two-months-later) Now—the options are Yours for the opting. What the Geezer Version maintaineth, deponent knoweth not, at least not for certain; I don't read *ev-*

*erything* the bloke writes, especially when I'm not shown it. But push *my* button and You get mine,

*To wit:*

That it was no biblical forty days till *TOFO II* was re-deluged off Ararat, but a mere and equally biblical three; and then not by any back-to-Square-One "Hurricane Aaron," but by an encore from the Heavy who'd nailed us on Thursday, 9/9/etc. 'Tis of Zulus I & II we sing, who lingered in Tropical Storm Mode off the Jersey shore till the weekend, then took a *very* deep breath and roared back usward as just-barely-Hurricane Z: first ever to blast Delmarva *southbound*, as if bent on rewinding Z I's track—down the Outer Banks, on to the Caribbean, back to Africa! Let's skip the Tempest scene (You can bet we put it in the show; check the tape of our MPT telecast): Suffice it to say that, apprised of the sucker's second coming, between the Jewish Sabbath eve and the Christian Sabbath morn we evacuated all hands (me'n Sher included—We're loyal, but not suicidal) except for Captain. Adam. Lake. Who steadfastly refused. To abandon the ark. That his earlier miscall. Had fetched to Ararat. Also Capt. Harry K., alone on anchored *Raven*, and Cap'n Elva not quite ditto aboard her *Dove*, as she had a New Thing going with our sturdy **SPECIAL EFFECT!**, who in addition to love-or-whatever had a professional interest in camcording Ma Nature's bravura setpieces. The twin tugs were, unusually for them, rafted cheek to cheek as we bade them our hurried bye-byes, their storm anchors vee'd out on long scopes and their towlines taut to *T II*'s bow-corners, just in case. Whatever his afterthoughts about 9/9/99 (Official Inquiry still then pending), Capt. Harry had his trusty fire ax reniched near *Raven*'s towline bitt, also just in case.

Then *Blam!* And, moreover, *Blooey!* Although Z II's eye remained offshore (wherefor thankee, Zeus), its winds outblew Z I's: trees and power-lines down all over the peninsula, the usual mobile-home parks smithereened, a humongous rainfall that not only ended Maryland's worst drought-year since Dust Bowl days but likely flushed the Bay of sea nettles for summers to come. And *après le déluge*? Why, the whoppingest storm-surge on our Chesapeake since Hurricane Hazel's in '54, when a certain novelist-now-emeritus, then still an Aspirant and summer-vacationing in his hometown from an entry-level college instructorship, monitored the flood from his all-but-inundated Choptank waterfront apartment while drafting *The Floating Opera*. That floater's sequel, so to speak, was by this surge lifted free of Ararat, whereupon it threatened to drag tugs and anchors and all up onto that same shoal, the winds being northwesterly at eighty knots, the seas ocean-size and steep, and the tugboats' drafts considerably deeper than the barge's. Where're *Helicon* and *Parnassus* when we need 'em?

But hey, no Storm Scene: Let's chase to the cut. In winds and seas like those, and short-handed to boot, Cap'ns Elva and Harry couldn't feasibly have gotten their anchors aweigh under full load even if they'd wanted to. To keep the tugs from bashing against each other, they'd long since unrafted and were now in something like their normal towing positions, Cap'n Harry straight on and Cap'n Elva angled off; their strategy was to throttle up their engines just enough to keep the hooks from dragging and then stand fast in hopes that Z II would ease off in time for them to haul *T II* clear of Ararat before the surge subsided and regrounded her. A dicey business for sure in such howling weather; one imagines Cap'n Harry having more than once to resist the Fire Ax Solution that Sunday forenoon, while his sister monitors her rpms and croons *Don't you worry, Abie baby* into the VHF bridge-to-bridge channel. In this landlubber's opinion, however (and that of several of the subsequent Official Inquirers), it had an odds-on chance of success — whereupon they'd've made their way *à trois* back up to Snug Harbour, reloaded us Arkade Players, and gone triumphantly on with our Final Postview Season and its Inner Harbor consummation. In any case, nobody then or since has come up with a *better* idea. . . .

Except, in his own opinion, our Capt. Ad. — of whom it must be said that the doubtless terminal hospitalization of his longtime Significant Other, Sher's mom, has had a deleterious effect on his captainly faculties. What with the heavy weather and pitching decks, **SPECIAL EFFECT!**'s camcorder tape leaves something to be desired as Tempest footage (although Greg Kim, our all-but-resident newscaster, worked clips from it into both Fox News's and CNN's follow-up coverage); it clearly shows, however, that at the peak of Z II's Chesapeake action — just after midday, when the Kanes had been at their balancing act for some two or three hours already — Capt. Ad. stepped forth. Onto *T II*'s bow. In his *Captains Courageous* sou'wester. Wielding the showboat's very own fire ax. And whacked those twin umbilici, first *Dove*'s and then *Raven*'s, without so much as a by-your-leave. And only *then* — while the tugs sprang forward as if slingshot on their anchor rodes, and their skippers leaped to throttle down and shift to Neutral, and *The Original Floating Opera II* wheeled hugely arse-to and slid off downwind — only then did Our Captain deign to ring up Channel 13 and bid the Kanes to mind they don't foul their props on those trailing lines. *No help for it, mates. Had to cut. 'R else* Dove *and* Raven*'d be stuck for keeps on Ararat. In place of TOFO Two. Not to worry: The barge'll fetch up on South Marsh Island. And then we'll just see.*

But the barge didn't — at least not on the outlying flats of that nominally uninhabited wetland Wildlife Management Area, as would have been the case in any normal storm. While Harry and Elva scurried to retrieve their towlines and anchors, dialoguing their joint dismay via whistle-toot and VHF, the barge sailed onto and right over those flats and ditto the marsh behind them. Surge or no surge, the tugs' draft was too deep for them to give chase and attempt rescue — not that either Capt. Ad. or the now-diminishing-but-still-formidable sea conditions would have permitted reattachment of their towlines. All they could do was patrol the too-shallow-though-much-deeper-than-normal water and watch "Abie baby" slide irretrievably far into the marshy isle itself: right over the storm-submerged cordgrass and spartina, right between isolated loblolly pines temporarily waist-deep in tidewater, right almost to the island's center, if so irregular and ever-shifting an entity can be said to have one. There it fetched up at last, no bigger on **SE!**'s camcorder tape than when GreatUnc Ennie first espied it four summers since, rounding Hail Point on the Chester River and turning himward to invade his creekspace as it had already his mind- and muse-space. By now the hurricane surge was noticeably subsiding;

likewise wind and waves in Z II's wake as the storm moved down to the Virginia capes and swerved inland to its rather swift dissipation. A comparatively high marsh-hummock, virtually an island within the island, arrested the barge's solo voyage before it could cross South Marsh altogether and carry on southeastward into Tangier Sound, across to the Annemessex River, to James Island State Park, Crisfield, wherever. By Sunday evening's low tide, *T II* and its solitary captain were, if neither high nor dry, much more spectacularly aground than ever on Ararat Shoal: aground in a labyrinth of marsh-guts no deeper than a heron's knees and not much wider than a muskrat house, surrounded by kilometers of saltmarsh in all directions.

*So we call it the Second Grounding,*
I proposed at our first postevacuation get-together, in Patmos Tower Conference Room 696 on that Monday Morning After. The tugs were back in Snug Harbour by then—nothing further they could do —and the Cast of Several's Core Corps, most of their belongings still aboard *T II*, had been billeted temporarily in DTE's harborfront motel while we sorted things out. Only Capt. Ad. remained aboard the showboat, whence he reported by radio that the barge had suffered no apparent damage. All systems operating. Should be reachable by airboat. Perhaps more conveniently than before. Without the bothersome transfers from boat to boat. He acknowledged, however, that he could see no prospect of retrieving the vessel from South Marsh Island. And we go on with the show, I proposed to Mort Spindler, the Captains Kane, and the closed-circuit countenance of our Arkangel-in-Chief.

Growled Harry Kane in my direction "You've lost it, man. Worse'n Cap'n Ad." He and Elva had made their case already to the virtual Andrew S. Cap'n Andy Todd Andrews Todd that, given Zulu II's significant waning-trend, another hour of their holding action would have permitted them to begin windlassing both their anchor rodes and their towlines and to get *T II* clear of shoal water and on her way home. And we had run **SPECIAL EFFECT!**'s videotape of the Second Cutting, uncut, to considerable effect.

I might have countered by asking Harry where he supposed Captain. Ad. had gotten his fire-ax inspiration from. But Elva left off brushing Sher's too-short-to-brush-anyhow hair and put a calming hand on her agitated brother's arm. "What show, Hops?"

"*The* show," my mate answered in my stead—for the team of Kit & Kaboodle had truly become in effect one person through this Final Season, especially after that August miscarriage, and We had spent an all-but-sleepless night considering Next Steps. "*Our* show." Her hand-gesture included everyone physically or virtually present: the whole Core Corps. The way We saw it, We then explained, was that whether or not FLOPCORP declared the showboat a total loss, and regardless of whatever marine-insurance settlement might ensue, the Arkade Players would no doubt now be disbanded—with a bonus payoff, one hoped and presumed, from what remained of ATC's Postview Season budget. But we all needed to get back aboard *T II* to collect more leisurely what belongings we'd not been able to take off with us in our hasty, storm-tossed evacuation; and some few of us would surely be staying on to oversee the dismantling, packing, and offloading of as much of the showboat's valuable equipment as could be salvaged. What We therefore proposed—and had tentatively broached already to our man Greg Kim, who'd promised to discuss it with his counterparts at Maryland Public Television—was to work up some sort of MPT special telecast of *CS!!!* TM as our Final Season Finale, in lieu of our hoped-for Inner Harbor climax. Assuming, of course, that the barge was indeed reachable by airboat or whatever, and that the logistics of food-supply and other necessaries proved feasible.

Mort was skeptical: Power, water, and sewerage should be no problem, inasmuch as *T II* had its own generators, auxiliary reverse-osmosis watermakers, and waste-treatment system. But to keep the company aboard and provisioned on the mere speculation of a possible one-shot telecast . . .

"*I like it*," spake the countenance of our Arkangel-in-Chief, and that was that. Captain Harry would reconnoiter the barge's physical situation and report on means and routes of access thereto. Captain Elva—who found herself elevated then and there to the post of Acting Director of FLOPCORP in Captain. Ad.'s absence and, shall we say (at least pending the outcome of DTE's Official Inquiry into Groundings 1 and 2), incapacity — would work out with her brother the logistics of returning to the showboat as many of the Cast of Several who so chose and of supplying them through, let's say, the rest of September, after which no doubt we'd have to make plans for permanent evacuation and salvage. Cap'n Andy Etc. himself would communicate pronto to certain of Greg Kim's counterparts' superiors our proposal for a telecast Final Performance; and Doctor Spin, per usual, would manage the publicity therefor.

"Zingo," that worthy not so much exclaimed as concurred. After another night's rest and reflection, however — and much confabulation among ourselves, and preliminary estimates from Elva of what would be required from the mainland to keep barge and players up and running in place, so to speak, for a fortnight — he regained some of his characteristic energy. On the Tuesday, word came from PT 666 that Cap'n Andy was sufficiently encouraged by his exploratory conversations with the public television people to greenlight our plan, at least provisionally; by the time we were all back aboard and squared away for script-modification and rehearsal, he expected to have a firm commitment-in-principle themfrom and arrangements for a shipboard visit from their technical people to discuss production matters on site with us. The Players greeted this news enthusiastically; if nothing else, it gave them time to consider their next moves. Indeed, the only discouraging word was from Captain Harry Kane, who — after overflying South Marsh Island by rented helicopter that same afternoon, nautical chart in hand, and then landing on *T II*'s roof to review with Capt. Ad. the barge's exact position and surrounding topography — reported that they could see no feasible way through that wetlands maze for a dozen-plus people with their baggage and supplies. Zulus I and II, it seems, had so reconfigured the anyhow ever-shifting waterways that the chart could not be relied upon; Capt. Ad.'s earlier pronouncement to the contrary notwithstanding, it was by no means certain that even a small airboat could penetrate the island-within-an-island whereon *T II* was stranded. The only sure connection was by helicopter, prohibitively expensive and limited to one or two passengers per trip.

So there went *that*, we gloomed, and wondered collectively What Now? Many of us had valuables still on board: my backup file of computer disks, e.g., which I'd left behind in favor of my laptop, unable in our hurry to evacuate both; **SPECIAL EFFECT!** 's tour-de-force Main Feature effects, together with the not-inexpensive equipment of their production; a fair fraction of Holly Weil's Wonderbra inventory. And what about our agenda down the road? Rent a shoreside facility in Baltimore, maybe, for our scheduled Final Performances? Do a studio telecast for MPT? But our show's whole sense depended on its constant reverbs between the Ark onstage and the Ark that contained stage, players, and audience as well—a conceit more central to our play's concerns than was the name of Shakespeare's Globe Theatre to his. Not for the first time, I envied the relative simple-assedness of novel-writing: Give your N.E. Character pen and paper (or your N.A. his faithful Pentium-chipped PC), a reasonably flat surface to set 'em on, and a spell of relative peace and quiet, and he's in business. No Cast of Several! No corps of techies, no sets and props and sound-and-light gear! Nor, to be sure, any thrill of adroit teamwork, or electricity between author/players and live audience. I missed those highs already—the more acutely given my entire unsuccess thus far in GreatUnc Ennie's medium. . . .

But on the Wednesday, like a cheap-shot *deus ex machina* by some Playwright Aspirant, *"FLOPCORP FLOPCORP,"* came radio'd word to Elva Kane's new office, formerly Captain. Ad.'s, where VHF Channel 16 was routinely monitored: *"This is TOFO Two. Over?"*

"FLOPCORP here, TOFO Two," responded Elva's secretary, who recognized her former boss's voice. "Go to Sixty-eight, Cap'n Ad, sir."

*"TOFO Two to Sixty-eight."* And when both parties had switched from the calling channel to their designated speaking channel, *"Cap'n Ad Lake here, FLOPCORP,"* the caller declared unnecessarily: *"We got a visitor on board. Wants to speak with either Cap'n Elva or Cap'n Harry. Over."* The former director of The

Floating Opera Corporation and skipper still of its principal asset sounded gravely pleased.

"Cap'n Elva here now, Cap'n Ad. Who's your visitor? Over?" Whereupon a different, not-unfamiliar voice rasped from the loud-speaker *"Jest call me Ditsy, Cap'n Elv; call me whatchadurn please. But like I told Cap'n Ad already, it's you folks is the visitors, not me—and I bidja welcome to Hick Fen Island! Over?"*

No fan of dialect-dialogue, I'll cut to the chase: That island–within–South Marsh Island whereto the storm-surge had fetched *T II* turns out to be the home bog of our once-and-future bilge-pump virtuoso and general maintenance-person, whose shack-on-stilts — damaged by Zulu II along with certain of its contents — stood (no longer quite vertically) just a mile or so hence. Its proprietor had of course noted and recognized the great hapless trespasser on his turf and had inferred what must have happened, but had been too busy salvaging and emergency-repairing his/her house and appurtenant systems, so he said — including the swamped johnboat *Nameless* and the improbable computer Big Bitsy — to get around till now to checking things out. And be durn if it weren't a right nice surprise to find Cap'n. Ad. himself aboard of her, and old *TOFO* in a lot better shape than some folks' cabins that one could mention! . . .

"The long and the short of it is," Captain Elva reported tri-umphantly to us-all after sign-off, "we're letting Ditsy live aboard till she gets her cabin back in shape. And—*Ta-da!*—she swears that no matter what the charts say, she can ferry four of us at a time from either Crisfield or Deals Island Landing right up to *T II*'s tran-som, and'll be happy to do it to earn her keep. How's *that* for some good news for a change!"

We agreed that Captain Elva (who always refers to Ditsy in the feminine) must have either cut her nails on the Monday or said "rab-bits" on the first day of the month, as was her occasional good-luck advice to us. And sure enough, that same day we strategized and pri-oritized (Mort's terms) our return to the showboat: The Kane twins first, along with the Galley and Maintenance Teams' chiefs, to check out all systems and assess our needs; me'n Sher'n Mort next; then Holly Weil, Jay Brown (at sixes and sevens because friend Ditsy had neither asked after him nor sent warm regards; could it be that that EARL guy had reappeared on Hick Fen?), **SPECIAL EFFECT!**, Heather, and the rest—including, we hoped, Greg Kim to cover The Animals' Return to the Ark, our tactic being to involve him and his employer as much as possible in our ongoing story. Boatload by johnboatload our grizzled Charon shuttled us from Deals Island Landing (its name a euphemizing of Devil's Island, its location a closer shot than Ditsy's "Crassfield" to his/her "Hick Fen"), three miles across choppy, crab-rich Tangier Sound and another mile or two at top workboat-speed through a dizzying reticulation of spartina-walled guts, storm-trash-littered tide ponds, and crisscrossing natural ditches, past our ferryperson's out-of-plumb cabin, through another and smaller maze within the first, to the virtual doorstep of *TOFO II*, whose dear white bulk we saw now to starboard, now to port, now before and now behind as we made our circuitous final approach. All truculent goodwill was Ditsy, events having more than justified those bilge-oil-smell-based apprehensions that had prompted his end-of-August jumping ship (I find I'm calling him/her a he; don't ask me why). Before Zulu II knocked out his generator, he had followed the televised reports of our grounding on Ararat Shoal, but seeing we were in no danger he'd been shy of visiting us there in *Nameless* lest he seem to be crowing I Told You So. On the questions of the First and Second Cuttings—Captain Harry's and Captain. Ad.'s—as on the First and Second Groundings, he discreetly reserved his opinion, except to declare (a) that the showboat could not imaginably be safer and sounder than where presently perched, and (b) that there wasn't a Popsicle's chance in Perdition of its ever being budged therefrom before the middle of the upcoming century, when rising sea levels from global warming might just do the trick. He was, for Ditsy, borderline effusive, hallooing us each by name as we emerged from the D-o-C van, embracing (a warily stiff) Jay Brown like, well, a longlost lover, and right pleased altogether to welcome each'n'ever' one of us to Hick Fen. A cynic might well have wondered whether, in our undamaged but irretrievable floating theater, he saw a prospective permanent dwelling-place much grander than his stormsmacked shack.

But we were too pleased at being back aboard to more than register and dismiss such notions. Capt. Ad., for one reason or another, had little to say to us; he seemed content to leave our welcoming to Ditsy and the overseeing of our settling-in to Harry Kane—who indeed had assumed the acting skippership of *T II,* as had his sister that of FLOPCORP. Early on in Ditsy's back-and-forthing, our captain excused himself to return on *Nameless* to Deal Island and thence to Dorsettown, to be with his ailing ladyfriend. For the rest of us, however, once the Core Corps were all aboard and our gear squared away by afternoon's end, it was party time on *The Original Floating Opera II,* courtesy of the Galley, Concession, & Bar Team. We would, we agreed, get cracking first thing mañana on a pared-down televersion of *CS!!!*TM—The New New New New Show?—and work on it right into the weekend, inasmuch as Mort Spindler, Holly Weil, and one or two others had requested shore leave for Yom Kippur on the Sunday and Monday. If no telecast materialized (but our Heather, in whom Fox News's Greg Kim had taken an amply-requited interest during his coverage of our First Grounding, was working her cell-phone connection himto on that subject, as presumably was "Cap'n Andy" with Maryland Public Television), we would consider Next Steps. Meanwhile, here's to the unsinkable Arkade Players: Long may we wave, and on with the show!

*That night,*
snugged together once again in happy postcoital lassitude in Our cozy cabin, my selfmate surprised her selfmate by asking, languidly, "Who are We, hon?"

He begged her pardon?

"You know. You and I: Who *are* We, really?"

It was to the back of his left hand she spoke, that arm being tucked under her head while the rest of him spooned against her back. Into her hair he ventured Me Kit, you Kaboodle? You Scheherazade, me Shahryar? Cathode and Anode? But he sensed the More on her mind: her stepping out of Ourself to size Us up, as it were, from a third-person P.O.V. Couple of improvisers? he therefore ventured next: A third of the way at least through Our separate stories without a helluva lot to show for it yet, but still in the opening chapters of Our Story? Whatcha have in mind, Sher?

"Oh . . ." She kissed my handback: "Like, Failed Writer and Failed Smalltime Actress-Director on Failed Showboat in Middle of Nowhere? That sort of thing."

Good a place as any to either turn the page or close the book, I heard myself declare — not to my lover's hair now, but to the antecedents of the pronoun Us. Want to pack it in?

I sensed her considering the question. "Not yet. No. You?"

No. But that Not Yet chills me to the soul, Sher.

"Me too, love."

It was that unexpected but immediately comprehended soul-chill, surely, that imbued Our following days and weeks with what I can only call a mellow, poignant gravity. With all former deadline-pressures off — no "Maryland Defenders Day," no float-parade up under the Bay Bridge to the Inner Harbor finale, no Next Season, and not all that much to be done in preparation for the proposed MPTelecast to wrap up this one — the spirit of our program-revisions and rehearsals was no longer Get It Done, but Get It Right, for no other reason than the doing of it to our personal/professional satisfaction. As Mort reported more than half seriously to Greg Kim, if nothing came of the telecast (which, however, we understood to be looking likelier all the time), we would videotape a Final Performance for ourselves — and for DTE's archives — before disbanding the Arkade Theatre Company and leaving the showboat to whatever its final disposition.

In fact the telecast took place, on the month's last evening, supported in large measure by a Special Grant from DTE's parent entity, The Tidewater Foundation. Sparked by the very lastness of it, all hands performed admirably to a house empty but for ourselves, the TV techies, and a handful of invited local reviewers. Media coverage was gratifying: Greg Kim, while not a drama critic, had been made aware by friend Heather of the new spirit pervading our company, and had duly communicated same where it mattered. People from the *Sun,* the *Post,* the *Times,* and CNN choppered or *Nameless*'d in, found complimentary things to say about the pared-down show, and made what they would of our situation's portentous symbolism: "the serene and cheerful seriousness," as Greg put it (with a

bit of cueing from Yours Truly), "with which this tightly bonded little band of players prepares for The End of Their World."

*Who are We, really?*

Not a question best answered by overmuch frontal pondering, perhaps. But as we Arkade Players, "bonded" indeed as never before in
our seasons together, calmly counted down the days to our very own
TEOTWAWKI, two events focused that question more intensely
for this narrator, without, however, by any means answering it. In
Ditsy's daily, sometimes twice-daily runs between Hick Fen and
Deal Island, he routinely picked up (along with choice Z II leftovers
from the marsh) the mail fetched down by van from Dorsettown.
One such delivery included the disk of *COMING SOON!!! THE
NOVEL?*, with polite regrets from my neophyte agent (my ex-grad-
school roommate Sybil, who, unable to score a proper academic ap-
pointment even with her Ph.D. in Queer Theory, switched from
"Feminist Soma[tics]" to flat-out text-huckstering, and is doing just
fine) that her placement efforts had been in vain. Even the minuscule e-fiction "trade," she concluded, putting the term in well-deserved quotes, evidently wasn't "ready for it yet." No surprise to its
perpetrator, who had long since surmised as much and was grateful
that an agent who had yet to make a dime from her efforts on his behalf had persisted for so long. But a set-down, naturally, all the
same. Gravely—with those eyes those eyes of hers that seemed to
me now unremittingly to ask that question that question of hers—
Sher comforted me. "Set it aside for a year, maybe, and then take a
fresh look at it?"

A year. Who were she and I, really, even to begin to imagine
where We'd be a year from now, and what doing? *Real* people, with
real vocations—my medical parents, e.g., or The N.E. Character
and his mate—knew such things, barring accident, but not us aging
mayfly youngsters. *T II*'s resting-place happened to straddle a tidal
ditch, *Nameless*'s final approach these days from the waters of the
world beyond. That same evening—the Saturday after the autumnal
equinox, full moon rising over Hick Fen—having resisted all afternoon the temptation simply to Frisbee my magnum opus into the
marsh, I saw fit to seal it instead inside a Ziploc™ sandwich baggie,

that inside another, and them inside a third. With a canned-beer libation to Poseidon and a toast to Whoever We Really Are, over Sher's objections I plopped the thing off *TOFO*'s stern into that then-out-flowing ditch and declared myself, to the brilliant impassive moon and my ontologically uncertain selfmate, to be thenceforward an Aspirant Emeritus, amen and fuck it.

Whereupon the gods of Heavy Irony saw fit, the very next day, to choreograph a surprise visit from none other than the *Emeritus* Emeritus: GreatUnc Ennie himself! Who since our 9/9/99 First Grounding had politely declined Mort's routine invitations to maybe do a Special Walk-On bit in whatever turned out to be our Final Performance, but who upon learning of our new and unequivocally terminal situation had himself requested a Last Visit to the showboat, if one could be arranged on such short notice. In particular, Mort reported to me that Sunday morning, together with these tidings, the guy hoped he might have a Private Word with me.

Whoever *that* might be.

"Don't dare tell him you just chucked your novel," Sher advised —urged, warned, whatever. "We've got no grudge against him, but I don't want to give him that satisfaction. He's probably coming to tell you that *his* version is finished and off to his goddamn publishers."

She and I, I reminded her, were one person, whoever *That* might really be. So hang around, and We'll hear what's what.

What was what, it developed—after Ditsy had duly ferried Our Chap over from Deals Island on that Sunday forenoon along with a brace of MPT types, and The N.E. Character had warmly regreeted all hands, tisked his sympathy for Groundings 1 & 2 and the position they'd left us in (together with his half-relief at having been spared after all the walk-on bit he'd rehearsed with us at Solomons against his better judgment), and declared his anticipation of the forthcoming wind-up telecast—was a good-humored confiding to me'n Sher (in the privacy of Mort's shipboard office, lent for the occasion) that as of 9/9/99 *et seq.*, after four years of intermittent labor upon his p-narrative *COMING SOON!!!*, he had abandoned that project for good and all, or it him. He was sufficiently old and experienced in the medium, he maintained, to recognize the signs and cease throwing yet more good money after bad; to cut his losses and devote to less refractory projects whatever musely time remained to him. For any other-than-amiable episodes in our ongoing competition, his sincere apologies to both of Us; for his part, he assured Us, the rivalry had from the start been more sporting than combative, a mere novel spur to his imagination. He respected my energy and talent, he declared, half envied me my youth, and wished me and my gifted partner successful careers and a good life. While still skeptical of the medium of electronic fiction, he encouraged my explorations thereinto. Whatever I might see fit to borrow, appropriate, reorchestrate, or flat-out steal from whatever I might have gathered of *his* now-abandoned version of our joint story, I was welcome to. As far as he was concerned, the proverbial torch had—he wouldn't say *passed*, for he still had a few promising notebook-notes to run by his muse for possible elaboration before his expiry-date overtook him —but *passed on* its fire to mine, as one might light another's candle with one's own. Mine now to take that fire and run with it, with his blessing: no longer (or for not much longer) a Novelist Aspirant, but a Novelist Emergent. His vows to the muse, he informed us, prohibited among other things the blurbing of blurbs except for first books by his former apprentices at our joint alma mater; he now went so far as to include my e-novel in that exception, should I see fit to have its publisher (if that was the right term in Cyberville) send him an advance copy, with instructions for its operation, and if, as he readily presumed, he found it blurbworthy.

Et cetera! Whereallafter, more or less dumbstruck, We thanked him, allowing as how We'd See About That when the time came. We then *abrazo*'d our reciprocal farewells (his not to Us alone but to the showboat and to showboats generally, he declared, which had served him well and sufficiently over the decades as a fictive subject and metaphor) and waved good-byes between *T II*'s stern and *Nameless*'s as Ditsy ferried him back down the winding *canaletto* whereinto, just the evening prior . . .

*"Bullshit?"*
We Ontological Uncertainties wondered to Each Other when he'd vanished 'round the bend. "Something up his emerital sleeve?" No

*way* he could've known I'd ditched my bid to snatch that goddamn torch of his and had moreover—what I was beginning already to regret—purged the ditched disk's original from my computer's HD as well, lest it tempt me back into its futile coils. "Me," nevertheless said Sher, "I half suspect he's been the fucking Phantom all along. Pulling our strings! Tweaking our plot!"

Not likely, in this Failed Novelist's opinion: For one thing, the guy would never allow so smashing a Cornball Ironic Coincidence this late in the tale. Remember his spiel that day at Solomons, that I told you about? Aristotle on Coincidence?

"Don't remind me. What matters is what We *do* with this little infobit. What now?"

What now indeed? Plus, I reminded her, Who *are* We, really, et cet? As to the former: What's now is, we-all put on our slam-bang Final Performance next Thursday; that's who We are till then. *Then . . .*

Then—which is to say, *just* then, even while I so bravely improvised—the full crunch of what I'd done crunched down. Okay, so the world wasn't ready for my cunningly hypertexted magnum opus, my e-pic; so couldn't I have maybe reorchestrated it for dear old fuddlyduddly print—as a faux–electronic narrative, say, the way my early-Modernist forebears imitated news headlines, "streams of consciousness," and sundry sorts of nonlinearity? Said I to my distressed self, Shit, man: Even without remarkable Cunning & Strength, Youth + Patience + Time are bound to overcome Age + Cunning + the whole emerital Kit & Kaboodle, no? Not that that silly rivalry any longer interested me. One had heard the cautionary tales (I forget them just now) of precious works-in-progress lost and rebegun from scratch. Could *I* possibly . . . ?

Forget it. *Where was my dear ditched disk?* What had I done? And while one's at it, who the fuck was I? Who would my Kaboodle and her Kit be, really, after Thursday's wind-up telecast?

*"Mellow, poignant gravity,"*
did someone say awhile back? Mellowpoignantgraveferocious *energy*, more like, on K&K's part (whoever *They* are, really) between that vertiginous Cornball-Coincidence weekend just narrated and

the Thursday MPTelecast. A brace of quietly desperate dervishes We were, Sher and I, goosing Ourselves, each other, and the Cast of Several to precedent-surpassing pitches in the empty theater. Never had the lively Corpse de Ballet so danced, the Pit Bulls so rocked and swung, the faux–steam calliope so faux-steamed. "What *is* it with us?" wondered awed Mort Spindler at some break in Thursday morning's final run-through before the evening's live broadcast. "Especially you two?"

Offered sweatsoaked Sher, "The End Of The World As We Know It?"

I say "live broadcast"; in fact, the format we'd settled on was a combination of live and taped segments, over which Greg Kim affably presided as master of ceremonies: film clips of *TOFO II* in better days and of our First and Second Groundings by the mighty Zulus; brief behind-the-scenes interviews with sundry cast-members and even the virtual "Cap'n Andy" (though not with The N.E. Character, who had Politely Declined); shots of our ferryperson ferrying the camera crew through Hick Fen, *Nameless*'s portside steering-stick in one hand and crabnet in the other, progging doubler-crabs and miscellaneous flotsam as he went and growling cheerfully *Call me Ditsy, call me whatchadurn please, just an old-time Chesapeake* progger's *what I am, and you'd be s'prised what turns up in these marshes after a blow*, etc.— just as he rounds the last bend and *T II* heaves hugely into view. All this to culminate (the viewer having inferred our show's general story-line from the taped set-pieces and interstitial commentary) in a live performance of the finale: Noah's Younger Daughter's sexy pitch to Scriptor John of Patmos; his Alteration of the Text; Apocaplyse Deferred until The Fire Next Time; then Hip Hooray for Y2K and You're the One, O One, O One!

May I say, in all modesty, that the sucker took wing and *flew*? We were Broadway that night in Hick Fen, every one of us over the top; old Charlie Hunter and Ms. Edna Ferber would've been tickled pink. In my Kaboodle's eyes eyes eyes (and she in her Kit's, she would later tell me) I saw a passion veritably apocalyptic as we soared way over our individual and collective heads: *After* this *and* this *and* this, *let come what may!*

Scary. And now it must be reported — what an abler novelist

would've established earlier — that in the absence of Captain. Ad.,
all other candidates for the role being multiply bespoken already or
having once again Politely Declined, the part of "Scriptor John" was
being played by none other than Call-Me-Ditsy, who needed little in
the way of makeup to pass for a grizzled hermit and had little to do
onstage besides pause in his drafting of the Book of Revelation
(which was also, You dig, the script of our show-in-progress), listen
frowningly to Holly Weil's eloquent song-and-dance plea, stroke his
fake beard a bit, and declare that while The End can't be *deleted*
from The Script, it might just possibly be postponed. Handing her
then the sheet he's been scribbling upon throughout the scene, "Play
*this* on your calliope," he instructs her, "and We'll Just See."

After which, all hands on deck for the hoedown.

Nor did I mention, as I should have done and now shall, that
Mort's choreography of this scene positioned Sher and me (Noah's
Elder Daughter and his Number-One Son, to whom Authority had
been Transferred during the preceding Tempest scene) not far behind Holly on Mount Ararat-that-was-also-Patmos, with the Corpse
de Ballet just behind us, gathered anxiously on the prow of our
grounded Ark/*Arke*/showboat/ Etc. while our fair emissary sang her
last-ditch pitch to The Author. Who, unbeknownst to us-all, had
made a little script-alteration himself: At the Big Moment, Ditsy
rose from the writing-stool, duly stroked his beard while looking
from Holly to parchment-in-hand and back again, delivered his
"possibly postponed" speechlet — and then, to our flabbergastment,
tossed the script-page back onto his writing-desk, progged with his
other hand into the brown folds of his robe, winked hugely at the
MPT camera, drew forth a baggied computer-disk, and handed
same to astonished Younger Daughter with the instruction "Tell yer
pal there to boot up his calliope and run *this* sucker on it, hon, and
we'll just *see* what's a-COMING SOON!!!"

Nonplused Holly dumbly took the proffered item and looked
wildly back to Sher for rescue as Ditsy John, beaming, stood arms
akimbo now before his Scriptorium. My selfmate squealed, sprang
Kid-Sisterward, snatched the disk herfrom, and held it aloft for me
and all hands to see, then herself launched the anthem "Thank You,

Author of Us-All" that was meant to be Holly's response to John's Script-Change, and which our soundtrack-tape had already fanfared. A seasoned trouper herself these days, Holly quickly recovered, linked arms with Sher, and took up the theme—

> *As it is written, so shall it be:*
> *But the Script's been changed—Hooray! Whoopee!*

—as did I, half a dozen beats later, joining the duo at Sher's jubilant summons and accepting from her hands my evidently still dry, triply Ziploc™'d treasure, which I held forth for the camera to close in tight upon:

> *It's Curtain Time, folks—but not to worry:*
> *What's COMING SOON!!! is in no hurry*

—and the Corpse de Ballet, on cue and in chorus immediately thereafter:

> *The rewrote Writ is the script we'll play:*
> *Our End won't come with Y2K!*
> *Come though it must (and soon enough),*
> *There's time yet for Love and Art and stuff!*
> *What started with Eve's Apple bitten*
> *Won't end until THE END's rewritten,*

et cetera—all as rehearsed except for my waving my baggied disk instead of the scripted script-page as we danced and sang

> *Thanks, Author, for this Second Chance.*
> *It's The Fire Next Time—but till then, let's dance!*
> *Rewrite us to Heaven, rewrite us to Hell:*
> *Our Second Chance is Yours as well!*

etc.

*"And vice versa,"*
Sher declared to me later that night, in Our berth in Our lights-out cabin, after the backslapping, headshaking, champagne-spritzing cast party with its toasts to all hands and especially to Ditsy—who

sure gave us a tense moment back there, but ultimately inspired a finale as full of genuine Celebratory Relief (once we-all were back on track) as of the stage-direction variety called for by the script—and after my heartfelt, soulfelt public thanks himto for my own Authorial Second-or-Anyhow-Next Chance (the entire Cast of Several appears to have known of my disk-ditching despair and of GreatUnc Ennie's ironically subsequent Passing of the Torch me-to), to which our "Scriptor John" had replied "You set yerass down'n *write* that sumbitch now, man—don't, I'll write it m'own self, and *then* you'll be sorry!" He too had gathered, he confided aside to Sher and me, what was what N.A./N.E.wise, both from his own observations and from certain recent ferry-trip remarks by that other Scriptor-John fellow—who, Ditsy assured Us, had sincerely wished me well, as he wished all his former apprentices, official and otherwise.

"Which don't mean," our Progger Extraordinaire ventured to add, "he mightn't have a card or two left up his sleeve. So if I was you, I'd hop right to it."

No more hopping right to it, I had told Ditsy then and repeated now to my mate vis-à-vis her above-ventured Vice Versa: that this novelistical Second Chance of mine could also be Our Next Chapter as a couple, now that Our showboat days were done. Set about it? Yes, vowed I. Get It Right this time? Yes-if-I-can. But no more Get Cracking, no more Hopping Right To It. Same goes for Us.

She me squeezed. "Whoever *We* are, really."

Declared I, We know who We are, love, until Gee Dash Dee rediddles Our script. We're Us Here Now, is who. Shall We get married, to make it official?

"Not just yet." But the suggestion earned me a resqueeze.

October! Lovely on the Hick Fen marshes after so hot, so drought-afflicted and then tempest-tossed a summer. By threes and fours the Cast of Several and their support teams, au revoired with hugs and waves and faux-calliope bye-byes, were Ditsy'd back to Deal Island Landing, Dorsettown, and whatever next episodes of *their* stories, while Sher and I lingered aboard between visits to her ailing mom: Us. Here. Now. Holly Weil, e.g., skipped off pronto to her fiancé, Mort's-brother-the-Salisbury-orthodontist, to enrollment in the state university's campus there for the purpose of Taking a Master's Degree in Something, and to prospective membership in the Spindler *mishpocheh*. Greg Kim returned to his regular Fox News beat in Baltimore, more or less accompanied by his new friend Heather, whom he steered to a gofer job at his studio while she auditioned for sundry storefront theaters in the city's Fells Point district. **SPECIAL EFFECT!**'s post-Postview-Season plan had been to make her way to L.A., the hot center of her specialty; but her new connection with Captain Elva—together with the attention paid to her videotape of Zulu II and our Second Grounding, the popularity of "savage Nature" flicks and even of Storm Tourism (fools flocking to the Outer Banks of Carolina in hope of hurricanes)— has got her considering the field of Ma Nature's special effects, while working officially at FLOPCORP as her lover's aide-de-camp. Jay "Obie" Brown, his peace evidently made with Friend Ditsy, remained aboard with us through most of the month while the two of them worked to repair the latter's storm-damaged house as well as their connection—although Jay made no more secret of his nostalgia for city life than did Ditsy of his intention to "prog" the showboat of everything left behind once FLOPCORP wrote the vessel off their books and Cap'n Harry completed his official salvage operation. Why not prog his old cabin instead, my Sherry suggested, and set up permanent housekeeping on *TOFO II*? "Wouldn't want to heat this sucker come winter" was Ditsy's reply. "Plus who wants a three-hundred-seat living room? Not *this* girl, thankee ma'am!"

And while I'm in this Regular Old-Fashioned Novelist mode, wrapping up and paying off my characters like ATC our Cast of Several, what about the others? Well: Captain Elva Kane officially replaced Captain. Adam. Lake. at the helm of FLOPCORP after DTE's Official Inquiry, which exonerated him in the matter of our First Grounding, but clucked its official tongue at his having "done a Cap'n Harry," as Mort Spindler put it, at the height of Zulu II. All which would lead one to expect that that latter skipper would be found similarly culpable in the matter of the 9/9/99 First Cutting and our consequent lodgement on Ararat Shoal, would it not? How came it, then, that H. J. Kane was not only excused and retained as

*Raven*'s captain (a not very meaningful post, as shall be seen) but charged with the overseeing as well of *T II*'s maintenance through October and its disposition thereafter? One can only conclude that Dr. Rachel Spindler's testimony to the four-person Inquiry panel ("Cap'n Andy," his ever-more-right-hand-man Mort, the marine-insurance adjuster, and DTE's legal counsel) must have been compelling.

To wit? Doc Rachel's statement—volunteered at her husband's suggestion—was unsworn and confidential, but both Elva Kane and Sherry Singer (who've been, one remembers, Very Close Indeed in time past) are among her gynecological clientele, and wives and husbands both actual and virtual share things, don't they. Thus am I positioned, as they say nowadays, to report that those twins, as Reader may've been told somewhere already, were originally trizy-gotic triplets. That the secondborn themof—Abe, nicknamed by his siblings "Abie"—emerged from their mother's womb umbilically strangled. That the cause thereof (just reporting the news, Reader, as reported to me by Never Mind Whom, as reported to Doc Rachel by her patient the firstborn triplet) was the trio's frolicking together *in utero* at term and pretending to compete for birth-position, although "they all knew" that Harry was to go first, Abe second, and Elva third, following the order of their serial conception. Which frolick-ing did lead to Brother Abe's entanglement—in his own umbilicus, so they three thought. That when his siblings' increasingly alarmed efforts to untangle him only garroted hapless Abe the more, Harry pushed Elva out first "to get help," and that to that end the newborn tried desperately to explain the emergency to Mom and Doctor but couldn't make herself understood themby, her speech issuing as mere infant-squalls that delighted all extrauterine hands—"like speaking through a dream," Elva put it to Doc Rachel, adding with a chuckle "Y'oughta hear the sounds Sherry wakes me up with now'n then!"

This being the period when she and my Sher were Very Close.

That—communicating then back to Brother Harry via her own umbilicus, she and he agreed that their brother's only chance was for said Harry to "cut him loose." That Harry forthwith did so (with his Swiss Army knife, one wonders, already ever-handy in the womb?) and then forcibly shoved the patient out for medical rescue, thereby accidentally strangling him in what turned out to be Harry's own birth-cord. Thus (quoth Elva, quoth Doc Rachel, quoth my informant) Harry's inconsolable howling upon his own emergence and for an uncommon while thereafter, despite Sister Elv's efforts to calm him with soothing proverbs as soon as her own cord was cut and her respiration proceeding normally: *"If two people knock heads bending over, they'll sleep together that night*, so you hush now, Harry hon; we did our level best. Anyhow, today's *the first Thursday in July*, which is when *all the toads turn pink from two till two-thirty*, you just watch and see, okay?" etc. That this early trauma doubtless accounts, as Reader will have surmised, for Captain Harry's skipperly disinclination ever to deploy *Raven* in the pushing mode; likewise — what follows less than logically for Yrs Truly, but evidently satisfied the Inquiry panel — for his disposition, in tangled or potentially entangling situations, to go for his knife, fire ax, whatever, and cut *all* cords before it's Too Late. Likewise too (not mentioned by Doc Rachel, but likely-seeming to others us-of) for Elva's pastimes of unknotting, unsplicing, de-macraméing, and forever brushing her own and others' hair, not to mention her croonings to *TOFO II* while berthing and unberthing same in seasons past. Further than this deponent saith not, and Case Dismissed (though none had ever been formally brought) against Captain Harry James Kane.

Which leaves (moving right along) . . . whom else?

*Us. Here. Now.*
Right. Aboard *The Original Floating Opera II* in sweet October-lit, mosquito-free-at-last Hick Fen: often just the two of Us, more often with Ditsy and Jay and one or both of the Captains Kane for company, occasionally with such visitors as Doctors Mom and Dad (Just checking, Son), or already-nostalgic members of the Cast of Several, or other friends, relatives, and associates, including of course Mort and his kids, although after the Inquiry their dad was busier than ever. Following Sher's grandma's death, her longtime partner

Andrew S. "Todd 'Cap'n Andy' Andrews" Todd shifted his residence up-tower to her penthouse suite, 999, generously bestowing his former lodgings in 666 upon the fast-sinking "Bea Golden" and her caretaker-in-chief, our former. captain., and elevating our former "Doctor Spin" from head of Promotion to acting director of Dorset Tradewinds Enterprises.

Us. Here. Now. Not all day every day, to be sure: With unaccustomed time on her capable hands and her problematical mother out of action, Sherry busied herself with the co-executorship of her grandmother's complex and considerable estate, and discovered in herself both a talent for and, more surprising to both of Us, an *interest* (beyond the financial) in such to-me-merely-tedious accountancy. "It's a whole new world!" she declared to me: "a regular *education*!" Wherein, her grandma's grandchild, she proved so apt and ready a student that by that fair October's ides she was in frequent, spirited, and canny virtual conference with the Arkangel-in-Chief himself, and toward month's end was vouchsafed — as even Mort had never been — a private personal actual audience with that worthy in Patmos Tower Special Conference Room 969. "Cute old duffer, really," she reported to us-all after, half breathless still and starry-eyed: "Fruitcake in some departments, maybe, but tacksharp in most. I sort of *liked* him! It's as if he really *were* my Foxy Grandpa."

Which, who knows, the guy just might be; she didn't get that middle name of hers from nowhere.

All this by way of saying that such business — together with sympathetic attentions to her mom — fetched her with some frequency from Hick Fen to Dorsettown-on-Choptank, sometimes to Jane Harrison's estate-lawyers' offices in Baltimore as well, upon which excursions my laptop and I usually accompanied her, and We would use the occasion to touch base with what We called the Five D's much missed (as Jay Brown will testify) by non-city-dwellers: good Doctors, Dentists, Department stores, Delicatessens, and Dining out — as well as to maintain Our Dorsettown apartment. In this benign Limbo of a Hick Fen October, Our needs were modest, and money was no problem: My mate had had grandparental trust-fund income since age eighteen, more than enough for basic subsistence, and looked to be coming into very considerably more once the estate was settled—without even counting her mother's share thereof, not far down the mortal road. It was because she'd never "had" to work, Sher liked to maintain, that she habitually worked so hard and so enjoyed doing it. My own parents had ever been generous to a fault, Q.E.D., and while I had declined their supporting me after undergraduate days, I could have maintained myself modestly for some while on their accumulated past beneficence. But there was no need for that: Sherry being otherwise engaged, Mort kept me on salary in her stead as acting director, excuse the expression, of the Arkade Theatre Company, to preside over its presumable shutting down and closing out (my first official act in this acting capacity was to respell *Theatre* Yankee-style). It was a job that could be responsibly done with my left hand, so to speak, and for the most part as efficiently by Remote Access from *T II* via phone and e-mail as from "my" office in Dorsettown.

While with my right? Reader, Reader: In that limpid October mudflat-fragrant marsh-light—to the pterodactylic squawk of blue herons and the skreek of ospreys and bald eagles; to the plash of muskrats, otters, and nutria, the plish of fish jumping for insects or their lives in the surrounding tidewater; to the omnipresent soft drone of bees going about their last bee-business before the first hard frost (and, it must be added, to the chug of *Nameless*'s bee-busy comings and goings, the distant racket of Jay's and Ditsy's cabin-carpentry, the overflights of F-16s from Patuxent Naval Air Station and A-10s from Dover Air Force Base)—I became a novelist.

By which I mean? Oh, that on the thousand-and-first go, let's say, at readdressing the narrative project that I'd been heartfeltly farting around with, and it likewise with me, since . . . 1995, was it?, and had more than once believed I'd finished in its e-version, and had more than once abandoned even before I'd bagged and ditched it, I felt (more than saw) the thing *come together*. Corny expression, to "find one's voice"—as if one's narrative testosterone had suddenly kicked in, testicles descended, or birth-liquid from one's newborn lungs been expelled by Doctor Muse's head-down spank so that one could draw first breath at last and, Harry Kane–like, sound off. But shit, Friend: Find My Voice is what I fucking *did*, on—Shall we make it Columbus Day?—amid a *T II* work-morning not outwardly different from ones before and to follow; found my voice almost in mid-sentence, actually, or anyhow found myself finding same. Some unanalyzable ground-shift of register, mix, timbre, stance—*et voilà*. Anybody who's ever hit upon how *really* to do a thing that they'd thought they had the hang of already and only in retrospect understood that they hadn't will know what I mean, if You know what I mean. Whatever the fate of whatever this new-found Voice of mine found to say, and in whatever medium it it said (good old-fashioned bookbound Print, my muse pretty clearly now foresaw, no doubt tricked out with souvenirs of the author's Electronic Period and calibrated echoes of his reluctant mentor), that voice was at long last not only mine but, as much as if not more than any other single attribute, *me*: was Who I was, really. Had GreatUnc Ennie, I wondered—with whom I discovered myself now feeling an odd and gratifying *atonement*—experienced something similar, somewhere way back? Surely so, as must everyone have done who ever lucked beyond *finding* his vocation to *realizing* same.

Which-all doesn't mean (I told my love that night in Our Hick Fen berth, vis-à-vis this voice-is-who-I-really-am business) that I'm not also Us. Okay?

"Goes without saying, love," replied she, and stopped my mouth with kisses—and not many minutes later, by our best subsequent back-counting, we reconceived.

Atonement, yes: not *penitence*, mind, for any Aspirant overstepping of bounds in our late competition, or for any unbecoming Oedipality in our voltaged connection, but *at-one-ment*, as if a certain scriptorial project truly was, after all, as much our collaborative effort (whichever of our names it bore) as the new life in my love's dear bod was the collaboration of that other Us. Amen, and screw Penitence.

We had—she and I and the Muse of Story that October—all the time in the world, We felt, and We made sweet-fruitful use of it.

Round about All Hallows Eve, FLOPCORP's Director Elva brought Us tidings We'd quite expected: that *T II* was to be evacuated for good and all by mid-November, whereupon Captain Harry's Salvage Team, co-advised by Ditsy and Capt. Ad., would commence the stripping and removal from it of everything (better say "anything," in Elv's opinion) both salvageable and worth the expense of transport from that inconvenient venue. After which, *Dove* and *Raven* would be sold, The Floating Opera Corporation itself would autodestruct like the Arkade Theat-E-R Company, and the surviving Kane triplets would be unemployed—"'Less'n we go with the tugboats or talk Mister Mort into building us a brand-new TOFO *Three* in time for O One O One," Elv added—only half jokingly, it seemed to Us: "'Cause *Eat corn out of a tomato-bowl this year,*" she concluded sagely, "*'n next year you'll eat corncake out of a muskmelon,* right?"

"I guess," guessed We. But Something told Elva (so she subsequently confided to her still-close-though-less-so-than-formerly friend Sher) that Brother Harry's salvage project would never, uh, get off the ground? Don't ask her how she knew (We didn't); call it telepathy from the ghost of Brother Abe (If you say so, Elv); her pit-of-the-stomach feeling was that at 11:11 on 11/11, *T II* would be smitten again and finally by its legendary November Curse, in the form this time of The Fire Next Time—leaving only the barge's steel hull to rust away into the new millennium unless floated off by global sea-rise "b'fore he's a-rusted right through, poor thing."

He? Ah, yes: the late brother's unquiet spirit—and so, perhaps, we have the Phantom wrapped up too, noted the Novelist usamong. Anyhow, thanks for the Curse Alert, Elv; We'll see to it We're ashore before The End. Will that be A.M. or P.M., by the way?

With a wink and a whistle, "*Kill a daddy longlegs and your cows'll go dry,*" replied Captain Elva.

"And *A woman that whistles or a hen that crows,*" offered my Sher as she and her Old Friend high-fived good-bye, and the pair then finished the proverb in unison: "*will have her way wherever she goes.*"

\* \* \*

*"That there's a Christ fact,"*

opined Ditsy one week later as he shifted Us and the last of Our on-board belongings across the Sound to Deals Island Landing, and We repeated the proverb himto (Our ferryperson happening to be a whistler) but chose not to pass along Elva's 11:11 11/11 prophecy, lest its repetition bring bad luck. The arch-progger of Hick Fen and his pal Jay Brown—the latter increasingly wistful and restless as the autumn advanced, it appeared to us—were more or less settled in their fixed-up cabin now, and not likely to be personally endangered by the November Curse, if and when. We Ourselves planned to move before long from Our D-o-C apartment to roomier and cushier digs in Sher's mother's now-vacant villa, where there'd be ample room too for . . . "Can We call him Abie if he's a he?" Our creature's ma had asked its pa, who'd allowed as how We'd just see.

No hurry, though; no hurry. The old die, as You may have noticed; the young grow old; the next generation comes (literally) to pass; and Sher goes about *her* newfound vocation while I put this sentence after the one before and, in no hurry, direct my attention to the next. When We phoned to tell Doctors M&D that We were shorebirds now, "Look here," they bade Us: "It's time you two took a holiday from showboats altogether, don't you think? We're doing Thanksgiving down at Caneel Bay in the U.S. Virgins. Come along with us, our treat, okay?"

We thanked them—*heartfeltedly? heartfeelingly?* How would GreatUnc put it?—and promised to consider their offer seriously, but found and find Ourselves inclined to stay home instead (that is, to set up housekeeping in "Bea Golden's" aforementioned Dorsettown pad, now Ours) and—one of Us, anyhow—to make thanksgiving sentences, sentences, sentences about *The Original Floating Opera II*, its Cast of Several, its story. We would just see. I had already a New Idea for the novel's opening: Old-fart Hick Fen progger of uncertain age and gender—a sort of sub-sea-level Tiresias with the twangy drawl of the lower Shore—finds Ziploc™'d diskette labeled *COMING SOON!!!* a-bob like baby Moses in the marshgrass after Hurricane Zulu. Retrieves same and (in no hurry) slugs it into the upscale PC that he happens improbably to maintain in his

pile-perched shanty. Opens with mouseclicks twain the icon that
forthwith appears onscreen:

Etc.

READ ME

Its closing mini-icon:

```
┌─────────────────┐
│    READ ME?     │
└─────────────────┘
```

*2311 EST 12/31/99:*

Say *what*? "Old-fart Hick Fen progger of uncertain age et cetera finds Ziploc™'d diskette labeled et cetera after Hurricane Zulu"? "Retrieves and slugs same into upscale et cetera in his pile-perched shanty"? "Opens with mouseclicks twain the icon that forthwith et ceteras"?

Fuhgeddaboudit! *Ditsy here*, let's just say: ditsy Ditsy, as has Been There, Done That. As has, let's just say, Seen It All. . . .

Or all but All. For here we sit — me and Big Bitsy and whoever You are that's seen fit to "open with mouseclicks twain" etc. — in the wind-up hour (by U.S. Eastern Standard Time) of the wind-up day of the ditto year of the ditso century (by popular Gregorian-calendric reckoning*) of the second millennium C.E.**: TEOTWAWKI a-Coming Soon indeed, if the flakes turn out to have it right; maybe soon enough anyhow if they don't, as is more likely but less interesting.

So, then: Can we talk? For if You've READ ME thus far, Friend, You may be a tad curious nonetheless about the Ditsy Version of What Happened Next to a certain showboat aground for keeps on a certain marsh island in a certain mid-East-Coast-U.S. bay, Your hav-

---

* There's them of course that hold with 01/01/*01* rather than mañana as the New Millennium's curtain-raiser, for arithmetically sound but party-pooping reasons.
** The "Common Error," Old Buddy EARL calls it, him being of the Faithless persuasion though Druidical in tendency.

ing scanned (a) "The Emerital Version" (Fuhgeddaboudit, that cock-eyed pipe-dream of a certain Pit Bull drummer, Script Team chief, and aspiring counterfeit novelist emeritus, in decreasing order of Mister Make-It-Hop's gifts, though he's right smart of a lad all the same) and (b) "The Aspirant Version!" (altogether likelier, it being in fact the ventriloquized confection of a bonafide and still-fully-fledged though GoldenAged noveleer). Herewith, then,

## C. The End?

according to Ditsy:

Just about this time of day just about seven weeks ago, the way I see it,* in all that Passing of their pesky Torch somebody must've up and Dropped the Ball—right into *T II*'s petroleaginous bilges, wouldn't You know, on the virtual eve of Capt. Harry Kane & Co.'s Salvage-Whatever's-Salvageable operation, tisk tisk. Most likely 'twas that there Phantom-fellow, don't You reckon? Good thing that "Kit & Kaboodle" had shifted ashore just a couple days previous with their belongings and their heir-in-progress; good thing too that the Cast of Several's Core Corps had pretty much reclaimed their left-behinds, and that me and my then sometimes bunkmate Obie Brown were shacked up in my "pile-perched" proggeria instead of on board.

Or so we would've been, him&me, if that nimble item hadn't just the day prior kissed me and Hick Fen *arrivederci* and headed home to the Inner City whence he'd sprang, declaring he'd rather brave the crackheads as'd killed his pet kid brother than weather a winter *à deux* with this old cracker out here in spooky Nowheresville. *Ich verstehe*, I assured him, and *Nameless*'d him across Back-water Sound to Crassfield—and a teary-eyed trip that was for fer-rier and ferried alike.** Maybe I'd come visit him from time to time

---

* *Id est*, aboard *TOFO II* @ 11:11 P.M. on Th 11/11 last.

** Fairier and fairied? Resist the poor pun, Mate: Obie swings both ways, as doth Yr narrator, and is as of this writing happily hooked up with gung-ho Heather, late of our troupe and no longer Greg Kim's gofer, but a bonafide sophomore drama major at Towson State U, waitressing evenings at the Inner Harbor's Planet Hollywood to pay her freight. Ditsy's blessings on 'em both: *Mwah! Mwah.*

in Homicide City? Fuhgeddaboudit, said I (a contagious locution I'd caught from Jay, who'd picked it up like an STD at something called a Newyorican Poetry Slam): Ain't had us a homocide yet here in dear Hick Fen, said I, nor for that matter in the entire Backwater Estuarine Wetlands Area Reserve that I know of, as'd surely be the first to know — and so here I'll take my webfoot stand, said I, with a faretheewell *mwah* to cher(e) Jay O. B. Brown.

But a lonesome stand it was, Mate, that night and next day, just me and *Nameless* and the marsh-critters round about, like in progging days of yore before I hooked up with that Original Et Cet Two — except now I had *that* great lunker perched practically on my doorstep, empty but for memories and spooks: the kind of company that makes a girl lonesomer yet. My instructions from Cap'n Harry were to shut down *T II*'s systems — power, water, heat, waste disposal, and what-all — and to drain all pipes against freezing after the Johnson/Singers had left and before his crew arrived on Monday, the fifteenth of November. But who had the heart, that eleven-elevenish Thursday, even to prog a prime souvenir or two before the Salvage Team got cracking,* much less to pull "Abie baby's" plug, in a manner of speaking? Went a-progging instead clear over to B.E.W.A.R.(West), I did, to keep the showboat out of my view — and thereby putt-putted myself right from frying pan to fire, excuse the incendiary metaphor, for I wound up hand-tonging me a mess of oysters amid the bombed-out ruin of a certain former estuarine aquacultural research laboratory,** where once upon a better time than Veterans Day '99 . . .

Yes, well: They say our brackish Chesapeake's nor more nor less salty than our tears,*** and so I reckon I didn't change its chemistry none, for all I must've raised its level just a tad. That night I shucked and ate them right-nice oysters and drank me two-three home brews and then booted up the Big B to take Ditsy's mind off ditto's blues

---

* Which'd've come close to stealing anyhow, in clear violation of P.C., the Progger's Code.
** See <u>Its opening mini-icon:</u> Read Me, *supra*, for the fate of dear EARL's E.A.R.L.
*** *Vide ibidem*, s.V.p.

for a spell in that Black Hole of Leisure Time, the World Wide Web, figuring I'd get to my showboat-shutdown chores next day. Let any squint-minded spirits who'd impute arson(!)* to old Dits bear in mind that it was exactly this down-in-the-dumps procrastination that saved the day that night, sort of: I had just settled into updating *T II*'s homepage, whose hit-rate was much fallen from back in Ararat-Shoal-First-Grounding days — <u>Last (party-)animals leave the Ark! Salvage operations to commence after Veterans Day weekend!</u>—when I saw in my onscreen windows a flickering that at first I figured was a voltage-flutter in my power system (as happens now and then when the diesel generator hands off to the windmills and solar panels or vice versa) but then saw to be a reflection from the literal cabin windows behind me, facing out across Hick Fen toward Oh shit, said I to myself, among whose still-salaried duties as Chief of *T II*'s Maintenance Team was to keep an eye out for Code-breaking proggers or other vandals as might interlope aboard: Those were *flares and flames* a-flickering yonder, no question, and inasmuch as your tidemarshes *per se* don't incline to spontaneous combustion beyond the occasional *ignis fatuus* and suchlike wills-o'-the-wisp, much less to pyrotechnics, those Fs & Fs must needs be Oh shit *shit!* said I again, and popped into my parka and *Nameless*'d posthaste thither. Black moonless night, but for those flares; black chilly-misty marsh-maze that however I could've navigated blind, the way I used sometimes to navigate half-gay Jay: hard a-port, then hard a-starboard, now dead ahead and skiptomelou and there she loomed, all right, three-four flares still a-flaring on her roof, which had itself took fire, plus what looked to be yet more flames a-flickering behind her upper windows, where the projection room and sound-and-light consoles were. Oh triple shit, said I, and lashed alongside and hauled myself aboard just as *voilà!* I heard the automatic sprinkler system kick in — which it sure wouldn't've if I'd drained and winterized the sucker as I'd been going to do till I up and got my Black Thursday blues.

Case dismissed? I reckon!

---

* Another big-time no-no, per P.C.

But there's still them freaking flames to be dealt with, yes? Not to mention whatever scalawag set them and might yet be skulking amongst the smoke! So I hustled up the outside stairway to the bow end of *TOFO*'s roof, where once upon a time a certain famous water-barrel is said to've sat* and more lately a proper fire-hose hung. *May the seawater-pump intake* (prayed I) *be duly still positioned in the marsh-gut whereinto I deployed the sucker shortly after our Second Grounding—for if not, old* T II*'s toast.* The Ditsy Douse-Plan, cobbled up even as I climbed, was to count on the sprinkler system to contain the fire or fires inside whilst I hosed down the roof-ones, after which I'd nozzle my way in and down from deck to deck. Unreeled me right smart of hose, I therefore did; opened the big gate-valve, and was relieved to hear the water surge and see that pile of flat canvas linguini writhe and fatten python-thick. Luckily for all hand, there was no wind to fan the flames; I braced myself against the back-pressure, opened the big brass nozzle, and commenced a-blasting my way sternward through the smoke and spray, zapping each flare and flame by the light of the rest whilst keeping an eye out for the dastard Perpetrator. In the nature of the case, if I may so put it, this meant that the whole scene darkened as it and I progressed, reeling off more hose as I went and side-to-siding my nozzle like a SWAT team leader his assault-piece or Father Time his scythe: The less fire, the more smoke and steam; the more S&S, the less light to see by, and so 'tweren't till I was maybe a third of the way down-roof from the bow, if You follow me, working my way through Cap'n Elva's old herb-and-vegetable planters, that I caught sight of myself coming meward maybe a third of the way from the stern—hose in hand, side-to-siding, a-etting and a-cetering just like me!

Talk about Smoke & Mirrors! I stopped in my tracks, my hose still pissing mightily at nothing in particular. That spitting-image mirror-me did likewise—but a beat or two later, and so I knew then what I knew already and would've known a moment later if I hadn't've known it twice by that time, if You follow me, when *that*

---

* *Vide exempli gratia* "C. Hunter's" *Show Barge* (the "One Drop" sequence), not to mention E. Ferber's ditto *Boat*.

one went back to mowing down the flares that for aught I knew he'd set himself, whilst I took a beat or two longer to undumbstrike myself and get back into the Fire Extinguishing mode.

Cut to the chase, Dits! For about two nannyseconds I thought Jay Brown might've had him a change of heart and made his way somehow back, just in time to help me save the let's-say Theater of Our Love? But aside from the bleeding unlikelihood of *that*, even in the fast-fading firelight I could see 'twas a stockier, less limber somebody hosing his way Ditsyward than either "Senior African-American Citizen Joseph" or "Young African-American James," to name just two of Jay's camped-up Darky turns in Hop Johnson's Floating Operations. Plus pinkfaced and swag-bellied, this one was, with a WWII-style graywhite crewcut: Improbabler yet, but I'm a son of a seacook if my fellow fireperson weren't a living dead ringer for "Now that I have your attention," growled (You guessed it, maybe?) longlost EARL — going right on about his firefighting business with no more'n a quick cock of his eye in the direction of me that once was apple of same — "what say we finish off this fucker and have us a little catch-up chat?"

By which F-word he meant, I hasten to interject, the fire in hand, so to speak (which in fact we did now have pretty well in hand), not the *Floating Opera II* that fueled it. And so whilst poor Ditsy all but fouled her foulies with astonishment before getting some half-assed hold of her heart and soldiering on, without so much as a proper *abrazo* or even a "Long time no see," my bill-capped* erstwhile bosom buddy went on a-spritzing, thoughtfully watering the about-dead planters along with the fire; and I, *faute de* fucking *mieux*, followed suit; and when the roof was finally firefree we hosed our side-by-side way indoors and put out what the sprinklers hadn't in the projection room and backstage and understage and here and there elsewhere — where-all the mini-fires themselves had done less damage than You'd expect, but the sprinkler- and hose-water had done more, like an operation that cures the cancer but kills the patient.

---

* Sorry to've withheld You from this identificatory infobit, Reader; can only plead that my incredulity withheld same from me. I grant that plea, however, to be one that — like certain other of EARL's and mine to follow — may not be coppable.

Then, by the light of *T II*'s still-functioning emergency lighting system, as EARL hosed out the last flicker and turned meward with that shit-eating grin of his, I let the darling sumbitch have it broad on with *my* hose: Knocked him arse over tincup, I did, whereupon with a whoop he snatched up his nozzle and gave as good as he'd got, the pair of us then water-cannoning each other to and fro across TOFO's stage like a brace of 'tween-acts clowns till at last we couldn't squirt straight for laughing and so shut our hoses off and sloshed into each other's soggy arms. . . .

Him first, by golly, as 'twas EARL as had dumped Ditsy, not Ditsy EARL, in his general pissed-offedness at the U.S. Department of Defense's blitzing of B.E.W.A.R.(E.) as a Persian Gulf War exercise, and who hadn't so much as postcarded his once-dear dumpee in all the years since. Where'd he fucking *been*? And up to fucking *what*? And "Well now," I managed after a proper while to ask, "what brings *you* to this particular formerly-floating theater this particular evening, *amigo mio*?"

"Long story," alloweth he, and just to fill in Your picture I ought to mention that *T II*'s stage was still set for Act Last of Hop Johnson's COMING SOON!!! THE MUSICAL: Mount Patmos/Ararat, with "Scriptor John's" hermit-cabin Stage Left and a painted Stage-Right backdrop of Ark/*Arke*/TOFO nudging the shore. Once we'd turned the house ventilators on to clear our smoke, EARL set himself down on the fake stone *Sitzplatz* where Noah's Youngest Daughter was wont to make her sexy plea for Apocalypse Deferred, and where Author mercifully accedes thereto by strategic diddling of Script. The irony was not lost on me, as they say, as old EARL stroked his stubbled chin (so familiar a gesture it twanged Yr narrator's very auricles) and pushed *down* his black-plastic-rimmed specs (ditto), the better to see over 'em, and cobbled up a trial version of his and my First Grounding, let's call it, to see whether 'twould float or be by me torpedoed.

"Well," said he: "I do fancy the occasional night at the opera, don't you? But after what they did to B.E.W.A.R. parenthesis E., I needed time to get my shit regrouped. Okay?"

*Not*, I let him know: Nine entire EARLless years gone down Time's tubes, out of howthehell many's he think we've got left at our age? First four-five I prog my heart's busted pieces from B.E.W.A.R. East to ditto West, till I can't stand the ghost-jammed lonesome of it and so hook me up with this here showboat; do my durnedest to forget there ever was such a pearl as my EARL, but get so lonely amid all those showfolks that I up and jump ship back to Hick Fen, till old Hurricane Zulu blows the Mountain to Mohammed, as some might say, and here I set. Now then: *¿Qué pasa, s'il vous plait?* What the mothering fuck?

"The Mothering Fuck, old girl," respondeth EARL, "would take another nine years to What—and that's just the *short* version." So why don't we just allow, proposed he, that the both of us've passed right smart of water in that interval? During which, since I asked, despite his grudge against the Pentagon and by extension against most things governmental, he shuttled his arse between the U.S.'s and the State of Maryland's Departments of Agriculture, Interior, and Natural Resources as an advisor on aquacultural and estuarine matters, losing himself insofar as possible in his work whilst he tried to get his mind around losing his E.A.R.Lab and his dear Ditsy. . . .

"Bareassed liar," I here interjected. "Your freaking fishtanks is what you lost and missed. But lie on, mate; it's your voice *I* lost and've missed. For one thing."

Ree-tired to Floriday, he did, EARL said on, merely wincing his starboard eyebrow at my critical interjection: flang himself more or less literally into the movement to save the Everglades from agribusiness and retirement-community developers. Got ever more nostalgic, there amongst the sawgrass and the gators, for dear old ecostressed Chesapeake spartina and crabs and oysters, and Hick Fen proggers of the gender-flexible variety—to the point where, when the 1998 Pfisteria ruckus* made news all the way to Key West and returned his attention tidewaterward, he followed that attention

---

* *Pfisteria piscida*, a noxious marine virus thought to be fostered by massive chickenshit runoff from poultry farms on the lower Eastern Shore, caused large-scale fishkills in the Pocomoke and neighboring waterways that summer, threatened the Chesapeake seafood industry generally, and triggered temporary memory-loss and other alarming symptoms among waterfolk working the affected waters. Has since receded in virulence but, like stage-villains and opera-phantoms as a class, lurketh still in its old haunts and possibly in new as well.

Back North, adjuncted himself to the Free State's Pfisteria Management Team, and discreetly scouted his still-cherished though lamentably neglected Belle of Hick Fen — his Belle-Buoy, maybe? Even sort of shadowed her, he did, off and on, and came thereby to understand that the old girl had got herself romantically involved with . . . a Younger Fellow, should he say? Horse of another color, maybe, no slur intended? And so maintained his heart-hurt but had-it-coming-to-him distance, whilst at the same time keeping a weather eye on his old flame's new spark. 'Nuff said?

Says I Not hardly, Ace! How came it he hadn't made his move sometime between late August, when I'd jumped ship and left sweet O. B. Brown behind me on account of certain premonitions, and our 9/9/99 First Grounding, after which I'd rejoined the party? *There* was a proper Window of Opportunity, if he'd been weather-eyeing the scene for such: fucking French *door* of same, more like!

"Point taken," calmly granted EARL. "But we're talking no more'n two-three weeks there, love: Hardly time for you to know your own mind on the matter, much less for *me* to know it. I mean, like that Hop Johnson fellow and that Sherry Singer gal kept asking themselves, Who *are* we, really, you and me? And the proof I did right to hang back is that when Zee Two blew old Tee Two off of Ararat Shoal here into Hick Fen, and your Cast of Several lit out for the Territory, and I watched to see what'd be next in Ditsyville, what do I see but a certain brace of lovebirds patching up a certain pile-perched nest?"

My my my, says I: You *have* been the busy little tabskeeper, haven't you now? The regular phantom of our fucking opera!

"Won't deny it, dear Dits," says he, and went on to declare — but let's put the EARL-o'-my-world on Hold whilst I remind You that we're having this little catch-up Alibi Review amid the still-soaked and steaming but fairly smokefree carcass of poor *TOFO II*, in whose Gally/Concession/Bar Team lockers we had found us a stash of left-behind Wild Goose Amber microbrews to suck upon at world temperature whilst Earnest EARL spieled and Doubtful Ditsy listened, all by the romantical glow of emergency floodlights — that when DTE had pronounced *T II* unsalvageable *per se*, it had occurred to Mister EARL (who then made himself and his credentials known to FLOPCORP's new Dorsettown-on-Choptank director, Capt. Elva Kane) that the stuck-for-keeps showboat was, in his expert estimation, ideally suited and situated for conversion into a wetlands EcoLab: the field HQ and showpiece of—excuse any seeming vanity, he here pled, as none was intended, only historical/bureaucratical continuity—an Estuarine (or, better, Ecological-) Aquacultural Research Laboratory II, which he himself would happily assume directorship of, whether officially, *ex officio*, or in some let's say emerital capacity. Good Cap'n Edna, he didn't mind boasting, had proper sprang for the idea—Right up her organic-vegetarian alley!—and had floated it to Mister Morton Spindler of DTE and presumably to old Andrew Whatsisname-Whatsisname Todd as well, up in Patmos Tower. So all had looked Go-ish indeed there for a spell—We're talking last week, week before?—and if I was to ask him whether this E.A.R.L.-Two sky-pie scheme was a round-the-barn excuse to reconnect with his much-missed Ditsy or vice versa (if that's a vice that's versable), he'd be durned if he could sort it out, and to hell with trying. What was certain was, he craved 'em both, declared our (temporary) narrator EARL. But aside from the Powers in the Tower (which Cap'n Elva reported to be Not Unreceptive to the EcoLab notion as a Y2K fallback, once the showboat *qua* showboat had been stripped by Cap'n Harry's crew), there remained for the scheme's proposer one major sticking-point, in the agile form of Mister Young African-American James. By this time last week, so swore EARL, he had just about made his mind up to come out of his closet, so to speak—his Second Coming, should we say?—and introduce himself to my pal Jay Brown as well as *re*introducing himself (figuratively speaking, Y'understand) to me. He would make his new grand project known to us, and, who knows, maybe even propose one of them French-style menageries of three, if all hands thereto inclined? But *alors et sacré bleu* et cetera: Almost as if he'd got wind of what was in the air, Young Goodguy Brown lights out just then for the city, leaving poor Ditso sucking the mop *encore* and depriving the former Opera's (possible) Spook of his chief spookee. Coast clear, in short, for Outing and Clean-

Breasting, for Contrition and Reconnection or anyhow Penance, in the form of offering his old love and sidekick the co-management himwith of E.A.R.L. Redux, if and when.

"I knowed what Cap'n Harry's salvage schedule was, see," declared my once-so-precious by way of wind-up, "and so I got my arse back out here, never you mind how, and I set myself down on *T II*'s sterndeck with a couple of these here Wild Gooses and waited to give my darling Dits the surprise of her life when she showed up to Shut Down our Systems. Waited the whole livelong day, I did, and when it came clear you was for one reason or another otherwise engaged—"

Broken heart, I believe they call it, grumbled Yrs Truly. And whatcha mean *our* systems, boy, anyhow? Whereupon EARL reached to pat my hand or knee or whatever—which pacification I was having none of, thankee, just yet.

"—I decided just for the fuck of it," he spieled on, "to light a couple flares up on the roof, where they wouldn't hurt nothing, just to get your attention? Which they did, Allah be praised, but not before things got a mite out of hand, and here we set." With his Wild Goose Amber he gestured around at the right-ruined theater, whilst scratching his brush-cut with his proffered-and-rejected other hand. "Reckon I burnt my own bridge out from under me, didn't I now? Butt-fucked myself good and proper." He grinned his shit-eatingest dear grin. "And all for love!"

Mm-hm.

*0101 EST 01/01/00:*

'Twas Mister H. D. Thoreau, I've heard tell, as claimed he wouldn't walk to the next streetcorner to see the world blow up. Respecting the Y2K foofaraw, You can count me and EARL in old H.D.'s corner. All the same, however, earlier this evening we liberated a magnum of Mumm's from *TOFO II*'s *cave à vin* (fortunately spared in November's fire), had us a flute or three thereof to salute TEOTWAWKI's possible approach, and then a spell of more-than-friendly *fin-de-siècle* frisking, now that we're more than friends again—whereafter my man woozed off at the eleventh hour. Myself being the sort that sex boots up rather than sedates, that's when *I* booted up Big Bitsy and set about recounting this account, with my lover's deep-sleep snores for soundtrack. Figured I'd spacebreak just before the Momentous Moment and boot *him* up for a final toast: to Us After All; to gone-by bygones and the newborn century that we'll die in; also, whilst we're about it, to *E.A.R.L. II.*\*

But then I fell to narrating, You know how it is, about *T II*'s November Curse and its blessed fallout, and next thing I know the new millennium's already an hour old! Seeing as how we're evidently all still here—my EARL a-snoring and me a-pecking away at BB's ergonomic keyboard, our Franklin stove a-crackling, our generator a-humming, and not so much as a flicker on Bitsy's monitor—I infer without surprise or regret that the world's still with us, mostly anyhow and at least for the time being, although I grant that if it weren't, we'd likely be among the last to know. Sooner or later I'll click up the news and see what's what. Meanwhile: On with the story?

Whereof, in truth, there's not a great lot left to be told. Needless to say, when I called Cap'n Elva on my FLOPCORP cell phone that dark November night to report the fire, there was much ado in Dorsettown-on-Choptank. Bright and early next A.M. (for I'd assured her the fire was out and no more could be done till then) EARL and I ferried her and Cap'n Harry over from Crassfield to inspect the remains. "All my fault," EARL acknowledged straight out—but then followed that admission with a cockamamie tale of Accidental Distress-Flare Ignition in the course of his more-or-less-authorized Preliminary Feasibility Survey, prior to Systems Shutdown, for *T II*'s conversion into the more-or-less-proposed Ecological/Aquacultural Research Laboratory (II). "If not for good

---

\* As E and I still intend to call it—like it's our child-in-the-works, You dig? Which, come to that, it fairly is. But its co-co-director-to-be, Capt. Elva Kane, inclines to speak of it as "Abie's Baby," and DTE's official name for the thing, so we hear, will be *New Ark*, the new baby of their New Ark Productions. *Chacun à son goût*, declareth Ditsy—who feeleth herself already to be . . . in an Interesting Condition indeed.

Ditsy here," said he with sigh and stroke of stubbled chin as we approached the Accident Scene, "we'd be burnt to the waterline. As 'tis . . ."

As 'twas, 'twas a right skeptical Brother Harry and a more-sad-than-skeptical Sister Elva that we conducted through the blackened carcass of their erstwhile Abie Baby. "You accidentally set 'em off *how*?" Cap'n H wanted to hear from EARL again (who I did a double-take to hear them call "Doctor Jensen"!), whilst Cap'n E caught her breath and fisted her mouth at sight of the charred ceiling and smoke-and-water-ruined stage. And from me, "You two knew each other from Before, I believe you said?" Ms. Elv did more shaking of head than pointing of finger as we toured the mess, "Doctor Jensen" all the while patting my shoulder and singing my praises as Marine Firefighter *par excellence* & Damage Controller *extraordinaire*. It occurred to me, in that second capacity, to venture a risky ecological analogue: that just as forest fires can be Ma Nature's way of clearing out the Old for the sake of the New, so maybe this Really Unfortunate Accident dot dot dot?

"The way I hear it," grumbled Cap'n Harry, "your Forest Service even *sets* them fires now and then on purpose, so they can control 'em."

"That there's a Christ fact, Captain," firmly granted Mister Doctor EARL: "But didn't nobody *set* this one, sir, and it's only thanks to Ditsy we even got us a barge left."

"Of course nobody *set* it," Cap'n Elva came down on her twin, "any more than you and I set about to hurt poor Abie. Sometimes the best intentions go wrong, is all."

Which shut *his* mouth. "'Preciate your saying that, ma'am," said EARL, and Harry allowed as how he'd meant nothing personal. "Just doing my job, Edgar."

*Edgar*?

Elv then observed further, as much to herself as to us-all, that the stage and curtains and orchestra seats and Pit Bulls pit and balconies and projection room and such would all've had to go anyhow if the Floating Theater was to be rebuilt as a Hick Fen EcoLab. Should that project go forward—as she was now more than ever personally determined it would — we'd just have to finish what the fire started and design a new superstructure more suited to our new purpose.

As she warmed to this theme, so to speak — music to my and Mister-Doctor Edgar-EARL-Jensen's ears, as it meant my forest-fire gamble appeared to be paying off — her own cell phone warbled in its belt-pouch: Mort Spindler from Patmos Tower, wanting a Preliminary Damage Assessment ASAP for him to spin into a media release.

"Gonna give you to the Salvage Team first," quick-thinking Elv came back, maybe to give herself time to think less quickly, "and then I'll speak my piece." She handed the phone to Brother H, who said straight out "Ain't diddly-squat left to salvage, Mort. Barge seems okay, but might as well declare everything from the deck up a total loss. Cost more'n it's worth to salvage any of it. Looks like I'm out of a job, huh?" Not hard to guess what Doctor Spin must've asked him next, as Harry looked from one to the other of me & EARL and said *Accidental ignition of distress flares during routine inspection before systems shutdown.* What? Yup. I expect the ad-justers would want to look things over for themselves if they hadn't already canceled their coverage; but seeing as it's us that takes the hit, I reckon our finding is the one that stands, and that's our finding. Roger that, Mort. Here's Elva now."

Who first seconded her brother's assessment and then suggested that in any statements to the media Mort ought to mention that thanks to the all-night efforts of the on-site Maintenance Team, the blaze had been extinguished before it could destroy the barge as well as the theater, with possible environmental consequences to the surrounding wetlands. He might consider too a comparison that had occurred to Doctor Jensen: that just as accidental fires in a forest are a natural factor in woodlands ecology, clearing the Old to make way for the New, so et cetera — Mort could work it out, how it fits with our proposed conversion of *TOFO II* into an EcoLab.

She paused while Mort responded, Harry shook his head, and the On-Site Maintenance Team nodded assent and tried not to wink each at the other. Then, *"Phoenix?"* she evidently repeated after him. "Like the town in Arizona? Yeah, sure, I get it, and we'll definitely put that name in the hat with the others. Plus I guess FLOP-CORP'll have to become ECOCORP or some such, right? But that's your department. I'm authorizing Ditsy to finish shutting down whatever systems are left, and he and Harry can decide what needs battening down for the winter while we get our plans firmed up for the spring. Hold on a second, Mort—" She muted the phone on her shoulder whilst I said what I'd signaled her I wanted to say; then winked and passed it along to Dr. Spin: "*Just like Mother Nature does at hibernation-time*, right? Maybe mention that to Greg and the guys, along with the Forest Fire bit. Gotcha, Mort; over and out." But she had no sooner clicked off and warned us that we would no doubt soon be seeing the newscopters overhead again like back in First and Second Grounding days, and that we ought to take any such media opportunities to promote the EcoLab Concept, than she said "Oh shit, excuse my French," and redialed Mort to urge him (via his secretary this time, whose boss was already on the horn with the press) to consider the possibility of our New Ark* as a sort of anchor to windward for the *real* Y2K, thirteen months hence. "Already thought of that, did he? Cool! Shows we're on the same wavelength. So have a good one, Doris."

And so it came to pass, like a replay of 9/9/99 *et sequentia*: the TV choppers, old buddy Greg and his camera team, soundbites by Noted Ecologist Dr. Edgar Jensen—formerly of the U.S. Department of the Interior's Fish & Wildlife Service and Maryland's Department of Natural Resources, currently Ecological/Aquacultural Consultant for Dorset Tradewinds Enterprises' proposed new Hick Fen research facility—about Nature's inclination to sprout new life from old, the way the mythical Firebird is reborn periodically from its own ashes.

*Doctor*? I'd started in on him soon's we'd fetched the Kane twins back to Crassfield. *Edgar*? *Jensen*?

"Don't mean squat, girl," had responded he—his old shit-kicking self again the minute their DTE van pulled off and we *Nameless*'d homeward. "Just call me EARL, if you don't mind. I've got right used to it."

---

* This was, in fact, where that appellation first surfaced in this connection.

Mm-hm. That same day we finished *T II*'s System Shutdown, most of which the Accidental Distress-Flare Ignition had done for us. To my professional eye it appeared that while Cap'n Harry's judgment about the theater's unsalvageability was sound from FLOPCORP's point of view, the place was a progger's paradise: enough progworthy stuff in there to give us a fair leg up, come spring, on *New Ark/E.A.R.L. II/Phoenix/Abie's Baby/*Whatever. Mindful of the hits my "pile-perched shanty" had taken from Zulus I & II, I even got to thinking that Mister Doctor EARL might consider designing more stormproof living quarters for the pair of us aboard his big-deal Ecological/Aquacultural Research Facility — if indeed we was a-fixing to be a coupling Couple again, which it turns out seems to've turned out to be the case.

And exactly that the good doc has since done, bless him, together with living space for a postdoctoral assistant or two and guest quarters for Cap'n Elva, she being very much on our team, or rather us on hers. Truth to tell, the "EcoLab" side of *E.A.R.L. II* sprouted mainly from Elva's (and Ms. Sherry Singer's) old fondness for growing herbs and tomatoes and such on *T II*'s roof, back when *that* pair was more or less an item, and then again on a larger scale after our Second Grounding, when the Phantom slipped a few MaryJane seeds in amongst the sweet basils and thymes and parsleys. What Elv has come to fancying is a sort of updated 1960s mini-commune: a little band of all-but-self-sufficient hunter/gatherers on the wind- and solar-powered New Ark, living off the marsh and what can sustainably be progged therefrom plus what they'll grow in *E II*'s high-tech fish tanks and hydroponic planters; a model community for the New Age if Shit hits Fan on the Big Binary, 01/01/01. Inasmuch as Yrs Truly is a seasoned hand at living just about that way (but with a diesel backup for the powerplant and the odd Beck's *Dunkelbier* to relieve the home brew and pot-grown pot), I was not only awarded a citation from FLOPCORP* for Meritorious Effort at Fire Extinction, but named Senior Consultant on Ecologically Compatible Wetlands Hunting/Gathering Techniques to boot. In short, just call me Progger-in-Chief, Matey — and we'll just see.

---

* Now named ECOCORP, sure enough.

As for Captain Harry James Kane—a chap on the whole more comfortable taking orders than giving them, seems to me, except from the pilothouse of old *Raven*—he'd been without honest work since our Second Grounding, and more so yet after our Accidental Et Cetera of 11/11. Naturally, Mort spun out job-descriptions for him: Co-Supervisor of Conversion; Expediter of *New Ark*/Dorsettown logistics; what have you. But when ECOCORP found a buyer down in Norfolk for the tugboats and contracted for Harry to deliver them, and Cap'n Elva for old times' sake took a holiday from administration to pilot her *Dove* one last time down-Bay beside her brother's *Raven*, their whistles tootling merrily back and forth as they left Snug Harbour and headed out the broad Choptank, only Elva came back in the DTE van that Mort dispatched to retrieve them. Cap'n Harry, she reported, had accepted on the spot the new owner's invitation to stay on as *Raven*'s skipper, nudging freighters into and out of their berths in nearby Portsmouth. Shoreside life purely didn't set well with him, she declared he'd declared. Although he would sorely miss the odd git-down session with Hop Johnson and such other Pit Bulls as still prowled Dorsettown-on-Choptank, he felt 'twas time (I quote his sister's quote) to "cut himself loose." . . .

"Hop Johnson," did I hear me say? Where in all this End Time, You may or may not be a-wondering, has our not-so-young-anymore Novelist Aspirant been, and up to what? Likewise his gone-straight mate Miz Sherry Those-Eyes-Those-Eyes Singer, and that Novelist-Emeritus type (our label, not his) that did his durnedest to keep us-all at arm's length, but found himself Tar-Babied proper usto as our seasons passed and the chapters rolled by? *¿Qué pasa* with that particular threesome from old *TOFO*'s Cast of Several?

First the sad news, heavily foreshadowed here and there already in these serial endings as if by M. le Fantôme, but left for us Systems Shutdowners to deliver: The good Doctors Johnson—heartman he and glands-lady she, professors of same at their beloved Hopkins and eminent private practitioners as well—set out together on Wednesday, 11/23, aboard never-mind-which air-carrier for a well-earned Thanksgiving holiday at Caneel Bay, St. John, USVI, whereto their only child and his pregnant pal had been urged to come along as their guests, but had declined in favor of staying on at Dorsettown to settle themselves into Sher's mom's vacated villa whilst Sher and Captain. Adam. Lake. looked after that ailing lady and Mister Hop got a-going on his All-New Version of—Ready for this?—*COMING SOON!!!* THE NOVEL! Through that foregoing stretched-out sentence, their stretched-out never-mind-what-aircraft banks and climbs to cruising altitude, leaves the mainland behind at Carolina's Outer Banks, and southeasts toward the Virgins whilst its stretched-out first-class passengers sip champagne and wish "their kids" had seen fit to holiday with them, though at the same time approving their responsible sticktoitiveness. . . .

Nobody knows exactly how their sentence ended. Blip suddenly gone from radar screens. No distress transmissions from flight crew. Some small debris-items found at site half a thousand miles SE of Hatteras or SW of (here it comes) Bermuda. No survivors; not even any bodies, major plane-parts, or flight recorder recovered. National Transportation Safety Board investigating. Nutcase theories all over the Wacko-Wild Web.

And Only-Child Johns truly *floored* with grief and guilt: that he had steadfastly spurned the worthy profession they so loved and wished him to follow. That he'd come to resist (though never ungratefully) even their relentless generosity. That they would now never see the grandkid they'd been so pleased to have in the works, not to mention the novel that, Muse willing, might go some way toward justifying their son's years of farting around on *The Original Floating Opera II*. Most of all, that his mom and dad—who, excuse the tired expression, had tirelessly Been There For Him through thick and thin, as for their innumerable patients and med-students as well—were suddenly, violently, and forever *dead and gone*: dead and gone and gone and dead! For some days the lad was in literal low-grade shock,* unable to do much more than sob from room to

---

* So cell-phoned me his mate and e-mailed me his erstwhile sort-of-mentor and half-pretend rival "GreatUnc Ennie," who maintains a benevolent curiosity re his "N.A. Character" as well as, for whatever personal or professional reasons, re me, Mr./Dr. EARL, and even our projected new ark *E.A.R.L. II*.

room of the family house in Guilford. Good Sherry's loving sympathy and patient nudging have got him now Working Through his bereavement, as they say, by immersing himself in the settlement of their very considerable estate, with its major bequests to their (and his) alma mater, its medical institutions, and other worthy beneficiaries ranging from the Chesapeake Bay Foundation and the United Jewish Appeal to, of course, JHJ himself: positioned, as they say, to become a financially independent Novelist Aspirant with a house in Baltimore's poshest neck of the urban woods as well as that right-nice pad in D-o-C. Word even has it—cyberword, from the source aforementioned—that he has been offered some sort of instructorship in the program from which he graduated not long since.

But of all this he's having none, is Mister Hop, at least for the present: no more, anyhow, than by his own reckoning he's entitled to. Doesn't *want* to teach amateur scribblers before he can call himself a true professional. Doesn't *want* a Guilford showplace that he did nothing to earn beyond outliving his workaholic parents, and so has progged through its furniture and assorted mementos, painfully consigned the rest to auction, and listed the place for sale at an appropriately high figure in the city's booming R.E. market. His share of their estate he'll take, of course and gratefully, out of his love and respect for them and because he's an all-but-dad these days—a hard worker himself, come to that, though not in the gainful-employment way. What dedicated hours he puts in (so phones his mate and Cap'n Elva, and so e-mails his "GreatUnc") on the opus he's now free and by his lights *obliged* to devote full time* to!

Through all which grave business, needless to report, Miz Scheherazade-on-Choptank's belly grows and grows toward term: "The *really* Big B just 'round the bend," Cap'n Elv calls it, and zips digital-camera cybershots it-of to *New Ark*'s Hick Fen website. What Mister Doctor EARL and Mister GreatUnc Ennie reckon is that the conjunction of deep loss and deep responsibility, of parenthood on

---

* Except for probate-court distractions and the running up of simulations for us on his new computer (by Hop dubbed The Even Bigger Bitsy) of our EcoLab's projected "story" with, let's say, varying missions, budgets, and casts of characters.

the heels of untimely orphaning, might just make Johns Hopkins Johnson N.A. into the Real Thing. On the other hand, they agree, so much financial independence could be the lad's ruin. To both possibilities, Yr Narrator nods Aye—but what do *I* know?

Let's just see:

*What Ditsy Knows.*

- That (as I have electronically advised The N.E. and N.A. Characters regarding that race to the finish line with their respective *COMING SOON!!!*s) the early bird may get the worm, but—per Capt. Elva K.—*it's the second mouse who gets the cheese.*

- That for those of us past age sixty, say, all that hyped-up countdown to Y2K—like the title of that shape-shifting NARRATIVE/NOVEL?/MUSICAL/whatever—has been mainly a pesky reminder of our *real* TEOTWAWKI (Coming Soon indeed, although we mercifully know not when), and of our surely evergrimmer approach thereto: I mean loss of friends and loved ones, and of capacities mental and physical; ever more discomfort, disability, dependency, and downright suffering; "second childishness and mere oblivion," per Capt. Wm Shakespeare. E.g., though he won't speak of it, my progger's eye and bilge-pumpmeister's ear espieth that not all's well with Mr./Dr. EARL, a-rumbling away in our yonder (queen-size) berth: Something renal or pancreatic, is Ditsy's guess, and oncological to boot—but what do I know?

- That such night-fears of Mortality and Its Discontents can be enough to make a girl half envy the Doctors Johnson their quietus: two minutesworth of out-of-the-blue out-of-your-mind terror, and then—.

- That, however, she must count herself blest who in the fleet meanwhile has known by far more health than illness, more capacity than in-, more sufficiency than want. More companionship, even, than solitude-except-as-chosen, by and large. Yea, verily, and more peace than harassment and hassle, more liberty than unreasonable constraint, more Less (more to my liking) than More. Not to mention tidemarshes! Sweetnsalty Hick Fen creeklets in every light and weather! Blue crabs a-tickling through the eelgrass! Softshell clams and Chesapeake oysters, workboats showboats herons ospreys, rock- and bluefish, summer T-showers and winter goose-music! Even skeeters and sea nettles, come to that, and sweatstinky dog-day heat indexes. Yea, even the several asspain hurricane-preps per season, if not the storms themselves. Ah! Ah!

That being the case, You may inquire, why not then in like spirit savor those several Death-Preps aforereviewed, if not dying itself— they being as much an aspect of Life as are volcanoes of old Dorothy Lamour South-Sea-Island-Paradise flicks and hurricanes of The Land of Gracious Living?

You kidding, Reader? Fuhgeddaboudit already!

- That, take it all in all, what Ditsy knows doubtless can't fetch tea for what Ditsy don't. But, *quod est* here & now *demonstrandum*,

- That stories, also, end.

**John Barth** is the author of numerous works of fiction, including *The Sot-Weed Factor, The Tidewater Tales, Lost in the Funhouse, The Last Voyage of Somebody the Sailor,* and the National Book Award winner *Chimera.* He taught for many years in the writing program at Johns Hopkins University and lives in Chestertown, Maryland.